COLLECTED SHORT STORIES

GUY   WILSON

First published in Great Britain in 2001
by: Benchmark Press
Little Hatherden   Near Andover   SP11 OHY.

A CIP catalogue for this book is avaliable from the British
Library.
ISBN: 0-9537674-2-6

Printed and bound in Great Britain by Henry Ling Ltd, The
Dorset Press, Dorchester.   DT1 1HD.

CONTENTS

BY THE SAME AUTHOR:

Brought up in Devon, Guy Wilson was educated at Marlborough College and Gonville and Caius College, Cambridge.   After a stint in the Royal Marine Commandos and a statutory attempt at being a schoolmaster, he determined to be a novelist.   He and his wife, Angela, set off to Spain on a motorbike. This was the start of an adventurous and precarious existence.   They spent three years in Spain, two in Algeria, three in Italy and one in Paris, supplementing literary income by starting and running English language schools.   Then they found themselves in charge of Padworth, the international sixth-form college for girls, which they ran for twelve years.   The Wilsons now live in Hampshire.

THE VILLA DES FLEURS BLANCHES

Pasquale Ducrois was a resplendent figure these days with his large healthy face and his heavily-oiled black hair, two curved glossy salients of which flowed up from a central parting like the bow wave of a ship. On Sundays the meat manufacturer always wore a black suit with a buttonhole for Mass. Afterwards he and Jacqueline Ducrois took a ritual drink at the Café de la Rose. It was the high point in the week for him to sit in this the most frequented of the cafes, Jacqueline beside him in her best, acknowledging faces he knew passing along the broad pavement of the Boulevarde des Platanes, the picturesque main street of his old Midi town. Sometimes a closer acquaintance would come to shake hands and exchange a few words. If it was a woman he would rise and bend his head over her hand in an old-fashioned way. For this was Pasquale's town, which had witnessed his birth and childhood, offered him the chance in life which he had taken with both hands, and which had now bestowed on him the just reward for his endeavour.

Pasquale had begun his career as an ordinary butcher, having inherited from his father the small shop in a side street. Here for fifteen years the Ducrois pair had, four times a day on six days a week, rolled up and down the metal blind which protected the door and the window, and here for nine hours a day Pasquale in a white apron had sliced chops, hacked and sawn joints and made his own sausages which regularly won the provincial cup that stood proudly on a shelf behind the counter. Here also Jacqueline had sat at the pay desk. By selling only first class meat they had managed to defy the supermarkets, but Pasquale had seen the writing on the wall. When the chance came he snapped up a semi-derelict canning-factory on the outskirts of the town and invested all the money they had in the enterprise. The old shop was let, but of necessity Monsieur and Madame Ducrois lived on in the flat upstairs.

The canning business lit like tinder under Pasquale's skilled and devoted management. He no longer these days got up at five to go to the big wholesale market twenty kilometres away to select and buy his meat. It was delivered in refrigerated lorries, and woebetide the suppliers if the quality was down. He no longer chopped and sliced on a wooden block scrubbed white. The machines in the factory scuffled, rotated and spun for him, a few white-coated staff with gauze hats tending them. Animal carcasses came in one end of the building, mountains of tins departed from the other. Among his numerous clients was a supermarket chain, deliveries to which included mountains of pet food as well as meat for human consumption, and he was rich.

Pasquale was not without ambition for those luxury possessions which can be bought with wealth. He already owned a new Mercedes, for example, which he kept at the factory. But he was at heart a traditionalist and remained deeply attached to the small property where he was born. It pleased him to walk home in the evenings up the narrow cobbled streets in the centre of the town, with their elegant houses towering above, and to renew contact with the familiar sights, sounds and odours of his youth. Jacqueline on the other hand grew restless. Though it had been hard work and long hours, she had treasured the thought as well as the practice of working every day beside her vigorous husband, in the evenings climbing wearily upstairs with him to eat their supper. It had compensated her for their childlessness. Now she had nothing to do but cook and wash and sew alone, and occasionally meet other unemployed wives in cafés. She fastened a good deal of her discontent on the shop below, which she felt intruded on their privacy and which, ironically enough, sold baby clothes.

Jacqueline was not of the town. She came from the north of France, did not speak with a Midi accent, and had had a better education than her husband. As a child she had been interested in painting and had been considered quite good. In a desultory sort of way, more to fill in her time than from any driving urge, she took it up again. She did still life, things she could do in the small back room of the flat. Then one afternoon, when she was coming back into the town on a bus after visiting a friend in a village, she saw that the Villa des Fleurs Blanches was up for sale.   Attached to the wall of the wild and unkempt garden was an estate agent's board.

She naturally knew the Villa.   Though it was privately owned and not open to the public, it was part of the heritage of the town, and merited brief mention in the guide books dispensed by the Tourist Office in the Place des Martyrs.   For it had been the house of Jean Baptiste Claude, the great Post-Impressionist, who was born there and in his later life returned to it to make it his work-place.   Jacqueline remembered reading that Claude had modified one side of the building to accommodate his atelier.

The matter did not seize her at once.   She thought no more about it that evening.   But the next morning she found she had woken with a strong memory of that 'for sale' board.   She found she had subconsciously recorded the name of the agent.   Even when later in the morning - as she thought, idly - she popped into the agent's office in town, she imagined it would be to enquire why it was that such an important monument was up for sale in this way.

She learnt that the owner, Claude's great-grand-daughter, had died childless.   It was her heir, who was not a member of the family, who had decided to sell.   Would not the town buy the property, Jacqueline asked - perhaps as a financial investment as well as from a sense of civic duty?   No, the woman told her, there was no talk of that.   Certainly no one from the Council had approached her office.

The words were out of Jacqueline's mouth before she realised she was saying them.   She would like to view the Villa, she said.

The place enchanted her before they were through the ill-fitting gate which was tethered with a rough chain and padlock.   It was not large, probably only four smallish rooms on the ground floor, each of which had a pleasing wide window framed in stone, contrasting with the red brick of the rest of the house.   Another piece of knowledge about Claude came back to her.   His father had been only a moderately successful 'avocat.'   The modesty of the place fitted with this information.   The garden, which she could only glimpse, was a small jungle, with the trees - cypress and myrtle she recognised - too close together, and parched grass uncared for. The woman opened the front door with two old keys and they went in.

As they entered the musty bare hall she felt immediately, uncannily, welcomed. It was as if someone who had waited for a long time and perhaps dozed a little, hearing the approach of footsteps had jumped joyfully to their feet.

'Oh,' she said - an expression of delight not intended for her companion. As she spoke, she looked up the stairs, which had a mahogany balustrade curving up invitingly into the shuttered darkness.

'It does need a little doing to it, I'm afraid,' the woman said - and then, as if to deflect criticism, 'the artist's atelier of course is on the first floor.'

This was where Jacqueline's love affair really began. The bare room was quite unlike the rest of the house, which gave a pinched feeling. It was huge and spacious, soaring up and swallowing the third storey. The whole of the outer wall was a window. Round the other three walls were two continuous wooden seats, stepped up from the floor, which must, Jacqueline thought, have been used by the artist to place the paraphernalia of his art - palettes, brushes, canvasses and so on - to pose his models, or even perhaps for him to take a rest from his easel and contemplate his work.

She must have stood there quite a time, lost in reverie, furnishing the place in her mind as it must have been when Claude was alive. It wasn't until she heard the woman rustling downstairs that she came to.

'You've had a good look, madame?' the woman said as she went down.

'Oh yes, thank you.'

'The bedrooms have very pleasant aspects, don't they?'

She blushed. She had not looked into the other rooms.

It wasn't until they were back in the office and she was about to leave that price was mentioned. The woman thrust the paper into her hands. 'In the circumstances it is very reasonable,' she said. 'It is very much against our advice, but the artist's possessions, which had been kept, were sold separately. The house would have been priced a great deal higher had it been sold as one lot.'

Pasquale could not remember precisely that he had made a choice in appointing Alphonsine Noisette. He recalled that his previous 'girl' - he never used the word secretary when talking to friends - had left him to get married, and that there were several candidates. He must, he supposed now, at some point in the conversation with Alphonsine have made it clear that he wanted her, but all he remembered was that at a certain point she seemed to be assuming that he had. She closed with the words, 'Well, Monsieur Ducrois, I shall be seeing you on Monday then, sharply at eight. I think you'll find me very punctual.'

It was by the same seemingly inexorable process that things developed. There was a day not so very much later when they began to use the second person singular. He was calling her Alphonsine not Mademoiselle Noisette, and reciprocally she was calling him Pasquale. The latter usage only took place when they were alone, however. She never called him Pasquale within the hearing of other employees or visitors, a circumstance which somehow made for an even greater intimacy. Their first act of love-making came about not much later.

He had to travel about a hundred kilometres to keep an afternoon appointment with a supplier of herbs which might be useful in the manufacture of a new line of terrine he was hoping to develop for the delicatessen market. He found himself saying to Alphonsine that it would be nice to have a second opinion on the quality of the herbs. The rest followed. They stopped for lunch at a rather expensive roadside hotel and restaurant and, after eating and drinking substantially, it was a relatively small step for Alphonsine to go to the public telephone in the street outside to refix the appointment for another day while he booked a double room. The progression to regular trysts in Alphonsine's small bungalow in a conveniently anonymous suburb of the town - again, usually in the afternoons - was similarly frictionless. Pasquale woke one day from a post-coital doze to realise he had a mistress and that no one knew about it or was likely to.

It surprised him a little at first. He had always imagined himself happily married and had never seen himself as the sort of man who would embellish his life in this way. But as it had happened so smoothly and as the arrangement did not in any way threaten the stability of his existence - Alphonsine seemed to wish everything to go on precisely as they were and never spoke of his married life - he supposed he had been wrong about himself. His surprise evaporated. He *continued* to be happily married, he told himself, and this was not inconsistent with the idea that a man in his position would at a certain time in his life take a mistress.

He gave to Alphonsine's good sense a lot of the credit for the uncomplicated addition to his life. One hot afternoon, when their intercourse had been especially rewarding to him and, judging from her behaviour, to Alphonsine also, he acknowledged this. 'My dear Alphonsine,' he said, 'you are so *intuitively* understanding.'

'Yes, Pasquale, since you mention it, perhaps I am,' she replied calmly. 'But then, in a way, it is not difficult - for our interests are so similar, are they not?'

Pasquale continued to enjoy the Sunday visits to the Café de la Rose in Jacqueline's company. He felt more deeply still a man of his town, his region, of his culture. And in a strange way he found himself experiencing more frequent waves of goodwill towards Jacqueline because of the new dimension in his life. How fortunate he was to be married to a woman of such excellent intellect and feminine skills. A wave of goodwill was in progress one evening when she brought up the question of their flat and how nice it would be, now he was doing so well, to find something more accommodating out of the centre of the town. When she came up with an actual property, and the price proved - though more than he would have contemplated - within his means, he found himself agreeing. If he was to be a town councillor, maybe eventually mayor, an ambition which had recently risen above his horizon, he had to concede to himself that a house such as this one was a more desirable residence than their present property, satisfied with it as he had always been hitherto. It was also on that side of the town opposite to that in which Alphonsine lived.

Did Jacqueline know of her husband's secret liaison or sense its existence? There can be no certain answer to this question, though it might be supposed she pondered the reason for an outbreak of unwonted generosity extended towards her by her husband at this time. She received bouquets of flowers in the evenings sometimes for example, when this had never happened before. Pasquale gave her a beautiful amethyst ring on her birthday, and then proposed and organised an expensive holiday abroad when they had never even contemplated leaving the country before. Most of all there was his easy agreement to the purchase of the Villa.

What is certain is that Jacqueline's absorption in her new abode was complete from the moment of its acquisition, and that her attention became centred on Claude's atelier. This being the only sizeable room, it was the obvious choice for the salon, but from the outset Jacqueline was adamant that it should not be. The rest of the house was painted, carpeted, furnished, a modern heating system was installed to keep them comfortable in the winter months, but under Jacqueline's firm instructions, the atelier was to remain just as it was - with its bare floorboards, its greyish walls, and its huge north-facing window which here and there had panes of a different glass, two of them coloured, where repairs had been done at various times. Pasquale mildly questioned her about this. When he did, she always said the same thing. 'No, it must stay like that until I can do something about it,' she said. 'I know Jean Baptiste wishes it.'

Her reference to the painter's first name, and her use of the present tense like that to describe his predilection, might have given Pasquale some cause for thought. But as has been made clear Pasquale had an in-built reason at this time for not questioning his wife's whims. She was making the rest of the house snug and delightful. He was content.

As time went by, however, Pasquale did receive more than an

inkling of his wife's intentions.   She was making strenuous efforts to recover the dead painter's scattered artefacts with a view, apparently, to furnishing the studio as it had been under his great granddaughter's care.   In this she was only in a minor way successful.   She discovered that the major items, the palettes, the brushes and the huge easel, had been sold to one man, a rich collector of memorabilia of this sort.   But her written request that he might resell the objects back to her 'in order that they may be returned where they belong, as Jean Baptiste would have wished,' was firmly rejected.   She recovered, from elsewhere, no more than some photographs of the artist, his wife and friends, a wooden bowl he had used several times in still-life paintings, and a notebook in which ideas and a few very preliminary sketches had been scribbled.   But among the photographs there were several views of the atelier from different angles.   These Jacqueline was able to give to an ébeniste in the town who made skilful copies of the six raffia-seated chairs, the easel, and a large armchair upholstered with what had apparently been crimson corduroy, as it appeared in one of the paintings.   It was difficult to reproduce exactly that patina the original objects must have had, but in a few months Jacqueline was satisfied that the room was as faithful a representation of the original as was possible. She then began a vigorous research into the painter's life and work, sending for books from various libraries and spending most her time reading them.

Pasquale had some misgivings about Jacqueline's new interest which, it occurred to him peripherally, had about it an obsessional quality.   It did not accord with an innate frugality in his nature, either, to see the main room in their new house turned into what he could only think of as a museum.   But he had always been aware that the abandonment of their old business had deprived Jacqueline of an occupation, and he was glad at least to see her fully engaged again.   The loss of the room was more than compensated for by this.   There was then a disquieting development.

One evening when he got home and as usual called as

he opened the front door, there was not the customary answer from the kitchen.   Entering the kitchen, he found she was not there and had not started their meal.   He went to the bottom of the stairs and called up.   Silence met him here as well. Alarmed, he went up.   Was she ill?   The bedroom, too, was empty.   He then had the strongest intimation, which he could not have explained, that she had not gone out - the next obvious conclusion - but was in the atelier.   He went in and there she was, dressed in an artist's smock, standing before the easel.   In one hand, her thumb through the hole, she held a palette, in the other a paint-brush poised in mid-air.   On the easel, confronting her, was a large blank canvas.

'Why, Jacqueline, didn't you hear me call?' he said, not without irritation despite the unusual sight before him.

Jacqueline had been in a pose of seemingly great tension, like someone taking part in a tableau aiming to capture some moment of high drama.   As he spoke, the tableau seemed to disintegrate. She lowered the brush and the palette, put them on top of a cabinet full of wide shallow drawers beside her and rose.

'Jean Baptiste has been speaking to me,' she said then.   'I now know he has work for me.'   She spoke in a matter of fact way, as if indeed 'Jean Baptiste' was someone living with them.

Pasquale was relieved there was nothing serious amiss, and confined himself to pointing out what the time was and to the fact that no preparations were yet under way for their meal.   But he found he could not so easily rid himself of the incident. Later, while they were eating - some rather indifferent frozen food had been provided which was not at all up to the standard of cooking he was used to - he found himself referring to it again.

'Jacqueline, I'm not sure you aren't overdoing this Claude business,' he said not without edge. 'It seems to be becoming an obsession not a hobby.'

She turned amazed eyes on him. 'Hobby?   But of course it's not a hobby.   Though I do think obsession is a very good word for it.   I *am* obsessed.   The poor frustrated spirit is calling me. He has work for me.'

'He has what?'

'My reading has told me that Jean Baptiste died before his work was completed. What came to me today is that I am to be his handmaiden.'

The following evening Pasquale had another premonition and returned home an hour earlier than usual. Again there was no reply from the kitchen. This time he raced straight upstairs to the atelier. To his horror he saw Jacqeline's crumpled form on the floor in front of the easel on which a fully painted canvas rested. The palette was still in her hand, two brushes lay scattered on the floor nearby. He thought she was dead, and with a wild cry rushed to her. He found that she was not dead, but breathing evenly, a slight flush - not unbecoming, he noted even at this anxious time - on her cheeks. Mad with relief he picked her up - with ease, for Madame Ducrois was quite a slight figure - and carried her to the bedroom. He laid her gently on the bed. She must have worked herself to exhaustion, he thought.

While he sat anxiously on the bed beside her wondering if he should call the doctor, her breathing stumbled, she sighed, her eyelids quivered, and she woke. She smiled beatifically.

'It has happened, Pasquale,' she said after a moment, staring at the ceiling. 'I am to be the vehicle. Something quite wonderful has happened today. I have begun to be used. *I felt him at my side guiding my hand.*'

'You're ill. Jacqueline. You have allowed this nonsense to make you ill.'

She lowered her eyes from the ceiling and looked at him with a directness he found even more disconcerting. 'Oh no, I'm not ill. A little tired perhaps, but I feel wonderful. You must listen to what happened.'

He was forced to. It had happened in the early afternon, she said. This was a curious thing - all her experiences so far had happened in the afternoon, never in the morning. She'd had an exact representation in her mind of the picture she was required to paint, but at first it had been as if her limbs were frozen. She could only stand motionless in front of the canvas, as he had found her doing the day before, 'while the forms and colours raged in my mind, screaming like frenzied prisoners at their barred windows for release.' Then, it must have been about four o'clock when the heat had begun to ebb, her arm made a movement as if it were a robot, remotely controlled. She saw it mixing a colour on the palette, it rose to the canvas, and she was astounded to see a long wavy line journeying horizontally in front of her eyes. It happened again with a different mixture of paint. Soon she was working frenetically. She went on until the canvas was covered. With the last stroke she must have collapsed.

It went on like this. She did not faint again, but every evening when he came home she had been in the atelier, producing a canvas a day, sometimes two. Often Pasquale had to get the supper - or rather, his supper, for Jacqueline often said she didn't feel like eating. He tried to be tolerant, strove to see it from her point of view. She had been too much on her own, he thought. They should get out at week-ends more, take another holiday abroad maybe. But underneath these thoughts he found he could not feel tolerant, only irritated. It was irrational, he argued, sentimental, even hysterical. He wished they had never moved out of their old premises. He thought wildly of selling the Villa behind her back and finding some other property.

He had not to this moment paid a great deal of attention to the canvasses, which insasmuch as he had looked at them he had thought rather meaningless - mostly series upon series of horizontal wavy lines, like the readings of some medical machine recording the heartbeats of a very sick person. The colours were quite attractive, but even in terms of abstract art, which was presumably the category into which they fell, zilch. Then one Saturday morning when Jacqueline had gone off to the hairdresser's - for in her obsession she had never ceased to look after her appearance, which if anything had improved - he went into the atelier to have a closer look. Examining the canvasses, he realised that not only was there a clear progression in what were obviously the more recent works but that they were becoming much more intelligible. The multi-hued wavy lines continued, but it was now possible to say that the pictures were clearly landscapes, Midi landscapes, with a suspicion of bare mountains, pine trees - in one instance what was obviously a field of lavender.

Looking at his watch he made a decision. He selected one of the more recent works which seemed to suggest a landscape of sparsely wooded hills. He wrapped it in brown paper and set off at a pace to the Claude Gallery which was in the centre of the town. He slightly knew Courtier, the director, whom he had several times supplied with specially prepared fresh patés for the *vernissages* of living painters who also exhibited from time to time on his premises. By luck he was in his office. Pasquale undid the package and revealed Jacqueline's picture. He held it upright on the desk for Courtier to see. 'I'm not going to say anything, but I'd like your opinion of this - off the cuff,' he said.

Courtier stared at the work for some moments. Then he took it from Pasquale's hands, propped it on a filing cabinet, and stood back.

'It's rather extraordinary,' he said. 'Are you sure you're not going to tell me how it came into your hands?'

'I'd like you to say what you think,' Pasquale insisted.

Courtier frowned, approached the painting to peer at it closely, and touched a rough area of yellow paint which stood up in relief. 'Well, it's by an amateur of course. But the extraordinary thing is that in places the brushwork, the technique, the colour, is almost exactly Claude's. That's why you've brought it to me, isn't it? Even the composition is in a very direct way his. It's almost as if . . .'

'Well, go on, as if what?'

'I was going to say that if Claude could suddenly be resurrected, this might be his first shot at painting - leaving out the obviously unskilled elements of course.'

Pasquale would not reveal who had painted the picture or how he had come across it but, in the sudden grip of an emotion whose dimensions he had never felt before, he abruptly and rudely left Courtier's office and returned briskly to the Villa.

Jacqueline had not yet returned. He went straight up to the

12

atelier and opened the window. In groups of two and three he began to throw the canvasses down into the garden. He then went down, made a stack of them on the grass, soaked them in some paraffin he found in the garden hut and put a match to them. In a few moments they were blazing. Only then did he begin to feel something nearer to normal. When the flames began to die down he went in, took the newspaper and, with his heart beating a little slower, went to sit in the downstairs salon.

He heard her come in. She went straight upstairs. He waited for her cry and again rehearsed what he was going to say to her - which he wanted to be, not emotional, but controlled, reasonable, even kind. Nothing happened. The heaviest of silences settled on the house which had the curious effect of making him feel he wasn't in it. Had she not seen what he had done? Had she not noticed her stack of canvases gone and the black smouldering ring on the lawn? He was forced to go up. She was in her smock at the easel, staring at a new canvas. She did not turn as he entered.

'This has got to stop,' he said. 'You're going mad. It's - evil.'

'You think so, Pasquale - evil?' she said. Her voice was light, almost humorous.

'I've burned the lot,' he said harshly.

'Yes, I see you have. But it doesn't matter. I'm still only learning, you see. In another month or two it will be different. In another month or two I shall have to protect the paintings, for they will not be mine, but his. If at that stage you were to burn those pictures you would be burning not my possessions but the heritage of France.'

He was seized again with the force of jealousy and frustration which had affected him in the Gallery. 'Stop it, Jacqueline, stop it this moment. I'm *commanding* you to stop it.'

She laughed tolerantly. 'But I can't stop it, even if I wanted to. I don't have the power. In two months it is the anniversary of Jean Baptiste's death. I somehow think that will be the day it happens. On that day I shall to all intents and purposes be one with him. It may even be that after that I shall not be troubling you for so very much longer.   My purpose on this earth will be accomplished.'

In the next days Pasquale was in such a turmoil he could not do his work.   For hours at a time he left the office on pretexts and went out for long walks out of the town in the countryside. Jacqueline *was* mad, he told himself, he should consult the doctor.   Perhaps a psychiatrist was necessary.   But behind these rhetorical thoughts he knew very well that he did not think Jacqueline was mad.   In some indefinable way, despite her antics, he felt she was as sane and as in control of herself as she had ever been.   Wasn't it the truth that Jacqueline had fallen in love, fallen in love with a ghost?   It was himself perhaps who needed help, not her.

Whenever he was in the house alone he sneaked into the studio to see the new canvases she had painted.   There was no doubt they were improving at an alarming rate.   Thinking about this and what it might lead to, tears mounted to his eyes.   He was being jilted, he thought, this great painter was taking his beloved wife from him, every day that passed it was drawing nearer a point of no return.

One afternoon, in an extremity of agitation he suggested to Alphonsine that they went to her bungalow.   In her usual way, she did not say yes or no, but began at once to make arrangements which would enable them both to leave the office and not return that day.

In these days of anxiety Pasquale knew his love-making had changed.   He felt his own physical urge no less impatiently but reached his own point of pleasure a great deal sooner than usual and without his usual regard for Alphonsine.   He said nothing of his trouble to her, and although he knew she might have realised he was not himself she had said nothing to him.   But today he knew, as he sat disconsolately in the armchair in his underclothes after another less than satisfactory performance, that he was going to have to say something.   Surely she would understand - perhaps give him some guidance.

'Alphonsine, you must have noticed that I have not been

behaving quite as usual lately.' Alphonsine was sitting up in bed, smoking. She regarded him, he thought, as if he were an object of mild interest she was looking at for the first time. It burst from him uncontrollably. 'I am a desperately unhappy man. My wife is becoming obsessive about painting, and I fear that she is ceasing to want to carry on as before. Alphonsine, I have to ask you - if, by any awful chance I should lose her . . . would you ever consent . . .'

'Would I become your wife, you mean?' He nearly wept for joy that she had said it, not him. 'No, I would not,' she continued after a moment. 'I would never want to be married to you, Pasquale.'

'But - I know it is perhaps indelicate of me at this difficult, perhaps tragic time - I am a man who needs stability. I shall of course do everything possible to avert such a dreadful outcome, but it would make such a difference to me to know that you . . .'

'Oh no, Pasquale, not marriage, not me. You should know that. It wouldn't work - our *living* together.'

It was a Friday. They never met at week-ends. Pasquale passed an impatient time waiting for Monday when he was sure he would have to renew his attempt to get things straight with Alphonsine. Surely, after she had thought about it, she would come to see that being his wife would have enormous advantages to her? If she consented, he thought, with an executive fierceness he was not accustomed to apply to anything but business, he would tell Jacqueline she would either snap out of her silliness or he would leave her.

Monday came. He arrived in the office early. Alphonsine did not come. He telephoned her bungalow, there was no reply. In an acute state of nerves he drove out at once to the suburb. He rang and knocked at her door. Getting no answer, he began to peer through one of the front windows. As he was doing so a woman next door came out of her door and saw him.

'Mademoiselle Noisette has gone away,' she said.

'Gone away, but she can't have. Where to?'

'To a relative, I believe. She said she would not be back for some time.'

When he returned to the office the post had arrived. Among his mail there was a letter addressed to him in Alphonsine's handwriting. He tore it open.

'*Dear Monsieur Ducroix,*' he read, '*I much regret that owing to family circumstances I have been forced to leave the town at very short notice. I do not anticipate returning for some time. Perhaps I shall not return at all. At all events I am forced to vacate my employment in your firm. I sincerely apologise for any inconvenience caused and trust you will quickly find a replacement. Naturally I do not expect any further wages than those I have been paid. Yours faithfully, Alphonsine Noisette.*'

Pasquale went out again, on foot. This time he did not wander in the countryside but in the town itself. He wandered for two hours in the labyrinth of small alleys, trying to find something of the atmosphere of the town of his birth that would comfort him.

He came at last, by accident not choice, to the street where he and Jacqueline used to live. To his mild surprise he saw that the old shop and the flat above it were up for sale again. He enquired in the shop next door, also owned now by strangers, and was told the people had gone bankrupt.

He was aware of a small interest stirring despite his desperate confusion. Noting the agent's name from the sign in the window, he went down at once to the Boulevarde des Platanes where the address was. Yes, he found, the property was for sale - at a price considerably more than he had got for it. He found himself putting in an offer at exactly the price he had received.

He thought no more about it. The bid wouldn't of course be accepted, his act had been a palliative to himself, no more. Back at work he slogged on, advertising for a new secretary, while at home Jacqueline continued with her weird obsession. But one evening, some week or two later, when he opened the front door a delicious smell of cooking was coming from the kitchen. He couldn't believe his nostrils. For the last month he had eaten nothing which required more than the most perfunctory preparation. Jacqueline was in the kitchen at work in her apron.

He imagined for a moment it was some new perversion of her inflamed imagination. Was Jean Baptiste Claude to join them for dinner perhaps? But he soon saw that some sort of a change had come over Jacqueline.

Half-way through the meal, when they were quite merry on a bottle of fine Brouilly she had bought, she referred casually to a phone call she'd had that day from a house agent. She understood he had made a bid for their old house. Well, the owners had accepted the bid.

He began to burble. He had thought, he said, that she no longer wanted him and that in the event of this being true he had thought he might go back to live there - where they had been so happy.

'But what a lovely idea, Pasquale,' he was amazed to hear her say, quite ignoring the statement about his feelings. 'Our old flat. Fancy. And we could convert the shop as we said we would and have a posh front door.'

'But - your painting, Jacqueline. You wouldn't want to leave here?'

'I can do my painting in the back room as I used to.'

'But Claude . . .'

'Oh, I think Claude has gone off me after all,' she said with a laugh. 'He tried hard to teach me how to paint, but I'm not good enough, perhaps not *faithful* enough. He has jilted me.'

The Ducrois sold their historic property very lucratively to the town council and moved back into their old dwelling, converting it into a small but very smart-looking town house. Jacqueline Ducrois became her husband's secretary at the meat-processing factory. Pasquale is now a town-councillor and likely to be mayor when his turn comes round. All the remaining pictures Jacqueline did she burnt before they moved, except one, the last one she painted. This was one which is quite recognisably a copy of Claude's celebrated portrayal of the Villa des Fleurs Blanches, which Pasquale insisted they kept. It hangs with suitable lighting at the top of their small precipitous staircase.

Visitors who know anything about art can almost be relied on to say how uncannily it resembles the master's work.   At this the Ducrois have been known to exchange the briefest of smiles.

THE ESSAY

In those days, not so long after the second world war, the ageing Rossiter was a power in the prestigious public school in which he had taught since the early twenties. Great schoolmasters - like great politicians, or great anything else - were not challenged so much in those days, their authority was not made accountable as it might be now.

At the time being referred to, if Rossiter were to make a rare appearance in the masters' common room - to bend short-sightedly at his pigeon-hole perhaps, or address a short remark to a senior colleague in his spare hoarse voice - younger beaks would exchange glances. They knew Rossiter was on a higher plane than themselves. He apparently never had boy problems other teachers and housemasters encountered. At staff meetings his brief contributions usually preempted further discussion. As a teacher there was no one in his league. History, his subject, was the elite among the sixth form 'disciplines'.

Rossiter had only one lung. He lost the other after being gassed in the first world war. He wore faded and well-worn but always neatly-creased grey suits, woollen ties, and highly polished leather shoes. He was a bachelor. In the holidays he went to stay with a widowed sister in the Lake District somewhere. His classroom was more like a chapel. A Victorian building, it had once been the school library and still had this function - for history alone. Books, many leather -bound, filled shelves high up the walls on three sides. The ceiling was a fine structure from whose stout cross-beams hung six ugly strip-lights on the end of long chains. The latter were needed even in broad daylight, for the few narrow gothic windows had stained glass. The boys sat at old-fashioned desks whose seats were joined to them. There was for Rossiter a flat-topped table which had casters and was covered with worn black leather, a tall-backed chair with a wicker seat, an old-style blackboard on an easel only ever used to write up French words -

Rossiter's pronunciation by his own admission 'never having crossed the Channel' - and the lectern.

Rossiter taught by lecturing. For three double periods a week his Upper Sixth listened in pin-dropping silence as relentlessly, lucidly, he encompassed Richelieu's ruthless subjugation of the French nobility, or unravelled the subtleties of James I - ' a much misunderstood man,' as Rossiter sympathetically described him. The lectern was rickety, for placing one foot on the base, clutching the top with both his bony white hands, Rossiter would rock it slowly from side to side as he talked, his large head tilted upwards to the rafters like that of an El Greco saint, as if it were from up there that he plucked down the words. Part of the tension he created indeed might have been the boys' concern that one day the lectern would collapse and send his aged frame tumbling. It never did, and the small voice went on, tip-toeing through the mysteries of the past, finding a line of thought which was powerful, illuminating and persuasive. It seemed Rossiter himself was in awe of his discoveries.

The boys took notes, which Rossiter never looked at. What Rossiter required of them were essays, one a week, informed from the matter of his lectures, from the standard textbook they all had, and from other books in the library he recommended 'for ampler study.' For the other two periods a week he saw them individually about their last essay while the rest of the class read.

Philip Lister, no scholar, had scraped into Rossiter's Sixth by dint of ardour and hard work. He was encouraged by the lower sixth master, who had more of a literary than a historical mind and saw that Philip had a love of words and writing, which might give him some armour for the daunting year he had ahead of him.

Philip had no father. He was an only child and a solitary boy. His mother had always encouraged him to read, especially history, which was her own passion. She had been a teacher before she married a rich glove manufacturer who had little interest in culture. Philip had noticed Rossiter one morning break when he was in the fifth form. At this time most of the school stood about in the huge central courtyard when it was fine. He saw Rossiter emerge from 'The Waverley' - which was the name given to the old library where he taught. Eyes down, his old brief-case tucked under his arm, hands in pockets, he set off with his rather trudging gait in the direction of his house. Boys seemed automatically to clear a path ahead of him. Philip had decided in this moment that he wanted to be in his sixth.

For the first weeks in Rossiter's class Philip was lost. He strained to understand the lectures, but it was like travelling in an aeroplane through broken cloud. There were sudden patches of bright clarity, then he was flipped back into grey nothingness with no visibility at all. It was the same with the textbook. Each sentence he could make sense of, but by the time he had reached the end of the paragraph he had forgotten the beginning and could gain no grasp of the whole thing. His first essay was a disaster. Words had always come easily to him and he covered three sides, but he knew it was just a patchwork of bits and pieces he had seized and written down, hoping like a lottery that they would somehow hold an answer to the question. There were no marks or comments on his manuscript, just a gamma minus scribbled in red ink at the bottom in Rossiter's thin handwriting. The second essay had a line through it and the caption, 'You do not begin to be relevant.' For the third he got a gamma without the minus. One of his paragraphs was marked with a vertical line in the margin and the words, 'pursue this line of thought and you might get on the map.' This gave him hope, although he had no idea why that particular paragraph had pleased nor what 'line of thought' he ought to pursue. He had not yet been called to sit with Rossiter and go through his work, so he could not ask.

One evening during 'free time,' when they had been set an essay on the causes of the English Civil War, Philip was in The Waverley browsing among the books on the shelf devoted to their period. It comforted him just to be in this room. He had a dream that Rossiter might come in when he was there and be so impressed at his interest that he would sit down and help him. He pulled out a smaller book, a somewhat worn paperback. The book was not upright on the shelf but stuffed along the top of the others as if it had not merited an orthodox place. Unlike the others, which had plain covers, it had a colour picture on the front. The picture was of a young girl - probably a princess, Philip thought at first glance. He was right. Sure enough, princess she was. It was a portrait of Henrietta Maria, Charles I's French wife, painted when she was a young girl.

He began to read. 'Charles Stuart first met his wife, to whom by then he had been legally married a month, at Dover. Who could have imagined at this moment that such a political marriage, the ceremony carried out in Paris by proxy, would be a love affair whose consequences would rock the kingdom and cost the lives of thousands of Englishmen?'

An hour later Philip was still reading, sitting on the floor by the shelf. He took the book out and back to his house. He devoured it that evening.

The next day he was filled with energy and excitement. The story of the proxy marriage moved him - the disastrous beginning, then as the magic of love began to weave its spell, the way in which Henrietta first supplanted Buckingham, hitherto Charles's favourite, then, renouncing her childish games, became seriously involved in the politics suggested by her Catholic faith. Was it not she who prompted Charles to rule without his tiresome Parliament, she, finally, as conflict threatened, who made Charles go down to Westminster from Whitehall Palace in the vain attempt to arrest the five members, those 'birds who had flown,' who had defied the royal prerogative? In the civil war, the love affair burned brighter still. And after it, Philip could hardly bear to read of Henrietta's last days when, her husband having been beheaded, she was forced to wander the cold corridors of St Germain Palace in poverty and despair, picking up the occasional small jewels Mazarin left about on purpose for her to steal, which she would have been too proud to accept from his hands.

The next evening Philip wrote his essay. He covered ten sides. Henrietta was obviously the cause of the Civil War - Henrietta, and Charles's love for her - this was his idea. In class the following day, when they had to put their essays on

Rossiter's table, instead of putting his at the bottom of the pile as he usually did, he waited until everyone had given theirs in, then placed his own on the top, neatly tethered with a paper clip. It was a thicker bundle than any of the others.

Lewis Rossiter rose from his chair simultaneously with his house prefects, who had been occupying the other easy chairs in his sitting-room. As they filed out silently and the last one closed the door, he moved to the marble mantelpiece where a heavy Edwardian clock, which spread itself in two elaborate scrolls on either side of a dial, sat complacently. It was its day for winding. Opening the glass gently with finger and thumb stretched, he fished for the key under the clock, inserted it into the face, and gave it a precise and fastidious twelve circuits. He replaced the key and refastened the dial cover.

The act released an emotion he was not prepared for. Unruly thoughts scampered ahead of him involuntarily like unleashed dogs. Less than two years now, he thought, and he would be free to roam the fells, free to read, to write, to think, to talk to his sister and enjoy her cooking. He reined himself back. For most of his adult life he had taught boys to concentrate on the matter in hand, to be relevant, concise, mentally honest. He couldn't allow himself, even in these last terms, to depart from life-long held principles. To his evening's work, he told himself.

As usual these days, not feeling up to the Common Room dining-room, he lifted the telephone to ask the kitchen to send up his meal, and first set about tidying the room. Books boys had returned were put back into the glass-fronted bookcase, the gown he had flung over a chair after evening chapel he hung up on the back of the door. Finally, the room immaculate, after a last glance at the headmaster's garden which he overlooked, he drew the curtains on the fading twilight and reduced illumination to the two wall lights and the standard beside his chair. He addressed himself to housemasterly correspondence at his desk.

'Lamb tonight, sir,' Gillespie informed him cheerfully as later, having knocked, he opened the door, the tray balanced on a raised knee. 'Mint sauce, new-*ish* potatoes, and an attempt at a trifle.   Worthy of a claret?   I took the liberty of adding a half-bottle.   I can take it away of course if you're not in the mood.'

Gillespie was the only person in the school he felt at ease with. As Gillespie took out a white linen table-cloth from the drawer and began to lay up one end of the polished table, he cast an eye on the tray.   With an unusual descent into the temporal, he lifted the metal entré cover.   'Oh, I think the indulgence could be made tonight, yes,' he said.

The ritual proceeded.   The meal laid, Rossiter sat and spread the starched table napkin on his knees while Gillespie drew the cork and poured a little of the wine for his tasting.

'Palatable,' Rossiter said, adjudging it with a chewing motion of his jaw.

'Will there be anything further, sir?' finished Gillespie.   He departed, pleased.   Gillespie had once worked for an earl.   To serve Rossiter he considered an equal honour, and coming up to his room was always a short relief from the banalities of school feeding.

Fed and wined, Rossiter felt fortified to tackle his main task of the evening, the Upper Sixth essays that lay in a neat bundle on the Queen Anne bureau.   When another of the men had been up to clear, he set about this work.

Six of the sixteen were worth teaching.   Four would almost certainly win Oxbridge scholarships.   He selected their work first.   He did of course now and then question his methods against the growing modern trend of socratic dialogue with the pupils.   There were times when he doubted the efficacy of lecturing.   The proof, he always told himself, was in the boys' essays.   He regarded them as a weekly inspectorate of his teaching.   He was not disappointed with the six.   All had, in various ways, squared convincingly to a complex subject.   It entranced him to see how their dawning intelligence had impelled them to tug at the tightly woven cloth of his own theses or those of the books.   Here and there they succeeded in pulling a strand or two loose.   Only one of them had simply registered what he had read, but even he had made an effort to present the material differently.   Another six months and they would all be ready for University.

He took a break to pour himself a glass of port before confronting the mediocre and the rubbish, each of which took double the time of the good essays.   It was always tempting to skip, but he read painstakingly, often re-reading, searching for coherent ideas which might be salvageable from beneath the mental detritus and literary incompetence.   One whole paragraph which fell into this category he rewrote for a boy, using as far as possible his own teenage language.   Having noted its extravagant length, he kept Philip Lister's essay until the last.   It was obvious what he had done.   Stung by his failure to date, he had thought to amaze with volume.   Probably he had paraphrased passages taken at random from several of the books in the hope of concealing his tracks.   The only interest would be to spot the books in order to teach the boy not to do it again.   Lister was a mistake.   He should have steered him elsewhere - into economics probably.

Philip spent the week-end in a fever of anticipation.   Monday afternoon was when Rossiter usually gave back the essays.   He was sure his work would have made an impression.   How could it fail to have done when he had felt so strongly for the ill-assorted couple caught in their lonely tragedy, particularly Henrietta who, so French, was exiled to a land she didn't understand or like.   Out of his own dislike of school life, he identified with her cruel fate.   He dreamed of seeing a beta, even an alpha, at the bottom of his work, with interested and interesting comments in the margins, embellishments he had seen on other boys' papers.   With Rossiter's smallest encouragement, how he would work, how pleased his mother would be.

Monday was wet.   Rain surged over the downs above the bleakly situated school, streamed callously from blocked gutters and pipes into the court.   By mid-afternoon all the classrooms had lights on.   Philip was heedless of the gloom.   His heart raced as Rossiter entered The Waverley, shook out his umbrella by the door and left it open to drain.

The period was to be for reading.   Rossiter sat at his table and began to call forward boys to talk to them about their work. Each time one rose to return to his desk, Philip's pulses started up again.   Rossiter fingered the diminishing pile of essays   It must be his now, surely.   But another boy was called, and another long murmured colloquy began.   With only five minutes left Philip's hopes were dying.   Perhaps, he vainly tried to persuade himself, his essay was so good there was no need for comment.   In a minute Rossiter would rise to distribute the remaining essays he had not time to discuss.

'Lister.'   His name was spoken like a pistol shot.   Philip almost fell out of his desk.   Hitching his trousers with his elbows with an awkward mmovement like a fourth-former he made his way forward.   'Sit down, sit down,' Rossiter said impatiently as Philip stood beside him.

Philip had never been quite so close to Rossiter.   He smelt faintly of antiseptic.   The white fingers, which were almost like those of a skeleton, were turning the pages of his essay.   The back of his hand, he saw, was blotched with large liver-coloured freckles.   Rossiter cleared his throat

'Where did you get this from?' he said in a spare whisper.

'From, sir?'

'Well, it didn't come out of your head, did it?'

'No sir.   I mean some of it, sir, yes.   I found a book, you see . . .'

'Doubtless you found a book, but which book?'

'Over there . . .'   Philip nodded, transfixed, in the direction of the shelf.

'Fetch it.'

Watched by the class he went to get the flimsy paperback.   He handed it to Rossiter.   Rossiter scrutinised its tattered cover, back and front.   He opened the first page and read.   Then he leaned to drop it in the waste-paper basket.

'I do not recall recommending this book.   Indeed it is not in the library.   If that is the shelf where you found it, I do not know how it got there.'

'You mean, it's no good, sir?'

He did not receive an answer to this question. 'Quite apart from the book you have plagiarised, Lister, there is no answer in your essay to the question set. At best it is a slice of biography. As historians we are not interested in biography *per se* - that is journalism. You have been assiduous - little more, I fear.'

'You mean my essay isn't right?'

This also was ignored. 'You will see I have indicated a few of the directions in which you might look to begin to try to explain the complex subject of the outbreak of the Civil War. If you examine these you may well come to the conclusion that the Queen's behaviour and her relationship with the King, though interesting and in some peripheral ways relevant, is a very small part of the matter.'

Philip Lister lacked everything, it seemed, except courage and persistence. Silently, alone, he wept in bed that night, but he recovered quickly to try again. By the end of the year he had learnt sufficient of Rossiter's doctrine of the relevant and the succinct to scrape a place at a tertiary college where eventually he obtained a second class diploma in 'modern studies.' His mother had hoped he would become a writer or a journalist with his interest in stories and his talent for writing - so, in his earlier days, had Philip. But under Rossiter's tacit and remote control he decided to become a civil servant. Surely, if he could manage it, Rossiter would approve of this? After taking an exam in which his sense of relevance was noted - and no doubt the eminent school he had attended - against expectations he obtained entry to the executive branch of the Home Office. Since then he has risen to a moderate level, and has indeed always been noted for his extremely clear memoranda and for his impatience with disordered thinking. He never reads fiction.

Rather late in the day, when his mother was dead and he was in his early forties, Philip noticed a not unattractive and sensible girl among the non-executive secretarial staff. He courted and married her. The honeymoon was in the Lake District. Remembering Rossiter had retired there, he looked him up in the phone book and was glad to find his name, coupled with that of a

Miss Ann Rossiter, living at an address near Keswick.   He phoned, made an appointment, and went to see his old history master, taking with him his new bride.

How old Rossiter was, in an invalid chair, his scraggy neck stretched even higher, the voice sparer, the metal half-spectacles perched more precariously on his aquiline nose.   He must be over ninety.   Philip had a rush of affection and gratitude for the old man who had played such a part in his life and who no doubt - he was more than prepared to concede it - had been the basis of that small success he had had in life, which he now modestly described.

As he spoke Rossiter strained his big head upwards.   Was he again seeing those massive rafters in The Waverley?

'Lister, yes, of course I remember you, Lister.   You wrote rather indifferent essays if I recall.   Civil Service, eh?   Strange. I wouldn't have thought you'd have chosen such an intellectual career.   More cut out for journalism or something of that sort I'd've said.'

LAST LEG.

She was glad to get out of the heat, but the cool posh hotel was disquieting - the way her two small suitcases were seized from her as she entered and taken somewhere, though she wanted to keep them by her, the contemptuous look the hall porter gave her when she asked where the 'buffet restaurant' was, as if she wouldn't be entitled to enter it.   There *was* a buffet restaurant, surely - Harold had said there was, where she was to have her lunch.

But when she had eaten, and was sitting in one of the comfortable white leather armchairs in the huge marble hall, she felt easier.   At the far end a sort of waterfall ran over an opaque glass wall into a pool at the bottom, the light sound was soothing, and she began to think that the knot of rich-looking Arabs, sitting on cushions in a group in their white robes and headdresses, no longer seemed sinister as they had.   She had some time ago observed they were not engaged on some important business, merely passing the time of day.   Paring and filing their nails, they eyed passers-by vacantly, as if they were at home not sitting in a hotel, and took endless cups of coffee from an Arabian Nights brass coffee pot with a curving spout set on a low metal table.   They came in for the air-conditioning, she supposed, outside it must be in the upper nineties by now.

She must have dozed off.   She dreamed of being at the school and that Robin, one of her asthmatics, was having a bad attack and that she couldn't find his breathing apparatus.   She woke with a start and, looking at her watch, saw with apprehension it was nearly four. She quickly drew out Harold's typed sheet from her bag, put on her glasses, and tried to smooth out the creases with the flat of her hand.   He had been, as ever, meticulous, going minutely into every stage of her journey.

'The only tiresome bit,' she read, '*is Dubai to Abu Dhabi, the last leg.   You can fly, but it's as quick, and quite a lot cheaper, to do the hundred odd miles by road.   Now you could get a car*

right away from the airport, but Bel and I are both going to be tied up most of the day and we wouldn't want you to arrive before we're home. You'll also probably feel like a rest after your flight. This is why I am routing you into town on your arrival, to the <u>Hyatt Regency Hotel</u>, which in my opinion is the best. I suggest you have some lunch there in the buffet restaurant (I don't imagine you'll want a full-scale lunch) and take a rest in the lobby. Then about fourish ask the doorman to get you an <u>air-conditioned limousine</u>. Now you must insist on the latter exactly as I have written, as if you don't the man's quite likely to fob you off with some lesser vehicle for the same price - whose driver of course would be a friend of his who'd give him a cut. The fare will be 500 dirhem (one hundred pounds sterling) so make sure you have that handy (this includes a tip, so add nothing for that). You must establish this amount before you start, but tell the doorman clearly that's what you'll pay and let him do the haggling with the driver, and give him a dirhem or two for his pains. Now don't pay the driver of course until you're right outside our villa - in fact let Bel come out and do it for you to make sure <u>he</u> doesn't get up to any tricks . . .'

There was quite a bit more - what seemed to be the exact reasons why Bel couldn't be home before five-thirty. Harold was also apologising again for himself, she saw at the bottom of the page - he had done so before - that he couldn't come over to Dubai to meet her, 'biz being biz, alas,' as he put it. She found herself putting down the page and taking off her specs. Her brother-in-law was immensely kind. It was kind of him to have suggested this trip in the first place, and even offered to pay - thank goodness she hadn't agreed to that. It was also true she had led a sheltered life compared with his and Bel's, that this was her first trip to a destination outside Europe where there might be pitfalls, but she surely wasn't quite such a dope as he implied, was she? It was in this context, she knew, she found herself now remembering the incident at Dubai airport.

She had been queuing at passport control. In front of her was a bearded young Englishman with a rucksack on his back. He was friendly and asked her what she was doing in Dubai. When she said it wasn't Dubai but Abu Dhabi she was going to, he laughed and said he was, too - he was at university, and his parents lived there. After a moment she couldn't help asking him if he would be taking the limousine, too - the thought had crossed her mind that they might share the fare. 'Good heavens no,' he said. 'Nobody in their right mind does that. Costs the earth. You go to the bus souk in a taxi, and then you get a minibus. They go every hour or two and it costs you under a fiver. It's just as quick.'

She had been a fool. She should have gone with him there and then, and perhaps would have done but for Harold's instructions lying in her bag like the Israelites' tablets. Because of them and her desire to conform and not cause a stir, it didn't occur to her. But now, a residual pride stirred. She wasn't surely the innocent Harold liked to depict her. She eyed the doorman lounging at this becalmed hour on the sofa by the glass doors. One hundred pounds against five, that was three weeks' food - and the return air fare had set her back. Then one of the Arabs got up. Adjusting his headdress which had become rather comically cocked sideways, he began to pad across the hall in his yellow sandals - to the toilet probably. Arabs were people like anyone else. Why should she be afraid? Harold and Bel would be annoyed but, she thought with an inner tremor of excitement, need they ever know?

She was on the verge of changing her mind when she had the doorman get her bags, which he had put out of sight somewhere. 'Taxi, where to?' he asked, holding a bag in each hand and backing through the glass door. She saw the driver of the first taxi in the queue outside sit up expectantly. It was a huge American-looking car, surely a 'limousine.' The heat puffed at her like a hair-dryer. She imagined herself settling back into the air-conditioned plush of that back seat, the last anxiety of her journey over. She wrenched herself from this cosy vision.

'I want a taxi to the bus souk,' she heard herself say.

She immediately wished she hadn't. The look on the

and started off, the taxi-driver, who spoke some English, wanted to know which bus she was taking. 'You go Sharja? I tek you. One hunnerd dirhem,' he said, looking at her in the driving-mirror. She wanted to check there *was* a bus to Abu Dhabi from this place. 'No, I'm not going to Sharja, but to Abu Dhabi,' she said, looking sideways out of the window to escape his eyes. 'Abu Dhabi?' he said. 'I tek you. Six hunnerd dirhem. Ver' quick.' He waved a finger horizontally. 'Bus no goot for leddy. Menny menny pipple. No aircondishning. Ver' hot.'

Perhaps if he hadn't gone on so she would have agreed, but he kept repeating his few phrases all the way to the bus souk. She supposed she got British about it. At the end of the journey he became surly. She was sure she had given him more than enough money, but he wanted more. She gave him another dirhem and turned her back. Mercifully it worked.

The so-called souk was daunting - a great un-tarmacked area full of people, luggage, livestock, and round the perimeter several ancient-looking ochre-coloured vehicles waiting like antediluvian monsters, and it was stiflingly hot. She fixed the strap of her handbag firmly over her shoulder, put on the wide-brimmed hat she had brought, picked up her cases and looked round her, bewildered. A man approached in a white embroidered fez, with carpets over his shoulder. 'Ver' nice carpet, leddy, you buy?' Another vendor lurked behind him with a monkey on his arm. 'Abu Dhabi?' she said to the carpet man. He didn't seem to understand, and threw a carpet open - thrump - at her feet.

She turned away and hurried off. She saw a European man in a battered straw hat and tried to get to him, but he disappeared in the throng. She wandered helplessly. Then in the corner of the square she saw a parked white minibus. The young man at the airport had said a minibus, hadn't he? A man beside it was shouting at the top of his voice, repeating the words over and over. Wasn't it Abu Dhabi he was saying? She approached.

'Abu Dhabi, are you going to Abu Dhabi?' she said distinctly.

The man stopped shouting a moment, jerked his head at a boy

'Abu Dhabi, are you going to Abu Dhabi?' she said distinctly.

The man stopped shouting a moment, jerked his head at a boy with a dirty brown sheish bandaged round his head and took out a leather wallet full of notes. While she paid the man - it was exactly the price the young man had said - the boy immediately jumped to seize her cases. Attaching their handles to a pole with a hook on the end he lifted them to the roof of one of the vehicles on whose rack another boy sat. The man was again shouting frenetically, and this time she made out clearly what he was saying - 'Abu Dhabi, Abu Dhabi, Abu Dhabi . . .' She felt like a fish that had been caught and flung into the hold.

The bus was half-full of men, all Arabs or Pakistanis - Harold had said a large percentage of the population of Dubai was immigrant. She thought she guessed the system. There was no timetable, they waited until they had all the seats taken before starting. Should she get in? Was it really the right bus? Would her cases be all right? Then she saw that one of the sitting people was a woman who held a child. Thankful, she climbed in and sat in an empty seat in front of her. She would need to reserve the seat or it would be taken. 'This *is* for Abu Dhabi, isn't it?' she said, turning to the woman. The woman drew her veil closer her face and looked away. But the man beside her nodded. 'Abu Dhabi,' he said. Simultaneously, another man sitting in the single front seat beside the driver's got out and indicated that she should take it. She would not have to be sandwiched in the confined space between two men. She was relieved. 'How kind, how very kind of you,' she said, bowing her head and beaming at the man as she clambered out of the bus again. The man showed no emotion but he had left the front door open for her. He spat for good measure and entered the other door.

She was at once ashamed at her apprehension. It was hot, and sweat was running down her neck into her cotton dress - why on earth did they cover the seats with sheepskins in this climate? - but she was greatly relieved. They were decent people. In a few minutes they would be off and there would be a breeze.

In twenty minutes they had their complement. She was rejoicing at her triumph in spite of the discomfort of the heat, when at the eleventh minute a man arrived to take the seat of the woman with the child, who must have been keeping it for him. She got out. Immediately all her worries were back. Among the last arrivals had been three young men. She was sure they were making remarks about her, they kept laughing raucously. Two hours of this, a hundred miles or more, of perhaps deserted road - anything could happen. Should she get out even now, return to the hotel and take a limousine after all? But it was too late, the driver was in his seat and starting the engine. Would he protect her if things got nasty? She couldn't think so, he wasn't much older than the youths.

For half an hour she sat looking straight ahead of her. The engine made it even hotter. The smell of oil and strong tobacco smoke was suffocating. The driver switched on the radio and the Arab music blared out with tuneless, tinny monotony. The sun was setting, it would surely be dark long before they arrived. As they left the town an utterly barren landscape opened of grey rock and soil. In a bout of real fear she imagined them turning off the road, raping her and leaving her to die. How could she have been so foolish as to think that what was all right for an undergraduate with a rucksack was right for her? Why hadn't she listened to Harold, who knew the Middle East and was so sensible?

Then once again her fears began to ebb. In the driving mirror she saw that two men were asleep. The young men were quieter. The engine droned on and did not seem likely to break down. There were other cars passing them going back to Dubai. Once or twice faster luxurious cars overtook them. In the space of a few minutes the heat relented as the sun sank fast in a fiery haze to the west. The desert was suddenly, briefly, beautiful in the encompassing rosy light. They passed a herd of camels eating something they had found in the wasteland. Some buildings appeared in the distance. As they approached the driver switched the radio off. There was a stir behind her. Apparently they would stop.

It was a broken-down looking café with a Cococola sign in English as well as in Arabic script. Another larger bus was parked. Beside the café was another shack. The men began to pile out of the bus and make for this shack. She presumed it was a lavatory. Out of the corner of her eye she then saw through the door. People were on their knees inside, praying. On the roof she spotted a crescent moon, knocked slightly sideways. It was a makeshift mosque, they were saying their sunset prayers.

Once more relief and delight flooded over her. It was all right. It had been all right from the start. She would arrive safely. They were honourable nice people. It was in England where rape and mugging happened, and Saudi Arabia, not the Emirates, where women didn't go out. How could she have allowed such unreasonable cowardice and prejudice to warp her mind? When later the polished lights of Abu Dhabi twinkled in the royal blue half-light she felt a surge of joy and confidence. She had done it. Just for once she was one up on Harold Rubin - though of course, if she could possibly avoid it, she would say nothing.

She had expected they would arrive at another 'bus souk'. But as they went into the town passengers were shed where they requested to be put off. Finally there was only herself and the three noisy youths when the driver suddenly did a U-turn into a sort of lay-by and stopped. It was near the crossing of two large boulevards of the modern concrete city, no taxi rank in sight. The driver tilted his head, indicating that she should dismount and himself got out to get her luggage down from the roof. The youths were already standing outside. It seemed they were waiting for her. She moved away. 'Town centre - taxi?' she said to the driver as he handed her the cases. He hunched his shoulders.

The young men approached, they *were* waiting for her. But face to face, they seemed almost shy. 'You - American?' dared one. 'No, English,' she said. This seemed to please them. 'Are - you - a - teacher?' another asked, spacing the words with pleasure as if each were precious and prize-winning. 'Yes, I am as a matter of fact,' she told them. 'I teach small children.'

They seemed impressed, as if this were the most honourable profession possible. It turned out they were learning English at a language school. After more halting exchanges they took her to a taxi rank. She showed them Harold's address which was written on his instruction paper for this very purpose, in Arabic script as well as English, and all three of them spoke urgently to the driver. They returned to her, one opened the door of the car and told her to pay only four dirhems. As she was swept through the tender warm night and the exciting lights, she sat smiling in the back of the vehicle. She thought of the boys as the centre-piece of an experience she had to see as rather humbling as well as triumphant. With their concern and politeness and jollity they could have been sons honouring their mother, and she had been casting them as hooligans.

The Rubins lived in what seemed a European ghetto on the outskirts of the town - an orderly area of new-looking bungalows, gardens, and, amazingly, some small trees. She realised she hadn't seen a tree since she landed in Dubai. The driver found the house all right. There in front of her uncompromisingly was the word 'Widdecombe', which she had written so many times on envelopes. She stopped the driver from turning into the drive and quickly paid him outside. All was well, nothing stirred in the house, though the lights were all on including a welcoming porch light. They would never know she hadn't arrived in a limousine.

She waited until the car drove off then focused her attention on the pleasure of seeing her elder sister and brother-in-law. It was a year since they had been home on leave. Bel opened the door, all concern. 'Jennifer, how wonderful, you've got here, we've been worried.'

Only for a fleeting moment did Jennifer feel at the usual disadvantage - Bel's tanned skin, her faultless hair-do, the expensive silk dress and gold accessories, the strong exotic-smelling perfume, and by contrast her own no doubt pale travel-soiled appearance on top of her usual comparative dowdiness. But Bel's welcomes and farewells, whatever happened in between them, were always genuine. They had been close as children. She joined in the celebration full-heartedly. They embraced warmly.

Bel remembered the car, looking at the empty drive. 'But the car, have you . . .'

'Oh, all taken care of,' she laughed. 'Thanks to Harold's instructions there wasn't a hitch.'

She was immediately offered a bath and time 'to rest up a bit' - Bel and Harold were full of American expressions. She did the right thing by saying she was fresh as a daisy and what she really wanted to do was to see the house, of which she had read so much in Bel's letters. She knew only too well how proud Bel was of the new wealth Harold's success had brought her and the things it bought, which was such a contrast to what they had come from. And why shouldn't prosperity be enjoyed, she thought? She was as appreciative as she could be at the modern kitchen with all its gadgets, the living-room with plushy Swedish furniture, the expensive carpets and mats, the dainty luxurious bedroom - the spare-room, too - the efficient air-conditioning unit, and the bathroom which had a jacuzzi and gold taps and fitments.

She was then allowed her bath and time to change. While she was re-dressing Harold came in. She heard his car and loud voice outside, then in the house. Harold welcomed her as warmly as Bel had done, actually embracing her which wasn't a thing he normally did. Drinks, however, were a bit of an ordeal. Harold started interrogating her about the flight - the exact timings, the weather at Heathrow, the type of aircraft she had flown in of which she hadn't the faintest notion. She had to say precisely what she had chosen to eat in the Dubai hotel - he seemed to know its menu by heart. She mentioned several delicious items she had noticed but not eaten, but he still suggested she had missed the best. When it came to describing details of 'the last leg' as he continued to describe the car journey from Dubai, she was afraid she might make some slip which would reveal the kind of vehicle in which she had really travelled, but it was soon clear that Harold was more interested in telling her what she would have seen than in hearing her account. His brow wrinkled momentarily when he heard that she hadn't got Bel out to pay the driver of her car as he had instructed. He asked her what she had paid. 'The fare was what you said it would be,' she said, the only lie she had to tell. It seemed to satisfy him. She musn't criticize, she reminded herself, it was only his unusual ration of energy and, again, his kindly interest in her welfare.

Suddenly, the conversation flagging a bit, he hit the palm of his hand with a clenched fist, and looked at Bel, not her. 'Right now, I bet you're feeling like some grub, Jenny. I know I am. Not too tired, I hope?'

'We thought we'd take you to the Club, dear,' said Bel apologetically. 'I should have cooked, I know - your first night. But it *has* been a day for me, I'm afraid, one way and another.' Why should she mind? The Club sounded immensely exciting, and now she'd had a bath, put on a more suitable dress and had a drink, she felt ready for anything.

She was horrified when she saw the prices on the menu - ten pounds for the starter alone - but she didn't allow herself to worry. She was on holiday. If they had invited her they could presumably afford it. Prices were always relative. She would do her bit here and there where she could, and enjoy herself. That was always the best way for a guest to behave. No host likes guilt.

They really did go to immense trouble on her behalf. Harold had taken the week off from his oil company, and Bel had cancelled a lot of her usual engagements. As they explained, they had also suspended their tennis-playing while she was with them, which they did early every morning before it got hot. After the first morning when she was allowed to 'sleep in a bit', they got up at six and something was organised each day. Harold was an engineer. One whole morning he took her round the oil refinery, explaining in detail how everything worked. She was certainly very interested, and tried not to show it when she found her energy flagging. Bel took her shopping twice, to two different souks. Bel made her buy a Kaftan and a gold bracelet she didn't really want, but she found the thronged shops and stalls fascinating. They drove around the town several times to look at important buildings. Being high rise and ultra-modern concrete, all looked the same to her, but Harold was a mine of information about everything. They saw ministries in which he had business, the new post-office which Harold explained had all the most up-to-date state of the art technology, the Sheikh's Palace, the sea front on whose concrete promenade there were flower-beds planted with specially selected thick-leaved plants and a few nice lawns, which had to be watered constantly, morning and evening. They visited a marine museum, and every day they went to the club for snack lunches and a swim. On four evenings dinner parties had been arranged for her at their friends' houses, all of whom were British. On the other nights they again went to the club for dinner.

Jennifer enjoyed herself, but she did have some private thoughts. Interesting as it all was to see, she reflected that the kind of life they led here would never have suited her. Everyone she met - and these were all Europeans - seemed to be so much the same, interested in salaries and what could be bought with them - the latter of which didn't actually seem to be so very much once the club had been mentioned with its various amenities. They were also fervent in running down the inefficiency of Arabs, who wouldn't have been able to achieve anything here, it seemed, had it not been for the ex-patriots showing them the way. Was that really true? And they seemed endlessly fascinated with gossip about their own community - who was sleeping with whom and the rest of it. She didn't allow herself to dwell on these private criticisms of hers, but she had to admit she was rather glad that through her local authority she had herself fixed to visit two state English language primary schools in Abu Dhabi. As they very hospitably sent a car for her in both instances, she had a few hours' breather from the busy programme. The schools were delightful, the children and their teachers alike so bright, so fervent. They were all eager, it seemed, to meet her and hear her speak what one of the Indian teachers called 'Her Majesty's English'. They questioned her closely about her school in England, as if education there was a kind of Mecca.   She could not help thinking, from her point of view, what a cultural oasis this was from ex-patriot life.

She wondered whether it wasn't these two visits which were responsible for the slight malaise which she sensed was appearing towards the end of the week.   There had always been a subcurrent between herself and Harold, which she had felt capable of keeping under control by a simple application of tact on her part - the avoidance of certain no-go areas, and a frequent demonstration of how much she admired Harold's achievements, which she didn't need to fake.   But from the start, the school visits seemed to cause a special tension.   She had naturally told Harold about them in advance by letter.   'But what on earth do you want to do that for on holiday?' he had written back, 'we've got a very full schedule worked out for you, you know.'   She really wished after this she hadn't made the arrangement, which Harold seemed to see as some kind of a slight on his hospitality, but by then it was too late to cancel them.

Perhaps the second mistake was to respond in any detail to the question Bel put to her about the schools during the dinner which followed the first visit.   It was only a perfunctory query to which she could have given a polite general answer, but as she hadn't had too much occasion to speak she thought it was something on which she could make a contribution.   She talked about the remarkable enthusiasm and also the achievement she had seen, especially in reading and writing, compared with her experience of British primary school standards.   A senior class of eight year olds had been reading selected bits of Shakespeare.   She didn't think such mild comment would tread on any dangerous ground, in fact she thought it would coincide with Harold's usual propensity for running down British life - unless it was the exported variety he was part of out here.   During her account she became aware that Harold was getting restless.

'Shakespeare, eh?' he said suddenly, grinning, interrupting her.

'Er - yes.'

'You realise it was put on for you.'

'Oh, I don't think it was, Harold.'

'Of course it was. Who was reading the Shakespeare? The teacher of course. It was going right over the kids' heads.'

'No, it wasn't like that actually. It wasn't the teacher reading, it was the children. They were *acting* the words as they read them. You could see they understood the meaning very well.'

'Then it was a selected school. Who fixed the visits?'

'The Ministry of Education.'

'There you are then. They made sure you saw the best - an English-speaking school. And you may be sure some jerk in an office told the head to be sure to put on a show to impress you. I do know my Abu Dhabi, Jenny.'

Should she proceed? It was probably true it was a particularly good school. Leave it here, a voice said, defer to him. She already knew Harold's views on the value of education, why incite them again? But just for a moment the wispy ginger hair, the pink complexion and freckled pudgy hands particularly irritated her.

'Even if it was the very best school, it was still impressive,' she said with a hint of starch she couldn't keep out. 'I found it heartening - *morally* uplifting.'

She knew as soon as she had said this word that she had launched a deadly missile. She could almost hear the thud as it embedded itself in Harold's muscley bulk. 'Moral, eh?' he said, with a sniffy laugh. 'A tricky word, moral.'

She was almost certain that at this point Bel touched Harold's foot with hers under the table. He looked at her quickly, and gave another small laugh. Bel got them off on another tack about the other people in the restaurant.

Jennifer was not convinced Harold had been quelled. While Bel talked he played with a spoon and stared at the tablecloth Had he ever shrunk from a challenge? The Indian waiter brought an elaborate cornucopia of fruit and ice-cream presented in artful baskets of spun sugar which Harold had insisted on for all of them. Bel's monologue was rudely interrupted.

'Now look, Jenny,' Harold said when the food had been distributed. 'I know Bel doesn't want me to say this, and I don't want to be a bore. I certainly don't want to criticise your profession in general - for which there is an obvious need. But I have to say what I mean about education *out here*, which I think I'm entitled to speak about. Just think of the future. What's going to happen is that sooner or later, and probably sooner, the fundamentalists are going to overthrow the Sheikhs. The writing's on the wall. Now what's going to happen then? Do you think that lot are going to care about general culture? Like hell they are. History and literature and the rest of it - even English, unless it's strictly technical English - will go straight out of the window. What they need is maths, sciences, business studies, not Shakespeare. And as for teaching anything to the girls, this is a total waste of time. What are the women going to do when the Sheikhs have had their throats cut? Stay at home, do their menfolk's dobi, and produce babies, if they've any sense. If they don't, or if they're educated, they'll probably have their throats cut, too.'

She only nodded at all this, eventually they got off the subject of education and the evening finished in reasonable order. It wasn't the point, Harold's clever politics were not the point, her mind shrieked behind her silence. The point was not at all Abu Dhabi and the Emirates and oil, which were his ground - on which he did have a right to speak. Her point was *him*, Harold, his motive, his general attitude to learning and culture which, under cover of possibly sensible remarks about Gulf politics, he wanted to denigrate. But it was pointless, counter-productive to dispute with him. He would always see her as single, female, and a teacher, the three ingredients which in his vocabulary were a definition of irrelevance. There were only three more days. Let them be harmonious, she decided.

She managed to pay for dinner on the penultimate night but - was it to go one better, she could not help thinking? - for her last evening Harold insisted on taking them to what he called 'an expensive restaurant.' Goodness, what was expensive if the club wasn't? 'It's dear, damned dear,' he said almost grimly, 'but the best. My position does allow me to afford it once in a while on special occasions, and this has to be one.'

She was again grateful, and felt really warm towards both of them. Whatever small annoyances there were, they were nothing beside the kindness and the fact that Harold *was* doing an important job and that Britain *did* need people like him.

It was a nice evening. They even encouraged her to talk a bit about her own life, which she hadn't had an opportunity to do before. Bel was quite complimentary. 'Must say I wouldn't know where to start, Jenny, even if I had the patience,' she said, 'faced with a pack of unruly nippers as you must be *these days.*' This was hardly an apt description of her pupils, who were lively, but for the most part easy to handle. But the gesture went a long way in terms of goodwill. Then right at the end of the meal Harold realised she was off tomorrow and that he must make arrangements for her return journey to Dubai. Holding his wrist-watch by finger and thumb, he stared down at the huge dial which, he had explained her, gave a lot of other information in addition to the time. 'Now I hate to think of your leaving us, Jenny,' he said, 'but your plane leaves Dubai at ten p.m. tomorrow. That means you'd better leave here, let me see, about five to be on the safe side.' He would order the car first thing in the morning to come to the villa at that time.

It could have been the extra drink or the niceness of the evening which had lulled her into a relaxation of vigilance. Indeed, the thought had crossed her mind that she might take a limousine going back to avoid a situation. But before she could censor herself, a reply had slipped out as if it had been there ready-made all the time. 'Oh no, don't do that, Harold. I think I'll go back the way I came.' Her voice was firm in a way which surprised her. This was, after all, *her* ground.

Harold's reddish face was looking at her in astonishment.

'The way you came?'

She realised her remark hadn't been a mistake on her part and that she had intended it all along. Though she didn't feel aggressive, certainly not defensive, the sight of Harold's face leaning towards her, the rather boyish pink hands clutching the edge of the table, confirmed her in a quite positive feeling that something had happened to her on her short journey. Would she ever be in thrall to Harold again?

'I have a confession to make,' she said with a smile. 'I didn't take a limousine in Dubai. I met a young man at the airport who told me he always came here by bus, which only costs five pounds. The bus took me into the middle of the town, then some nice Arab boys helped me to get a city taxi to your house.'

They both faced her like a firing squad. 'But that was incredibly foolish,' Harold said. Bel nodded vigorously.

'Was it?'

'Anything could have happened.   Nobody - no European woman - does that.'

'Well only nice things happened, and this particular European woman *did* do it.'

'You cannot possibly go back this way.'

She was briskly insistent, and in the end, perhaps because she in no way presented her decision as a defiance, but simply as an eccentricity if they liked to think of it that way, Harold concurred. 'Well you teachers sure are a crazy bunch of cookies,' he was brought to say finally, shaking his head in some semblance of good humour.   Was this a breakthough?

They took her to the bus stop in their car.   On the way she again warmly thanked them for her holiday, their thoughtfulness for her entertainment, their generosity, and also, she added, the fact that the trip had undoubtedly 'widened her horizons a bit.' She thought afterwards that phrase might have been quite Solomon-like.   Harold would think it was himself who was responsible for the enlargement.

Stopping on the opposite side of the boulevard to where the bus stop was Harold wasn't quite sure if the waiting bus was the right one.   She was able to put him right on this.   She could see the driver standing on the pavement, a boy and a mounting pile of luggage on the roof.   Lowering the window of the air-conditioned car, she could hear what the man was shouting. 'Dubai, Dubai, Dubai.'

She insisted Harold and Bel didn't come across with her, which they couldn't do anyway with the car and the traffic regulations.   Installed in the front seat again, which as it was vacant she took on her own initiative this time, she felt almost at home.   It wasn't the same driver but on the pavement she had paid him confidently what she knew she owed. When she looked across the street, Bel and Harold were standing by the car just where they had said goodbye.   She waved, they waved, and just for a moment she thought how stranded and sad and beset they looked among the traffic and the tall shining buildings, and how - at the start of her journey home to England - in an odd way it was they who were behind the times.

ON THE BRIGHT SIDE

Competitions were advertised each month in the magazine Paula Gregory took. The latest was called 'Put Them On Their Feet.' There were photographs of six pairs of feet and the names of six celebrities - three men, three women. You had to attach the feet to the names.

'I'm going in for this one, Arthur,' Paula said. 'It says you win a luxury week-end.'

Arthur was reading the evening paper he had bought on the way home from work. He didn't expect to be interested in anything Paula read out from her magazine, but they were on the sofa together. Without moving the paper he turned his head and read over her shoulder. In a moment he gave the laugh which was famous in several E.C.2 pubs.

'I'd save the stamp. Hundreds'll get that right. There's no skill attached.'

Paula quietly sent in her answer. To her surprise a gold-edged envelope arrived. She had won. A twin or two single rooms for two nights with all meals in a 'high-comfort hotel' to be chosen from a list. Later, in the current September issue of her magazine were their names and address - '4, Archery Close, Ruislip, Middlesex.' Not the least of Paula's satisfaction was that Arthur had to eat his words.

As a matter of fact he ate them quite cheerfully, though not to Paula to whom he continued to express humorous scepticism. 'We'll see what "high comfort" they supply before I count any chickens,' he told her. But to his fellow workers at the textile firm, where he had been a buyer for thirty years, he struck another note. He had a reputation for producing the unusual in their not over-eventful existence, and saw conversational possibilities in the windfall.

'Off to Pembrokeshire for the week-end,' he mentioned in a give-away voice over their lunchtime pint and individual steak and kidney puddings. 'One of these magazine stunts. Thought we'd have a shy and - lo and behold. Get a lungful of the old ozone if nothing else.'

Under eager questioning he expanded the story. Yes, it would be first class accommodation as he understood it. All the trimmings, all lux found.

In his private imagination he went further. He didn't know Tenby, but the 'Bonnington Hotel' conjured for him spacious reception areas, a snooker room for sure, plush carpets, a welcoming bottle of champagne in their room and a corsage for Paula. They would dine by candlelight with a live orchestra playing Strauss, and there would be dancing on a little polished square between tables. He and Paula had used to dance a bit before pop mania set in. By the evening of their departure even his reserve in Paula's direction had broken down. 'Best get the old DJ out of moth-balls, Paula, as well as the suit. You never know, it does sound to me the sort of place where they still go in for a spot of dog.' Paula was sceptical now. He swept her doubts aside. 'The Magazine wouldn't dare provide less, it'd tarnish their image. I'm not looking dowdy.'

The weather worsened as their not new Escort sped them west along the M.4. It didn't dampen their ardour. 'Blow, blow, thou winter wind,' laughed Arthur, who had done a bit of amateur dramatics in his time. By the time they reached Tenby in the middle of the afternoon it had set in good and proper.

They didn't bring the address of the hotel, it wasn't necessary, Arthur said. 'It'll be in a number one position on the sea-front of course, with fine ocean-views.' But when they passed The Imperial, apparently the only large hotel, he began to be concerned. There were one or two smaller places in the short block of terraced houses on the waterfront, none was The Bonnington. They had to ask.

It was right in the middle of the small town. Arthur knew as soon as he saw it the dinner jacket wouldn't be necessary. It was a detached building, however, and could be quite old, he thought. Should have been called 'The Coach and Horn' - something like that. It had two stars, and RAC and AA signs. Being the optimist he was, he began to adjust his expectations.

Inside he decided it must have been an old inn. A central area which would have been the courtyard had been glassed in to provide a lounge and bar. At reception a large male figure stooped in a greenish tweed suit.

Paula said cheerfully, 'We're the Gregorys.' For answer the man swivelled the leather-bound signing-in book in Arthur's direction and handed him a biro, nodding downwards. 'We're so excited to have won the Open Sesame Prize,' Paula tried again as Arthur began writing. After all, this needed clarifying in advance.

'Number Seven,' the man said, handing Arthur the key which he had unhooked from behind him.

The key was screwed into a cricket ball. Perhaps what was needed was a subtler male touch, Arthur thought. There had been apology in Paula's voice. 'Not quite cricketing weather though,' he said, pretending to shine the ball on his upper arm.

'Not the *country* for cricket,' the man said in an unmistakeably exiled English home counties accent. He turned away from them to reenter the office behind.

In their room they found a typed catechism of prohibitions tucked into the mirror. 'Do not throw tea-bags down the lavatory but into the receptacle provided.' 'Do not use coathangers for any purpose other than the one for which they were designed.' There were others. The note was signed, 'W. and M.S. Hampden-Smith.'

Both read these but neither spoke. They made plans to brave the rain and walk round the town. Find a cup of tea maybe. Privately, Arthur made another adjustment. A modest hostelry certainly, the distinction would have to be in the cuisine. He imagined Mr W. Hampden-Smith in the members' seats at Lords. Of course good hoteliers didn't have to be garrulous when they knew what they were up to. He had spotted the dining-room through a glass door. It was tastefully set out with oak tables and chairs, red table-cloths. Style, he had thought - it fitted.

When they got back from their walk they had showers. The notice said 'Dinner at Seven.' They gave it until seven-thirty.

When they went down the lounge-bar was fairly full. Most were sipping drinks or studying menus which had been brought to them. 'Just what you'd expect,' thought Arthur, no hurry, civilised. But when a woman approached him and suggested they also sat down and had a drink, Arthur said no, if it was all the same to her they would go straight in. Drink was not included in the Open Sesame offer, and they had decided upstairs to have just a bottle of wine with their meal. The woman seemed disconcerted by this suggestion.

'Well, you *could* go in directly if you want to,' she said in her sing-song Welsh. 'The waitress will take your order.'

As they settled at a nice table in a corner Arthur winked at Paula. What he meant to convey to her was that by his resourcefulness they were ahead of the sheep. There was only one other table occupied, two couples embarking on scampi and tartar sauce starters. They would steal a march on the others.

They chatted about the weather - it had to clear overnight at this time of year, was Arthur's opinion. Meanwhile he took in the cooking and service arrangements. The chef appeared intermittently behind a serving counter, his operations being divided, it seemed, between a visible turning spit behind the counter under which four large steaks were spluttering and, out of sight in what must be the kitchen, what sounded like a deep fry. Twice there was a rage of noise as food was committed to it. Then Arthur noticed a curious fact. The sole waitress spent most of the time leaning across the counter talking to the chef and made no attempt to come across to them. On the chef's instructions she then went out into the lounge to bring in a tableful of diners. As soon as these sat down, she went to fetch their food from the hatch, which was ready for them. There was then another bout of the waitress talking to the chef. In other words there was a queue, she wouldn't come to them until it was their turn. They might as well have been lining up outside a fish and chip shop and, having come straight in as they had, they probably weren't in the queue. God knew when they would be served.

The evening was a disaster. They waited fifty minutes until

they were brought two bowls of tepid vegetable soup when they hadn't even given their order despite several desperate attempts by Arthur to catch the waitress's eye. When Arthur pointed this out, the woman looked perplexed.

'But you're table d'hôte,' she said.

'We're what?'

'You're "Sesame", aren't you? Set menu.'

The soup was succeeded by two very indifferent pork chops and a vegetable said to be ratatouille - onion, courgette and tomato were identifiable, swimming in oil. There was a trifle heavily biased towards custard, and some ready-cut squares of cheddar with two biscuits each. When all the diners were seated a woman who must be Mrs Hampden-Smith had come round in a long purple skirt, talking to everyone. She didn't come to their table. The wine arrived half-way through the meat course.

In the morning it was still pouring. Arthur was on the point of suggesting they went home. He had not slept well and his usual spirit had left him. He felt deeply disappointed and depressed. Only a dogged quality made them both press on. 'We'll look at the darned cliffs even if we don't walk on them,' Arthur said grimly when they'd had a reasonable breakfast.

They found a deserted beach along the coast overlooked by a ruined castle. There were no other cars in the small park. It was practically a gale blowing. They sat facing the sea, watching long lines of surf moving towards the beach like waves of an invasion. A large bus arrived only half-full of late-season holiday-makers peering through misty windows. One or two got out to use the conveniences. They were immediately blown to bits. After a minute or two they re-boarded hurriedly and the bus moved off.

Something came back to Arthur. They had spent their honeymoon thirty years ago walking on the Cornish cliffs. This memory lay behind their choice of Tenby from the other venues offered. He had been thinking how he would explain the week-end at the office. 'Darn it, Paula,' he said suddenly, 'we're here. We've got to walk a few yards at least. Come on, we're getting out.'

Paula was game. She took a time buttoning and belting her purple mac and tying on the waterproof hat, but then, locking the car, they set off.

They trudged across the beach, bending forwards to stop themselves being bowled over. The rush of the sea, the moan of the wind, made it necessary to shout. Arthur stopped. 'What do you say we make for that headland, Paula?' he yelled. 'There's a footpath.' Paula looked. There *was* a thin red line which wound its way through the low thicket of growth. For answer she started walking. 'That's my girl.'

They battled for more than an hour. Paula tore her stockings several times on brambles. In places, where the rock came through the red mud, the going was treacherous for their leather-soled shoes. They had to help each other. But they kept going and at last stood upon the point where the magnificent coast was visible both ways. They watched the huge seas lifting on the rocks, the massive swelling of water that ran and erupted into the gullies, and breathed in the warm salty air.

'Film set for the Gods,' Arthur shouted, his hand cupped beside his mouth.

When they reached the car they were wet and tired, but triumphant. As Paula undid her hat they both laughed. Their feet and legs were sopping. Paula said she had water running down her back.

They didn't think the hotel would take kindly to the mess they were in. At the door they took their sodden shoes off. As it was, their wet feet would probably leave a trail across the carpet. They would creep upstairs perhaps unnoticed. The lounge was full of people drinking. An odour of beef pervaded. They began to mount the stairs. But a man in a tartan jacket spotted them.

'I say, you two've been getting the local colour.'

He had a loud voice - Arthur fancied he had sunk one or two. In a second the whole room had them in focus, halted half-way up the stairs, their shoes in their hands. 'Experienced the odd

51

spot of the elements certainly,' Arthur said, grinning.

The woman who had waited at table came running up to them. 'Here, let me take your shoes,' she said. 'Soon dry them off in the boiler-room.'

The Gregorys did what they had never done in their lives before, they had hot showers before lunch. When they came down in dry clothes everyone was eating. It was a set lunch for all, it seemed. Most would be locals tucking in, Arthur thought. As they moved to their table people turned and smiled. The waitress came at once to their table, blushing and smiling, with a bottle of wine and two glasses on a tray.

'Compliments of Mrs Hampden-Smith and she says that tonight you can choose what you like on the menu.'

That evening they were almost the only diners and they had a long talk to the waitress, who told them about her husband and three children.

'What a very nice lot of folks we've encountered here, Paula,' Arthur said as they went to bed. 'It's been a memorable day.'

Back at work on Monday, Arthur was besieged with questions about his week-end in the posh hotel.

'Oh, very pleasant,' he revealed easily. 'Not *quite* the refinements of the Ritz, but when all's said and done you wouldn't expect it down there in the provinces, would you? But very civil all round. The red carpet treatment par excellence. A nice break.'

They all laughed. 'Trust you to hit the jackpot, Arthur,' a salesman said, slapping him on the back. 'What'll it be?'

'A whisky if it's offered then,' Arthur said. 'The odd sniffle developing I fear. The Atlantic air most likely.'

CATS

The cats were practically the Logans' only joint possessions. It seemed to the few people who came to the small terraced house in Fulham that the things they owned separately were a good half of their problem, they were constantly quarrelling about them. There were not only two sets of inherited furniture but between them the acquisitions of three spent marriages. Added to this were all Humphrey's books, which occupied shelves built into every nook and cranny, and on every surface which offered stood the 'detritus', as Humphrey described it, of Sally's pottery. 'Have a sale of everything - except the books and the pots of course - and start afresh,' a friend advised. Neither Logan would hear of it. Each would have cheerfully disposed of the other's stuff, but neither would entertain the idea of a joint moratorium. Every day there was an incident of some sort. The cats threatened to be one.

They were Burmese. Sally brought them in, yeowling in a basket. A fellow stall-owner in the market had gone on holiday and Sally was doing her a good deed. Humphrey was furious. 'It's just typical of your sloppy, mindless sentimentality,' he said. But even as he spoke, taking no notice, Sally was opening the lid of the basket. Up came their heads in tandem, outraged but instantly curious like two people looking out of an open car. It wasn't the Logans who interested them but the place. Their heads twisted, one one way, one the other, critical. A brown paw came up on one side of the basket, two brown noses twitched at the alien scents. Then, together, as if in one movement, they took the plunge and leapt out. Crouching, all tensed muscle, their heads low, their tails making low sweeps, they began to examine the room like detectives. They disappeared behind the huge sofa. One leapt suddenly on to a shelf of pottery. Sally leapt to her feet, too. She needn't have bothered, the cat nosed the objects disdainfully, sure-footed.

'The little tigers,' Sally said. Humphrey scowled, but he was watching, too.

In a couple of days the cats had taken over the house. When they were having a meal in the kitchen, the Logans heard two plops in the hall and a frantic scampering on the staircase Sally rushed out. 'It's all right, it's nothing, only Matt gone mad,' she called happily.

Humphrey tried to keep his hostility, but when on their second evening Mark, the smaller and more affectionate of the two, hopped into his lap, settled, and purred loudly, he was won. It was the guiltless insolent occupation of their property which did it, the immediate seizure of their possessions as unquestionably, inalienably, the props of their own comfort and play. Sally had been told by her friend the animals would eat anything. Humphrey wouldn't hear of scraps for them. The cats' menu became an annexe of their own. Sally and Humphrey liked their food, the cats ate fish, chicken. It was as well that when Sally's friend came home and saw what had happened she offered them for sale. It was doubtful if they would have put up with scraps again. A hundred and fifty pounds was exchanged for the pair.

Humphrey was a medieval historian at London University, his specialisation illuminated manuscripts, especially those pertaining to the Carolingian renaissance. He wasn't a popular don, undergraduates found him walled into a chronic ill-humour. He was a poor lecturer. Suffering from catarrh badly he cleared his throat constantly and it seemed the very act of speech was an effort, even when engaged on his own subject. They wrote him off as a neurotic cross-patch who had got through two wives, or more likely they had got through him. Brilliant of course - his reputation in his field was world-wide - but not made for normal human intercourse.

The idea of the symposium wasn't his. It came from Edgar - 'the tout' as Humphrey called the man the College now employed to rove the world and sell the place as if it were merchandise. But the British Museum had an exhibition of manuscripts coming off. Humphrey had been called in to advise on them. Why not combine the exhibition, suggested the eager Edgar, with a series of lectures by world experts, which would be open to the public?   Humphrey would surely give one of the lectures himself, and with his recommendation the College Council might well agree to share the costs with the Museum out of the promotion budget, as this would vicariously throw a spotlight on the College, which would figure jointly with the Museum in the billing.   Humphrey still detested the publicity aspect, but on reflection did see it was an academic opportunity. He agreed, so did the Council and the Museum.   It was at this moment Humphrey thought of Jacqueline Beautemps as one of the visiting lecturers.   He would offer to put her up, he thought with a frisson.

The day after this was fixed on the telephone, Humphrey had a new row with Sally about her purchase of a huge chamber pot with an absurd green dragon painted on the side.   She said she had bought it because she had been sorry for another stall-owner who had sold nothing all day.   She'd had a good day herself.

'And what possible use have you for it, pray?'

'I thought it'd come in handy for flowers.'

'It isn't worth pissing into.'

'That's what you would say, being artistically blind - and vulgar to boot.'

'Are you calling that thing art?'

'It's homely,' defended Sally.

He chose this moment of exasperation to tell Sally that a professional friend of his, Jacqueline Beautemps, would be coming to stay.   In consequence, for a couple of days there might be the faintest chance of some conversation a few inches off the bottom levels of banality.

'Beautemps, who's she?' asked Sally, wide-eyed.

'Among other things Jacqueline is an authority on the Utrecht Psalter, which will figure in the exhibition and upon which she will lecture.   She is at the Sorbonne.'

After their meal, Sally retired to her hut in the small garden.   She needed to get her fingers into clay.   Until she had them coated with the creamy substance, the pot turning on the wheel, she couldn't think straight.   It wasn't the rudeness which got to her -

she was used to that and she would hardly be living with him if she gave much importance to it. What was it then?

In a moment or two she realised. It was the two words he had used - 'upon which'. 'Upon which she will lecture.' He was having a go at her lack of education compared with his of course, trying to glorify lecturing and all the other things he did at the University in contrast with her 'artefacts' as he contemptuously called them. But it wasn't like him to give credit to another don. He must have met this woman when he went to Paris a year ago. Of one thing she was certain - it wasn't academic awe he was feeling.

In the market the next morning business was slack. She could watch her stall from Marjorie's. She went to sit with her. Marjorie was knitting. Marjorie, who made and sold basket-ware, was the previous owner of the cats.

'Well, how are they, darling?' she said. 'I miss them, you know. Great mistake of mine, that was.'

'Oh they're fine,' Sally said distantly.

'I say, you're broody today. What's up?'

'Do you think it matters, Marge, the intellect?'

Marjorie looked at her anxiously. 'You know damn well it doesn't, not Humphrey's sort anyway. What's he up to this time?'

'Perhaps he does miss it in me.'

'Bollocks. He's bored to the arse with all his intellectual stuff - as they all are. Look what happened when he married the last one, the blue stocking - lasted six months. We know what they all want, carried nemeni con.'

'"They" isn't necessarily Humphrey, Marge.'

'Near enough. Men are all much of a muchness if you ask me.' Marjorie paused. 'Come on then, what *has* he done? Though you know what I'll say in advance - I think he'll be lucky if you stop with him two minutes if he's playing about.'

'She's French this one.'

'Oh, so he *is* up to something. What's French got to do with it?'

'She's a visiting professor.'

56

'So what? You've got enough where it matters to see off any old froggy egghead, male or female.'

'Have I?'

'Of course you have.'

The conversation did her good. She thought she did have what it took. Just pre-menstrual whatnot probably, she was being maudlin. Give her art every time. Where life was concerned these eggheads usually hadn't been beyond the end of the street.

She lashed into him afterwards. The next day she let him get his own dinner, saying she had work to do. He was furious. What could she possibly have to do that was more important than his dinner, he said? She just laughed. Mark was sitting on top of the dresser at this moment, Matt had his bum on the ironing board - the warm bit where she had been working. Two pairs of china-blue eyes regarded her complacently. She had fed them. They thoroughly agreed with her, she thought. As she laughed, Matt yawned, licked his chops, then stuck one leg in the air and began to lick his stomach. This perfectly expressed the whole situation.

From the Customs Hall travellers began to issue. Humphrey held back behind the crowd which moved forward to the barrier, but he was worried he wouldn't recognise her, or worse, she him. Perhaps he should have had a placard like these hotel and taxi people. Blood seemed to be pumping in his mouth. How would he fail to recognise her when he had thought of her so often?

In the event there was no question. She appeared, dressed in a smart light-weight suit, her almost jet black hair styled in a long forward-slung salient *à la Parisienne*, carrying a bag and an expensive-looking briefcase and looking for him. The year which had passed vanished like a conjuring trick.

'Jacqueline, s'il est possible tu es encore plus charmante . . .' The rehearsed phrase clattered dead to the ground. He didn't think she even heard. For a moment her eyes hesitated - *was* it him? - then her own verve took over. 'Oomfray. 'Ow are *you*?

Lovely to see you again.'

He didn't speak French any more. Seizing the bag, which she lifted slightly for him to take, he walked lamely by her side all the way to the car while she chattered in her excellent English. Only the syllable stresses were awry, and her r's and l's which had the richness of garlic and camembert about them. It amazed him how many talking points she had gathered in the half-hour flight. They lasted until they were well on to the motorway. Meanwhile, anaesthetised by an exotic perfume, he observed the loose movement of the white coat over slithery satin and imagined the tethered flesh it contained.

He only wished Sally could have been absent. The street, with its differently painted doors was upwardly mobile, but Sally had put on the whole armoury of Hampstead artiness - a flimsy purple skirt which came down to her ankles - the inevitable response to anything she thought was an occasion - a fussy creamy blouse upon which metal clinked liked harness. She looked huge and dowdy, indeed like a drayhorse. While the two women went upstairs he made a plan. They would have to eat here tonight, but tomorrow night, after the symposium, he would take Jacqueline out to a night club.

The women were ages upstairs and he heard both voices. What on earth were they finding to talk about? He could imagine Sally rabbiting on, but it was definitely a duet. They came down still at it hammer and tongs. 'We're going to see the studio,' Sally said. 'Jacky's very interested.'

He looked at Jacqueline to learn the degree of her tolerance. 'You did not tell me your wife is a *potier*. I am fasc*i*n*a*ted,' she said, giving nothing away.

He gave them five minutes. Let Jacqueline get a speck of clay on her spotless suit. Or Sally would overdo it - since when did someone like Jacqueline suffer fools gladly? Tomorrow evening, he thought, he would be able to intimate - with a sad tilt of the eyebrows perhaps - what he had to put up with. It would be the unspoken basis for . . . whatever developed. He had thoughts of a hotel. He went into his study.

But an hour went by and there was no sign of a return. He

went back to the kitchen.   Dinner remained a thought, its ingredients yet dispersed in the fridge, on the untidy shelves. He drew the curtain aside with a finger. They were still in the shed. He looked at his watch. Seven-thirty. Anger spurted. Only the cats saved him from rushing out there. Both animals were off their favourite shelf behind the aga. They began to bombard his legs with their cheeks and backsides.   Matt looked up and yeowled.

'All right, you buggers,' he said aloud.   'But you're not the only ones starving.' He put the tin under the opener and wound. He turned out the meat on to the two platters Sally had made specially for them, one with a fish painted on it, the other a chicken leg.   It made him feel marginally better to see them wolfing the food in great hunks, half-standing, half-sitting.   He still felt annoyed, but less so. He went out to the hut.

Jacqueline was wearing a clean white overall Sally had lent her. She was at the wheel, her hands filthy with clay, and a spot had fallen apparently unnoticed on to the shiny black of her shoe. Sally, behind her, was holding her hands to show her the way. Both were absorbed and didn't see him.   Suddenly Jacqueline stopped pedalling and giggled in the most surprising way.

'Oh I cannot do *it*.   I could never do it.   You are a genius, Sally, a magician.'

They saw him. 'Jacko's jolly good,' Sally said. 'For her first time, she's amazing.   Real talent.'

'Oh, do you think *so*.   You are surely flattering *me.*'

It nauseated him particularly when, after he had suggested that some dinner might not be such a bad idea in view of the hour, Jacqueline said there was no hurry - this was such a fascina*ting* experience for her - and Sally gave him a withering look.

He thought to take Jacqueline into his study while Sally got the dinner, but Jacqueline suggested they sat at the kitchen table for drinks so they could all talk.   He started to speak about her work on the Psalter. She interrupted him. 'Oh, not that now, Oomfray, we shall bore Sally,' she said. She held aloft her wine glass and helped herself to a home-made cheese ring.

Matt and Mark had digested their food. Out of the corner of his eye Humphrey saw Matt stand and stretch, his impertinent eyes looking for trouble. He saw him pace stealthily along the shelf behind Jacqueline. Jacqueline hadn't noticed the cats. She was holding forth about Carolingian ceramics for Sally's benefit - as she thought - while Sally shook herself and the frying-pan at the stove. Between manicured fingers now immaculately clean of clay, she held aloft a cheese-ring. A second before Matt pounced, he knew what would happen. Jacqueline screamed as the food was snatched. Matt leapt triumphantly on to the highest shelf of the dresser with the spoil.

'Cats, I cannot bear cats,' shrieked Jacqueline. 'I am aller*gic* to cats. Take them *a*way.' She rose, knocking the chair back. At which point Mark made a secondary attack on the plate in front of her. She screamed louder and backed into the corner, her palms held out in front of her face.

They had to lock them in the study, which they succeeded in doing after a mad chase which took them up and down the staircase several times and under furniture, while Jacqueline cowered in the kitchen with the door shut. The evening was not a success. The cats started a chorus of complaint. Sally had eventually to turf them out into the garden and wedge the cat door shut in the kitchen. Then they yeowled outside.

In the morning Sally got up early, fed them, and got them outside before Jacqueline came down. It was an embarrassment.

But the morning went well for Humphrey. Free of the house and Sally's asininities, his feelings of the previous day returned. Jacqueline's lecture was well-acclaimed. When she returned to sit beside him she was pleased with herself. There was a buffet lunch for the participants. He took a risk and suggested they went off together to a place he knew where the food was excellent. No one would notice they weren't there in the scrum, he said. Was she looking forward to receiving congratulations for her lecture? For a moment she hesitated, but then agreed.

It was an expensive fish and wine bar. They had a bottle of good muscadet, fried prawns and brown bread, followed by Dover soles. They talked shop until a moment when they were both sipping the wine and their eyes met over the glasses. 'You remember our walk in the Bois, Jacqueline?' he said.

'When I think you were just a little naughty, yes.'

'When I *felt* more than a little naughty, and maybe, you did a little, too?' He paused. 'Jacqueline, my dear, my life, as you see, has become difficult.' He saw her pick up her knife and fork. As she readdressed the fish her hair fell forward seductively. His mouth and throat were throbbing again. 'Shall we go out tonight?' he said in a rush.

Her face lit. 'Oh, but what a perfectly lovely idea,' she said.

'I thought, to some sort of a night club do?'

Through the afternoon session at the Museum he wrestled with the logistics. They would have to go home first. Should he invite Jacqueline's connivance in some kind of subterfuge? He rejected this, which would be messy even if she would agree to it. The best way was surely to tell Sally point blank - Jacqueline and he had things to discuss, they were going out alone for the evening - he would think of something. Just before they got back in the taxi, he said shortly, 'I shall tell Sally we have matters to talk about tonight.'

She did not reply, merely turning her head to look out of the window. His spirits leapt in anticipation. Wasn't this so typically French? No fuss, no hypocrisy, just down to earth practicality. He had a supporting brainwave as they went in. He would tell Sally privately it was also the cats. He might also say Jacqueline had suggested it.

Jacqueline went upstairs, he went into his study to do a few chores. Suddenly he heard Sally coming downstairs like a beach-ball filled with stones.

'Humphrey, Jacqueline tells me we're going out to a nightclub. How super. But what am I going to wear?'

He was furious. He couldn't have made it clear enough in the taxi. He thought he would cancel the whole thing. But how was that possible now? How could Jacqueline have misunderstood - after their conversation at lunch, too?

They went to a ghastly place just off Piccadilly. It was the only one he knew of - he had heard a student talk about it. It was a dungeon, pokey, crowded with rich idiots and appallingly expensive. The worst was that both women seemed to enjoy it. The meal was awful - the steak had the resistance of biltong, what was said to be champagne was rubbish. They both said how delicious it was. He danced once with Jacqueline on the crowded dance floor - he had the impression they were clinging to a lifeboat - and decided that was enough. He suggested going. Jacqueline wouldn't hear of it. Sally, he considered, was drunk, though what on he couldn't imagine. She was floundering about, giggling at Jacqueline - who was revealing a side of herself he couldn't have imagined. She was behaving like an elderly schoolgirl. She got up suddenly.

'Come on, Sally, we'll dance,' she said. 'Old Oomfray 'ere is fatigued.'

He was astounded. Sally was a bit taken aback, too, he could see, but she went. In the semi-darkness he glimpsed Jacqueline's face under the absurd turning bracket of amber lights. It was hard, ghoulish, ugly, turned upwards like a death mask or something in a Bosch painting. The thought came to him for the first time - why was it Jacqueline had never married? The slowly beating music, the heat, made him feel sick. He decided he would go, even if they wouldn't. He must go.

He had actually stood up, when Sally came running from the dance floor, knocking over a chair at another table in her haste. 'We're going home now,' she said. Jacqueline followed, cool, not at all perplexed.

The taxi ride was totally silent. He sat on one of the retractable seats, the two women facing him. Both gazed outwards, either way. When they got in Jacqueline went straight upstairs. 'Goodnight,' she said with aplomb, indifferently leaving the situation behind her.

In the kitchen Sally wrenched open the back door - the cat door had been wedged again to keep them out. 'Matt, Mark,' she called. They needed no bidding. They were past her legs before she had finished calling them. They made straight for their plates and tucked in to the half meal they had left. Sally poured milk into a soup dish and lowered it.

'What happened, Sally?'

'What do you think happened?'

'You mean she . . .'

'I mean yes, she did. So much for your Utrecht Psalter.'

He went to the fridge and got a beer. 'Do you want a beer?'

'Something clean certainly.'

They sat with the two cans, not bothering with glasses. There were a couple of faint noises upstairs. Mark sprang on to the table, licking his whiskers. In a minute Matt followed. They curled their tails and sat, very upright and proper. Mark began to purr, rasping ratchets of sound. His eyes closed, then slowly reopened. They were back, things were normal, he seemed to say.

Sally began to laugh. 'The way Matt snatched that cheese-ring,' she said. 'Frightened the daylights out of her.'

He, too, felt a delicious diffusion of mirth. Matt had begun to clean himself. He laughed, too. In a moment or two they were both helpless. 'I am aller*gic* to cats,' he mimicked. 'Take them away,' she capped. Their laughter rose like leaven through the house. They didn't care if she heard.

The cats were indifferent. Mark settled down into a comfortable crouch position, his shoulder-blades protruding from his sleek fur. Matt was licking his chest just under his chin, with arched neck.

FESTIVAL

As the evening angelus began to boom, the golden air was alive with screaming swallows and the warm streets of the lower town were thronged. Between the browning chestnuts in the main boulevard and square hung banners and balloons, and at the Palazzo Municipale stood two handsome thickets of black and yellow triangular flags.

Nori, a young liceo teacher, was waiting near the bus stop outside the railway station. She was looking about anxiously for her friend Giorgiana with whom she had arranged to go up to the old city for the evening. She had bought the bus tickets, but as usual Giorgi was late and in some inadmissable way the festa unsettled her. She became aware of a well-dressed foreign couple standing beside her, who had just arrived by train apparently, without luggage. They, too, were looking about them uncertainly.

'Perhaps we should take a taxi,' Nori overheard the woman say in very English English.

'Can I help you?' she said.

She watched the diffident grey eyes of the man turn to her. 'Yes please. We're hoping to find a bus which will take us up to the old city on the hill. La Città, I think you call it?'

She laughed, she wasn't sure why. 'Well that is easy, I am going there - this is the bus stop. I will show you. But before this you must go into that building over there to buy the tickets. In advance,' she added proudly. English was her subject.

The man was nice. He thanked her courteously and went off. She turned to the woman, whom she saw at once, like her husband, was *signorile* in a particularly English way. Her clothes were expensive but discreet and she was immediately friendly and natural.

Nori was about to say, 'Is this your first visit?' Instead she said more humorously, 'You have chosen a crowded evening to visit our town.' This got them talking about the festa. Nori was proud of the place where she had been born and grown up, and launched into a description of their 'Festa dei Fiori' and the interesting things which were to be seen in La Città during the week. Probably she was talking too much, she thought, but the woman nodded frequently as she spoke and her intelligent eyes seemed to absorb everything. She was so involved with her chance encounter she didn't see Giorgi.

'Papa è imposibile,' she said, barging into Nori's conversation as if the Englishwoman didn't exist. She stood with her back to the stranger as she related at the top of her voice what a 'peasant' her father was, how he had come back from work covered in the usual 'disgusting' white dust and had insisted she run his bath for him, knowing she was going out. 'E medioevale,' she finished with that theatrical syllable stress she gave to every other word.

Nori was fond of Giorgi. She liked her for her very excesses. But for this moment, seeing her through the Englishwoman's eyes, she was ashamed of her - the tarty scarlet dress hanging precariously from her ripe body, the bright lipstick, the glossy black shoes which were fastened in front with a black bow. She was ashamed of Giorgi's single-minded indifference to anything which didn't immediately concern her.

'Er - Giorgi, this lady and her husband are from England,' she began in English. The man was just returning. Barely acknowledging the lady, Giorgi turned her full attention on him.

'Buona sera,' she said in quite a different voice.

Nori thought the man would be put off, but if he was he didn't show it. 'Buona sera, Signorina,' he said, smiling broadly.

They got on the bus together, the couple first. They sat in a double seat on one side. Giorgi let Nori take the window seat of the pair which were level with these so that she could be on the aisle next to the man. As the bus crawled through the crowded town centre and then began to climb the winding road up the hill, she took on the duty of guide in her threadbare English. It was like a fourth-rate travel brochure, Nori thought. 'The beautifulness of our dear old city,' she said once, 'which we love with all our hearts.'

Staring of the window Nori fumed. What did Giorgi care about their city, which in her mind was a provincial prison keeping her from Milan where real life was? How could any man be taken in by such a stagey performance?

The old bus lumbered, exhausted, into the cobbled piazzetta. With a dying gasp the doors sneezed and clattered open. In the last moments Giorgi had been losing interest in the couple. Her few phrases of English, brought out with such a flourish, had been spent, and she made little effort now to conceal her boredom with the efforts the man was making to speak Italian. Having got off the bus, she turned her back, and began to look round to see if she could spot anyone they knew in the square. Nori had a sudden wish to keep the tenuous contact. The words were out of her mouth before she could consider them.

'Would you like us to show you round?'

The couple exchanged a quick glance. Of course not, Nori thought, of course they didn't want to be shown round by a couple of boring Italian girls they had somehow got entangled with. It was a matter only of which polite formula they chose.

'But you don't want to spend such a lovely evening with two old people like us,' the lady said.

'I expect you have friends you are meeting,' the man added.

They were both looking at her intently and she realized they were taken by her idea. She felt a surge of defiant confidence. She didn't look at Giorgi. 'We would like to be your guides,' she said. 'Andiamo, we start with the Duomo.' She was already walking.

Nori felt borne on a tide. It wasn't at all to spite Giorgi. Never had the cathedral appeared more lovely to her. Mass was being celebrated at the high altar. The intoned words of the priest mounted in the incense-heavy air into the void of gothic darkness above them. In a corner fluttered the humble yellow light of candles. For moments they stood in silence. Nori remembered the everydayness, the unreligiousness of protestant services in England. Surely whatever they thought about religion, the emotion of this scene would affect the English couple as it never failed to affect her. When she thought it was the right moment she moved them to see the two treasures of the cathedral, a Donatello statue and a Tintoretto.

She showed them next a much smaller church which had Visigothic connections, and then the great hall of the castle which had an exhibition of modern paintings. They finished in the loggia where there was a huge display of chrysanthemums and dahlias. These were the finest blooms of the province, for it was a competition and a centre-piece of the festa. Nori surprised herself with the amount she knew and had to say, not only about history but about modern Italian life.

The English couple offered them a drink in one of the piazza cafes. As they sat sipping they continued to ask Nori questions. During their tour Giorgi had made no effort to hide her annoyance. She had sighed several times, and tapped her foot. Now she gazed at the girating parade of young people where but for this tedious irrelevance, her whole manner asserted, they would have met someone they knew by this time.

Nori felt guilty. She had hogged the floor, using English Giorgi couldn't compete with. Because of Giorgi's behaviour, some element of rivalry, she knew, had now crept into her performance, and she relented. She wanted to bring her in. Georgi could talk Italian, and she would translate. But the couple were looking at each other again. The man turned to her.

'Look, you've both been most kind to us and I expect we have already taken up much too much of your time. But if by any chance you are free, my wife and I would love to offer you some dinner somewhere?'

Giorgi tossed her head and flushed, and just at this moment spotted two boys they had met briefly recently. One worked in the same factory where Giorgi was a secretary. The boys approached then, seeing the English couple, checked. Giorgi rose.

'Ciao, Leonardo,' she said loudly. She made no attempt to introduce the boys and went off with no more than a perfunctory glance at the couple. 'Grazie,' she said over her shoulder.

For an instant Nori was furious. Really, Giorgi was a child. Couldn't she accept not being the centre of attention for a few minutes? 'I expect you'd like to go with your friend,' the woman said kindly. 'No,' Nori found herself saying much too harshly. 'That is to say, if it is all right with me only, I would like very much to accept your kind invitation.'

Nothing was said about Giorgi's's behaviour. Nori felt they understood. With their understanding her annoyance died. If Giorgi preferred to throw away a new experience, which was different and interesting, for the unlikely chance of some encounter with a dream man, that was her funeral. How many evenings like this one, starting with such hope, had fizzled into predictable disappointment? Perhaps, she even thought, her friendship with Giorgi was silly. What did they really have in common? The events of the evening illustrated the gap.

She did like the English couple. The man, who said his name was Andrew 'by the way', and his wife's Elizabeth, asked her to recommend a good restaurant. She didn't know what to say. She had seen they weren't poor, on the other hand she wouldn't want them to think she was being greedy. She mentioned three restaurants, hoping to indicate by her voice that they were in descending order of price. Andrew chose the Leon d'Oro, the first.

She had never been here. In the discreet candlelight the waiters moved like efficient shadows. How kind of two complete strangers. She told them how much she loved England, its order and kindness, especially how she loved her family in Walton-on-Thames with whom she had stayed twice as a paying guest while she went to the language school. She told them how, as a teacher in a liceo - which was a kind of grammar school, she explained - she hoped to prepare people younger than herself for the hard life they would face when they left school. Andrew questioned her about the Italian education system. Elizabeth's smile and interest also encouraged her, as if she were someone important. They made her feel important.

Later she realized she was talking far too much again, the teacher's disease. No one could be indefinitely interested in other people as Andrew and Elizabeth seemed to be. Fortified by the wine, she leaned back in her seat. 'What is *your* job, Andrew?' she said.

Andrew looked a bit taken aback. He touched his lips with

his napkin. 'Well, I suppose I'm a sort of politician.'

'Davvero? You mean you are a Member of Parliament?'

'Yes.'

'What is your constituency?'

'I'm in what we call "the other place" actually.'

'You mean you are a Lord?'

He smiled. 'That sort of idea.'

Giorgi felt savage. She would never speak to Nori again. She had done it on purpose of course, dull spiteful little schoolmistress that she was. Nori didn't want to walk in the square because she knew she couldn't compete, that's what this was all about. Culture, how she disliked all that stuff. And that English couple, how typically boring they were - the man, too, with his superior air. Good thing for his wife she hadn't had him alone.

For a blazing minute, standing in the centre of the medieval piazza, she imagined herself a princess. Leo wore a green doublet, a bronze poignard slung at his side, and a magnificent, sloping, feathered, green velvet hat - his friend the same in flaming scarlet. Both were paying court to her. The whole square was paying court to her, watching what she would do. Would she bestow on the young suitors a smile, or arrogantly kick her dress and turn on her heel?

'Senta, Giorgi, vuoi prendere una pizza?'

As her vision faded Giorgi realised the boys had had a whispered exchange and were offering her a meal. The total banality. 'I'm not hungry,' she said. 'We're going to Fantasia. I'll pay for myself.'

In the crowded cellar she felt better. She by-passed a couple hovering ahead of them, and the two young men, trailing behind her like dogs saw her grab three seats as they were vacated. They sat round the upturned barrel which served as a table, and Giorgi ordered a bottle. 'On me,' she said. When Leo began to protest she jumped to her feet. 'Come on, I want to dance.'

They joined the small box of humanity which in the restricted space was trying to compete with the strident demanding music.

Somehow Giorgi's energy cleared a space for her and her partner. She began to live again. Between the whitewashed walls, hung with chains and instruments of torture, was a solid block of red light. Into this a twisting light threw down a confetti of white squares. It was snowing in hell, she thought, and she was the devil's mistress. Leo sprouted pointed ears and a tail. The rhythm changed to slow and she was in his arms, gently swaying as if they were borne on a great river, gently turning on a never-ending journey. She closed her eyes.

When they returned to their seats the other boy had gone. Leo looked dismayed. 'All to the good - just us,' she said. Leo continued to search for his friend.

Just at this moment she saw another man looking at her. He wasn't suited and polished like Leo. He wore black tapered trousers, a black shirt with a yellow handkerchief round his neck. He was swarthy, meridian, incredibly handsome. She knew her split second look and its contents was enough, she felt his interest in her kindle across the room. She knew he was approaching. He felt his hand on her waist. He didn't even speak.

Like a ballerina certain of her partner's position, she turned into his arms. She was aware of the darkness of his clothes and the red of her dress. Apart from that, she had no thought but for the music and their movement together.

They danced, it seemed to her, all night. He bought champagne. Only when she asked him, he said he was 'in the film industry.' He worked in Milan but was up here visiting his widowed mother. His name was Silvano. Apart from these scraps of information they talked entirely in the present. She told him how she had started the evening, how she had escaped from Nori and the tourist couple and how she had used Leo to come here. He laughed. 'I can see you get what you want,' he said. 'I could see that as soon as I noticed you across the room.' She was dimly aware, under her largely thoughtless ecstasy, that what was different about him was that he asked none of the usual questions. He didn't ask where she lived or what her job was. It was just *now*, and only now - the way she had always thought life was. Only in now was there eternity, only now did not stop to count and measure. If only in this world there were no measurements, if only people could look neither forwards or backwards.

They were almost the only couple dancing when the place closed. They walked out into the narrow empty streets. They walked to the narrow park which ran under the castle wall and sat on a bench. Below them spread the sparse night lights of the lower town.

She let him kiss her and felt, what she knew already, that he knew her exactly. He knew she wouldn't allow him to touch her tonight and she knew he wouldn't press it. She felt the gentleness and patience of his experience. He was quite a bit older than herself, she guessed over thirty. Was she falling in love?

'Tomorrow I have to spend with mother,' he said, 'but we could meet on Sunday. 'We could drive to the lake for the day.'

She withdrew a fraction. What did she know of him? But as if divining her thought, he added, 'you could bring your learned friend. I will bring Lucca. Lucca teaches chemistry at the university.'

Nori had a last glimpse of them in the first class compartment as the train pulled away, Andrew raising his hand in farewell. They were 'staying with Italian friends,' Lady Elizabeth had said. Nori imagined a noble Palladian villa with an estate. As she turned to go, her spirits fell. It had been an exceptional evening. She had felt brushed and smoothed by their quality, so benignly bestowed on her. But now their grand life had passed on ahead of hers. She would never see them again, even though Andrew had given her his card and told her he would show her round Parliament 'when she was next in England.' She knew she was unlikely to be able to take him up on it.

They had wanted to deliver her home in the taxi they had taken to the station, but she said she only lived round the corner. Why had she done that, she asked herself? Why had she unnecessarily given herself a mile to walk? Because she hadn't wanted them to see the ugly block in which her family occupied a small flat? And why was that? Because it destroyed the illusion she had briefly had that she could belong to another world?

How had she said only a couple of hours ago that she loved this city? As she walked briskly, a couple of teenagers tried to proposition her. They trailed her, giggling. She turned on them viciously. 'Go home to your mothers,' she shouted. Their cracked, adolescent laughter wounded her. Why hadn't she gone with Giorgi after all and not taken on the role of a silly guide? Giorgi would now be furious with her and would be quite likely to sulk for a week. She told her mother and father about the evening and for a moment, knowing how interested they were, relived it. But when she went to her room, she lay on her bed in her clothes and wept. She heard the clock on the municipal building strike midnight. It seemed like a life sentence.

She got up late and found she felt no better. It was Saturday. Normally she would be meeting Giorgi this morning, going for a walk, then having coffee in the lower town square. She didn't feel like phoning her. She didn't know why she was friends with someone who was so shallow and selfish.

When she was making herself coffee in her dressing-gown, the phone rang. Her mother answered. 'It's Giorgi,' she called. She could barely drag herself to the phone.

'Ciao Nori,' came the cheerful voice. 'Look, something quite amazing has happened.' Yes, really, she said. No, she couldn't say on the phone, it was too precious and might disappear. The square at eleven?

Nori's gloom thickened. A silly escapade Giorgi had got herself into - surely not Leo, elevated to dream status under threat of her friend's having a more interesting evening then hers? However, she found a little spirit did begin to stir in her. All right, if this were the case, she would let Giorgi have it, she thought. She would tell her what a lovely, memorable evening she had had with an English Lord and Lady who had invited her to visit them in London, and she would say how stupid Giorgi had been to flounce off with Leo like that. She would mention a few home truths.

For once Giorgi was there first, her cafe solo already in front of her. She was sitting inside the cafe, as the morning already carried the first chill of winter and outside the seats were still turned on top of the tables. Nori felt so devastated all of a sudden, she knew she was not going to be able to carry out her plan. What was the use of being cross with Giorgi or of lying to her? They were playing in the same orchestra, weren't they - different instruments but the same tune? She slid out of her coat and rehung it on her shoulders.

'Well, how was your dinner?' began Giorgi, limbering up for the false excitement of her own account. Nori decided to be flatly honest.

'Oh, it was nice, really nice, I enjoyed it - until they'd gone. Then it seemed, I don't know . . .'

Giorgi's excitement couldn't be contained any longer. 'It's happened, Nori darling, at last - or I think it has. The most superb *man*. And maybe for you, too. Tomorrow, we're going to the lake, all four of us, in his car. His friend teaches at the university. And I'll need you to tell me if Silvano's all I think he is, you're so much cleverer than I am. Oh, Nori . . . he lives in *Milan* and he's in *films* . . .'

In her mind Nori mustered all her scepticism. How naive Giorgi was to think that such a man, met in such circumstaces, could possibly be what she wildly imagined? And why should *a* man, who happened to teach somewhere, be *her* future? And yet, as Giorgi talked, she felt her resistance involuntarily dissolving. What she wanted to do, she realised after a few moments, was to laugh, not with scorn but with joy. Giorgi was extraordinary - so everlastingly hopeful, so irrepressively gay. Effortlessly she created hope and gaiety, she saved them both from the dismal and the predictable.

Of one thing she was certain. Giorgi was a good friend. She would look forward to the outing tomorrow, too. Who knew?

MISS WHEELER

'Ask God for a judgement on that,' said Trent.   He threw a glossy file filled with neatly-typed sheets on to his partner's desk and put his arm along the mantelpiece.

The office was in an older building in the middle of the timber yard, small, overheated by a modern gas fire and crowded with furniture.   Both men had their desks facing each other.   Miss Wheeler sat at a table at the side - between them, like an umpire.

Miss Wheeler watched Kenilworth's slow reaction.   Trent was short, jaunty, bursting with energy.   He wore a sports jacket and fawn-coloured whipcords.   Kenilworth, as always, wore a dark suit and toning tie pulled to an immaculate white collar.   He finished what he was writing, screwed the cap on his fountain-pen, and only then picked up the file.   Opening it, he raised his eyebrows, readjusted his glasses, and blew out his cheeks as if he wished to imply that anything given him to read by his colleague would probably be a waste of time.   In the silence of his reading a circular saw sang briefly outside, and a hibernating tortoiseshell butterfly, awakened by the heat, fluttered lightly at the window.   When he was half-way down the second page he switched impatiently to the last, where figures were laid out.   His face began to change colour.

'This is quite out of the question,' he said, throwing the file down.   'Much too large a sum for such a risky venture.   It'd take all our liquid assets, it'd be folly.'

Mark Trent gave a quick dangerous laugh.   'Folly - like the extension of the yard, the new lathe, the prefabs business, I suppose?'

'Those were logical extensions of the existing business.   This is a blind plunge into a market unknown to us.'

A violent argument broke out.   In the normal way Miss Wheeler wouldn't have been too worried about this.   It was the way the two men worked.   Trent, the busy volatile salesman, the one with the ideas, Kenilworth, slower, surer, who had judgement   and   looked   after   the   money   side.   Their complementary combination was the success of the firm. They played each other's strengths instinctively, in the common interest, like two stags locking antlers but each knowing finally when it was his turn to give way. Trent's proposal - he had already told her about it in confidence - was to buy out a stumbling hardwood door and window-frame company, which would take them into the luxury market. But it wasn't the details of this which Miss Wheeler listened to on this occasion.

It was Mr Trent's manner which worried her. She heard a shriller, more personal element in his speech - which wasn't like him. 'The trouble with you, Tom,' he was saying, 'is that you spend too much time on your knees and can't see what's above the pew. What's the point of thinking about the next world, which doesn't exist? This is where the action is, here and now. Money - that's what I'm after. Money, which buys kicks and pleasure. What bugs me is that you like it as much as I do when I make it for you.'

Kenilworth's face was now scarlet with rage. He made a not very disguised reference to Trent's private life. Miss Wheeler went to the toilet at this point. She didn't like to listen to any more. It was no longer business they were wrangling about. It was personal.

She guessed she wouldn't be allowed to hide from the row, and she wasn't. The next morning, when Trent had gone out to an appointment and she was alone with Kenilworth, she knew his mind was no longer on what he was doing. He stopped work all of a sudden, pushed his chair back, and crossed his legs.

'You know I'm very worried about this proposal of Mr Trent's,' he began. 'He hasn't thought it through. The plant he wants to buy, and the goodwill, will be very costly - it would certainly involve a mortgage of some sort - and we have no idea if we can obtain the skilled labour. How do we know also that the outlets are there for selling the goods? The firm is probably in difficulties because their market hasn't been satisfactory.'

Miss Wheeler abandoned her machine, folded her arms, and looked at the ceiling, a posture she normally adopted when as, not so infrequently, a listening role was asked of her on a subject which was taxing one of her employers.

'I shouldn't say this,' Kenilworth went on, 'but of late I have noticed a somewhat frantic note in Mr Trent's behaviour as if he were trying to *prove* something.   I mean, we all know how splendidly inventive he can be, and ebullient.   I am the first to say how much we have profited from these qualities.   But this is not good business, this suggestion of his.   I fear it does not arise simply from a sense of business enterprise at all . . .'

Miss Wheeler knew Mr Kenilworth was not asking her directly for her opinion.   It wasn't her place to be asked and she would have been embarrassed if that were to happen.   She felt her role was as a sounding board.   She had noticed quite often that this was a contribution she could make.   Was it by her sympathetic listening - and hopefully by having her feet on the ground, where she always tried to keep them - that in some way the two men were better able to make up their own minds?   She lowered her gaze from the ceiling, allowed her head to nod slowly twice, but then finished by leaving it slightly to one side. 'It is certainly out of the blue,' she said, 'and of course *none* of us should be personal in our work.'   Would he conclude from this, she wondered, that it might be too early for a final judgement, that from *both* their points of view business sense must be separated from personal factors?   She thought he just might, he was at root an honest, fair-minded man.

A few days later Mr Kenilworth's wife phoned to say her husband had a touch of flu and wouldn't be in.   Mr Trent was out all morning, but at about midday she heard his Porsche.   He burst in in his usual bombastic way.

'Miss Wheeler - all alone?'   She explained that Mr Kenilworth was ill.   'Splendid,' Trent went on, 'then this is the perfect situation for a suggestion I have to make.   We shall break our habits and have a good lunch together.'

In the shadowy luxury of the Blue Lagoon restaurant she wondered if she should have accepted.   It had never happened before.   What would Mr Kenilworth think when he knew?   She had imagined a sandwich in a pub, but this place had a plush carpet, discreet music, lowered lights, and fish in a glass tank.

They were almost the only clients. In the street, at the door, she had said, 'Oh, Mr Trent, I thought it would be just a quick snack somewhere.' 'Certainly not, we're going to have a slap-up lunch,' he had replied. 'Heaven knows, you deserve it, and I'm ravenous. Hope you are.' His push, enthusiasm, and infectious humour won her. Though no less anxious, she admitted to herself it was nice. Her life wasn't so full of surprises.

He took her grey coat with fur on the collar and hung it up, stealing the waiter's job from him but not making a fuss about it. 'Now I'm having a gin and tonic,' he said then, rubbing his hands. 'What are you drinking?' She asked for a tomato juice. 'Bloody or straight?' he said, and made her laugh. Thank goodness she knew what a Bloody Mary was. He chose the table, short-circuited the waiter's wish to explain the menu by choosing almost at once what he wanted - a curried chicken dish which had an exotic name. He said it was excellent, that he'd had it before, and so made the choice for her, too. 'And bring us some of your splendid red plonk,' he said to the baulked waiter as he folded and took back the menus. She had always liked this about Trent, an almost comic directness which left most people standing. She admired a man who knew his mind.

She began to enjoy the food. He talked about his latest journey to Scotland where he had been investigating a new timber source. Half-way through the chicken there was a rapid switch of subject.

'You don't go to church, do you?' he said. She had her mouth full and shook her head. 'Of course you don't. And if you did, you'd be sensible, you'd go for the company and for a good sing - nothing wrong in that. You wouldn't take it seriously, as Kenilworth does. In Kenilworth's case, it's a substitute of course, a substitute for life.'

She lowered her eyes. She had expected there would be some reference to the matter in hand but certainly not such a direct and personal one. She was aware that he put down his knife and fork, wiped his mouth quickly with his napkin, and leaned towards her. 'Kenilworth isn't looking at this hardwood proposal with a business eye, it's coming from his persona. He daren't act in business because he daren't act in life, and the older he gets the worse he is. Look, I know I shouldn't be talking to you like this, but you've been with us a long time and I believe you are a very astute and understanding woman. I'd like to know what you think. Tell me, do you think I'm exaggerating about Kenilworth?'

Miss Wheeler didn't know which way to look. In the office it was easy to deal with confidences, she had her routines. But in this place, taking this expensive lunch from him, it was different. She wondered how she was going to swallow the food in her mouth. To make it worse he waited for her to do so, watching her every movement.

'Religion can be a solace to people,' she managed at last.

'But he doesn't need solace. What he needs is to live.'

She thought he looked a little mad at this point. They said he had women, one after the other. She could believe it. It was a much more difficult situation than the one she had faced with Mr Kenilworth. She made a great effort. 'I'm quite sure,' she said, 'that as far as business matters are concerned, you and Mr Kenilworth will *together* find the answer to the problem which faces you, as you always have in the past.'

He was disappointed, she knew. He wanted her to take sides, to condemn Mr Kenilworth personally, which she would never be prepared to do. The rest of the meal wasn't so much fun. He continued to joke in a lively way, but she knew he couldn't wait to get back to the office.

She heard no more about it, but one afternoon about a week later she had to go out into the yard to check in a new consignment of pinewood. This was part of her job, a safety measure Kenilworth had instituted against 'timber with legs,' as he put it. She stood off from the lorry as usual with her clipboard, noting the quantities of wood as it was unloaded by the crane and fork lifts and taken for storage.

'Should be plenty for a coffin for Kenilworth in this lot,' she heard Ben say. Ben was the youngest of the men, who had a reputation for repartee.

'A bed of nails more likely,' said another man.

'Can see Mark Trent fixing the nails in himself,' said a third.

The worst thing was she was quite sure it had been intended she heard the remarks. She had to go to the foreman's office when she had finished, to check her findings against the delivery notes. Stuart Bailey, a Scotsman, was a sensible man and they got on well - she would never have dreamed in the normal way of discussing gossip with him, especially if it referred to the directors. But in the circumstances she felt it was her duty to break the rule.

'Stuart,' she mentioned in a different voice as they concluded their business, 'I couldn't help overhearing some remarks just now. They were talking about a coffin for Mr Kenilworth.'

Stuart gave a short laugh. 'I can guess what that was all about,' he said. 'The yard's abuzz of course.'

'Abuzz?'

'About the row between Trent and Kenilworth of course - the new door and window business. Don't tell me they haven't informed you about it?'

She hesitated. 'I know what might possibly be in the wind, yes,' she said guardedly.

'"Possibly?" That must be the understatement of the year. It's going to be Trent or Kenilworth, isn't it, a showdown? Which side are you on?'

Miss Wheeler felt breathless. 'I certainly know of no showdown,' she said.

'Then you must be the only one Trent's left out. Probably afraid you'll tell Kenilworth. He's been at the rest of us like a politician.'

In her long service with the firm she had never known anything like this, such casual overtness - and Stuart appearing to think it was all a bit of a joke. She collected herself. 'Do you mean Mr Trent's being talking to the men about his project?'

'I'll say, though it's cost him a few pints, I can tell you.'

'And you're saying he's been implying Mr Kenilworth's against the project?'

'Hardly implying, Miss Wheeler. Not that that will do him any good. Trenty's made up his mind all right, that's plain enough, and if he's decided, things happen, don't they? We've all got to move with the times, haven't we? Kenilworth'd have us left high and dry.'

It was this last sentence of Stuart's Miss Wheeler thought about most when she got home that evening. Stuart, the Scot, was the acme of caution, but he had spoken, she realised, with an unaccustomed energy, *an energy not his own*. She suspected he had borrowed Trent's phrases - 'left high and dry,' for example. There was a forced defiance in his voice, as if he needed to persuade himself. She couldn't sleep. Of the rights and wrongs of the new proposal she was in no position to judge, but of one thing she was now sure. That Trent should start canvassing the work force in this way only went further to show that personal factors were featuring in a most disturbing way.

Kenilworth was back in the office two days later. After a lot of thought, she decided to let him know that the hardwood scheme was being talked about in the yard. She left out any idea of the fact that it might be the result of Trent's activities, but it was only fair he knew what was going on. Trent was out. At about four o'clock she realised a fog was coming down outside. This seemed to lend a kind of cover for what she had to do. She put the lights on and drew the curtains. She was just about to say what she had planned when Trent came in. He hung his coat up as usual and sat at his desk, hands in pockets. She knew there had been a new development. Trent was looking at her, not Kenilworth, and looking very pleased with himself.

'Well, it's in the bag, signed and sealed,' he said.

Kenilworth had been searching for something in a drawer. He was not conscious of Trent's demeanour. 'The Simmonds contract? Good,' he said absently.

'Not the Simmonds contract. The hardwood firm. I've bought it.'

It was a moment or two before Kenilworth registered what Trent had said. He abandoned his search in the drawer, leaving it open. 'You've *what*?'

'The machinery and remaining timber stocks arrive next week. I've already set in motion advertising for specialist staff. We'll rationalise our timber-space, clear the south barn for action, and with luck we'll be in some kind of production within a month.'

Kenilworth's eyebrows had converged into a single thicket of intensity. 'You cannot have bought a business without my counter-signature on the cheque,' he said thunderously.

'I thought you might come up with that. In the normal way of course I couldn't have, could I? But we've been a bit careless of late, haven't we, signing blank cheques before MissWheeler has filled them in? There were two the other day which came to me for my counter-signature, still left blank.'

Miss Wheeler swallowed. It was her job to make out the cheques. It happened sometimes when the two men were both busy or one was going out that she would tell them how many there were and get them to sign before she filled them in. This had happened recently in the case of these two cheques, which were passed to Trent second after Kenilworth had signed. Trent had been in a hurry, on his way out to an appointment. He told her he would fill them in and post them when he was out.

Kenilworth was realising the enormity of what Trent had done. 'This amounts to fraud,' he said.

Trent laughed. 'The Nelson touch perhaps. Do I recall a telescope and a blind eye?'

'I'll take you to court.'

'I doubt if you will. Because it would do neither of us any good. Your word against mine? It isn't the first time you've had cold feet and wanted to go back on a decision.'

'I've gone back on no decision. Miss Wheeler will attest . . .'

'That you signed two blank cheques?'

'Miss Wheeler knows that I signed them in the knowledge that they were normal payments of small amounts.'

'Does she? Does she know of our private conversations, in one of which - alas, but momentarily - you overcame your innate and tortoise-like caution and agreed to make this purchase?'

'I did no such thing.' Trent's shrug was almost imperceptible. 'How much have you spent?'

'A mere two hundred grand. It's a bargain. We could sell the new plant for a lot more than that.'

Mr Kenilworth exonerated Miss Wheeler completely - the signing of blank cheques was a routine he himself had suggested, he pointed out, in view of his complete trust in her integrity. She should not blame herself in any way for the dishonesty of his partner. But she could not accept this. She felt responsible - and quite decimated by Trent's act. She considered resigning. It was only because to have done so would have seemed like desertion of the firm at a time of crisis that she didn't. Was there not still some way in which her accumulated knowledge of her employers might enable her to assist in a happy outcome?

The next month or two was a period of almost intolerable strain. Her employers spoke to each other via her. Trent was almost never in the office. Kenilworth's firm-lipped silence was monolithic.

But then Miss Wheeler was able to detect a subtle shift in her spirits. Trent was not much in the office, but he spent more of his time than usual on the premises dealing single-handed with the new business - with which Kenilworth would have nothing to do. His energy was phenomenal, supervising the installation of the plant, appointing the new staff and monitoring their performance. She had even seen him helping to operate the machines in the shed he'd had converted. His enthusiasm had transferred to the whole staff. Then the products began to come off the production line. They were beautiful, precision-made.

The question was of course whether the goods would sell. Miss Wheeler began to share the common view that if they, the staff, thought highly of them so would their clients, who would show their appreciation with their cheque-books. Miss Wheeler's opinion was not consulted these days but, had it been, she thought, she would surely have come down on the positive side. Shockingly as Trent had behaved, his enthusiasm surely deserved to triumph over Kenilworth's sulky gloom. Maybe when Kenilworth saw that success was coming he would change his view.

One morning she realised how far he was from this. Kenilworth came in and sat at his desk. He didn't look in a very good frame of mind, and began to open the mail. There was one letter, she noticed out of the corner of her eye, which he seemed to ponder over for some time.   Then as he put it aside she saw him give a quick smile.   When he had finished looking at the letters he passed them to her.

'Nothing which isn't routine, Miss Wheeler, you can deal with them all.'   Definitely, there was an element of levity.

She glanced through the letters.   One caught her eye.   She knew Trent was awaiting the outcome of a crucial tender he had made to re-window the headquarters of a Swiss bank in the City with their new products.   The contract would be worth sixty thousand pounds which would tide them over the immediate cash-flow crisis.   The envelope had the bank's name on it.   She read the letter.   It turned down the tender.   Before thinking, she exclaimed.

'Oh, Mr Kenilworth, I'm so sorry about this.'

'Sorry?'

'That we don't have the bank contract.'

Kenilworth was writing.   He didn't stop, and frowned to hide his satisfaction.   'You thought we'd have it, did you?'

'Well, I thought we might.   Mr Trent was very optimistic.'

'Mr Trent is well endowed with optimism.   It is, I'm told, the quality most shared by bankrupts.'

'Mr Kenilworth, do you mean . . .'

'I mean the sooner we realise the folly of this venture, cut our losses and get back to normal routine, the more likely we are to survive.'

She tried to think of something to say, but couldn't.

The following day Trent burst into the office in an unprecedented fury.   'Have you been talking to Stuart and the others?' he said to Kenilworth.

Kenilworth didn't interrupt his writing.   'Would you be surprised if I had?   It is a practice you are familiar with, it seems?'

'It's sabotage.   You told them the luxury business is failing?'

'If they say that they misquote.'

'You told them the business is touch and go.'

'It's all touch and *no* go as far as I am concerned.'

Trent sat down. For once words didn't come readily to his lips. 'You're incredible. You would sabotage your own business and sow discord among your employees?'

'Salvage is a better word than sabotage.'

'You negative, mean, treacherous sod. And to think you profess to be a Christian. I always knew your so-called religion was phoney.'

'You'd have to think that, wouldn't you? In view of the morally baseless existence you lead.'

They were off. Miss Wheeler would have escaped if she could, but Trent was now leaping about the room like a monkey in a cage and she feared collision. She entertained no doubts at all from what she heard that the quarrel went far beyond business. Kenilworth was remarkably well-informed. Trent had recently been deserted, it appeared, by a woman he had hoped to marry from whom he had concealed his past. It was also clear between the lines that, whatever he said, Trent envied the settled happiness of Kenilworth's family life. And perhaps Kenilworth had begun to wonder in the inner recesses of his mind if he had not missed things in life. Both men had passion. They could not therefore both be right, or wrong. As in the age of religious intolerance, rival dogmas clashed swords for the right to enter heaven.

Miss Wheeler felt she had unwittingly strayed on to a field of battle where cannonballs flew about her head and smoke and noise raged. She was confused. How could she intervene, she was but an employee? They were arguing figures now. It appeared money would need to be borrowed immediately to keep things alive until several pending orders materialised. They would have to have a small extension of the loan they had negotiated from the bank, Trent said. With their collateral there should be no problem.

Miss Wheeler realised there was a crisis. With falling spirits she heard Kenilworth pronounce his triumphant words. There would be no request for any further loan. It would need his signature, which would most certainly not be forthcoming.

The smoke cleared momentarily. They had fought each other

to a standstill. An idea came to Miss Wheeler of such proportions that for an instant she couldn't breathe. Of course the idea was senseless she debated - she, a mere secretary. But it would not step down, she found. She continued to think it even more strongly. The business had been her life as well as theirs.

'Mr Trent,' she said, 'I hope you'll forgive me if I speak for a moment as a private individual and not as an employee. The firm is, I understand, in need of some ten thousand pounds for a venture which is on the brink of success. I had a small legacy recently. I have the amount at present in an accessible savings account. I would very much like to invest what is necessary to save the firm in its hour of need and at the same time to give myself the chance of increasing my capital. What I'm saying is that, if permitted, I'd like to buy a share in the new business.'

Trent's face lit. 'You would, Miss Wheeler?'

Kenilworth's eyebrows contained menace. She hurried on. 'I would - and I will - lend the money in any circumstances. But as a shareholder I'd feel a lot more secure if the dual management which has made the firm what it is were fully restored. Mr Kenilworth is, I think you might admit, Mr Trent, a great deal sounder on figures.'

Whatever happened, she thought, she would enjoy for some time to come the look of pure astonishment which had appeared on both men's faces. They looked like schoolboys caught red-handed. Kenilworth was the first to recover his voice.

'Oh no, Miss Wheeler, there's no question of your doing such a thing.'

'With respect, Mr Kenilworth, you really cannot stop me if Mr Trent agrees.'

'You might lose every penny.'

'The risk, I admit, would be greater if you continue to oppose the hardwood venture.'

Trent looked at Kenilworth. For once he wisely kept his mouth shut. Kenilworth spread the fingertips of both hands on the desk as if he were playing a chord on a piano. 'I'll not have Miss Wheeler risking her money,' he said. 'I'd rather borrow it from the bank.'

'You mean you agree to an extension of the bank loan?' Trent said.

There was a long pause, after which, to Miss Wheeler's astonishment a slow smile began to spread across Kenilworth's face. 'What I mean,' he said at last, 'is yes, you're right, I think Miss Wheeler has me over a barrel. What she is indicating to me is that I have probably been overcautious, and certainly in recent days malicious. On reflection I accept this. But what I think you don't fully realise, Mark, is that in a different way she has you over the barrel, too. Neither of us has been behaving very well lately and, wise lady that she is, what she has been doing in the most modest way is point out to both of us how wrong we've been. Yes, I do agree to the bank loan. But on Miss Wheeler's other suggestion I do not agree. I think we should *give* her a share in the new venture as a token of our gratitude for the service she has given to this company over a great number of years.'

THE HAPPIEST MAN IN THE WORLD

The heat of the Roman afternoon was suffocating. The cypresses in the garden of our villa stood like sentries, even the cicadas were taking a siesta. On the edge of sleep I dimly registered the frantic tinging of a bicycle bell. There were footsteps and William Buglass's voice shouted from just below our window.

'Darlings, come out from wherever you are, I bring you tidings . . .'

William slaloms in and out of our rather staid diplomatic life. We like him, just because of his eccentric ebullience and unpredictability. But this was not his most welcome visit. Groggily, I went to the window and said we would be down in a minute.

William is small and, though only thirtyish, is balding and seems older. He has a natural tonsure, a little halo of fluffy grey hair encircling a salmon-pink pate. He is often unshaven and his clothes are invariably crumpled. He is perpetually excited, immensely energetic, and always laughing - like a clockwork toy which never needs rewinding. When we went down he was sitting on the balcony mopping his neck with an enormous spotted handkerchief one of his students had given him for his birthday. Sweat stained a large area of his shirt under his arms and across his chest. Sue gave him iced lemonade.

It was quite possible there was no news, nothing of importance. The chances were, despite the heat, he had just had an impulse to peddle the six miles out of the city to see us. What he had to say would be a trumped-up excuse. This was why we were in no hurry. Sue asked him if he would like a cold bath and one of my shirts before we had tea.

He had been undergoing our courtesies with visible impatience. I don't think he heard them. 'But my news,' he interrupted, 'I have startling news. Darlings, you my dearest friends, are the first to know. I'm to be married.' We must both have stared. 'It's true,' he giggled. 'True. True. True.

A miracle has come to pass. Buglass is to be spliced, hitched, handcuffed for life to the most beautiful girl in the world - my golden girl, my Rokeby, my Venus. Her name is Maria Luisa Columbino. She came to our private tutorial this morning with *flowers.* We sat on the sofa together and *twice* she let me put my arm round her waist.'

Sue looked at me, then incredulously back at William. 'A student?'

It was difficult not to be affected by William's fervour. *Was* it possible? But when he had gone we got things into perspective. A supplementary teacher of English at the University, William's students and colleagues, especially the women, loved him for his humour and kindness and old-fashioned manner, but no one doubted he would remain a bachelor all his life. And Luisa must be at least ten years younger. A hand round her waist - was that all? Like his other fantasies, this one would have its hour and fade into the next.

But we were to be witnesses to the 'divine intervention' - this was how William described what had happened to him. The next day he phoned to say he had invited Luisa and her friend Donatella to spend Saturday on the beach at Ostia with him and Luisa had accepted. Wasn't this the definitive proof of her feelings, he debated, if any more were needed? Would we come, too, he asked, then we could see for ourselves. It would have been difficult to say no, and we had to admit to curiosity.

One thing was certain. Luisa was beautiful. In her white bikini sensationally so. Brown skinned, small hipped, small breasted, she could have been a model any day she wished to walk into a fashionable photographer's studio. What a contrast with her plump, dowdy and rather silent friend Donatella, who came, too, and who like Luisa was being coached by William for her thesis. Luisa was also, it was at once apparent, a very gracefully-mannered girl - uncomplicated and genuine. '*Che piacere*,' she said respectfully and warmly when introduced, what a pleasure to meet William's closest friends.

Meeting her immediately scotched two possible explanations I'd had - that she was out for a few expensive meals or, worse, that it was some cruel *dolce vita* student bet.   Luisa seemed an innocent.   There were further confirmations.   All day William rushed about like a madman, fussing and giggling and joking. Luisa seemed to like it.   She kept looking at Donatella and laughing.   In the sea she took William's hand, unbidden, and William, in an access of gallantry, raised it to his lips.   Luisa blushed and laughed again.   Later when William went off with Donatella to buy ice-creams, Luisa told us with gravity how marvellously kind William was to her and Donatella and how deeply she admired him.   William had published a few books of literary criticism and poetry.   She began to question me about these.   Was he '*molto celebre*' in England, she asked naively, her admiration plain.

Sue and I began to construct an identikit background for Luisa and, thus, a credible explanation for the love affair.   Obviously, she came from a rich background.   An only daughter, a secluded and protected childhood?   This seemed to be along the right lines when we heard in the next days that Luisa was very religious.   William was also a Catholic but had hitherto been an erratic churchgoer.   Now he began to accompany her regularly to mass.   'She is deeply spiritual,' he annnounced, 'and she is going to reform my dissipated life.   It's a *Damascan* conversion.'

William came almost every day to report 'progress' as he called it, and increasingly for advice.   Just how quickly should he press things?   He confessed he had never 'really' had a girl before.   Should he kiss her?   If so, in what circumstances? Would she misunderstand, would it offend her religious sensitivities?   Should he propose first, before the kiss?   He went through an extravagant phase of thinking Luisa might prefer a celibate marriage.

The Victorian niceties were beginning to get tiresome, even mawkish, when there was a dramatic development.   Quite unprompted, it seemed, Luisa had asked William to accompany her to her home in a seaside village 'some way up the coast.' He was delirious.   It could of course mean only one thing.   'It is the Italian way,' he explained joyfully.   She was virtually proposing to him.   Or rather, he amended quickly, she was telling him she wouldn't be averse to his proposing to her - if her parents accepted him of course. He asked a great favour. Would we go with him? He needed our support and 'sophisticated counsel' - '*in the field*,' he added with a giggle. He had another point. With roguish candour he explained how if Luisa's parents saw he had friends in the British Foreign Service this would clinch matters. In addition to common charity, we felt we owed William a lot in terms of the lively entertainment he had given us in the past. The Colombinos indeed lived some way 'up the coast'- to be precise in San Remo at the southern end of the Riviera. Sue booked us into a hotel there.

But the next day William arrived, brimming with joy. The hotel was out of the question, he said. We must cancel our reservation at once. When he had told Luisa we were coming she had immediately spoken to her parents on the telephone and we, too, would be most welcome. Wasn't this fantastic? It wasn't what we would have preferred, but it seemed churlish to risk tarnishing William's exuberance. It might also seem standoffish to the Columbinos if we declined their kind hospitality.

We had pictured an affluent background for Luisa - a palazzo or something near it had seemed on the cards. William had certainly given no other impression. But it turned out to be a small pensione the Columbinos ran. There was of course nothing wrong with this, but it was embarrassing to find they had cancelled bookings to accomodate us. We had been given one of the best rooms with a view over tamarisk trees to the sea - William had been given similar treatment. At the height of the season goodness knew what loss of income this represented. If we had known the circumstances we would certainly have insisted on the hotel. But when we said all this to William he laughed. 'It is kind of them, immensely kind, but look upon it as an investment on their part, an investment in Luisa's future happiness. That is how I see it, at least. They plainly want to please us. Why not let them? I will repay them a hundredfold in the years to come in my devotion to their daughter. There will be no regrets, I assure you.   Give the matter not one thought more.' He giggled yet again. 'They see you, of course, *in loco parentis* to me.'

We had been seriously wrong about the grandeur of Luisa's home, but we had correctly guessed another aspect of her life. Luisa *was* an only child, and both her parents doted on her. When we were once alone with the Columbinos, their conversation centred entirely on her charm, her beauty, and her intellect. Signor Colombino - who wore gym shoes and a singlet with blue and white horizontal hoops - kept tapping the side of his head and saying '*Luisa, molto habile*' - unlike himself and his wife, he added modestly. A brain had been bestowed, it seemed he wanted us to believe, by immaculate conception. They had made great sacrifices to send her to Rome University, but how they had been rewarded.   And what student could have been luckier than Luisa to come across a teacher so eminent, so sensitive, so understanding, as *Il Professore Buglass*.

Sue and I began to think we were superfluous. If the purpose of the invitation was to get an embassy opinion of their daughter's suitor, surely there was no doubt of the outcome? They behaved to William with unctuous servility.   '*Dottore*' this, and '*ilustrisimo professore*' that.   William was ecstatic. Signor Colombino wanted to settle Luisa's tuition fees.   'But there can be no question of *fees*, Signor,' William said.   He was hurt to think the idea could be entertained. He grew bolder.   'It is all for love,' he burbled, with emotion that spewed out like champagne from the magnum of a racing-driver.   'For love all things are possible.'   There followed, in English, the lines of a Shakespearean sonnet whose full significance surely eluded the perplexed but genially nodding heads of the Columbinos.

William knocked on our door as soon as we had gone to our room that evening. He couldn't contain himself.   'We've done it,' he burst out.   'How can I deserve it all?   There can be no doubt the Colombinos approve.'

The next day Sue noticed something about the behaviour of the Colombinos towards us. They were no less attentive to William, but all morning we were getting significant looks from them.   At lunch, as he served me with a noticeably generous helping of '*fettucino al pesto*,' Colombino gave me a stage wink. Later, William and Luisa decided to have a lesson.   Sue and I were asked in a whisper if we would consent to come into the kitchen.

We sat round the plain scrubbed table.   Signora Colombino looked uncomfortable.   She crossed her small plump arms and looked over them at her feet as if there were something on the floor beside them of great interest.   Signor Colombino cleared his throat and began an elaborate overture in English, though Sue and I both speak passable Italian.   He began by setting out the situation, stressing again how unusually kind William had been to Luisa, though he could understand this as she was such a talented pupil.   At last he came to the point.

'Signor, Signora, I will not *prevaricare*.   I must to tell you now the most profound secret.   Luisa is fallen in love.   Yes. The man is rich, handsome, *di buona famiglia*.   The boy, he is also *licensiatio*, an *inteletuale*.   It is for this reason, more even than others, that Luisa has need to do well in her exams.   Now you know well, Signore, the state of our education system here in *Italia*.   Degrees are given for *merito* naturally, but also - you will understand - is important *la potenza*.   Signor Buglass is a fine teacher.   He is well-known in the *Facolta*.   But he is English. We wonder - perhaps you can confirm us - that he is *suficientemente potente* in order to . . .   You will understand, Signor, I am not a rich man.   I need to know the money I spend for Luisa will get her a degree . . .'

Somehow we escaped the interview.   Yes, I said, I could confirm that Signor Buglass had influence, both in general terms and in the specific sense Colombino meant.   I said I doubted if William went as far as some teachers did, for gain, and wrote their pupils' theses for them, but if Luisa was good enough - and I had no reason to think she wasn't - I was sure he would see her thesis and exam were viewed in the most positive light.   (I am, after all, trained in diplomatic mumbo-jumbo).

The next morning I invented a crisis at the embassy.   William was sorry at our premature departure but he was not distraught.

For he had 'weigh', he chuckled merrily, lovely 'swashbuckling' weigh, which would 'freewheel him to paradise'. He would return to Rome by train with Luisa. As we took our leave, he put his head through the window of our car. Who knew, he said - he might return to Rome, the Rubicon crossed. He had bought the ring.

We knew it was cowardly of us. We should have told him before we left. It was also selfish. We just couldn't face the thought of a shattered Buglass all the way to Rome.

William returned to Rome unchanged. He had not popped the question. He had decided, he said, that Lusia's thesis must be finished first. There could then be double celebrations. For once he didn't ask our advice. Was he already, we thought hopefully, beginning subconsciously to sense the truth? And if this was so, wasn't it gentler to let this process go on so that he would have time to prepare his inner defences against the inevitable disaster?

We did do one positive thing, however. Sue discovered where Donatella lived, and consulted her. Not entirely to our surprise she was entirely au fait with the situation from her own observation. She confirmed that Luisa was entirely unaware of William's real intentions, so were her parents. Luisa was very idealistic and easily blinkered by her romantic ambitions, she said. She simply thought William was being kind in a fatherly way. She agreed it would be a mistake to tell William or Luisa at this juncture. It could cause Luisa to fail her exam. She undertook do what she could to prevent Luisa from giving unwitting encouragement to William, though this would be difficult, for Luisa was extremely fond of him and grateful for everything he had done for her.

Our hope that William might subconsciously have realised the situation evaporated, for his ardour did not abate. One day he announced that that evening, Luisa's exam or not, he was going to 'do the deed.' The proposal would surely inspire her? We really thought he meant it this time. There was a new seriousness and none of the usual effervescent self-mockery.

Following this there was a silence. Sue and I happened to

have a rush of work at this time, and no doubt cowardice on our part further explained why we did nothing immediate to contact William. But after a few days the silence became ominous. We telephoned his villa twice and got no answer. The University knew nothing - as far as they were concerned he was still on leave. What fools we had been. William could have put his head in the oven. Not very rationally, we got in the car and drove like the furies.

Pulses thumping, we rushed up to his door and rang. There was a movement, definitely a movement inside. Something at least was alive. After a long pause Wiliam opened the door. He was eating an apple.

'Oh hallo,' he said.

'William, we just had to know . . .'

He seemed reluctant to let us in. He gave a shifty glance behind him. For a moment he looked like a stranger, even hostile. Then suddenly he ignited into his usual self.

'My darlings, come in, come in. As a matter of fact you've come at just the right moment. I'm the happiest man in the world. I'm to be married. Yes, Buglass has pulled it off. You can't believe it? Champagne? There must be some somewhere. My love, come. Come and be congratulated by my oldest and dearest friends.'

We filed into the sitting-room, and there was Donatella, getting sheepishly to her feet but ready to accept our congratulations like an Empress her tribute.

Hand over hand we pulled in the story. There had been 'some difficulties in a certain quarter', which had temporarily 'thrown' him. But Donatella had moved in her first aid services pretty rapidly, it seemed. We got the impression she'd had them ready in the wings for some time.

'And now, my dears, a banquet, don't you think? A marriage feast, in the garden, *a cuatro.* Candlelight? *Canelonis? Abacchio al forno*? Wild strawberries? A good Orvieto? Yes? Yes?'

We didn't see Luisa again, and William never mentioned her. We heard from Donatella that she got her degree. Donatella was not sure if Luise had married her well-connected Croesus - and cared little, we were to understand. The Italians can after all be as skilled as the French at combining the practical with the romantic. So under their tutelage, it would seem, can be the English.

THE OTHER DEATH

The old man's death caused little stir. For fifteen years he had lived in one room of the house, widowed, morose, senile. To all intents and purposes he was dead already.

Villagers saw the house from the fields, its big mullioned windows staring lidlessly, no smoke curling from its copy Tudor chimney pots, no discernible movement except an occasional flutter in the west wing where Reg Hobart and the other man lived. A gardener who mowed the two lawns once a week had caught sight of the old man through a downstairs window recently. He had seen a pathetic, pyjama-ed figure, poor soul, in a wheel chair, unshaven, bent, nodding. At the funeral it was just the two men who accompanied the vicar at the graveside. They both wore suits, bowed their heads and held their arms down in front of them with hands clasped as if they were giving a leg up to someone mounting a horse.

But the will? The thought of this provoked more interest. Perhaps there was an heir who would be young and vigorous, who would restore the house, repair it, purchase, employ. There would be functions, parties, and the village would understand again why the house was there. Then the rumour started. There was no family heir. Reg Hobart, who had come to the place out of the blue eight years ago, had scooped the lot, the house and its contents, and would sell.

In a few days this was confirmed. Large notices appeared in the national newspapers, the expensive space taken by a well-known London firm of auctioneers. Comment said the contents sale would be the event of the decade for anyone knowing anything about antiques. Great Choke house itself was not the excitement. It had been built as a hunting lodge by an early Victorian steel baron, the younger sibling of a much larger dwelling. Some casual observers, and the villagers, thought the house rather romantic with its thick mantle of ivy, its tall red chimney pots heavily ornamented, set as it was rather secretly in a wooded depression in the rolling Warwickshire countryside.

Cognoscenti sneered. 'A hybrid monstrosity that has plundered the styles of every epoch since Elizabeth I, it is fortunate the vegetation and its low situation denies a view from all sides until one is upon it.' So read one passage in a highbrow guide to great properties. But about the contents there was no dispute. The five descendants of the founder had vied to fill the place with treasures, not only of previous ages, but of their own. Apart from the Great Choke chest reputed to have been King Alfred's, there was a unique collection of Gilberts, one of the finest cabinet makers of the Victorian period, and an outstanding collection of glass, porcelain and pictures.

The auctioneers saw to it the sale had the widest publicity. A glossy brochure printed with a colour photograph of the chest on the cover went to dealers and known art collectors far and wide. To make more space for the prize items, a huge marquee was erected with pink stripes and a frilly frieze. Into this were moved the lesser artefacts, crockery from what had been the servants' quarters, a collection of military uniforms and swords, a table full of prints in large folders, garden and estate machinery. Another smaller marquee was for refreshments, which included champagne and smoked salmon sandwiches. Up and down the country, prospective buyers, small and great, amateur and professional, planned, calculated, speculated - and on the appointed days converged.

Esther Petrie drove the small vintage Talbot doggedly through the summer rain. With both hands on the wheel she sat slightly forward peering through the small aperture the wiper cleared. Some miles from their destination she saw the first yellow AA sign: 'GREAT CHOKE SALE.'

'God, their outriders have penetrated far and wide,' she said.

Her husband, Lionel Petrie sniffed. He had a chronic sniff. Sitting beside Esther in a neat tie and a light-coloured jacket, he appeared the smaller of the two, though he was a head taller. He seemed to contemplate a reply but said nothing. He, too, was peering forwards intently. The wipers ploughed audibly.

'I'm quite sure that lawyer sent the letter to us deliberately late, hoping we wouldn't be able to come,' Esther said. 'I've decided. To teach that grasping pervert a lesson I'll settle for the Gilberts, no less.'

Lionel stirred. 'You mean *all* the Gilberts?'

'The set. The will states quite clearly "an entity". What could be more of an entity than that furniture? Now I think about it, I'm quite sure that was what was intended. My uncle had to encode his instruction to get it past that monster. And quite apart from the legalities, it would be an aesthetic crime to break up such a collection as it almost certainly would be in the sale.'

'But Esther, we couldn't possibly find space . . .'

'We'll give it to the University,' Esther snapped. She had been lying in wait for Lionel's point. 'Take one or two smaller pieces perhaps, and donate the rest. Quite apart from rescuing it from rapacious dealers, it'll make Hobart appear in his true colours and put him in his place. He's bound to try to kick up a fuss.'

Lionel's academic mind was quietly fastening on the salient point. Could the word 'entity' possibly be so construed? He doubted it. Indeed the phrasing of that part of the will implied one object and *not* a group of them. Probably the words had been chosen carefully by the lawyer. But so many times Esther's drive and certainty had brushed obstacles aside, and she had got away with it. He sniffed again, and remained silent.

A temporary entrance had been made, it seemed, through a five-barred gate into a field. They encountered a queue of cars.

'I shall use the main entrance,' stated Esther, and pulled out to overtake the queue.

She was stopped where the cars were turning into the gate by a mackintoshed figure wearing an armband and wellingtons. 'Sorry, madam, no through traffic on this road today. There is a sign further back.'

'I'm not through traffic. I'm using the main entrance to the house.'

'Sorry, madam, the main entrance is blocked for the sale. This is the entrance.'

Some inkling of Esther's feeling of outrage seemed to get to the man. Maybe it was in deference to them rather than because of the impractibility of her turning round that he waved her though the gate ahead of the other cars. Two hooted. Flushing, Esther turned the car with an angry burst of acceleration on to the grilles they had laid across the sodden churned grass. She was forced to slow, however, as she joined the spaced flotilla of cars making steadily for the parking area. The Talbot was involuntarily added to the anonymous phalanx of dully gleaming metal and the Petries were coralled into a further procession, this one pedestrian, making its way in the rain along a green canvas strip to the marquee.

'Entrance by brochure only,' a sign announced. Esther ignored it and swept inside, but she was stopped again, this time by a well-dressed man in a dark suit sporting a red carnation who motioned her politely to a girl sitting at a desk on a raised dais beside a pile of brochures.

'How much are they?' she asked the man loudly.

'Ten pounds.'

'What?'

She would have given vent to her feelings. Ten pounds charged for her to enter the house where she had spent her childhood? It was outrageous. If they knew who she was . . . But for once Lionel quietly had his way. Reaching for his wallet, he was already approaching the girl. 'Not worth the fuss, you'll lose,' his quick look communicated. 'And after all, what will ten pounds look like if those chairs. . . .'

While he paid, she tossed her head away to observe the crowd circulating round the long rows of trestle tables. The accents, the clothing, communicated to her at once the class of people who had come. They were turning over the goods in that insolent way all sale-goers have, as if what they handled was already theirs. By rights all of this belonged to her. They were violating her property.

The brochure proved useful. It listed and numbered every lot. Most of the good items had photographs as well. Each had also a description and an estimated value. Lionel read with his usual patient concentration.

'The Gilberts seem to be mostly in the dining-room and the library,' he said.

Esther knew every inch of the place. Leading, she took some vicious satisfaction in barging past hesitant people finding their way. Identify and make a note of the stuff, then beard Hobart and deliver her message, that was her plan. Almost certainly he would be gloating in that wing he had purloined for himself and his pathetic little consort. He couldn't guess what was coming to him.

She exclaimed with pleasure over Gilbert's furniture, which she had never noticed before. In those days it had just been part of the place, taken for granted. There was a magnificent table, fourteen feet long, twenty-four matching chairs, two sideboards, several small tables, beautifully inlaid with native woods, bookcases, all with the same distinctive style. Lionel discovered there were more upstairs. A four-poster bed and two sets of bedroom furniture. She made him tot up the 'suggested' value in the catalogue. The figure was staggering.

'It's a truly exquisite collection,' she said. 'And they'll have to withdraw it today, right away. If Hobart won't agree, we'll get an injunction. It will of course wreck the sale,' she added with satisfaction.

The door to the wing was locked. They had to retrace their steps and go round the house. As they left the marquee the sun came out. Esther accepted its light as the illumination of victory. What a revenge.

Sam was uneasy. He hadn't liked it from the day these superior people came from London with their well-tailored suits and expert knowledge. Though the house was falling into decay, and though he got no recompense for it, he had kept the better furniture and treasures dusted and polished. Was it now to be broken up, was all the thought and love and care of a century and a half to be dispersed? Above all he was uneasy because of Reg. It seemed to Sam that Reg had been in a kind of frenzy ever since the old man died. To Sam's way of thinking, Reg deserved what he had been left. He had been conscientious, and no one else had cared. But there was an element of revenge in his mood, as if it were an old score he were settling with the whole of his previous life. All right, Reg was on the point of realising a dream - a Carribean island, tuxedoes, cocktails at sunset beside a blue swimming-pool and the rest of it. People were entitled to be excited when their dreams came true. But did he have to be so aggressive about it?

Today for instance, the first day of the preview, Reg had been going through that door every other minute, rudely bullying the auctioneers' men who had been planted about the building to keep an eye and to answer the public's questions, then coming back to tell him what he had done. There was one incident with a dog. He had caught a lady with a pekingese under her arm. Dogs were not permitted for obvious reasons. 'I just seized the yapping little beast, held its silly muzzle, and threw it under the canvas flap. "Can't you read notices?" I say to the woman, "you'd better go straight out and rescue the animal and lock it in your car before my wolfhound eats it." "Who are you, I'll sue you," she says. "The owner," I say, "sue away." It was exaggerated, Sam thought, unnecessary. Would sunshine and palm trees ever calm him down? Would it ever be the same again out there, would they themselves be?

He had just finishing dusting sugar on a sponge cake, when the sun came out through the last bits of scampering ragged cloud. Good, he thought, tea in the garden perhaps, maybe that would calm Reg a bit. Then round the corner came the trespassers, a couple, the woman striding ahead of the man. Oh Lord, he thought. Reg was in the lounge at his desk making money calculations. Should he call out to the strangers? Better not, Reg would be bound to hear and go after them, making an unnecessary scene. In a moment they would surely realise they had strayed where they shouldn't and retreat.

But they came right up to their front door and knocked. Pulses broke out all over Sam's body like a troupe of tumblers in the middle of their act. It was the niece, he saw, he hadn't thought it would be her. So she *had* come. He left the door for

Reg to answer, he couldn't face it. Perhaps they would have a conversation, perhaps the couple would go and he wouldn't be involved.

The voices sounded quite calm. Then Reg stuck his head round the kitchen door. 'It's the Petries, we'll give them tea,' he hissed. Sam could tell he was hyper-excited - and *pleased*. This was worse than anger.

When he wheeled tea into the lounge they were hard at it. She was a small woman, but vehement. She threw her arms about to compensate for her size and her eyes seemed to bulge. 'An entity,' she was almost shouting, 'the will says an entity, it's perfectly clear.' And there was Reg, so tall and good-looking sitting in his favourite pink high-backed chair, his hands clasped in his lap, looking as cool as a judge.

'One object is meant, one object only. If I were you, I'd take it now while you have the entitlement. The day after tomorrow it'll have been sold and you'll have lost it.' For the second time that day Sam heard the word sue. She would sue Reg. No she wouldn't, said Reg. No lawyer would even take it on. He had taken advice as to the meaning of the will and it was plain.

The row got worse and Sam couldn't listen to it. To keep his mind away, he thought as kindly of Reg as he could. It wasn't true what the woman was going on to say. He had always believed what Reg had told him, that he had come to the house originally about insurance - he used to be in insurance - and while he was there the old man had some sort of a fit and he'd had to cope as there was no one else. Who could blame him for accepting accommodation and an income in return for looking after the invalid? Reg had never liked insurance. And he had looked after the old man, both of them had, feeding him, comforting him when he was down, cleaning up his mess, bringing him books. *She* hadn't lifted a finger. Only visited once to see how the land lay. She was shrill, this woman, her rage was ugly.

But he couldn't keep himself from criticising Reg, too. Really, the two were as bad as each other. Couldn't either of them see the tragedy they were participating in? An old house was being dismembered.   Item by item its limbs were being severed and borne away until only the carcase would be left.   It was like squabbling at a funeral.   In the end he went back to the kitchen on a pretext and stayed there till the Petries had gone. He only felt for the man - a university professor, wasn't he? - who sat there mute in spite of his eminence, watching impotently.

Numbers exceeded all expectations.   The place was thronged for both viewing days.   During this time passion was muted, concealed, dispersed, as objects were fingered, smoothed, transported in private imaginations to be tried out in positions in other houses.   In the rooms there was a constant hum and clatter but little talk, as if a vow of silence had been taken.

But on the day of the sale it was different.   All this dispersed emotion was concentrated in one place, the library.   There was a packed tense expectation, the only movement, it seemed, that of the auctioneer mounted on his rostrum and of the two white-coated assistants who displayed some of the more expensive and movable objects like the pictures - and the flick of a bidder's brochure.   Long arpeggios of price mounted, each one rising from the apogee of the last until again the lot was gavelled down and amazed excitement rippled back across the room that such prices could be paid.   The King Alfred chest reached just under half a million.   Item by item the house was emptied.

Late in the day the withdrawals began.   Removal vans backed up their yawning cavities to the front door.   Individuals bore off their spoil to cars and shooting brakes.   By dusk the halls and rooms and corridors, even the cellars, were void.   On the dingy wallpaper were brighter squares marking the graves of departed pictures.   Some of the fitted carpets, too worn and dirty for sale, bore the spore of cabriole legs and bronze casters.   A damp mustiness, for some time at bay, seemed to rise up more strongly to take possession.   The house, raped and ransacked, was moribund.

Esther Petrie, going for all, got nothing.   Her attempt to gain an injunction from a local magistrate failed.   She was too proud to take her legitimate legacy of one item. All she got was the right to tell the story for the rest of her life of how she had been cheated out of a fortune by an unscrupulous insurance agent turned nursemaid. Perhaps this was a rewarding enough compensation for an individual of her psyche. Reg and Sam went to Bermuda.

Great Choke was sold a few weeks after the other sale. It was a low-key affair and went to the County. It was to be a centre for short-term teacher refresher courses. Cleaned, repaired, rewired, overpainted, the house became 'premises.' Signs went up on the doors - 'refectory', 'lounge,' 'lecture-room.' The rooms were minimally furnished with modern bric-a-brac. Droves of teachers came and remarked on the architectural style of the building with the same caustic phraseology used previously by aesthetic publications.

Only Sam perhaps remembered the place as it was, just at odd moments when he was preparing a lobster thermidor or putting final touches to a caviar salad. For as he tried to say to Reg one day, the old man after all lay in the churchyard under a fine tombstone and had a bronze plaque in the village church to be remembered by, but the house? Who remembered the house in the fine state in which they had kept it, the noble proportions outside and the grand furnishings within?

ON THE PEAK

'In my view the Colony will retain its prosperity through 1997,' said Philip Lavington. He coughed into a clenched hand and turned to serve himself with 'king-prawns marinated in a garlic sauce', which the waiter was offering him on a silver platter. 'The Beijing Government aren't fools.'

Laurie's nerved attention was divided, for Mrs Purser chose this moment to fill his glass with white wine from an elegant decanter. As she did so she leaned towards him in a certain way and he could see quite a long way down her dress. Below her sun-tan her lightly-tethered breasts were milky white and shapely. Lavington talked on. Was her act a challenge to his solemnity? It seemed like it. Laurie's dislike of Lavington focused.

'Will you be maintaining your personal investments here then?' he asked into the next conversational space, knowing this was lésé-majesté. Lavington, he was sure, would expect school-teachers, even headmasters, to keep station and certainly not intrude into matters such as private finance.

It seemed he was right. Like something undesirable in the street, his remark was coldly by-passed. They listened to personally-gathered evidence of Beijing's intentions, related in the same even tones. Lavington, whose family had been in the Island before the war, was the senior partner in an accountancy firm which advised the Government at the highest level.

The restaurant was lavish and air-conditioned. Built out into the harbour, it was like dining on a moored luxury liner. Through the closed wide windows, the lights of junks and other craft moved at one remove. Inside, islands of discreet light grew from candles on   the tables. Waiters glided over soundless carpeting.   Here the Raj was living out its last days, Laurie thought, determined not to flinch until the end.

'Well now, and how are the offspring coping,' said Jock Purser when Lavington had finished. He had the air of a number eight batsman coming in to slog when the classic players had departed. Yet he commanded both couples' interest. It was after all what they had invited Laurie for, what they were paying for.

Laurie relaxed. They had come to his ground where, he knew, as long as their children were under his command, he held them to ransom. He took the Lavington boy first, and with him executed a small revenge on his father. 'Oh, Richard's fine as ever,' he said tolerantly. 'The ploughman plods - and not so wearily, especially on the cricket field.' He was only sorry for Jane Lavington who turned on him a sample of her chronic anxiety. For her benefit he elaborated a little.

'And what about ours?' boomed Jock when he'd done.

Laurie turned with his speech-day smile to Pam Purser, and effected the perceptible change of tone. 'Ah now, *Nancy* is shaping very well. A considerable intellect growing to maturity. Come university application time this autumn I think we can be very sanguine.' With a glance he included Jock in his conspiracy, and out of the corner of his eye saw Lavington dab his lips fastidiously with his napkin.

For the rest of the meal he had them under his thumb as they discussed education in general and, finally, careers. Richard Lavington, he supposed with an air of undisguised inevitability, would do accountancy, and Nancy, with a Bsc in her pocket would have a range of choice. She was talking at present of oceanography, an interesting and unusual choice. Certain of his views, convinced of the rock of liberal morality on which they were based, armed with his objective knowledge of their children, he strode with a charmed life among the minefields of the colonial establishment.

There was an obligatory return to Lavington's sphere. Coffee and liqueurs were served. As he talked, Lavington quietly flicked his fingers and was instantly attended. He wanted the bill. *He* was paying, it seemed - for the Pursers as well. The waiter reappeared, with paper this time, not prawns, on the silver plate. A brief perusal, a quickly squiggled signature, and the final assertion of superiority was made. In recognition, a liturgy of gravely murmured thanks were offered across the table.

Lavington turned his head aside, as if in pain.   Like a hired minstrel in a gallery, Laurie felt he had been playing for them after all, to be dismissed at Lavington's pleasure.

They rose.   The women went to the Ladies' room.   As they descended the carpeted stairs, Purser and Lavington conferred on some Island matter.   Laurie trailed behind them.

Outside, the men still conferred, standing by Lavington's Jaguar.   Tropical heat had reclaimed them.   Starkly, Laurie felt this unique oriental place about them - the glittering skyscrapers, the teeming streets, perhaps the real centre of the world now, where careers had been built, wealth accumulated, the wealth that paid private school fees.   For a moment his few culture kites seemed paper things to fly.   Absorbed, he did not hear Pam Purser approach.   He started as she took his arm above the elbow.

'Laurie, you're such a very interesting man.   You *are* going to have lunch with me before you go, aren't you?'

He felt her breast against his arm and caught a whiff of her refreshed perfume.   Her voice was lowered, denied to the others, even Jane Lavington just behind her.   Accepting, he kept his own voice down.   She gave his arm a squeeze.

The evening put a match to a fire that Laurie could not quench. He ran with buckets, smothered the flame, but it smouldered on and fiendishly burst out again in another place.   All the next day at the Education Fair the conflagration threatened while he interviewed countlessly the identical anxiety of earnest Chinese faces.   He began to dislike these students as he sat urbanely, legs crossed like an education guru.   They were lemmings.   Why did they want education on the other side of the world?   Why should he supply it?   Why should anyone want education?   Why was he a schoolmaster?   He thought he had chosen to be.   Had he? Who said he didn't want what Hong Kong money could buy, the status the business world could bring?   And a hundred times he thought of Pam Purser's breasts, so heavy yet tender and humble, and her several little attentions during the meal.   And what did her invitation mean?   'Have lunch with *me,*' she had said.

Would Jock be there?

That evening in the hotel, promptly at eight, his wife, Marjorie, phoned. It was her turn. Her cheerful inventory of English commonplaces calmed him like a bromide. But an hour later, dining alone and a little drunk, the fever was back. Could his ideology stand if it were tested? Did he want it to? He had phoned Pam. Lunch was fixed for tomorrow.

The weather had changed in the morning. Among the skyscrapers the sun still shone, but moodily. It was sultry, and cloud, level as a tray, pulled across the peak, protruding either side like a conjuror's trick, obscuring the dwellings of the rich. The taxi sprinted the lower slopes, then settled to a graver gait like a lone mountaineer attempting an Olympian summit. They swerved round bend after bend. At each a new volume of cicada noise opened and dropped below. Who did these nobs up here think they were, Gods?

There was a wisp or two of mist, then - snap - the astounding view was severed. They were plunged into a new world of looming shapes, large houses each seriously perched on its chosen crag. By one a Union Jack hung limp at its staff, and a white child on a tricycle stared through an iron gate. They swung into a dripping courtyard of modern houses. But for the acacia trees and sulking hibiscus it could have been Switzerland.

A Chinese maid opened the red door. He was shown into a long room that spanned the building. At one end was a polished table of Chinese rosewood. Only *two* of the red-seated rosewood chairs were drawn to it, two places laid. A pulse began to hammer in his throat.

The maid had said nothing. She had gone upstairs. A door opened, there was a brief exchange, she descended. It was deathly quiet. The mist came impertinently right up to the picture window. He stood in a daze of uncertainty.

'Laurie, you've come. I was so afraid there'd be some last minute necessity - with your busy schedule. I see you are looking at my totem.'

He had not heard her coming. She had not made a sound coming down the thickly-carpeted stairs. She didn't shake his hand but stood beside him, staring at the naked male effigy on the mantelpiece.

'I found it in Canton. Jock had to go there, and took me. I think it's a little wicked, don't you?' She took it down and ran her fingertips over its rough surface. 'I always hope he will bring me something - new.'

They moved to chairs and she brought him sherry. Again she leaned forwards, so near him, to pull a small table from a nest and place a glass. She wore silk clothes, a blue skirt and yellow blouse, and she'd had her hair done that morning, he guessed. But there was a difference from last night. She was confident. This was her home. All the objects in this room she had chosen and placed. Surges of sensation swept through Laurie.

She was waiting for him to say something, now they were seated. 'Sad it's misty,' he said, turning his head but not his eyes to the window.

'Oh, I rather like it sometimes,' she said. 'Shuts off the bloody place for once in a while, like a curtain drawn.'

'You mean you don't like it here?'

She stared with her rather thyroid blue eyes, and he saw she could be open, direct - flagrant? 'What do you think?'

'I, well, I suppose I hadn't thought really, except to imagine . . .'

'Look at poor Jane Lavington for example. Frightened to open her mouth, married to that big shot. Of course he's *not* a big shot. *You* know that, I could see you did. You don't like him, do you? In London he'd be a nobody. Yet look how he and his kind treat poor Jock. Jock's a civil engineer. He, and people like him, are building the place - and mostly they're Chinese of course - but for Lavington they're nothing - trade - and all just because he was born here.'

She laughed, swallowed half a glass of gin at a gulp and dashed the glass back on the table. 'But I haven't got you up here to talk about Hong Kong, have I? As I said, the curtain's drawn on that today.'

He swallowed. 'Jock's . . .'

'At work,' she snapped. 'Has to be in the New Territories all day. Shall we eat?'

She rose and called 'Sue Wong' in a voice which required no answer. There was none and they advanced to the table.

Quite honestly he was beginning to find her slightly vulgar. She had a small brass bell beside her plate, which she lifted rather prissily between courses and shook with a short vicious vigour between red fingernails too perfectly groomed. Sue Wong's impassive face shed silent resentment as she stooped to serve the food. Was Pamela Purser any different from, any less materialist, than the others, except that her husband, and therefore she, was not high enough in the pecking order for her liking? Her idea of England, the subject she chose to talk about, was theatres, hotels, parties, and 'fun.' Yet with every inflection of her suppressed Midlands accent he felt the noose tightening, perhaps because of it. It could not be serious, and that was why it was feasible. That little on the side, taken and forgotten, that he had so often talked about in others with humorous scorn - though none the less tempestuous for that. The only difficulty was the Chinese woman.

On her request he refilled the wine glasses. The third time he didn't get up but leaned across the table with the bottle. She didn't mind. Her finicky manners were slipping, he thought. Any moment there could be a vulgar joke and a ginny laugh. She watched him fill her glass with her attentive stare, wiping her mouth sideways with her napkin absentmindedly, leaving a red smear. The fumes of the wine licked higher.

'You can go when you've washed up, Sue Wong,' she said as coffee was served.

When the front door closed, she rose. 'Come upstairs,' she said. 'I want to show you something.'

The bedroom was a foam of white, white curtains, a white lace bedspread, frilly white lampshades. There was a pale pink carpet with inch high pile. By the window was an easel.

'Not an etching, but a watercolour.'

She stood looking at her work, in front of him. He thought he would put his arms round her waist from behind, slip the buttons of her blouse.

'But it's no good, is it?'

He drew closer, looked over her shoulder. He could feel her body warmth. A slight movement and her hair would brush his cheek. Blurred, he saw a harbour, masts thickly clustered.

'It's not bad.'

She swung round. 'It's terrible, Laurie. I have no talent. I've got you here under false pretences, you know. Please forgive me. You see I'm so desperately *isolated*.'

'I understand.'

'I must do something or I'll go mad. I can't paint . . .' Hands on her shoulders now, as she had turned, sliding over her back to a full embrace? 'I want you to help me.'

But suddenly she sat in an upholstered chair and pointed to another at the end of the bed. 'Sit down, Laurie. I've just got to talk to you. You know where Nancy's mind comes from, don't you? It's mine. I've got a brain, but it's unused. Fallow all these years. I want to educate it. I want you to educate me - with book lists. I've thought of the Open University, but it's not a degree I want. I want to read. History and English Literature. Will you help me?'

In the three evenings left, he walked out into the streets after dinner. He couldn't face talking to Marjorie, how could he keep his voice normal? On his return home he would plead invitations from potential parents. The streets of Wan Chai weren't like the down-town area. They were filthy, teeming - great ugly blocks with crowded iron balconies and, below, pavement arcades, open shops, smoke, neon lights, street vendors, endless grimy faces, and the perpetually angry-sounding Cantonese language. Commercial grins, vulgarised by poverty, loomed at him and discarded his blank hostile stare with contemptuous indifference. This was the East, he didn't belong here, they said to him. None of the British belonged here, and were going. Out here one's whole metabolism was thrown into malfunction.

He was thankful to be at the airport. As he heaved his cases on to the scales and set the dials whizzing, an attractive wholesome girl in a saucy tartan cap smiled at him.

'You're the wee-est bit overweight, but we'll perhaps be looking the other way,' she said with her Scottish accent. 'Presents for the family no doubt?' She did the paper work. 'Had a good time at the Education Fair?' she asked as she handed him back the remains of his ticket and his boarding card.

He started. 'How did you know I'm a teacher?' he said.

'A school address on your luggage? And if you don't mind my saying so, sir, it's written all over your face as well, and that's by way of being a compliment. My Father's one.'

She could have pulled him out of the ocean. This was when his convalescence began.

HELD TO RANSOM

To all who worked at the Institute 'Geoff and Hal' were two names inseparably yoked, like pepper-and-salt or mustard-and-cress. A fused light, a silenced boiler, trouble on the roof, the response was the same. 'Get Geoff-and-Hal to deal with it.' Major Winston, the bursar, hired them on a fixed contract three days a week.

Hal was the better plumber. His build suggested it. If shortish, he was stout, and the long convex curve of his stomach was pure muscle. His thick arms and large hands seemed constructed for the manipulation of copper pipes and brass fitments. When he had been in a room he left a twin odour of tobacco and metal, of which the latter was the senior partner. Hal didn't have much to say but, sitting in the pub, he and his plump wife, Elsie, reigned as monarchs of normality. Only after several pints would Hal sometimes talk a bit. He had been in a mercenary army in Africa and hinted at violent but necessary deeds.

Geoff was different. He was the electrician. He was taller than Hal and looked older. A coil of anxiety seemed to lie beneath his alert good-natured frown. Faced by Major Winston with a knotty problem, while Hal's bland silence suggested no problem, Geoff's, you knew, covered a busy reconnaissance of the matter and a search for a possible solution. He was the brainier of the two. Winston sometimes talked to Geoff alone without Hal's knowledge.

Geoff married a beautiful and delicate Indian girl whose parents, recent immigrants, had both died. Hal was content with a two-up-and-two-down Council house. Geoff and Meira moved into a nice modern bungalow which had a goldfish pond in the garden. He loved the Indian food Meira prepared - and which Hal and Elsie secretly endured when they, rarely, went to eat with their friends. He grew to like Indian music. He had always wanted more contact with culture. Meira brought it to him. Hal and Elsie mocked sometimes, in private, when Geoff refused a Saturday night at the pub. 'No, he's off to the snake-charming again,' said Hal.

Since Geoff's marriage, things did not go on in the same way in the Major's estimation. One tried to be fair. Fairness was surely what people looked for in an army officer. The fact was, Hal was no longer pulling his weight. There had always been a tendency in his case to leaning on his spade - the odd late arrival, the extended cigarette break. Things came to a head over the redecoration of the new Principal's flat.

Geoff and Hal were hired full-time on their daily rate until the job was finished. It was true Hal had had a minor accident. He slipped on the step ladder while paper-hanging, Geoff confirmed it. He could have pulled a muscle and was off two days, during which Geoff worked on alone. But then Hal came back and he made no attempt to conceal the standing about. Winston would do his rounds, and there was Geoff hacking away or painting or plastering and Hal wasn't there - he'd had to go out for materials Geoff said - or he was there but not actually working. Once he was sitting against a wall watching Geoff putty in a window-pane.

Winston let it go for a day or two more. Maybe Hal's back wasn't quite mended. But one morning Winston found Geoff alone again. 'Where's Hal, Geoff?' he asked, trying to keep his voice unaccusatory.

Geoff didn't answer. He was painting a long slow line with the smaller brush, where the pink wall met the white ceiling. Winston thought he was concentrating. When he finished the line and dipped the brush in the pot he repeated his question. 'Your guess is as good as mine,' was the surprising reply.

'You mean he hasn't, so far as you know, gone for materials?'

'We need no materials, Major. They're all here.'

'Another job then, an emergency?'

There was no answer. Geoff was back with the big brush now, making long handsome careful strokes so as not to splash at the turns.

Winston had no doubt what he had to do. The next day, seeing Hal arrive at 09.44 hours exactly, he sent his secretary to ask Hal to come and see him in his office.   An hour passed, nothing happened.

He went across to the flat himself.   For once Hal was working.   He was rendering a wall and putting his back into it. Stripped to the waist, he was making bold sweeps with the board. Hal had always been a good renderer, and of course knew it.

'Did you get my message, Hal?'   Winston asked as bluntly as he could.   He had spotted before a tendency in himself to placate Hal.

'I got it,' Hal said.

'Then when can I expect you?'

'You can expect me when this is finished.   Can't waste wet cement, can we?'

Winston was quite sure his secretary had given Hal his message before the cement was mixed, but he wasn't getting into that.   He ignored the surly tone.

'Very well, but before eleven please.   I have to go out.'   He went off at once, saying nothing to Geoff.

At ten past eleven Hal knocked on his door and came in simultaneously.   He had a vest on but not a shirt, which he knew was against what was expected.   He sat uninvited in the basket chair across the desk. The basketware complained at the unaccustomed burden.

Winston could see Hal knew what was coming - the eyebrows were already raised disowningly.   He put his pen down beside what he was writing.

'Hal, you know, I hope, that I try to be fair, but I'm afraid I have a point or two to raise with you.'

'Oh?'

'This morning for instance.   09.40 hours arrival?'

'Well?'

'We start at eight.'

'Do we?'

'You know very well we do.'

'So?'

Major Winston flushed slightly.   He knew where this was leading if he allowed it to go on.   Hal would say he had planned to stay late in the evening.   'Now look, I don't want to bandy words with you.   Getting into niggling arguments of fact won't get us anywhere, we've known each other too long for that.   I'll tell you straight out what's in my mind.   For whatever reason, just lately I don't think you've been pulling your weight.'

Hal was playing with the paper-weight, turning it over and over.   'You're entitled to your view,' he said.   It was as if they were having an academic discussion about someone else.

'Which I can see you don't share.   Well then, it is my simple duty to warn you.   I've got to see an improvement, rapidly . . .'

When Hal had gone the chair continued to crackle as if it needed time to recover from the ordeal of bearing his weight. Winston felt exhausted.   Hal's cool, cynical complacency was like a landslide across the road, impassable.   He would lose them both, he thought, and where else in a country district would he get men of equal omnicompetence?   He would finish up paying more for less, even with Hal's shortcomings.   Where would he then be with the Principal and the Board?   Surely he had been rash to act.

He hoped Hal would go without sacking, leaving him Geoff. But he didn't go.   The next day he was in, exactly an hour late. It had to be deliberate.

He hoped that it might correct itself.   After a day or two of petty remonstrance Hal might take the hint.   Geoff might help. Winston couldn't imagine he took kindly to rowing both sides of the boat.   But it was soon apparent that nothing had changed. At three o'clock in the afternoon Hal wasn't there when Winston went over.   He was glad, for he had already made a new decision.

'Care for a cup of tea?' he said to Geoff.

He chose a quiet corner of the canteen.   It wasn't pleasant trying to split working partners, and risky.   But while he spoke Geoff blinked and nodded his head in an understanding way. Winston could hardly believe his luck.   Yes, Geoff would stay, come what may.   Geoff agreed Hal wasn't pulling his weight. Winston wrote the letter that evening and posted it.   He didn't mention Geoff, but made it plain it was an ultimatum to him, singly.   He gave Hal a week.   He assumed of course that Hal would discover from Geoff that he was on his own in the matter. The next day at half-past nine Hal knocked on Major Winston's door. He looked normal. He wouldn't have had the letter yet, Winston thought. Again he sat uninvited in the empty chair.

'Geoff's not in,' said Hal. 'I phoned Meira as I didn't hear anything before leaving home. Geoff's in hospital.'

'It's not serious?'

'Taken ill in the night. Bad pains. Meira didn't like the look of him. He's had a bit of pain recently.' For once it was apparent there were bricks missing in the rampart of Hal's complacency. But he grinned. 'Probably too much of that snake music.'

It was a growth in the kidney. They thought they would have to remove it - 'though there was no reason to think it was malignant.' Which of course meant there was every reason to think it was. They operated. Geoff went home to be looked after by Meira. Winston went frequently to see him. His face was grey and emaciated. They had taken far more than the kidney with the knife. Half his personality, too.

Hal joked about it, now he'd had time to remember to play the tough, realistic mercenary. 'He's had it, hasn't he?' he remarked once. Winston thought of Meira, her pain invisible, quietly and gently serving her husband and the fate his condition represented to her. He reflected that the East was an older civilisation than their own and might have more understanding.

Hal continued to work at the Institute. Neither he nor Winston referred to the letter of ultimatum. Winston didn't know whether Hal knew he didn't have the support of his partner in the matter. Hal's attitude to his work did for a time show some change. That, and the indelicacy of discussion in the circumstances and, quite frankly, from Winston's point of view, the fact he couldn't be left without anyone, confirmed him in his silence.

Geoff died some months later. They took on another contracting electrician, nothing like as good as Geoff. Hal continued to give his three days and was soon back to his old ways. Winston made discreet enquiries to find another man but failed. One evening he dropped in to the local to get some cigarettes. Hal and Elsie were there, well-ensconced at the bar, and well down on their beers - not their first he guessed. Hal was in one of his rare loquacious moods.

'Why, if it isn't the Major,' he said. 'What'll it be now? Brandy and ginger, is it?'

Reluctantly he accepted half a bitter. Hal was expansive. His wife gave her ginny laugh at everything he said. He talked of Geoff. 'Never thought he'd pull through right from the start - that first morning when I phoned Meira. The writing's on the wall, I thought. No stamina really, old Geoff. Meira didn't help, I'd say. I mean, nice girl, a beautiful girl, but behind it all there's your Indian acceptance, isn't there? No fight.' He paused, but only for an instant. 'Then there was your letter, Major, wasn't there? Best forgotten that, eh? *I've* forgotten it. For in the end it's the stayers you want, isn't it? That's what went through your mind, no doubt. All respect to Geoff, but it's the man with the stamina who counts, right?'

They both looked at him, man and wife, no more than mildly curious to see his reaction, like parents viewing a child. Then they looked at each other. Hal winked at Elsie, grasped the handle of his glass, raised it to the level of his nose, then down again to his thick lips.

It didn't seem fair, thought the Major. That's what stuck in his gullet. One tried for justice but got headed off. Why should he be held to ransom by this self-satisfied, bullying loafer? What had Britain come to these days?

ON HER MAJESTY'S SERVICE

One of the things the American tourists liked about Maximilian Brown was his old-fashioned style. As one of them said once in a farewell dinner speech, he played on the English language like a musical instrument.

'I thank you, sir,' said Maximilian in his reply, 'for a most gratifying compliment. I have to confess that one does try for the odd verbal felicity.'

It wasn't only the Americans who appreciated him. At the office in the Haymarket he was acknowledged for the all-round professional he was. The boss, little Heinz Schmidt, a Swiss by birth, called him his 'flagship.' 'Get Maxi,' he would say when there was an important group coming through. 'I want class on this job.'

It was said he had trained for the stage. He had a good voice which, deep and plummy, came up effortlessly from mysterious depths. In the Abbey at the height of the season he didn't have to compete with the others, shrieking like hecklers around him. 'Now ladies and gentlemen, if you'll be kind enough to foreclose an inch or two?' They smiled - 'foreclose' - delightful. And they heard every word about Poets' Corner or the Tomb of the Unknown Soldier.

His success was also because, however many times he had done it before, his talks communicated a kind of passion. He always made them personal and amusing. In Oxford, for example, when it came to which of the colleges they would visit he always gave them the option of seeing Christchurch, which was scheduled on their itinerary. Or, if they so wished, he would add after a pause, in a very different voice, if they so wished they could see the ugliest college in the University, Keble, 'where once upon a time, in the days of yore, I had the honour to be an inmate.' Of course they always chose Keble, and delighted in his colourful recreation of undergraduate life.

He made much of the small window where 'gentlemen made their entrances after eleven of the clock.' And actually, as Maxi well knew, they didn't find the bare Victorian brickwork ugly, it being so much nearer their own 'ancient' buildings. When, in a certain way, he ran it down, they were delighted, because to them this was plainly just the understatement and phlegm of an English gentleman, the real thing.

Maxi lived in a street of semi-detached houses in Harlesden. He had a wife, Doris, who worked as a clerk in the Social Security office, and a daughter Shareen, who was training to be a hairdresser. He didn't enjoy life at home. Doris constantly mocked him for his work, which she considered 'flashy'. She repeatedly reminded him of her drudgery, on which they depended for their regular income - in the winter Maxi had to take jobs where he could - and said it was all very well for him 'putting on airs' for rich Yankees to satisfy his ego, pretending to be cultured when he wasn't anything of the sort, and eating four-star dinners. She had the home and the family to support. In former times Maxi had had a largely silent rapport with Shareen, but this had disappeared of late since she had started at the hairdresser's. She had learnt her mother's contempt. He faced now a double barrel of female hostility.

So when on a spring or a summer morning he took out the better of his two suits, which still, he thought, had shape despite a few imperfections, and selected one of his silk ties, his spirit began to break free. As he closed the cartwheel gate and struck out towards the tube station he felt he was an ambassador representing his country. He was on Her Majesty's Service.

One such morning when he got to the office some half an hour before it opened - he had to be at the hotel to meet his group by nine and needed to pick up vouchers and other papers - a surprise waited for him. The whole staff was in, travel desk as well. He didn't have to use his key, a girl was waiting to let him in. As he entered, they were standing in a circle and began to applaud. Most surprising of all, beside Fifty-Seven (Heinz's inevitable nickname) was Mr Slemen B. Hunter, American chief of the company, over from the States, beaming and bringing forward his huge handshake.

'Maximilian, thanks a million,' said the voice which went with the hand. 'This is a great day. Twenty-one years with the company. We think you're tops.'

There was a cake with twenty-one candles, rather a ragged and embarrassed rendering of 'happy anniversary to you', a cheque, and a speech by Mr Hunter in which there was much about 'Maximilian's example to us all with his long years of devoted service.'

This was entirely unexpected. Maxi was absorbing it and composing a few suitable words in reply, when Hunter went on. 'And finally, Maxi, to mark the occasion, I would like for your good wife and your charming daughter to join your good self on the Hunter Midsummer Night's Dream Tour of the Heart of England today, which it will also be my pleasure to personally attend and enjoy. We also hope your wife and daughter will join the afternoon tour of Oxford.'

Maxi was thrown into a panic. 'Oh no. No, that won't be possible, I'm afraid, Mr Hunter, though I thank you for the thought. You see, my wife . . .'

'But that *will* be possible.' Grinning, Hunter did a scan of the circle of faces to let them know what a human touch he had when he chose to apply it. 'That will be entirely possible. I just called your wife, and also spoke to her boss at the Social Security office. She will take the day off from her job. Also your daughter - a coiffeuse, I understand. I am sending a car. We shall all be joining you at Stratford-Upon-Avon for luncheon.'

Maxi was shattered. As he talked into the microphone on the way to Warwick he kept visualising them there, half-way down the bus, looking at him in that mocking way. Why had Doris accepted? It couldn't have been her natural inclination. Obviously what she intended was to embarrass and humiliate him in front of the Americans and in front of his employer. She would lose him his job. Maurice, the driver, noticed his preoccupation, as they sipped coffee together at the roadside hotel where they stopped mid-morning.

'Feeling all right are you then, Maxi?' he said. At the Castle, and later in Stratford, he did his job by instinct, but by the time they got to the Hamlet Hotel just outside the town, he was emotionally exhausted. He prayed something had gone wrong and they would not have arrived. But there in the entrance hall was Hunter and Heinz with Doris and Shareen in attendance. Both women were done up in their best.

'Why here he is,' said Hunter, handshake at the ready again. 'Here's our conquering hero. And all you lovely people. Yes, it's Hunter - Slemen B. Hunter, folks, here with you in person. Got over here to welcome you and to honour our number one guide here, his twenty-first anniversary with the company - and Mrs Brown, Miss Brown, who have joined us. It's a special celebration in which you are all going to participate.' He flicked a finger as four waiters and waitresses were already moving forward with their trays of poured champagne.

A pandemonium broke out of 'ohs' and 'you don't says' and 'you old meanie, Maxi, holding out on us like this, you didn't say it was your anniversary.' He was seized by the hand, toasted a dozen times. There was another rendering of 'happy anniversary to you' - much better than the one in the office. Someone shouted for him to kiss Doris for a picture. As the flash-bulbs went, he felt like the blind man in a game of buff, pushed and pulled and twisted.

When Hunter called them to go into lunch, he escaped to the Gents. Let it all die down, he thought. He would slip in in a minute or two, perhaps sit with Maurice at their usual table for two. For fortification he went to the bar and had a double whisky on top of the champagne.

When he went into the dining-room he saw Hunter had arranged a top table for five which had an empty space. For a moment he had a view of them, half-way through the *paté-maison*. Shareen was deeply in conversation with Fifty-Seven, her back as straight as a rod as it always was on the rare occasions when she was on her best behaviour. And there was Doris, her chin into her neck, watching Hunter lean across her to fill her glass as she slightly pulled away sideways. Hunter's encircling arm simultaneously touched her left shoulder.

Then Hunter spotted him. 'Maxi, we wondered what kept you. Another minute and we'd have sent out a search party. Not that I've been suffering. Doris here . . . your Doris is a very lovely lady. You're a lucky man, Maxi.'

In silence he ate the silly toast and paté. The whisky had done nothing for him. Was he the same man? Was he the same man who normally at this time would be handling the hors d'oeuvres with brisk confidence, holding up a finger for the waiter to bring the wine list for a tour member who had asked for it, showing the Americans how entirely au fait he was with four star hotel manners? Yet here he was, deafened by the racket of crunching toast, watching his wife being vamped by this athletic American, and his daughter vamping his London boss - who wasn't objecting. What was he then, a mere recording that someone put on, part of a charade for which someone else had written the lines?

It got worse as the meal progressed. The wine percolated. Shareen began to giggle. Hunter got louder and more daring, Doris less and less bothered to parry his absurd sallies. Did Hunter not realise the woman beside him in the flowered dress was on any weekday morning to be seen stamping papers and upbraiding the unemployed? Did he not see what a killjoy she was? As soon as they got home she would 'see through' Hunter, as she saw through everything. What she was enjoying of course was his own discomforture. Her laugh broke out suddenly, the way it did in the public house when she heard a smutty joke, knowing and superior. She knew his job would never be the same for him after this. She had got into the one free zone of his life and had dirtied it. That was what she was up to. And there was the afternoon to come. That was what he dreaded most.

Hunter and Fifty-Seven departed after lunch, Hunter with a crescendo of elaborate compliments to Doris and Shareen. He kissed Doris's hand in full view of the tour and talked again to Maxi of his very lovely lady wife. Like the American President going aboard his plane, he waved his last before he disappeared into the hired, chauffeured car.

The Americans took their cue from Hunter. They swept up

the two women into a renewed notoriety and excitement. On the way to Oxford they sang American songs from the sheets provided. Doris and Shareen sat in different seats, each with a tourist beside her.

Maxi decided what he was going to do. Keble was what he had dreaded most of all, until a simple solution offered. Today there would be no option. It would be just as it said on the itinerary. And he would let them have it, solid culture, shorn of any personal anecdote. But as Maurice pulled them up outside Big Tom and he announced the visit to Christchurch he heard Mr Buckmaster's voice at the back of the bus.

'But it wasn't Christchurch, this isn't the place.'

The hydraulic doors hissed and folded inwards. He rose. He saw the whole busload hanging back, uncertain.

'This isn't the place my friend said, Maxi,' said Buckmaster, a small man with a large tartan cap. 'They said you took them to your College last summer, off the record. Keble College. I saw the pictures they took.'

He was going to say he was following the itinerary, but they beat him to it. Those who had half-risen sat down again. 'Your College, we want your College,' they began to chant. Maurice moved his hand towards the ignition switch and looked at him. 'That's it, Maurice, you take us there,' said a lady in the front.

He looked away and Maurice started the engine. 'Impossible. New traffic regulations. College shut for repairs.' Such lies suggested themselves, but again it was too late. For the first time in his life the tourists were manipulating him. He dared not look towards Doris.

As it was, they cheered as Maurice pulled out into the traffic again. Buckmaster, not a favourite, was having his moment of triumph, telling them more of what his friends had said about their visit to Oxford with Maximilian last summer.

Over the years Keble had acquired for him a kind of beauty. Victorian vigour, enthusiasm, functionalism, was in the very bricks, as it was in the American psyche. But today he hated it. As they stood in the prison-like quad he gritted his teeth. All right, he thought. Facts. He would snow them under a deep mantle of facts, as the other guides did. He would give Doris not a round of ammunition. He gave them the Tractarians - Newman, Froude, Pusey, Keble, the lot. In almost a delirium of fury he would have recited the Thirty-Nine Articles verbatim at them if he had known them.

With grim satisfaction he saw how they began to wear that drugged, slugged look he had seen on the faces of other groups. But then, there was Buckmaster putting in his oar again, as he moved them into the dining-hall.

'But what about this window where you climbed in, Maximilian? You haven't said anything about that.'

'Yes, and show us where you studied, Maxi,' said another. 'Buckie here told us you once had to run from the . . . what-cha-call-it . . . proctors.' 'And where you got your degree' - this latter was entirely new territory.

He looked for Doris. He couldn't see her. She was there somewhere in the gloom, waiting no doubt and hoping for this, the dénouement.

For a moment he wavered, and for a moment he hated himself for the half-lies he had told over the years, the falsehoods becoming the truth from repetition, cemented in with the applause they always won. He almost began to hate the Americans - for their gullibility, their predictability, for their ritual enthusiasm, their regimented jollity. He thought he would tell them how false he had been in the past, how he had never been an undergraduate, just done a two weeks' guides course during the summer vacation.

Then a new feeling gripped him. Damn Doris, he thought, damn Shareen, with their pompous, smug superiority. What was wrong with a bit of style if it amused people and made them feel better? It was the entertainment business, wasn't it? If they were going to sneer, let them. He wasn't going to cease being a pro just because they were there. He told the Americans all the usual stories, took them to the place where the undergraduates used to climb in, showed them the room he had slept in, and left in all the innuendoes of his involvement in undergraduate life. They loved it, as always.

When they got back to the hotel he didn't stay to help them off the coach but rushed into the cloakroom. When he came back into the hall they were still there, talking to two of the women. He scribbled a message out of sight by the porter's desk and told a page boy to deliver it to the lady in the blue dress. He slipped out of one of the emergency exits.

He didn't have to go again to the office but he couldn't face the journey back with them in the tube. Somehow he imagined that if he arrived after them he might be able to create the illusion to himself that he was coming home after a normal day. Maybe little would be said. Maybe like a dream or a miracle it would all vanish and be as before.

He gave them an hour. The sky was set out with a pattern of small clouds like a woman's permanent wave, the air washed and gentle. When he came out of Harlesden station he didn't allow himself to notice the dirty pavements, the noise that fell out of the pub, the endless drift of grim faces. He opened the front door of his house and heard them in the kitchen.

He went into the lounge. An amazing sight met him. The table had been pulled out, as it was for Christmas. It was laid, with mats, for three - glass, silver, placed. In the centre of the table was a vase of gladioli.

Shareen came in. She was still wearing her low-cut dress. 'Hallo, Dad,' she said. She bore the silver cruet set which was kept in a polystyrene bag all the year. It had been polished.

'What's all this, Shareen?'

'Well, Mum said it's a celebration,' she said. Her voice had a clipped excitement.

Doris came in with what appeared to be a cottage pie   The dish had crinkled paper round it like a choir boy's collar.

'But . . .' began Maxi.

'They gave us the glads, Dad,' said Shareen.   'They really were ever so nice to us.'

Doris stood with her hand on the back of the chair.   'Come on, now, it's not getting any hotter.   Shareen, Max, take your places.'

'Couldn't we eat in here every night, Mum?' said Shareen,

blowing discreetly on her forkful of steaming potato.

Doris spoke briskly. 'Now Shareen, eat your food and less fuss about it.'

But there was a lift in her voice. Was this another charade? Surely not. By the time the rhubarb and custard arrived in a cut glass bowl (a wedding present) a timid hope was born.

He felt a surge of goodwill. 'Well, this is very nice, Doris,' he essayed, touching his lips with the red paper serviette. 'Very nice.'

Doris lifted her eyebrows as she served. 'Glad it's appreciated,' she said, as tart as the fruit. But Shareen grinned at him.

'Happy anniversary, Dad,' she said, raising her glass.

THE VISIT

The computer in the walnut console could programme the stereo, make calculations about the journey, and give detailed reports on the functioning of the engine. It had been custom built to Boris Luke's specifications.   Noting the readings on the clock, the mile and speedometers, he stretched a gloved finger and touched three buttons.   Red figures tumbled obediently on the dial.

'Estimated time of arrival fifteen hundred fifty-eight, Anthea. We'll be there on the dot.'

Anthea Luke had put on her spectacles some time ago and was reading a large National Trust publication on country houses. Her answer was on the fringe of her attention.   'Your mother's probably forgotten we're coming.'

Boris wriggled backwards into the comfortable upholstery and stretched his arm along the fawn-coloured door rest.   'Not today,' he said. 'I didn't tell her exactly when I rang, but hinted something special might be in the wind.   She'll be agog.'

Anthea came to the end of her historical researches.   She removed her spectacles and tucked them into their case.   'Agog isn't a word I'd ever apply to your mother,' she said.   She leaned forward to the dashboard pocket and took out an opened box of peppermint creams.   She removed from the top layer one or two unoccupied doilies, reclosed the lid, and leaned to add this additional item to an already crammed basket riding on the back seat.

The toy village seemed designed to test the Bentley.   Boris had to reverse twice to negotiate the sharp corner by the pub, watched by several pairs of critical eyes.   It was held up further down by a tractor whose driver had stopped to buy cigarettes from the shop.   When at a leisurely pace the man climbed back into the cockpit and proceeded, a salvo of clods flew backwards from the giant tyres.   Two of these struck and adhered to the windscreen.

The village was Boris's birthplace in which at every corner lurked memories of a rustic childhood.   He didn't recall them kindly today. Once the place might have been a pretty hamlet grouped about a medieval church, but it was surely a malignant lack of taste which had built that chapel, little more than a Nissen hut, the concrete pub with its absurd garland of half-fused fairy-lights, and the fish and chip shop from whose open door wandered blue smoke and a reek of vinegar and scalded fat. Supreme among the ugliness was the cantonment of bungalows whose cracked and unpainted stucco walls were greened with moss, in one of which Mother lived.

As Boris lifted the small iron gate, which had a hinge missing, Mrs Luke Senior came into view. She was sitting on a little patch of lawn on a wooden chair she had brought out from the kitchen. She wore a black dress and sat with her legs parted. The fine masculine head of untidy grey hair was erect, but her eyes were shut and her mouth ajar. Boris closed his ears to the vigorous snores that were competing with the other sounds of nature all around. What a lioness of a woman she was, he thought. What could she not have achieved if she had not at the age of seventeen married an amiable wheelwright entirely lacking ambition. For a moment he dressed her as a duchess presiding over a beau-monde of savants. He rededicated himself to his mission. Her days of privation were over. She would spend the rest of her life in the luxury she deserved.

'Mother, wake up, it's us,' Anthea was saying firmly.

The hostile eyes dropped open like a doll's. 'Oh it's you already, I've only just had my lunch.'

Anthea laughed, knelt in front of her, and began to unpack the basket. 'Look, we've brought you some goodies.' There was a small ham, a jar of home-made pickles, another of marmalade, a cake, two bottles of good wine, and the chocolates.

The old lady's eyes fastened on the food with greed. 'But I shan't be able to eat all that. How do you think I could, even if I wanted to, with my gums? I've told you not to bring me things. I've everything I want.'

'Of course you have. But these are just a few extras. And if you don't want them you'll be able to give them to someone in the village, won't you?'

Boris was prepared to stand off and watch in these early stages of the visit. He conceded that Anthea did have skills in removing the detonators from Mother's combustible nature. Mother stood ready to destroy anything she could convict of being 'new-fangled,' especially food. With her soft-spoken unrelenting logic, Anthea preempted her fears by explaining that the ham had been cured on their own farm and that she had made the cake, the marmalade and the pickles herself. They would soon be through to that exchange of platitudes, to that harmless barter of information shorn of fractious subjects which left everything just as it was, and which Anthea considered to be the mark of a successful visit.

'Well, it's nice of you to think of me, Anthea dear,' Mother was brought to say finally. 'It's more than most people do nowadays. Most people think only of themselves and how much money they can make.'

By this time they were having tea, admittedly extremely delicious home-made scones, plum jam and cream and a moist-looking cherry cake to follow. Boris ignored the undoubted provocation of Mother's last remark and concentrated on eating. As Mother was now waiting for him to say something, he referred, with his mouth full, to the 'riot of bloom' in the single flower bed. This was a safe subject. The flowers were nasturtiums which had seeded themselves more prolifically than usual this year. Some had begun trespassing journeys onto the grass. Mother approved of nasturtiums which she considered robust wild plants.

The opportunity came unexpectedly, as it so often did, though he had already thought the new car might be a good lead in. Mother liked cars. She raised herself in her seat all of a sudden and narrowed her eyes. She had caught the one view of pale blue metal visible through the unkempt privet.

'Is that yours, Boris?' she said loudly.

'Is what mine? Oh, you mean the car. Yes, it is.'

She stood up fully. 'I thought you had an English car.'

'That is an English car.'

Her old face tightened with interest. 'It doesn't look English to me. It's foreign, isn't it? Hired, I suppose.'

Tantalisingly, she sat down with a bump. She had plum skin stuck to her gum and began to rummage with her finger. The obstacle released, she seemed to forget the car.

Boris took a risk. Lose the chance now and it might not reappear. 'Mother, the car is mine. I've just bought it. It's a superlatively comfortable machine. I think, with your very informed eye for cars, you will think so, too, when you ride in it.'

The wrinkled jaw, greenish and hairy like a mildewed walnut, wriggled with excitement. 'Ride in it?'

'Yes, I thought we might drive into town and back after tea.'

'I'll do no such thing. If it'd been a decent size I might have considered it. But not in that. It's too large. People don't need such large cars.'

He moved gently. 'Mother, I wonder why you always rail against comfort when it's at hand.'

'Rail? I don't rail at anything.'

'Yes, you do. You did just now for example, over the food we brought you. When we've gone you'll enjoy the wine and the other things. Why not admit it? Just because you've never had many luxuries, why not enjoy them now?'

'I've plenty to enjoy, thank you very much.'

'Do you? Do you, Mother? That funnily enough, does raise the point I want to put to you. *Do* you have plenty to enjoy? It can't be much fun having to hang out the washing when you could be using an up-to-date machine. You have no central-heating in this jerry-built bungalow. And what does the village offer in the way of entertainment . . .

'Mother, we've got the most wonderful idea to suggest to you. You see, we've just had the lodge house done up on the estate. Central-heating, wall-to-wall carpeting throughout, all the best utility machines. We thought at first we would let it, but why don't you come and live there? You'd be as happy as a lark, and you'd have us round the corner when you wanted us. Now what. do you say?'

The old lady stared. She began to wiggle from side to side like a bird settling on its nest. This was always the sign of intense thought. 'What do I say? I say rubbish. What on earth makes you think I'd wish to leave the place where I've spent all my life and where all the people I know live? Of course I shan't move to your lodge.'

'But Mother, you're not getting any younger, you know . . .'

'Neither are you, neither is anyone. What's that got to do with it? The trouble with you is you're too rich. You can't imagine that ordinary people can be quite content with what they've got. And underneath, of course, you're guilty because you know all your luxuries are worthless and you've wasted your life getting them.'

'This is nonsense, Mother, you know it is.'

'Is it? Why then are you getting so excited?'

'I'm not excited.'

'Very well then, we can leave the subject, can't we, and everyone'll be happy? Anthea understands if you don't. Have the last scone, Anthea dear.' Anthea refused. Triumphantly she took it herself.

Going home, Boris was morose. He could think of nothing to say and Anthea was silent. For the rest of their visit Mother had been unusually cheerful. Her Parthian shot was to give Anthea a mixture she had concocted out of wild herbs. 'Give it to Boris regularly,' she said, 'he always was prone to bowel trouble.'

Boris knew he had made a tactical mistake. Relations with Mother were like a game of ludo. A bad throw and you were back at base. Throw a six or two on the other hand and you could be back in the running. He would do better next time. But in spite of this liberal and positive adjustment, he still felt irritated. What was Anthea's attitude? She seemed as happy about the visit as Mother had finally been.

'Mother's incorrigible,' he said, by way of a sounding.

'Exactly. I wonder then why you bother to try to change her.'

'I don't want to change *her*, but her circumstances.'

'The same thing.'

'They're not the same thing. If Mother lived in our lodge, she wouldn't stop being disagreeable but she'd be disagreeable in comfort.'

'But she doesn't want to move. It's you who is disturbed at the way she lives, not her. It offends you in some way - for yourself.'

'Of course it doesn't.'

'Why then did you start lecturing her when I thought you'd decided to be subtle?'

'I made a slip there, I agree. But next time . . .'

Anthea's voice was running as smoothly as the Bentley's engine. She had been rummaging in the console pocket again as they spoke.

'Have a sweet.'

He looked at the proffered box and wavered. 'No, thank you,' he said, returning his eyes doggedly to the road.

'All your mother wants is for us to go and see her sometimes and perhaps take her a few goodies. She's happy. You can't change her.' She helped herself to a butterscotch, her cheek bulged. 'If you ask me, you're a pair, you two. Kindness is *doing* what people want, not saying what you think they ought to want.'

Mrs Luke Senior shuffled back into the kitchen. The lawn was in shadow after six, and the midges always seemed to have a grudge against her. Anthea had unloaded the food on the table. She began to take up each item and scrutinize it. When she reached the first bottle of wine she held it thoughtfully by the neck and looked at the label. Then she went to the wall and unhooked a whistle hanging on a string and nail. She opened the window, blew two sharp blasts, shut the window again, and hung up the whistle. She sat in the rocking-chair and set it in motion.

In a while the gate whined. There were heavy steps and the front door opened. 'Are you there, Florence?'

'In here.'

John Melly was as old as she was. Like her, he had a mane of grey hair. He wore a shirt with no collar, and a black waistcoat, shiny at the back.

'What's up then? Family gone?'

She nodded at the wine. 'Get a corkscrew and open that, John,' she said. 'Bet you could do with a glass. I know I could.'

Later she was telling him indignantly what Boris had suggested. 'If he wants to change my life-style, as he calls it, why doesn't he put central-heating in here? They're all the same, the young. Want to own you.'

She made him a bacon omelette. They discussed the pros and cons of central-heating and she decided she didn't want it anyway. Dehydrated you. There was nothing she wanted she didn't have.

'Don't worry, if you get decrepit I'll come and light your fires for you,' John said.

'Now don't you start. It's more likely it'll be me lighting yours, with your hip.' She held up an empty glass. 'Now this is a good wine. What do you say to the second bottle, John?'

A TRAVELLING ASSIZE

The clattering of the shop door alert gave Roger Vermont the usual dual sensation, hope that it might be a sale - Christ, he needed a few - and annoyance that he should be sitting here like a beggar waiting for custom. He'd been on the point several times of bashing the bloody bell off its screw. There was a fine choice of weapons for the job.

Out of sight in the inner room he opened the brass fender box and slid the bottle in. He emptied the Waterford tumbler into the nearest receptacle, his throat, and reunited it with its posse of fellows on a Victorian sideboard.

He stood leaning in the doorway into the front room. They were Birmingham. He could tell before the woman opened her mouth. 'We'd like to have a look round if we may.' The state of funds cautioned moderation, but that 'may' indeed. She was already putting her filthy fingerprints all over a silver teapot he had shined up that morning. She didn't even bother to look at him as she spoke, so busy was she giving the place a once over, as if she were the bailiff come to collect.

He fought a losing battle. Fucking nerve, fucking Midlands. Collecting junk for their junky homes. They wouldn't know something beautiful if it were stuffed under their noses with a label attached. He preferred the trade. You never made a killing with them but at least they knew what they were buying.

'What are you asking for this warming-pan?' the man said, also not looking at him.

'Naturally, what's on the label.'

At last the eyes came swivelling up. They were dead, glintless, a good match for the phoney grin. 'Come on, now, cough up a decent price. We know you've stuck on two hundred per cent.'

The homey, knowing dialect got to him. He mobilised as much of the southern counties as he had still got. 'The price, as I say, is what is on the label.'

'All right, keep your shirt on.'

A bit later, when she was standing right in front of him, she caught him looking down her dress. If he concentrated on what she had in there, he thought, he might just about suspend judgement on the mental accompaniment above for the time a sale took. But simultaneously she caught a whiff of his breath. He saw her nostrils twitch as if he had stuck a bottle of ammonia under them. 'Come on, Billie,' she said. 'There's nothing we want here'- open, brazen, the false manners blown off at the first puff.

'Nothing for people like you,' he said audibly, as they made for the door. She gave him a last terrified look over her shoulder, as the two of them fled to the brand new Porsche. The village got the decibel equivalent of all three litres of sex substitute as the machine roared off, but quickly absorbed the violation. The roar became a thinning hum, vanished, and they were back to the mid-afternoon components of tedium - sparrows in the eaves, a tractor clambering wearily somewhere in the distance. The village clock with supreme effort dropped one castrated chime for a quarter past. He endured moments of desolation.

He saw them then, the Parish Council, coming out of the vestry door. Outside, they clustered round the asinine Cuthbert in his cassock, who was shaking hands all round as if they had just written the Nicene creed. He knew what had happened before they divided and La Tribe began her victory roll past his door. Masochistically, he watched her, the turban hat bandaged into a Rembrandt-like upward salient of hideosity, the ill-fitting pink dress and the sea-captain's daughter's walk, back as straight as a 1910 car, and the jaunty roll, one shoulder forward then the other as if she were pushing through a crowd. She walked right past the shop and under the offending item with not a deviant glance, though she knew he was there. 'Order restored, mammon repulsed,' her manner declared, 'the Great God Harpic appeased.' Filthy bitch. He felt a quickening of delicious doom.

Victoria Tribe rose at six every morning. She had no need of an alarm clock. Regularly, summer and winter, her eyes fell open at this time. For her there was no twilight between sleeping and waking. She was one or the other - at six precisely awake.

This was symbolic of her personality. She had never liked shilly-shalliers. One of her cherished lines in the Bible was: 'He that is not with me is against me.' As she woke, her left hand travelled to the edge of the duvet, drawing it back to permit her immediate entry into another day.

Invariably, a busy day. It was impossible to imagine this active spinster not doing anything. After routine but extensive operations in the bathroom - rites described them better - she donned clothes she had decided on the night before and placed ready. She then bent her head to open another notch the small lead-latticed window in order to cast an inventory-checking eye over the sleeping village. She noted that the flycatchers nesting in her neighbours' house had hatched, and made a note to warn her neighbour, who had noisy children, to be careful not to disturb them. On the house opposite a branch of apricot had broken loose from its espalier mooring in the night - she would offer its owner the use of her step-ladder to restore it. Then she saw Vermont's flagrant perpetration.

Most of the matters her vigilance raised were the result of minor backsliding. Backsliding implied sloth more than intention. This was in another category. This was deliberate, provocative, an ultimatum. It brought out in Victoria an emotion she seldom experienced - anger. He had done it in the night of course, stealthily, almost certainly having boosted himself with drink. There it was, an insult to the beauty of the risen sun and the splendour with which it knighted the Cotswold village and countryside, slung limply, amateurishly, across the street. He must have painted the letters on the cloth himself - 'ANTIQUES' - and a gross black arrow pointing downwards to the shop.

Her first act was to traverse the banner to its further terminal. Who would knowingly have become a party to such an assault on the community? Then she realised. The property was that of the Hofmeisters, who were not yet back. This calmed her. They, of all people would be horrified when they knew, for who was more appreciative of English rural beauty than these two anglophile Americans? They wouldn't have chosen to make these biannual migrations from their (presumed) Californian paradise if it were not deeply important to them. Victoria subsided further. The banner was not worthy of anger. Vermont's malice had for once outrun the cunning with which he normally applied it. She ended with a thought which was almost charitable. The truth was that Vermont's rudeness, and the consequent effect on his business, was driving him to desperate measures. He would soon be *out* of business. He would be institutionalised. And that would be a case for pity not wrath.

It would have been proper to make the Vicar her first port of call, but being proper in Cuthbert's direction was not always a recipe for action. Precisely half an hour after she had seen him draw the curtains of his bedroom, Victoria knocked first on the door of Colonel Quinton, fellow member and Chairman of the Parish Council. He hadn't of course seen the banner, and had to come out into the street before he would drop the look of outrage at her violation of his privacy at this hour. But Victoria had calculated right. Quinton was still wearing his slippers and an upper garment she thought was his pyjama top, but he could react to an emergency when he saw one. (She pictured him at Omdurman or Mafeking somehow, rather than Caen). By the time, installed in his kitchen, she was half-way down a coffee that was proffered, he was agreeing that in the circumstances she had acted correctly in coming to see him so promptly, that a Parish Council meeting was essential that day, that the offending bunting must be grounded before nightfall.

This didn't prove so easy to achieve. At the meeting, Quinton said he was sure the by-laws gave the Council power to enforce the removal of 'any obnoxious commercial display', and there was no disagreement about this. But the Reverend Cuthbert - offended, Victoria knew, that she had gone first to Quinton and not himself - insisted that he, not the village constable, would deliver the ultimatum to Vermont. 'In charity,' he said, 'Vermont should first be given the chance to remove the banner himself. Vermont might not have grasped the offence it caused. And who better perhaps to sound this out - if he could state this, in humility - than himself, the representative of Christ's

138

church?' Victoria Tribe doubted, she was sure Quinton doubted, how little Christ's jurisdiction operated in Vermont's domain.

The scepticism was swiftly vindicated. It was learnt later that day that Cuthbert had been rebuffed, insulted, even physically jostled by the antiques-seller. Yet he still wouldn't give way. 'No, there need be no recourse to the law,' he said at a further meeting of the Council. 'We shall simply await the return of the Hofmeisters. They will, almost without a doubt, decline to be connected with the banner which has been illegally attached to their property. Unhooked if needs be on their side of the street, it will flutter peacefully to the ground. You must concede, good people, that if there is a non-confrontational way, it must be preferred. Is this not Christ's own teaching?'

The good people didn't think this - two of them at least did not. But what could be said to spiritual blackmail of this order? The only consolation was that the Hofmeisters were signalled. They were due the following day.

As the aircraft turned, whining, into the arrival bay, Eva Hofmeister fought off moments of unexpected dismay. The crossing in the bright sunlight had made it easy to confirm the vision of England that in the Californian half of the year always grew so strongly as they described its more enviable features to envious friends. But the sun had left them at ten thousand feet. Rain was silently streaking the aircraft windows.

'S'what keeps the grass so green,' said Milton in a sing-song voice and with a rueful shake of his head. He'd had the same thought as hers.

She felt better. What Milton said was true. She remembered that, when she put her mind to it, she liked rain. She liked to put on her rainproof and go for walks in it. She liked the gentle warmth of summer drizzle as she crossed those lush Cotswold fields with hedgerows alive with small surprises. One could grow tired of unremitting sunshine which, like the American character, could become too single-minded sometimes. She composed herself again for joyful renewals, especially with their lovely village friends.

Milton particularly made friends easily.   Within a week of moving into their little house he had met half the village and apparently won their approval.   Eva needed a little more space and time, but she followed along close behind.   She had her thoughts, and sometimes mildly and silently qualified some of Milton's kind enthusiasms, but on a broader front she went along with him.

She and Milton were busy looking to either side as they came up the main street in the local taxi they always fixed to meet them at the airport.   Neither noticed the banner which in the rain had become even more unsightly.   It had bowed and sagged and the 'Antiques' had run.   They didn't see a soul, but that would be rectified soon enough, they thought, as they set about getting the three big suitcases upstairs and unpacked.   The place was clean, the air unstale.   Mrs Capsid had been in and fixed everything just fine.

They certainly didn't expect Vermont to be their first caller, but Roger it was, one sharp rap at the door as if that would do it if it were loud enough.   Milton went down and there he was.

'Welcome back, both of you,' Vermont said, stepping in. Milton had to make way in the narrow entrance.   He was carrying something in a newspaper.   'Brought you, literally, a house-warmer, or an assistance to one.'   He revealed from the paper, which fell to the floor and stayed there, a brass poker, shovel and tongs.   'Not that you have fires in the summer, but I remembered you didn't have any and they'll look nice in the grate.'   Eva was cautiously descending the precipitous stairs. 'Eva,' said Vermont, 'you're more gorgeous than ever.   Pacific sunshine, I suppose.'

This was out of line.   Eva wondered what was cooking. There had been questions in her mind about Vermont, but he was Milton's acquaintance more than hers.   She kept any opinions she might have to herself.

'S'pect you noticed the perpetration as you came in,' Vermont said - quite a lot later when Milton had brought out their duty-free whisky.   'Fact is I've got to do something during the tourist season.   Beam ends, or somewhere near them.   Cheek on my part, I know, attaching it to your property without asking. Take it down at once if you object. I just thought maybe there's the remotest chance you might not object.'

They opened the window to look. Eva thought frankly it wasn't quite right. She didn't object to the umbilical element joined to their bricks and mortar, but it wasn't surely quite the Cotswold village touch, and the frontal bribery Vermont had used was more American than British. But Milton was looking at her. 'Well, I don't see we'd have any objection?' he was saying.

'I reckon it's not going to tow us away,' she found herself agreeing.

Vermont had a second whisky. 'Of course some elements in the village are in a ferment,' he went on confidently, over the hurdle now. 'Victoria Tribe's staked her thermal underwear on bringing me to book. The Parish Council held two meetings extraordinary yesterday. Quinton's involved. Only Cuthbert stopped me being lynched. He's obviously persuaded them to wait till you arrive and say no. 'Fraid you'll be getting a deputation . . .'

Eva was never cross with Milton. They were so in tune they both knew what the other was thinking most of the time, and this pre-knowledge, coming in by radar as it were, preempted rage. 'I've landed us in a pretty pickle, haven't I?' Milton said the moment the door was closed.

'Never mind, you couldn't have helped it, the way he put it.'

'I could've been more neutral. If Cuthbert comes what the hec'll we do? We've told Vermont it's OK.'

Eva didn't know what they would do.

Even less when not Cuthbert came but Victoria Tribe. Eva didn't care for Victoria. Victoria's point was she didn't see why the Hofmeisters should be put in such a situation (she had seen Vermont visiting and was given an account of what happened). The Hofmeisters were villagers it was true, Victoria debated - the same as everyone else - but still, in her view, in matters such as this, they were visitors, and hosts should not put guests in this sort of predicament. The matter should be resolved without the

Hofmeisters. She suggested that when Cuthbert came they should say they really didn't feel they could unhook the banner just like that, when Roger Vermont's business wasn't too good and he had requested them not to. 'In other words,' Victoria finished, 'I think you can safely leave it to the Parish Council. We can handle our Mr Vermont.'

So when Cuthbert came, hooing and haaing in his delightful English way, this was what Eva Hofmeister said. She gently proposed, equally obliquely, that perhaps Cuthbert could find yet another Christian way, he had such fine diplomatic skills. Surely then, when Vermont realised the whole village was against him, he would give way?

The next days were very distressing for the American pair. Milton tried to double-track a bit and persuade Vermont in the amiable atmosphere of The Bunch of Grapes. Vermont became very loquacious about Anglo-American accord on the principle of the rights of individuals. Magna Carta was mentioned, and the recent ceremony at Runnymede, quoted in the newspapers, when the American Bar Association came to pay its respects to this supposed common denominator of freedom. The Hofmeisters threw their usual arrival drinks party, and the occasion was spoilt. No one, it seemed, could talk of anything else, and in the middle, Vermont, who had arrived late, had a stand-up row with Victoria. Vermont was drunk and called her, among other things, a pompous bitch. Victoria, white-faced but calm, said she was unmoved by such insults because they were uttered by a man who was mentally ill and would soon be removed from civilised society. She said she was sorry for him. Meanwhile the banner remained. An attempt by the village policeman to unhook it on the Hofmeisters' side of the street, had been abandoned when Vermont threatened both legal action and violence to the ladder if he proceeded. The owners of both properties consented to the banner, he said. It was perfectly legal. It seemed recourse to the magistrate's court would be necessary.

Eva felt more distressed than she thought she would have been. It was proving impossible to be neutral. Vermont had represented it that she and Milton were on his side. The village was beginning to believe it. Milton even suggested one evening that they should simply unhook the darned thing. Vermont was a drunk. The thing *was* hideous. It was under the stress of this, and the possibly violent retribution that would ensue from across the street if they did, that Eva had her idea.

She didn't even tell Milton. She quietly went off to Evesham and transacted her business. She explained the haste, and the object was delivered the next day.

'My, you're a genius, Eva,' Milton said, admiring. 'Nobody, but nobody, is going to object to that. Tasteful.'

They went over right away. The shop was shut and they thought Vermont was out. But they rang again, they heard a noise, and eventually he came, looking not too good. At first he didn't seem to know what they were talking about. But finally he agreed to come over and inspect whatever it was they had in their small garden.

It was an elegant double board painted black with white gothic lettering. 'ANTIQUES AND BYGONES,' it said on both sides. It would stand on the pavement.

'Now no one can take offence at that,' Milton said. 'The Bunch of Grapes has one advertising food.'

The banner was down that evening. Cuthbert was delighted. 'An act of such Christian inspiration,' he boomed. 'A vindication of the principle of non-confrontation. Our American friends are to be congratulated for teaching us all a lesson.'

Other views were less ecstatic. Victoria Tribe, cheated of the showdown she had hoped to monitor, thought Vermont should be made to pay for the board. Needless to say, he hadn't offered to. Later she was heard to say it was all very well for Americans, who thought everything could be solved with money. What *had* been solved by the donation of the board? The banner was down, yes, but was Vermont a jot different? How long would it be before the next incident? And it was true that as soon as the Hofmeisters left for the winter Vermont was crowing at the bar that he had forced them into it. In Victoria's view the banner hadn't been the cause of the problem, it was a manifestation of it.

The problem of Vermont and his obscenities remained.

As for the Hofmeisters, they were happy. Through the winter they told the story to their American friends of how they had been privileged to play a small part in an English village feud. They were all such characterful interesting folk. Their vision of England was once more intact.

CANDIED FRUITS

'You'll be all right then, Maudie?' Bruce Paterson called down the narrow garden. As per usual she was down in the jungle at the bottom, which she wouldn't let him clear. 'I'll only be an hour or so.'

He heard, he thought, a reply. 'She's pleased I'm going,' he thought. 'An afternoon with her book.'

He wasn't going to let that upset him. He gave his ordered May display a final sweep of approval - red tulips and forget-me-nots to the left, yellow tulips and forget-me-nots to the right, and the willow unloading its veritable cascade of green over his new rock garden. He backed the four year old Fiesta out into the trim street - crabs and cherries in full bloom. What a place to live.

Dilly lived twenty minutes' drive away. When her husband, Jake, died and things got worse, he had agreed to visit her regularly. For after all, when all was said and done, if he didn't who would? Penny, that sister of hers, and her husband Roland? Hardly - even though they weren't short of a bob, those two.

But as he drove the familiar route, which steadily deteriorated after passing the gas works, his thoughts also travelled in a familiar direction. Just because others didn't do things they should, that didn't stop you trying to do your best. Poor kid - he saw Dilly now as a kid - more helpless by the day, and in proportion to her helplessness, it seemed, more disagreeable to her neighbours, a vicious circle. The other day she swung her stick at her neighbour's dog which had got into her garden. The yelping had brought them out apparently. Couldn't they see, *this* was the disease - terror, inconsistency, violence even, followed by the abject? She had once hit Jake with an iron poker.

He twisted left and right through the battalion of terraced houses ranked, as with a sergeant major's pacing stick, one behind the other. He turned into Dilly's street - St Anthony's

Way. There were a lot of saints in the street names in this neighbourhood. At least Dilly's was the end house as if it had almost broken free. He parked outside the overgrown privet and the little lawn, knee-deep in floribunda dandelions. As usual the house stood brooding, curtains drawn, in thrall to its sick occupant. He sat for a moment, donning mental vestments like a priest in the sacristy.

He knocked and felt the blows assault the beaten gloom within. Not a sound, until the shuffle, the two bolts pistoling, the rustle of a chain and the rodent eye.

'Hall-o, Bruce,' the querulous beggar's switchback intonation as if this were a surprise visit not a ritual. A further wrestle with the door and she was bared momentarily to the blinding vitality of daylight. He bent to make the brief kiss which once - not so long ago - he had looked forward to. Now he feared it. She had clutched him one day, fiercely, crushing her breasts against him, her fingers clawing as she pinioned his arms. He pecked, smelt the sourness of the sunless air on her skin, and hurried into the living-room.

'Brought a few goodies,' he sang like a canticle. Putting the basket on the table, he unpacked a cheese, a brown bag full of cherries, a pot of honey, a bought cake.

'Oh Bruce, how kind of you.' The slippers pushed forward, the stick searching out ahead of her, the unchanging nylon overall. 'You shouldn't. Bless you.'

The tiny voice irritated him to the point of sadism. He kept out of range of it with a jaunty air. 'Oh yes, I'm very blessed. No doubt about that. And I've brought something for the said Pushkin.' He brandished the final object, a tin of *Velvet Paws*. 'Caviare for his lordship.'

The neutered beast, asleep on the window-sill, made a neutered response to his bounty. It slept on, its pearly head tucked upside-down into the furry nest of its stomach. He made the usual mistake.

'Well, how are you, Dilly?'

How many times had he resolved not to use that phrase. He was given the full inventory, the arthritis in the knee, the 'upset tummy', the sleeplessness, the headaches - none of this helped of course by the orchestrated barking of the dog next door, the trains which thundered over the viaduct, and the street thugs, so thinly at bay, who watched her house in the evenings.

He saw her eyes lock then, and travel to the party wall. He knew what was coming. She lowered her voice. 'They want to kill me, you know, next door. I heard them whispering.'

There had been a period when he had argued with her, trying to encircle her fancies with logic. 'How could that possibly be, Dilly? Can *you* hear *them*?' He had learnt now to go with it, permit a short innings, and change the subject. He jumped up.

'Now what about those accounts of yours?'

He had taken power of attorney. Roland and Penny had agreed. Typical of them, washing their hands. 'It's just so good of you, Bruce,' Penny said. 'She trusts you, you know.'

Did Dilly trust him? Intermittently perhaps. Often not. He suspected she checked out his handling of her affairs with a great deal of expertise. It was certainly remarkable how she kept within pence to her small income. And she hated his strictures of course, almost became normal when he told her the drink bills were inching higher. The stuff was brought in by the home help who shopped for her. He had seen the bottles in the dustbin.

While he worked, she fussed about him. He had drawn back the heavy curtains to give himself light, and opened the window for air. She re-drew the curtains and shut the window. 'Pushkin'll get out,' she said. There was a bank statement missing. She cried at the onset of this crisis, and he had to go upstairs to the drawer she kept locked to look for it. It had slipped down at the back. It all had to be locked up again, though she would be putting the papers back in a minute.

For brief moments there was a glimpse of the past and of what would have been but for . . . She managed after fumbling in the kitchen for twenty minutes to produce a cup of tea. Sitting there, for an instant her twitchings, sudden convulsions as a dog barked or a hooter blared in the street, ceased. She looked what her mother had been, what she would have been, a woman of intuitive style, connected to those past generations, to that instinctively sensitive and graceful living, association with which he craved and felt entitled to. It was nothing she said - purely physical. The way she held her head, moved her hand, blinked her eyes, poured the tea. There was so much surely, with - yes, it was no disrespect to him - with Jake no longer with them, which they would have had to share . . .

Then the last act of the charade set in. She became aware of herself as a lady. Deciding to play the pining widow, she seized Jake's photograph. Dressed in the suit no doubt Dilly had made him put on, he held a pipe an inch from his mouth - Baldwin's pose, wasn't it. 'I miss Jake so very much,' she said. 'I'm so desperately lonely, Bruce.'

What lies. She had despised Jake, made his life hell - undermined his pride in his skilless labour, mocked and broken like sticks one by one the few words and phrases he lived by, until finally he had released himself in death, the one definitive act of his own, one felt. He remembered the dead face on the pillow, happy, let out for the first time.

He left in a rage of indignation, yet kept his mask, gave the second kiss, joked about her expenses being dead right again, saying she had nothing to worry about, that he would be there again next Thursday and would cut the hedge and slay the dandelions. Good works, that's what one had to do if one called oneself a Christian, didn't one? Good works regardless.

'I feel one ought to visit her, it must be a year since we did.' Penny had to shout to get the words into Roley's ears.

'Ought one?'

He gave his irresistible grin as he accelerated and left a juggernaut doing seventy in the middle lane as if stationary. His yellow kid gloves were perforated in the palms and the open ends were turned back at the wrists. Penny admired anew the reckless dance of his hair in the stripstream of the open Aston Martin, like wind in the grass, and yet the ordered perfection of the silk tie she had bought for him.

She brooded for moments, her head turned away. She saw the dingy street, that unthinkably ghastly interior, and Dilly, who must be worse. An old gust of anger tugged. The spoilt youngest, selfish, weak, half of it was put on, all of it self-induced. She sent her cheques twice yearly, what more could she do which was not counter-productive? She would only preach to the girl if she went. And was it fair on Roley? It wasn't his problem. He was waiting for her decision.

'At least we could pop in to Bruce to see all's well - as we'll be so close.'

It relaxed her, too, to see the tension in his brow release. Did he know the tiny frown was there, giving her these early warnings? If she had insisted, he would have gone and nothing would have been said but, as she always felt, a black mark would have been inserted in some inner notebook he kept.

As it was, he took it out on Bruce by imitating his voice. 'All right, Penelope,' he mocked. Bruce always used their unabbreviated names.

'Don't mention it, Roland,' she capped. She had made the right decision.

In the quietly blossoming suburb, Roley flung the vintage car about like a shark in the shallows. He revved menacingly at the corners.

'Whichever bloody street is it?' he said, craning his neck ill-humouredly at the dinky street names. A startled gardener frowned on them, a hand to shield his eyes from the sun.

They found it at last by trial and error, having tied nooses of angry sound round the neighbourhood. As they sat, acclimatising to the fact of being stationary, Bruce's worried glasses peered at them through the latticed window.

Bruce was fast enough to recover, though. 'Good God, it's you two,' he said, bounding out in a flash. 'I thought it was. I say, what on earth . . .'

Penny, struggling to get out - she had never quite mastered the problem of keeping dignity during this operation - at last extricated herself and recovered her expertise.

'Bruce, it's unforgivable of us, I know. But we're on our way to town - you know, last minute thing - and we thought . . .'

'You've been to see Dilly?'

She was for the immediate present saved by Roley, who came strolling round the beetle-black bonnet. 'Hi there, Bruce, we thought you'd be good for a cup of tea.' There was enough social bromide in the tone to keep the topic at bay until a more propitious moment.

Precisely until, on the handkerchief of a back 'lawn', tea was - what - spread, deployed, exhibited? No, none of these, or rather all. Penny thought that if Bruce went inside for yet another variety of jam or a spoon for the sugar, which that barmy wife of his, Maudie, had 'forgotten', she would scream at him for God's sake to sit down. For once - a difficult choice of dislikes - she preferred Maudie who sat in monolithic complacency, sipping from the cup she held level with her breastbone, speaking (and living apparently) in spaced monosyllables. 'Your garden's looking nice.' 'Yes.' 'What delicious buns - yours?' 'No, bought.' 'How are the goldfish?' 'Hungry usually.' Older than Bruce, her only noticeable activity was reading - public library trash to judge from the three titles she had seen in the hall waiting for return. Penny didn't risk this topic. Meanwhile, in between his rushes into the house, Bruce received a lecture from Roley on the capabilities of Aston Martins.

This latter topic, Penny saw, was beginning to work on Bruce's not inexhaustible nerves. She knew Bruce was capable of only a finite quantity of encirclement. He could break out. Having at last exhausted his repertoire of tea items to be added, he was on the brink of doing so, she thought. Given the advantage he increasingly held, she decided to preempt.

'And how *is* Dilly?' she said.

The shots at Fort Sumpter or Sarajevo had no more dramatic effect. She watched Bruce as a mongoose watches a snake.

'You didn't go then?' he said, flushing, lowering his eyes and voice.

'No, we didn't. We thought we'd talk to you.'

That took his wind a bit. 'What do you want to know?'

'How she is?'

'She's much the same, I suppose.'

'Eating?'

'I imagine.'

'Finances all right?'

'Fine.'

'You *are* good to her, Bruce.   You know how grateful we are.'

It was on the edge of his tongue, she could see, to ask why he should take on everything, when after all he - now Jake, Maudie's brother, was dead - was now not once but twice removed.   But she had judged the strengths exactly, the energy she had given her flattery, the ruthlessness with which she had excommunicated any question of guilt on her part.   She knew now that at the door she would be able to say, 'Give Dilly my love when you see her next,' with no fear of an outburst.   He had been sweet on her of course, probably still was in some dogged way.

They stayed an hour.   They had seats for the theatre, and had to pick them up beforehand as they had booked by phone.   On the motorway again, Penny felt renewed.   What she was able to do was in its way a form of care - behind the scenes.   She would sometime make another adjustment to her will.   Roley had been marvellous.   Thank God for sense, and control, and health in the world.

Dilly always woke to fear.   There was the question - why had she woken?   Something must have caused her to.   They had broken in downstairs, got to her drawer in the spare room, were in the room somewhere, under the bed, in the cupboard - though she kept the doors of the cupboard open now.   This morning - oh God - there were footsteps, coming closer, closer.   She sat up in terror, endured seconds of blind paralysis, until she realised the footsteps were relentlessly even, neither nearing nor retreating. She saw the sky through the chink she left in the curtains to tell her it was day.   It was still and grey, as if a deed had been done and the world was in shock.   Was it over, was she dead?   Was that why nothing materialised?   Then she remembered that the gutter leaked.   It was dripping in a rapid tattoo on the concrete outside the back door.   It had rained.

She began to worry about the drain, still full of rotting leaves from the autumn. The water, dammed up in it was corroding the metal. She had seen flakes which had fallen. She would have to speak to the Council - no, to Bruce. This led her to the inventory of breakdowns - the gas stove the meter man had said was dangerous, the rates bill surely twice last time's, the broken hinge on the outer gate, certainly vandalism . . .

Only slowly, hand over hand, she brought herself out of the night. The clinking of the milkman's bottles in the street helped, and a child's laugh. That would be Maggie's boy, who lived opposite. Maggie was good to her when she had the time, which wasn't often, poor soul, she and her husband had to work themselves to the bone. By the time she had managed to dress herself, get downstairs and make a cup of tea, she was better. More familiar sounds reassured her. She went each time to the front window to confirm them, standing well back of course - they could see you otherwise. And by now she had remembered there were two people coming today.

It was a different woman from last time. The last one had been kind, though ineffective. None of the things she had talked about doing for her had happened. But that didn't matter. Couldn't they realise, it was having someone come which mattered, someone with some normal decent human warmth? This one was older. When she opened the door to her her eyes were already darting over her shoulder seeing what she could see. In the living-room she drew a notepad out of a leather bag she carried, which had a leather fringe along the bottom like the accoutrement of a cowboy. She spent a lot of time wetting her finger and turning the pages. When she had found one to write on, she dived into her bag again, brought out a sheet and began to read it. Dilly had chatted during the beginning of these operations, saying about the trains going by over the viaduct and how noisy they were. Then she realised the woman wasn't listening. Apparently she was meant to sit there in silence and wait.

'Now, Mrs Caulder, I see from my colleague here that you have complaints about your neighbours?'

Dilly felt near to tears.   The other woman - girl really - hadn't had a notebook.   She hadn't asked any questions, but just let her talk, nodding her head sympathetically.   She could see this one was going to cross-examine her.   She couldn't speak at all for a moment.   Down went the busy head.

'A barking dog, I think you said . . . and malicious remarks?'

Tears did now come to her eyes, she couldn't stop them.   'It barks all evening sometimes when they're out,' she managed to say.   'I can't go to sleep.'

'And have you spoken to them about it, Mrs Caulder?'

'Yes.   They say they can't do anything.'

'Are they unkind about it in your opinion?'

'No.'

'But you did say they make malicious remarks.'

Oh no, not that, Dilly thought.   Not with her.   She wouldn't understand as the girl had.   She set her jaw defiantly.   'They do,' she said in a different, lower voice, defying her.

'Could you explain?'

'They want to kill me.   I hear them saying it.'

'You mean - often?'

'Often.'

'Where do you hear them saying this?'

'In my bedroom.'

'Through the wall, you mean?'

Her tears had receded.   Dilly felt angry.   Silly bitch.   What did she know about anything, sitting there as if she owned the place?   She drew herself up.

'If you had any idea how these houses are built, you'd know the walls are paper thin.'

The woman looked for a moment the nonplussed idiot she was, then overlay her annoyance with a frown.   'I see,' she said. She blew her cheeks out in an unpleasant fashion and began to write in the book with little frenzied rushes.

She asked more questions.   Dilly answered them as shortly as she could.   She wanted her to go before she got tearful again. She could see every predictable thrust of her pedestrian mind. 'Ill, mentally ill,' she would be writing.   'Inform the doctor.

Query the treatment. Maybe rehousing?' Dilly had known it all before. There were two ploys. Reason - try to reason with her - or pass the can to another department. How could they know, unless it was by accident, that she didn't care which it was, that if they just gave a little ordinary kindness . . .

'Well, it was nice talking to you, Mrs - er.' She couldn't even remember her name. 'We'll have to see what we can do, won't we?' At the door, as an afterthought, she put her bony fingers on her wrist for a moment and patted it. 'And try not to worry, dear.' She was off to the car parked outside, the strap of her silly bag over her shoulder.

She looked forward to Dr Hearne coming, rare as this was. He was busy, naturally, she knew she couldn't complain. He alone, it seemed, understood her. He had recently changed the drugs the psychiatric people had prescribed because they made her sick. She liked the fact that he smelt slightly of ether, called her Dilly, didn't make jokes or bright remarks, and concentrated on her physical ills, which was all she wanted really. She went on feeling the effect of his visits for a day or two afterwards, almost as if he were her father, taking her cares away with him in his battered black bag.

He was due at three. At four he still hadn't come. Then she made a discovery. She had been upstairs. Coming down, she saw the package in the letter cage on the door. Her pills. He, or someone, had been and not even knocked. Inside there was a scribbled note on one of his surgery slips. 'So sorry, can't make it today. Someone will deliver these for you. Should put you right.'

She sat on the stairs and wept.

It was a bad evening. She knew it would be. While she had her tea, the sun went behind the viaduct. Steadily, the night furies would move into position. She nearly called Bruce, but she knew she would break down if she did, and he would be cross. Damn Bruce, damn Penny, who never came near her with her rich happy life. Why were people so cruel, so selfish? She had no friends, only Pushkin.

When she had fed Pushkin she scooped him up and took him

to her bedroom, cuddling him, putting her cheek against his fur. 'Oh darling Pushkin, what would I do without you?' She squeezed him too tightly, he took fright and ran out of the room. She heard them laughing at her next door, waiting for her to undress. They stood in the garden, she knew, and watched her put on her nightie. Her curtains could be seen through. With trembling hand she took the bottle out of the drawer and poured a tumblerful. Later she took her three sleeping pills.

When Penny and Roland had gone, Bruce felt very cross - cross with himself most of all. He should have put his foot down. He would write to Penny, he thought, pointing out that Dilly needed a sister's care, at the very least a telephone call once in a while. How dare they call in like that without notice, as if he were a kind of paid bailiff and not a retired bank manager who had dealt with all sorts all his life. Perhaps he shouldn't bother with Dilly any more. 'Withdraw his labour' - wasn't that the phrase?

He went in to Maudie about it while she was cooking supper. 'Maudie, do *you* think it's right?' he said.

'Eh?' She stood back from the onions she was chopping and wiped the corner of her eyes with the back of her wrist.

'Do you think it's right Penelope taking no responsibility for Dilly?'

'Right?' she said, as if he had said something unfathomable. Good lord, sometimes she was as dim as Jake had been.

'That's what I said. Wouldn't you say she should, Penelope being Dilly's sister?'

Maudie threw the onions into the fat. They made a scalding hiss. 'She's all right,' she said after giving the pan a shake.

'Who's all right?'

'Penny.'

'I didn't say she wasn't "all right". I said don't you think she ought to take more responsibility for Dilly, why should I do it all.'

'You like it, don't you?'

That really got to him. Was that what she thought, the old . . . that he did it because he liked it? Let her go and find out how

155

likeable it was, she could take the bus. Dilly was her brother's widow. He went into a sulk for the rest of the evening about it. He *would* write that letter.

The next day when he was doing the shopping - Maudie's leg was bad again - he had more sober thoughts. It wasn't the whole story by a long chalk, but there was some truth in what Maudie had said. There had been a time when he had enjoyed Dilly's company. Was that why he went now, when there was no enjoyment, when he knew that the more he did for her the more she would cling and exploit him, when rationality was receding, when each time it was a little worse?

He didn't honestly think it was. But it had probably started like that. So wasn't that an additional reason why he should stop going? It didn't have to be all at once. He could begin to space out the visits. Let the care services cope, the doctor. That's what they were all paid for, wasn't it?

He was in a delicatessen shop while he had these thoughts. His eye fell quite fortuitously on a bottle of candied fruit. He hadn't seen them for years. He remembered Dilly used to have a passion for them. His hand was reaching for them before he could stop it. He checked it in mid-air.

Here I go, he thought, an automaton, a creature of habit. He imagined himself giving her the box. 'Oh thank you, Bruce, bless you, how kind you are to me.' He had a convulsion of distaste and didn't buy it.

He was a sidesman in their C of E church. On Sunday during the collection, as he stood waiting for the purple purse to pass along the pew, his thoughts reached a climax. What was the point of it all, all this ritual and pretence? He felt a withering blast of scorn for the people in the pew who put in their coins while continuing to sing from their hymn books, passing the bag along hurriedly as if it were a game of hunt the slipper and they might be caught with it when the music stopped. Superstitious ritual, that's what churchgoing was. No wonder the modern age rejected it. What had it ever done for him? Penny and Roland weren't churchgoers. They simply crashed about doing what pleased them. Why should one 'do good' to one's neighbour?

Where did it get you? It was just part of the national conspiracy which kept the proles in place while the rich got richer.

Thursday came. He wondered if Maudie was watching to see if he would go. Much more likely, she had forgotten. Dilly had phoned on Sunday. He hadn't phoned her.

He found, though, that for some reason his anger had subsided. After lunch he looked out of the kitchen window and saw there were several things which needed doing in the garden. Maudie was down at the bottom again, reading. It would be nice to get to work with the thought of her there, and tea coming up later. But he thought he would go. Dilly would be expecting him. You had to keep at things, didn't you, even when they weren't quite what suited?

On the way be bought Dilly the box of candied fruits.

QUITE UNAPROPOS

The missile whirred inches from his ear. He heard it thump against the wall-blackboard behind him and fall to the rostrum floor. Aggressive laughter stirred. He knew what it was, a pellet of folded paper propelled by an elastic band. Not moving his head, he looked at his watch concealed below the desk. Two minutes. With any luck he could avoid the pointless act of detecting and punishing the culprit. He continued the mindless ticking of exercise books. Only one left, thank God. Nothing to take home.

The bell brought common relief to teacher and pupils. He locked the corrected books in the desk, took up his old suitcase, which still had a scratched and torn sticker depicting the Taj Mahal seen through a fretsaw Moslem arch, and wasn't the last to battle his way out of the classroom.

Reaching the sanctuary of his small Fiat, for a moment he just sat, beginning the unravelling of the day's tensions. He watched two colleagues approach another car. They were holding hands, and when they got into the car began to embrace. He reached forward with the ignition key. What decency was there any more? Teenage life was an open national orgy, and colleagues set no example. How many had any real respect for learning?

However, his spirits rose as he passed through the gate. Life began for him at four o'clock. He stopped briefly to buy his supper from the supermarket, frozen fried haddock pieces, frozen peas, and raspberry-ripple ice-cream, a partnership which occurred at least once a week, and he bought a new bottle of Cyprus sherry. He had a bit of a conscience about the latter item. It had been joining the company rather more often of late. Never mind, he thought. Tonight, if all went well, there would be something to celebrate.

When he got in he put the food in the fridge and went immediately into the small cluttered sitting-room. As he often did, he stood in front of the large painting which hung over the mantelpiece. Though crude and amateur, it showed a good-faced white man with silver hair, in a topee and khaki drill shirt and shorts, standing beside a group of Indians half his size. Behind them was a long, single-storey building on stilts, and beside it a flagpole with the Union Jack. In his arms the man held a child. All the faces were looking forwards as if it were a photograph and they were facing the camera. On a plaque fixed to the bottom of the frame were the words: 'Dr Gordon Findlater, Founder and Principal of the Marjarapore Temple of Ophthalmic Health, among his patients the year before his death 1938.' The painting had been given to Lester when he went out there to visit. The artist had been a bearer at the Clinic.

Nodding his head as if to confirm something, he went to the table in the window where there was an old electronic typewriter and twenty-three completed chapters of his work. The last chapter, which he had called 'The Consummation,' was done except for the last scene, Findlater's death. This was to include the famous words: 'Carry on, sister, would you? I'm just going up the hill to watch the sun go down.'

He sat down and looked out of the window as he had done so many times in the last months. His view included an area of scruffy wasteland between the high rise blocks. Narrowing his eyes, it wasn't difficult to transform it into that simple dusty village where Findlater lived, and he could conjure, almost at will, the full compassionate personality of his great uncle, so much had he absorbed from Findlater's own diary, from what many others of different nationality had written about him first hand, and from his own visit. He also remembered, verbatim, snippets of what his grandfather had said of his brother. These phrases and sentences had acquired almost Biblical significance. What a life of devotion and dedication to others, what purity of spirit, what skill, courage, what steadfastness and, yes, self-denial. For how many desirable women must have looked on that strong kindly face and wanted to possess him, to lure him from his work to their domestic webs? He must sometimes have been tempted, too. There was no reason to doubt he was a normal man with normal appetites. And yet he had lived like a priest and accepted total celibacy. If he had been a Catholic he would have been created a saint by now.   He was a saint, a modern saint, with no halo or miracles but just his work to speak for him - the giving of sight to countless Indians, and with that sight, unconsciously, the giving of a hopeful vision of life and how to live it.   It was said he was still spoken of in villages all over the Decan.

Lester Findlater knew he was but a pale reflection of his great ancestor but he felt he understood him.   He was determined that England, this very different callous country of nowadays should be reminded of its great hero.   The amazing thing was that, well-known as Findlater was, there had never been a biography. He set about his evening's work with passion.

Sally's colleague in the library reading-room rang the bell some half a minute before seven.   She kept her finger on the button and looked round the room fiercely.   At the newspaper table a ragged tramp-like man, who had been absorbed in *The Times,* which he had to hold up to his eyes, looked askance, startled, as if he would be arrested.   Sally also had cause for haste this evening, but she always hated closing time.   It seemed churlish to uproot people when they were absorbed.   On her clearing-up round she went to talk to the man, who had lingered, and allowed him to detain her further.

She had to run most of the way to Paddington and the guard was about to shut the doors of the train as she rushed onto the platform.   She flopped panting into her seat and won a smile from the man opposite, who lowered the evening paper and peered over his spectacles at her.

It was the first Friday in the month, the day she had supper with Kate.   Kate would never have confessed to minding if she were late.   But the small oak table would have been laid for some time in the window, the statutory bottle of wine placed with its attendant corkscrew, the food would be ready in the kitchen. Whatever she said, Kate would be anxious.   Sally wanted each of their evenings to be an unblemished pleasure for her.   There weren't necessarily so many more to come.

She got home, kissed her mother in the kitchen, went up to change, and was round to Kate's cottage just as the village clock was striking eight-thirty. Kate was at the door.

'My dear, like clockwork, I do hope you haven't rushed.'

Kate was an outgoing woman. She thought almost exclusively of others. Their conversations were about Sally's life. Sometimes Sally had tried to alter this by questioning Kate about her past. Kate would talk briefly, and usually amusingly, about her husband, Philip, and the people she knew and had known, but she always brought the subject back to Sally. Sally decided it was how she liked it to be. She drew pleasure perhaps from hearing what a younger person was doing.

Sally gave Kate the box of chocolates she had managed to get at Henley station. Kate asked her to uncork the claret and said 'I thought we'd have our favourite tonight.' When they had eaten the delicious salmon and mayonnaise and the fresh sweet rolls Kate had baked, she looked out of the window at the River Thames which bordered the small garden. For a few moments she was silent, as if her thoughts were being borne away by the smooth green current.

Her attention returned. 'You know, I have something to tell you this evening, Sally dear,' she said. 'I don't know if it's very important really. But for some reason I've never told anyone about it - except Philip of course. I'm certainly not ashamed of it. Very much the contrary. I suppose it's really because my guardian thought it should be that way - people were like that in those days. She didn't tell me until I was twenty-six, and when she died not long after that I went on being silent about it. My parents didn't die when I was young, as I thought and as I have allowed people to go on thinking ever since. My mother was an Anglo-Indian girl who came to England to put me in a convent. She then disappeared and never returned to see me. My father was Gordon Findlater, the pioneer of eye-surgery in India. When my guardian told me this, Findlater was dead. I suppose she delayed telling me until then on purpose.'

Kate paused. 'There, I've said it, and it *isn't* important. But I wanted to tell you. I suppose it's because you're very dear to me, Sally, almost as if you were my own daughter. And all of us has a dynastic streak, I suppose, as if life were a kind of relay race. So, you see, I've given you my baton. You can put it on the shelf and look at it sometimes when I'm gone and say "I knew Gordon Findlater's daughter." I should like to think of you doing that.'

A few weeks later Kate died, peacefully, in her garden chair.

It was six months later Sally saw the Findlater biography. It was among a batch of new books which came into the library and she was busy registering them and getting them ready for the shelves. She took it home that week-end and read it at a gulp. It deeply moved her, not only because of Findlater's personality, but because she saw so much of him in Kate. She also admired the author, whom she realised must be Kate's distant cousin. He wrote with such zeal, such sincerity. What intrigued her, however, was that he clearly knew nothing of the liaison which had produced Kate.

She had decided to keep Kate's secret, to put it as she had suggested on the shelf. Wasn't that what she had meant her to do by using the phrase? But her librarian's impulse for exactness about information was aroused by this strange omission in the book, and she began in consequence to wonder if Kate had after all wanted her to keep silent. Hadn't she been, in fact, telling her she wanted her story to be known one day after she had died? For days she debated the matter, then made up her mind. She would go and talk to Lester Findlater. He was so obviously a person of discretion and integrity. He wouldn't, she was sure, make any improper or sensational use of her information. He would be the best person to advise her - more objectively then her father or mother would. He would also, she thought, be interested.

With difficulty she got the private number from the publisher. After work that evening she went into a telephone box with her pulses racing. She had rather a shock.

'Hallo, who's that?' said the voice rather crossly before she had said anything. It was a nice voice, but the tone was definitely hostile.

'Hallo, my name's Sally Stringer. Is that Lester Findlater?' There was no answer, but she was sure it was him. 'I happen to have read your book, you see, and . . .'

'I'm not interested in journalists,' snapped the voice.

She thought she only just stopped him putting the phone down. 'I'm not a journalist,' she got in quickly.

'Well if you aren't a journalist, you must be a reviewer. If so, speak to my publisher. They deal with all that sort of thing.'

'I'm not a reviewer, either. I'm not anything. But I happen to have some information about Gordon Findlater which I think may interest you. If you could spare the time I'd like to come and see you.'

An instinct told her not to say what the matter was. From the long silence which ensued she thought he was interested. Why didn't she write, he said. She told him it was because it wasn't just the information she wanted him to have, she also wanted his advice on a personal matter involving Findlater. Finally he reluctantly agreed to an evening later in the week and gave her the address.

She was rather surprised at the kind of place he lived in, a huge soulless block of high-rise flats north of Islington, with no attempt at grass on the surrounds, only weeds and brown patches, and a lot of graffiti on the walls. Because of the name Islington, somehow she had imagined one of those posh and fashionable regency houses.

When he opened the door she liked his face at once, even though he was hardly welcoming. She thought it was sensitive and strong. But he turned his back. She had to follow him in and close the door herself.

'I had a bit of difficulty finding you,' she began, just for something to say. 'I had to ask.'

'Surprised you got an answer at all in this area. Lucky you weren't mugged.'

As soon as they were in the cockpit of a sitting-room he turned and said: 'You have something to tell me?'

'Well, yes. But can we sit down?'

She decided he must be nice. How could he be otherwise

when he wrote as he did? That meant his gruffness was shyness and perhaps gaucherie. She was used to people like that in the library. This thought gave her confidence. She took her time and let him catch her looking rather shamelessly at the sherry bottle on the sideboard. When he had rather reluctantly offered her one and poured another for himself, she began. 'I knew Gordon Findlater's daughter. She died six months ago.'

She almost laughed, he looked so startled. 'That's impossible. Findlater had no children,' he snapped.

'Apparently he had at least one. Her adopted name was Kate Slade. She lived near us in Henley for as long as I can remember.' She told him the story of their last meeting. She was intent on keeping her facts strictly accurate and didn't fully take in the effect she was having on him. When she finished she saw that he had turned quite pale. He jumped up.

'All this is absolute nonsense,' he said. He swooped up his glass and went to refill it. 'Findlater had no children. He never married. He lived a life of total dedication and celibacy. Everything I know about him points that way. I'm sorry, but there's some other explanation for your story.' He stood with his back to her, drinking the sherry in little quick gulps like medicine and looking out of the window.

She began to feel some doubts about him, and a certain resistance. Really, this was ridiculous. Of course there might be another explanation, but what kind of a scholar was he if he condemned, out-of-hand, evidence which didn't fit with what he already believed?

'Are you suggesting my friend wasn't telling the truth?'

'Not necessarily, no. That is to say, she may not have been lying. But she could have been wrongly informed by her guardian. She could have misunderstood what she was told. Any number of explanations is possible.'

'But doesn't it occur to you to ask whether Kate might *look* like Findlater?' She began to take the photograph of Kate from her bag.

The back continued to confront her. Then he gave her a quick sideways look. She held up the photo. 'I've seen the photos in your book, of course. You see, the setting of the eyes, the shape of the nose - and above all the cheek bones. As a matter of fact, I think you've got them, too, haven't you? And that picture - isn't that Findlater?'

He marched to the sideboard, put down the glass and turned to face her. 'Look, I'm sorry, Miss - er -'

'Sally Stringer.'

'I'm sorry, Miss Stringer. I'm grateful of course that you should think I'd be interested. But I'm not. I'm a schoolmaster, and the time I have for my research is limited. I'm already embarked on another work. If you'll excuse me, I'm afraid I must ask you to . . .'

She got up, flushing. This wasn't gaucherie but straight cowardice. 'I'm sorry you take this attitude,' she said, a little stiffly, at the door, 'I really thought after reading your book that you'd be interested. I'm sorry I bothered you.'

He didn't quite shut the door in her face but came pretty near it.

She made up her mind very fast what she would do. First, she involved her parents. They were delighted at the news about Kate's father. Her mother said she had always felt there was something different and distinguished about Kate. They quite understood Kate's discretion over her origins and Sally's delay in telling them. They agreed that Lester Findlater's public error should be publically corrected, if not by him then by other means. Best of all they came up with some facts. When they first knew Kate and her husband, Philip Marks, Kate's old guardian, a Sister Martina, had been alive. Kate used to go off and visit her at the Convent sometimes. They racked their brains and remembered the name of the convent and that it was in Southend. Sally found it was still there, went to the place, and discovered Kate Slade's name in their record. 'Admitted March 1913. Age: 6 months. Parents: unknown.'

At first sight this seemed rather a dead end. Presumably, at the time, Sister Martina was either guarding her knowledge of the parentage or learnt of it at a later date. Then something else occurred to Sally.   She remembered something in Lester's book.

She could hardly wait until next morning.   The first thing she did when she got into the library was to rush to the shelf.   In the book, sure enough, was the information.   It was reasonable to assume that if Kate was born in September 1912, she was conceived in December 1911.   Lester had recorded that between September 1911 until early in 1912 there was a gap in information about Findlater's life.   He had left the Clinic during this period with the explanation of 'having family matters to attend to.'   Lester offered no explanation of what these matters might be.   Kate had almost certainly been conceived during this time.   It wasn't proof, but certainly circumstantial evidence that Kate's story, told her by Sister Martina, was the simple truth.

Sally then had another idea.   If there was a registration of the birth it would presumably have been made in India.   She found there was a record office in the Commonwealth Office.   There were two likely problems.   Given the later behaviour of the Anglo-Indian lady who had been willing to abandon her child, it was unlikely she had bothered with such a bureaucratic chore.   And even if she had registered her child's birth, it was by no means certain that her name was Slade.   She might well have invented that for the nuns.   However, it was worth a try.

The records were arranged in Provinces.   She looked first at the Province in which Marjarapore was.   She found it at once in the volume for December 1912.   'Kate Ethel Slade: Father unknown.   Mother: Mrs Christine Slade of 19, Railway Close, Brahmatra.'   Christine's childish signature in faded light blue ink attested the document.

Sally rushed back to the library and took out the big world atlas in the reference room.   Brahmatra was marked.   It was some twenty miles from Marjarapore.

It was still not conclusive, but enough, with the photographs, to convince her.   But to her surprise Sally found herself at this point of apparent triumph unaccountably lacking in elation.   While the chase had been on it had been exciting.   Now, the dead quarry in her hands, it seemed a limp unexciting object she had been pursuing.   As Kate had said, it was not perhaps so very important. So, a great man had had a temporary lapse during an otherwise exemplary life. What did that matter? It simply made him more human. And perhaps it had been a beautiful love affair. Why did one assume the contrary? It was possible he hadn't even known he had a child and hadn't therefore condoned her banishment without funds to an orphan's home in England. To quote Lester: 'Any number of explanations is possible.' She did nothing more.

On August bank holiday, one of the other librarians asked her to go sailing with him. She didn't feel like it and made an excuse. During the afternoon she was reading in the garden at home on the canopied swing seat. It was hot and sultry. In the herbaceous border butterflies fluttered. Sparrows cheeped regularly in the creeper which clung to the walls of the house. She heard the garden gate whine behind her. It was a man in a blazer. As he approached, she saw it was Lester Findlater.

She half rose in her seat. It seemed he had made an effort with his clothes. He looked a lot smarter than when she had seen him before. There was a bow tie with orange and yellow stripes, and a sharp crease in his lightweight blue trousers.

'You live in a very beautiful part of the world, in a most attractive house,' he said.

She felt heckles rising. 'Oh hallo,' she said.

'There were three Stringers in the Henley telephone book. Somehow I knew "Orchard House" would be you. Can I sit down, it's hot?'

Without waiting for an answer he sat down in one of the basket chairs, took a large coloured handkerchief from his pocket and wiped his forehead. She sat back in the swing seat and set it in motion.

'I've come to make an apology,' he said weightily. 'I didn't receive you with any courtesy when you came to my flat a couple of months back. You see, the information you imparted was something of a shock. When one has studied, as I have, for three years - I even visited Marjarapore, you know, as part of my research - when one has studied for three years and has formed, slowly and meticulously, a view of a great man . . .'

'It's a shock to have to change it a bit?   Is that what you've come to say?'

He laughed, a little rapid laugh.   Then he straightened his back, like a gymnast who has completed half his routine and braces himself for the rest.   'Well no, that isn't quite it, not exactly.'

'You mean you haven't changed your views?'

'Apart from apologising for my behaviour, which I've done, what I've come to say is that there is, of course, a perfectly obvious explanation of the story told by your - er - acquaintance, one which I'm sure she believed to be true.'   He paused impressively.   'I've no doubt there was such a lady as the one she mentioned, perhaps an Anglo-Indian lady.   But probably she lived in England.   Many Anglo-Indians, those who could afford it, came to England to live to avoid the unpleasantness of the way they were regarded in the sub-continent, by both races.   No doubt she had a child and wished to dispose of it.   Now it would be quite natural for a woman of her background to name to the orphans' home the most illustrious person she could think of as the father.   I believe it's quite a common practice.   What name would spring more readily to her lips than that of my great uncle, a household word at the time?'

He paused, and wiped his forehead again as if delivered of a great weight.   He seemed to recover authority.

'But the Anglo-Indian lady didn't live in England,' Sally said tartly.   'At least I very much doubt if she did, and she was certainly living in India when her baby was born.'

'I beg your pardon?'

'She registered her baby in a town called Brahmatra in India. Her name was Christine Slade.'

Lester smiled indulgently.   'I see you've been at work.'

'I have.   I went to the Commonwealth Records office.   The town of Brahmatra is twenty miles from Marjarapore.'

She observed him closely. The eyes fell and the thick sable-coloured eyelashes blinked rapidly.   His hands flew to his tie.   'Really?   Most interesting.   Well perhaps she did live in

India then. That makes it even more understandable that she'd cast Gordon Findlater as her child's father. She had every reason to know of him if she lived so close to the Clinic.'

Sally looked away. 'There's another thing. I went to the convent where Kate was brought up. I found Kate's arrival date and how old she was when she was left there. It fits with her birthday, in mid-September, 1912. She was therefore probably conceived in December 1911, or thereabouts. You'll appreciate this was the period you said Findlater disappeared.'

'I didn't say disappeared. I said we have no knowledge of him at that time.'

'As you wish. But you must admit there's a compelling combination of circumstances at the very least.'

'Compelling?'

'Compelling one to believe what the photograph I showed you, compared with your photos of Findlater, and that portrait of him you have, makes obvious.'

His attention seemed to wander. He turned towards the house. 'Those chimneys of yours are very fine,' he said. 'They must be unique.'

She had a sudden feeling of ruthlessness. Was he impervious? '*Makes obvious*,' she repeated.

He turned slowly back to her. Was there at last a small shadow of doubt on his face? 'Sally - I may call you that? I do appreciate your interest. You've been very active.'

'But you still don't agree?'

He managed to smile. '"Still" not? No, I don't think I ever could agree. You see, I *know* my great uncle. Sometimes a biographer must decide from instinct, not just from reason. I just know Findlater was incapable of such a deed. All his life he held women in great esteem. He couldn't possibly have stooped to so dishonourable a liaison.'

'What you mean is you've formed your opinion and solidified it into a book and you won't change it. But you can surely never be so sure of a person when they're dead.'

'I quite disagree about that in this instance.'

'You can't know someone as well as that even when they're

alive. You know what I think?' She was overcome by a rash desire to expose him. 'I think the truth is you don't want to find that your ancestor was human. I think what you're doing is trying to embalm him - in a kind of viscous treacle of your own ideal, the ideal of saintly male virginity. Why shouldn't Findlater have had an affair? It may have been a beautiful one.'

It was as if there had been an explosion. What had impelled her to such an enormity? He was medievally embattled in his certainties and why should she care? With head ducked and ears covered she heard the heavy thud of objects returning to earth. She would have been quite prepared to see him on the way to the gate. But when she looked up after a few seconds the motionless walnut tree was still there, the butterflies continued to play like the endless twirling of a mobile over the catmint, the sparrows cheeped. Lester was still there, but staring at her with a look of incomprehension and - what was it, fright?

'Are you suggesting there's a connection between my personal attitudes and my view of my ancestor?' he was saying. She couldn't answer. 'I think you are. I think you're saying *I* have some ideal of celebacy. But I don't have such an attitude at all. I've always envisaged the possibility of love and marriage - to the right person.'

She was sure he would now get up and take his leave. She honestly rather hoped he would. He had been so unbearably pompous, and now she had allowed the situation to get out of control. But he didn't move. Instead, he looked at her unflinchingly for several moments.

'You really are an extraordinary girl,' he said.

'I don't think so.'

'I came here quite convinced I was right, and you've challenged me on a fundamental point.'

'Does that make me so extraordinary?' She didn't conceal her irony.

'Well, it does actually. To me. You see I live and work alone. I don't get any challenges. It's a new experience for me. And the funny thing is, I don't think I dislike it, not from you because I can see you're sincere. Yes, maybe I should look at this evidence about Kate Slade.   Certainly I will, if you'll allow me to.   It's really your material, not mine.   Perhaps you should publish something.' He paused, and she fancied a smile twitched his lips.   'Something else is occurring to me. I think this afternoon I completed the best bit of research I ever did.'

'What's that?'

'Finding Orchard House in the telephone book - I mean, quite unapropos of Gordon Findlater.   Does my saying that completely rule me out of court?'

She found a response to this difficult.   It was in the absence of any reason why not, that she found herself agreeing to let him take her out to dinner.

CRÈME DE LA CRÈME

As soon as Laura entered his office Leonard White knew the manuscript of the book under her arm was an alibi.

'Leonard, it' so *good* to see you again,' she said, 'and angelic of you to receive me at such short notice when you're now so important.' She walked the last paces as she said this, right hand outstretched. The outdistanced secretary who had intended to announce her, retreated and quietly closed the door.

She put the manuscript on the desk and turned her back to offer him the luxurious black mink coat loose over her shoulders. It was typical of Laura that she took no notice of the anti-fur lobby. As he placed the perfumed coat on a hanger in the cupboard he had the usual sensation of disadvantage. Surely into her eighties now, four discarded marriages in her wake, by any standard a bit passé, but here he was, not exactly on the bottom rung himself these days, with all his old apprehensions in her company rekindled in a moment.

'You really have done well, Leonard. I seem to read and hear of you every other day. Your father would have enjoyed your success. Poor man, he didn't have too much himself, did he? You've climbed - literally, it seems - to the top of the tower.' She walked to the view twenty-five floors above London at which she glanced peripherally. 'Do you *feel* important? I do hope so.'

This question, he knew, didn't need an answer. It was her usual trick of belittling any achievement which wasn't her own. Oil, she was saying between the lines, *so* fundamental, *so* necessary, but such a banality set beside the arts, and in particular the production of literature. How did she still get away with this in the millenium?

She soon exhausted her enquiry into his 'success'. She returned to the desk and took up her book in both hands, like a priest about to elevate the host. 'Well now, this is *my* new little triumph - perhaps, I have to say it, really my *best* triumph. It is a little gratifying after all these years to be *asked* for one's autobiography. My publisher did, you know, with no prompting. But as soon as the book was done I thought of you - with your Russian and your knowledge of the wider history of the period. You must tear it to bits. Promise me?'

'I shall read it with great interest, Laura,' he said.

They sat in the chintzy armchairs. One of the girls brought tea. Laura talked once more of those first childhood experiences among other Russian emigrés in Paris, whence her parents had fled in 1917, and about her subsequent career, on and off, as a freelance journalist on Soviet and now Russian affairs. Undoubtedly risking her liberty and possibly her life, she had flitted in and out of the Stalinist dictatorship, and since Gorbachov she had been making hay. Her latest report was an astonishing insight into the new St Petersburg mafia into whose inner cabals, if she was to be believed, she seemed to have breezed with lofty unconcern. For a moment Leonard forgot the personal implications. However much she invented, however much she tried to elevate her journalism into 'literature,' she was a highly interesting woman and deserved more fame than she had won. He was even quite pleased she had asked him to criticise the book. Couldn't this be taken as some indication she thought the world of commerce not so totally alienated from culture? Then she made her slip, probably on purpose. The book was to come out next month, it seemed.

'Oh, I see,' he said, puncturing her flow of speech.

His tone checked her. 'You see, what, Leonard dear?'

'The proofs are all done with.'

He watched her rather mean blue eyes register the point. 'Well, yes, the donkey work is over, thank God. What I now need is an informed judgement, you see . . .'

'Which will be too late to have any practical value.'

He scored momentarily with this. Her face reddened round the two prominent cheek bones. 'That's true,' she said in a more minor key. 'But I do value your opinion, and of course there may be a second edition.'

Her embarrassment was short-lived. He saw the swift change to aggression and realised how right his first intuition had been.

Her real intention came at him with no further preliminary. 'And quite frankly I confess I *did* have another motive in coming to see you,' she went on. 'I noticed on Sunday that your firm's advertising for a secretary. I made an enquiry and found it's the top brass which is wanting someone. The advertisement said "a senior executive". That couldn't be you, could it?'

'Yes.'

She looked away with a kind of irritable disinterest. 'It's Fanny again. The boy's getting into trouble at the comprehensive. He needs to go to a boarding school. She's not earning enough to pay the fees. She has skills, and a degree. That must be what you want, isn't it? You pay well, I see.'

'We pay well.'

'With the right handling I think Fanny is crème de la crème. You'd understand her, she'd work her heart out for you, and you'd save that boy.'

'It's a junior post. She'd be ten years older than the others and have to take orders from two of them.'

'She wouldn't mind that - for the money, and for Jamie. Leonard, I know you won't consider this - you probably can't in your position - but I have to mention it. I think your father would have wanted you to take her on. Your father did always have the right priorities whatever else he lacked, and I'm sure you've taken after him.'

Having agreed to interview Fanny, with others, he knew barring some blatant disqualification he'd probably appoint her. Laura knew it, too. Her final words assumed it. 'Good boy. You'll be the making of that girl.'

He hadn't seen Fanny since they were both teenagers. He had gathered from his father there had been a marriage problem, but he liked her on sight. For a start she had none of her mother's overbearing confidence. She had obviously tried to pretty herself up for the interview, but the black dress, which didn't seem to fit her, could have been borrowed. It certainly didn't fit the tough leftiness he had somehow branded her with from reports. She came in all apologies, with a curious neurotic bunching of her shoulders and a turning aside of her head.

'I feel desperate with shame, coming at you like this,' were her first words. 'I could have slain mother, and wouldn't have dreamed of applying if it hadn't been for Jamie. Though . . .' She brightened as she looked round the room. '. . . Though I can't say I'd be sorry to leave my present job. The firm isn't exactly in the Stock Exchange top hundred.' She swung her head up suddenly in a parody of her mother. 'Tell me, have I any chance at all?'

'Well, as I told your mother. . .'

'I mean, I really don't mind what I do within reason. Make tea, type technical memos and letters, be pleasant to bores on the phone, take succinct minutes. I'll even vamp your clients if you want me to, not that I've so much to vamp with these days. But I'm talking too much. I'm sorry. I'm not really like this, it's nerves. Are you really considering me or just being polite?'

He put into action the plan he had decided on, the same as for all the others. She seemed to be quite good on computers, held up, just, on dictation. She responded favourably to the what-would-you-do-if test he had designed, even with some flare. She was obviously sharply intelligent. She spoke some Arabic and could read it fluently, which would be of use. Her ex-husband, a mineralogist, had been working in Aden. And, crucially, the other girls liked her. 'She's amusing, and unassuming,' they said. If *they* weren't afraid of a middle-aged woman . . . He told himself if they hadn't liked her he would have turned her down.

He hardly saw her in the next month, except once or twice at meetings. She seemed au fait with the petroleum jargon, she followed the discussions with ease, and her minutes were excellent. She couldn't resist a touch of irony here and there, but it was well-disguised and, even if it hadn't been, as long as she didn't get cocky it might just make the bores think twice. Her best irony was to reduce a twenty minute speech to two sentences.

One evening Mary, his PA, said Fanny had asked to see him if he had a moment. Naturally he agreed, though he doubted if he could have avoided it anyway. Fanny was lurking in Mary's office next to his and appeared before Mary was through the door. She came in and shut the door behind her. She was obviously making an effort to smarten up, he thought - but the too long mauve skirt had a sagging hem, the cream blouse was creased, her hair looked winnowed at the back. She sat on the chair across the desk.

'Leonard,' she began, then checked. 'Oh sorry, I mustn't call you that, must I?'

'You can call me that in private.'

'Yes, of course. I mean, thanks, I'll be sure only to do it when we're alone. Look, it's dreadful, I *feel* dreadful, but I can't live on my salary any more. I've had to get Jamie into Francis Holland and it's crippling what they ask. I've had to sell my jalope to pay the rack rent I'm charged, and it's in Chiswick, not Kensington.'

'You're asking for a rise after a few weeks?'

'I want more responsibility. I don't want to be immodest but I can run circles round these little chicks. I mean, couldn't I be conference secretary for several departments? I'm good at that and you wouldn't then have to promote me over this lot.' She jerked her head at the door.

An old hackle began to stir. 'You're putting forward an odd principle, aren't you?'

'Principle?'

'That the company rewards its employees according to their needs. Don't I seem to have read that somewhere?'

'But it's not just needs. The same book also talks of work according to ability. It just so happens in my case the needs and the ability go together.'

She wasn't like her mother, he kept telling himself. Laura never pleaded, she didn't need to. This was a cri-de-coeur. He saw that her fingers were writhing in her lap like asps. And when he gently turned her down she burst into tears, or rather sobs. Her whole body heaved and shuddered with the effort of her grief. 'I'm such a mess, Leonard. I've made such a mess of my life. Even Jamie hates me. Please, please, help me.'

He felt wrenched by her. He got up and went to the cupboard where he thought there were some tissues. There weren't. He returned, put his hand on her back, and offered his handkerchief. She snatched it out of his hand.

'I won't give in. I won't give in.' She snorted, partially stopped heaving, then recovered. 'But Leonard, *could* you do something else for me. If I can't have a rise, I understand. I didn't expect you to give me one, really. Why should you? But - do you think you could somehow have a word with Jamie? It's *hell* not having a man about the place. He's getting so rude and abominable. If you could just speak to him he might reform . . . the little sod.' The expletive seemed to exorcise the last of her tears. She looked at him defiantly, wiping her cheek with the back of her hand.

There was something faintly comic. He couldn't help liking her. She was in one way so completely hopeless, in another courageous. And he had another, darker, thought. Was there any wonder there were difficulties with a mother like hers? Laura was right. He could do something for Fanny. He could supply, to start with, just a little common concern. He doubted if Laura had ever managed much of that.

He spoke to his wife, Jenny, and they agreed to invite Fanny and Jamie to spend the day with them, with their own two. They went to Longleat. From the children's point of view it was a success. After a period of appraisal, both their girls decided they approved of Jamie. If Jamie was a bull, they acted upon him like a couple of steers. His behaviour was golden all day, certainly there was no call for heavy admonitions. Fanny's behaviour, as ever, was ambivalent. At one moment she seemed almost cross Jamie was being so normal. 'It must be a cake-walk bringing up kids when you have a full complement of parents,' she said fiercely. And there was another even bitterer reference to money and the wheels it oiled.

But mostly she was relaxed. A bit over-vehement on the subject of animals - their 'incarceration' in this park she thought 'criminal,' a subject which led on to vivisection and blood sports - but she enjoyed the house and its contents. When they parted she thanked them genuinely, without gush.   Again, how unlike Laura.   She solemnly shook hands with all four of them, and made Jamie do the same.

There was another fallow period.   Mary reported well on her work.   She was contributing as more than a secretary, apparently. She produced ideas.

Every Friday the divisional heads met him for an informal chat.   At the end of one of these meetings one of Leonard's colleagues brought up the subject of Fanny.

'By the way, Len, you have an interesting lady in your coop, haven't you?   Came to see me the other day.   Wants to be conference secretary for the whole company.   Says it's a particular skill which she thinks she has.   Must say, though obviously intelligent, she has a bit of a Hampstead air about her, hasn't she?   I said she should have come to you with it, but said she didn't think it was important enough and wondered if I'd raise it at this meeting.'

So much for Fanny's discretion.   When he got back to his office she was waiting for him in Mary's room.   He thought of telling her he couldn't see her now, but the sight of her eagerness aroused his interest - or was it his sadism?   He was furious. Did she really think she could get away with this sort of thing?

'What did you all say?' she asked at once, closing the door behind them as if they were plotting together for her advancement.

Was it Jamie who needed lecturing?   He found himself playing the big executive.   He didn't answer immediately.   He went to his desk, opened his brief case, and threw papers into different baskets.   He was aware of her standing there like an excited schoolgirl.   He sat down, interlaced his fingers on his stomach, and frowned.

'Has it not occurred to you I could fire you for this?' he began.

Her face changed to horror.   'Fire?'   She advanced a step as if she were playing grandmother's footsteps.   'But Leonard, you must let me explain.   I realised of course you might feel . . .'

'Then it's a pity you didn't act on your realisation.   Do you really think a company of this sophistication is going to put up

178

with junior secretaries lobbying for their own interest in this childish way?'

'You mean, nobody thought it was a good idea?'

'Of course they didn't. For a start - quite apart from the impropriety of your method of going about it - how could one person serve all the departments? Meetings constantly overlap.'

She dropped into the chair with a wallop and hit the side of her head with a clenched fist. 'Oh God,' she said, 'of course.'

'Quite apart, as I say, from the impropriety. You had already approached me about it and I'd said no.'

It took him twenty minutes to get rid of her. There was a torrent of self-abasement - how could she have been so stupid after he had been so kind to her, and the rest of it. He was still sorry for her. It so obviously hadn't been devious. But he kept up the heavy boss act. In the end he said he was very busy if she didn't mind. She sloped out like a whipped dog.

The annual company ball was held at The Dorchester. Leonard always enjoyed the occasion. It was an opportunity to talk in a purely social way to colleagues, their husbands and wives, and to the secretaries. People were so much more than they appeared in the office. He was talking to Mary and her husband and another girl when Fanny came up. He saw at once she was drunk, or worse. She looked dreadful. The out-of-date dress - a Laura cast-off? - sagged on her slackly as if it were on a hanger, her hair was adrift.

'Good old Leonard, doing his stuff,' she said loudly, spreading her fingertips on the table for balance. 'The great capitalist expiation, cake for the people.' She slewed into an empty chair. 'Goddam it,' she yelled at the two girls. 'Can't you see through all this codswallop? Can't you see it's all a great bloody cover-up? They give us all this silver service, because they know they've got us by the knackers.' She giggled. 'Or the female equivalent. Take your hands off me, Leonard White, your filthy do-gooding hands. You're just like mother when the chips are down. Though at least she's honestly a selfish bitch and not a lousy hypocrite like you. Don't you realise I despise you?' she screamed.

Half the ballroom came to a stop.

It would have been easy to delegate the job. The Dorchester has people to deal with this kind of difficulty. Leonard felt he had to do it himself. With a mixture of force and coaxing he got her finally out of the limelight and into a quiet corner of the lounge. He thought she was drugged. She would droop for long moments breathing deeply, then rouse herself again into a new spasm of violent abuse. Jenny and others had offered to help, but he thought it best if he stayed with her alone. He knew it was the last service he could render her.

In twenty minutes she seemed calmer. He suggested home. He wondered about the boy and said something to this effect. She flared up. 'That little ponce? Why should I care about him? He never cares for me. He can live his own life. He's fourteen.' But soon after this he got her moving. He loaded her into a taxi.

It was a basement flat. A light was on. The boy was up, reading by the electric-fire. He didn't seem surprised to see them. Together they got her on to the bed, took her shoes off, and covered her. She seemed disposed to sleep. It clearly wasn't the first time something like this had happened. 'She'll be all right in the morning,' Jamie said. The adult calm of the boy moved him. Was he really so difficult? If he was, he had every right to be. But he was more like a resident nurse.

He didn't have to sack her, she resigned. It was a charming letter. She apologised for her behaviour. She realised that he couldn't possibly go on employing her. She didn't know what had come over her that evening, only that she had been depressed and taken a few drinks. 'Probably the wrong mixture.' She thanked him for his decency and concern, when he had all those other people at the dance to think about, and was sorry she had so let him down. With her qualifications she would get another job all right. Probably a better one. After this sentence there were several exclamation marks.

He talked it over with Jenny, and they decided there wasn't much they could do. They either had to do an awful lot, or nothing, half-measures would be useless. He checked with the social services in her area and found they were aware of her as an intermittent problem, but it didn't seem to be drugs. They thought she was basically all right. In the end, pretending it was her due from the company, he sent her a cheque for a thousand pounds. It would perhaps help her until she got another job.

He didn't realise the full effect of the affair until by mistake he saw Laura being interviewed on TV about her book. There she was on the screen suddenly, confident as ever, laying down the law about what should have happened, talking of the great and renowned as if they had been her daily companions and not just people she had interviewed.

He felt a gust of distaste. How could his father have admired her? Had he admired her in fact? He had only Laura's word. He had read her book. It was good - clear, perceptive and, on matters he could judge, accurate. But it made no difference to his feelings. He then realised he had a hostage in the form of her book, which he had done nothing about returning. He should send it to her by post with a note, but he had a better idea. If he hung on to it there was a chance she might come to collect it. He took it back to the office and locked it in a cupboard, when Mary was there to witness what he had done.

She came to the office mid-morning one day when he was in a meeting. Mary slipped in to say Laura only wanted the manuscript. Wasn't it in his office, and couldn't she give it to her without disturbing him? 'No,' he said, 'ask her to wait. I'll be back in my office in a minute.'

She was sitting in one of the chairs still in her coat. 'At last. Why didn't you send it by post? And the girl could surely have given me the book without all this fuss.'

He took his time. 'In a hurry, are you?'

'Madly.'

'There's always time for a few minutes. Drink?' He poured, handed her the glass and sat down. 'I enjoyed the book. Very crisp, and of course the material was always fascinating.'

'Glad you liked it.' Her voice was half-way down the lift shaft.

'The TV interview seemed to go well?'

'I am told it did.'

'You seem very disinterested about it all today, Laura?'

'I tell you, I have an important date for which, thanks to you, I'm going to be late.'

He realised he wasn't going to have time for any preliminaries. He put down his glass untouched. 'I realise you used your book when you came last as an introduction to the subject of Fanny. I'm doing the same, there seems a kind of symmetry about that. You heard what happened?'

She shrugged. 'You sacked her.'

'She resigned actually, though she would have had to go anyway.'

'Well I'm sorry. How was I to know she'd be as daft as that?'

'I'm not blaming you, I'm not asking for an apology. I appointed Fanny because she was a competent secretary. I wish it had worked out.'

'So?'

'She needs your help, Laura, your attention . . .'

Laura rose. She did so with a kind of leisure, like a cat after sleep. 'You can't account for other people's genes. Fanny is just like her father. There's nothing I can do.'

'I think there is.'

'Leonard, if you please, I must go. The book - you have it here, I gather.'

'You mean you take no responsibility for Fanny's troubles, for their cause or their care?'

'None whatsoever, certainly not their cause.'

'Nor for Jamie?'

'Jamie's Fanny's affair.'

'Hasn't it occurred to you that Fanny might be as she is because of the way you've treated her and not because of her genes? Her genes may be as much yours as her father's for that matter.'

She actually smiled as she pulled on her gloves. 'You're even more like your own father than I thought, except he was more outspoken. When he pleaded with me to marry him and I turned him down he called me a bitch.'

'If he called you that perhaps he wasn't so wide of the mark.'

'Never mind, Leonard,' she said as she took her leave. 'In spite of your rather spiteful attempt to lecture me I do forgive you. I realise that to a liberal like you Fanny's behaviour must represent the failure of your ministrations and you have to take it out on someone. You should give up your rather sweet idealism and become a realist like me. You'd certainly be a lot more fun.'

When she had gone he sat at his desk. Her unfinished gin stood on the table and her strong perfume lingered. He had asked for it, he supposed. What did he expect, that she would suddenly collapse and babble to him of a life misspent?

But he supposed he should feel some satisfaction. He had tried at least to perform a last act of decency for Fanny. But he felt only, illogically, as he always did with Laura, a sense of disadvantage. He remembered an old history book he'd had in the fifth form. Prehistoric man, it had said, was divided into two groups, the great majority, who lived in static groups and practised agriculture, and the few who were nomadic food-gatherers, eaters of berries and pluckers of fruit. Laura, he decided, was one of the latter. It was the best he could do to make a case for her. It didn't eliminate his impotent sense of defeat at her hands.

KID BROTHER

The yellow Mercedes convertible zig-zagged from the road and stopped dead by the pump like a toy electric train. Simultaneously the door opened and loud rock hit the forecourt where several other cars were filling.

Billy - tall, trainered, shaggy-sweatered - grabbed the silver nozzle and drew the heads of other motorists, dazed by motorway speed. In the pay-shop the girl had eyes for him as on the way to her desk in rapid succession he picked up two large boxes of chocolates and two teddy-bears. It was as if they had been put there for him to collect.

'Damage for this lot?'

'Sixty-three pounds to you,' she intoned suggestively. 'For yours?' she added, as she took the card, nodding at the bears.

'Nephew and niece.'

The unfulfilled potentiality for fatherhood pleased her. 'You can buy me one next time,' she said as she handed back the card with the receipt.

'Buy you more than a bear.'

The exchange did something for him. Last Christmas he had opted for the Gstaad chalet with the gang, this year they were off to the Bahamas. Several times on the road he had questioned his decision. 'Kiss or kin?' Brenda had mocked when he told where he was going. No doubt she would be bestowing her kisses elsewhere now. But blood was thicker than water, wasn't it - especially with the dimensions of what he had in mind? After the stop he began to believe in himself again. Plenty of fish in the sea.

What had happened to them all? When Mum and Dad were alive - what Christmases then in the crowded suburban house. Other people noticed. 'Well, the Clunes, what would you expect?' was the half-smiling, half-envious response on hearing the noise they made. Endeavour, laughter, pranks, talk, the house always hopping with friends they all brought in - *family solidarity*, that's what they'd had. It seemed then they were all sailing together into life like a convoy.

It was Dad's case of course which started the rot. It was not like a convoy at all after that, but a sunken sub lying on the bottom waiting to be rescued. Within six months, bankrupt, Dad, then Mum, were dead because of it. He was grateful that Gordon and Claudine took up the responsibility - after all it was Gordon who got Uncle Dick to pay for the 'little school in Dorset' he went to - Gordon always called it that, never by its name. But the family seemed to lose vitality. As well, he felt, unlike Mum and Dad, they always belittled him. OK, he was their kid brother and he hadn't their much better education and brains. It was also true that Gordon became an editor in a prestigious publishing house, and Claudine, unmarried, got a good job in the BBC. He'd had to make several changes in what he did. But, all right, now he'd made it big, and there was the chance to put things right.

'Oh no Ana,' said Claudine, 'not at the last minute like this. It's typical of him.'

Ana Clunes, who had come out to help her sister-in-law in with her things, laughed in her hospitable Swedish way. 'Oh, I don't mind. I'm glad he can come. There's plenty to eat, my mother and father love him, and the kids are ecstatic.'

To hide her chagrin, Claudine dived into the back seat of the car for the plastic sack of neatly-wrapped parcels. Ana's last remark crystalised her disappointment. Billy excited the children in quite the wrong way in her opinion, and she had been so looking forward to her quieter, more auntly cherishment of them. What on earth had suddenly made him desert his jazzy friends? Emerging from the car, clutching the sack, their breath billowed on the frosty moonlit air. 'You're so wonderfully tolerant, Ana,' she said. Ana laughed happily.

Ana went into the kitchen. Gordon said nothing of Billy when he greeted her. But later when she was seated with her gin and tonic, and he in his invariable spotted bow-tie and brown corduroy jacket - attended gravely by Emily and Harold handing him things - was standing on a chair to fix a last ornament on the tree, she brought up the subject.

'I hear Billy's coming after all.'

'I believe we are to be graced, yes. We are preferred to the West Indies, I believe, despite his new-found riches. We should preen ourselves.'

'A girl has let him down most likely.'

She wasn't sure if Gordon registered this. 'There,' he said, descending. 'finished.' He looked up admiringly at his handiwork, humourously pushing up his spectacles in the way which always reassured her. 'Pretty good, children, don't you think?' Harold gave a jump, Emily did a pirouette - her arms out, like a ballerina. But Gordon had heard all right. 'I daresay you're accurate about our own dear Billy,' he added, turning his head aside to her as he went to wash his hands.

She relaxed. Thank goodness for Gordon, who was so solid and reliable, Claudine thought. He of course would administer any necessary bromides if Billy got out of hand. Her premonitions were groundless. She felt even more secure in this thought later when, in front of a wood fire prancing in the grate, Harold grappled at her feet with bright plastic and Emily, snuggled by her side, drew with her crayons. Sipping a second gin, a Bach Oratorio in the background, she answered genial questions about her work from Ana's parents, Susanna and Gustav, over from Sweden.

The multi-tone hooter shattered the set-piece. Emily threw her drawing to the floor. 'It's Billy,' she shrieked. Harold scrambled after her, Gustav's eager face accepting defeat just as he was developing his views on Swedish broadcasting compared with ours. A door banged and Ana came running downstairs.

'Happy Christmas, darlings.' Joyful bedlam broke loose in the hall. Claudine heard Ana's warm welcome, Emily's clamouring to see the car, and at last Gordon's sardonic 'a prodigal appearance.'

Billy entered, the old couple rose sharply, like choristers bid by the conductor to sing, Susanna smoothing her hips as if to remove an inch or two. Billy after momentary hesitation kissed Susanna - it was only their second meeting - and shook hands with Gustav. Against her intention, Claudine also rose and was embraced.

'And how's Auntie?' she heard, in the routine, sing-song voice Billy always used to enquire after her work at the BBC, as if this were her only interest in life.

'Wheezing, but reasonably sound, I suppose,' she heard herself say, also a stock kind of reply.

Billy had already turned to the children. 'Goodies, darlings?' He had dumped two baskets in the hall. Fetching these, he distributed a teddy bear each, a ham and a cheese to Ana, chocolates to herself and to the elder Swedes.

'But presents are tomorrow,' chanted Ana, stricken.

'These aren't pressies, darling, only the horsey derves. Get the party going.' He reached for the last items, two bottles of champagne. 'Ice?' he said to Gordon's look of neutral spectatorship. 'No ice? Never mind. Then glasses?' Already untwisting the wire, he looked to Ana.

'To the family - both sides of the North Sea,' he toasted as, primed, they stood like a ring of waits singers.

Claudine grew interested. Something new had happened, she saw. This was not the usual inferiority complex, the smart display based on money he had borrowed or on some small and ephemeral success. There was a new confidence and excitement about him, as if - yes - as if holding the centre of the stage was no act of aggression *but a permanent natural right*.

He did not long keep them uninformed. Susanna said how generous he was to supply the champagne. Billy revealed how in the last months he had led his firm of estate agents into the recent London property boom, and that he had 'trawled a crumb or two from the great gesump.' She could believe it - believe also that he had played a leading part. Could it be that in the sale of property he had at last found the natural habitat for his talents?

She was pleased for him. If he was suddenly going to be rich, perhaps he would settle down and not be so compulsively lively. But his ubiquitous shallowness, flitting here and there, began to alarm her again. Why was this, she struggled to understand?

An uncomfortable explanation offered itself. Were not Billy's excesses in reality not vanity and inferiority at all - as Gordon had always said - but the result of a greater dynamism, more *joie de vivre*? If it was, she feared how Gordon might act. Last week he had been passed over for a more senior post.

But it seemed it was, as usual, Gordon to the rescue. Hand over hand, by remote control, he brought Billy back. No part of his regulatory contempt could be proved, yet there it was in every silence, in each manipulation of his eyebrows, in the faint grin which held the rather vulnerable mouth firm. The few shafts there were were heavily alibied, could even be thought humorous.

By dinner the situation seemed stable. The kids had at last been sealed upstairs, more exhausted than pacified, food was neutralising the champagne, and Gordon was being sagely frugal with the table wine. With Billy safely corralled by the Swedish steers, she was able to have a good discussion with Gordon and Ana about Gordon's latest publications.

She was aware that Gustav was talking politics, not Billy's forte, she sensed Billy's impatience, but she was not ready for the stark way in which he tore free.

'This house is too small for you now, Gord,' he said loudly. 'It's the Gawd's truth, ha ha.'

Gordon made a manful appearance of not hearing, and continued for a phrase or two on his explanation for the dominance of women novelists in Britain. It was like a soloist continuing when the orchestra had stopped.

'You need a bigger place,' Billy reiterated.

Claudine watched her elder brother as if her life depended on it. Surely he would cope with this in his stride. 'Or do we, I wonder?' he said, picking up his cheese knife unnecessarily and putting it down again.

'Your two little crotchets grow by day. What you need now is to move out of town. I've been in to it. Only half an hour out of the Great Wen. There are still bargains if you know where to look. What you need is an old rectory.'

'Really, I'll speak to my advisers about it.'

'You don't have to.   Look, I was going to tell you this tomorrow, but no time like . . . etcetera.   I've got just the thing for you, not yet on the market but going to be very soon.   Didn't have time to case the joint, but from the bumph, and from our man in Hazelmere, it looks ideal.   Solid Victorian, it's got everything.   Derelict tennis court, overgrown herb garden, four reception, six beds.'   He leered at Ana.   'Room for three more, darling.   Three acres and a cow, and all for three fifty.   You'll have to modernise of course, eighty grand should do it, I'm told.   Hang on, I've managed to get the prospectus, just out.'

He rose and bounded from the room.   Ana looked to her parents, exchanging their pleasant surprise.

'A very friendly tip-off,' Gordon said to anyone listening.   'And accompanied, no doubt, by a miraculous loan from on high to pay for it.'

But Billy had heard.   'Right in one,' he said, returning more quickly than expected.   'You've hit it.   A heavenly loan *is* at hand.'   He threw the quite glossy brochure in front of Gordon.   'I realise you might be a bit pinched, publishing not necessarily being in the jack-pot zone these days.   Here it comes.   I'm prepared to offer you two hundred grand of it sans interest for as long as it takes.   It's been my year and "push it around" is my motto, you know that - as the mule on the treadmill said.   You can pay it back when you publish your next best-seller.   It's my Christmas present to you both.'

There were tense moments.   Gordon's grey cheeks were faintly tinted.   Claudine prayed he would not allow the tension to continue, prayed he would gently lance it with some effective levity or, at the very least, take the amazing offer seriously.   He did neither.   'As always, how delightfully absurd you still are,' was what he half-muttered, returning to his food.   For once wit had deserted him.   She could see that he was, nakedly, furious.

Billy turned to Ana.   'He doesn't believe me, Ana.   I tell you, the money's there, rotting in the bank.   *You* believe me, don't you?   It's only right.   The money game's a lottery.   Dad hit a land mine.   It could happen to anyone.   I've hit it lucky.   I share it round the family, who looked after me when I was a kid.   The most natural thing in the world.   It's what families are for, isn't it?'

The air was black.   Claudine was going to say something anodyne, but Gordon's fury broke.   'You ignorant ass,' she heard.   'You haven't learnt the first thing about life, have you? Do you really think, even if you have robbed enough house-hungry people to cover such a sum, that I'd . . .'   She put her hand on his sleeve but he ignored it.   'That I'd be a party to your dubious enterprises?   You're certainly a fat chip off your father all right.'

'Father?   But I'm proud of Dad, Gord.   It wasn't his fault the market turned against him.   And isn't he your father for that matter as much as mine?'

'Father was a crook.   Are you too stupid even to realise *that*?'

'He was innocent of those charges.'

'*You're* innocent if you think that.'

'He was framed, caught without cash for a period because he had been generous.'

'He cheated and defrauded.   If his associates hadn't been frightened of their own necks and spilt the beans, they'd all have gone to gaol.'

She saw Billy gather himself in a way she could not have foreseen.   He was not angry, she saw, only *concerned*, concerned for Gordon.

'It might be, you know,' he began, his voice calm, intrepid, modest, above all curious at itself.   'Might just be it's you who isn't being quite honest at the moment.'

'And what's that supposed to mean?'

Billy hooked his arm amiably over the back of his chair. 'Well, isn't it possible that after Dad's misfortune you had to dig in rather, go head down for what you knew you could do - and do well, I'm not saying that, and you kept us all going - but forgetting . . .'

'Forgetting what?'

'Forgetting we were once a united family . . .'

It was Boxing Day.   The house had stilled suddenly - Billy had left early, Gordon had gone out to see someone, Susanna and Gustav had taken the children out. Claudine was in the kitchen with Ana. Through the window a high winter sun watched distantly through a hazy veil of cloud. Claudine strove to adjust herself. New patterns had emerged.

One of the new things was her relationship to Ana. She had always seen Ana, and her nice straightforward parents, as something Gordon, and herself to a lesser extent, had taken on as an annexe. Even Ana's children were not entirely her own, as they saw them. They were Clunes, Ana their carrier merely, a hired accomplice. And yet the very way Ana was humming now, so relaxed as she deftly diced the meat, stripping out the little pieces of fat and gristle, told her how wrong this was. This was her house - she, Claudine, the visitor. The Clunes, with one exception, had behaved badly, abominably, yet here was Ana absorbing it all, forgiving, placing it, understanding. The Clunes were the outsiders.

Claudine took the first consignment of floured beef chunks and pushed them into the pan, for she was helping with the cooking. 'It was nice yesterday, Ana, really nice, despite everything.' She hoped this sounded convincing.

'Oh, it was lovely.'

'The children were enchanted,'

'We all were.'

It wasn't easy for her to yield position, put the truth out to tender like this, but she must persist. She moved a step nearer. 'I'm glad you persuaded Billy to stay until today.'

'I wish he could have stayed longer.'

'He was hurt of course.' Ana was silent. She plunged. 'Would you yourself like to accept his offer, if the house is nice?'

'I don't think Gordon ever would.'

'I know that. That wasn't my question.'

Ana hardly paused. She knew her mind. 'Yes - *if* the house is what we'd like of course. And not only for myself of course.'

'You mean for Billy?'

'For Billy, yes. Also for Gordon. Perhaps for all of us.'

'Why?'

'It would expiate something, wouldn't it? What's the English expression? "Redress the balance."'

'How do you mean that exactly, Ana?'

'Well, the effect your father's case had on you all. You *are* a very united family, you know, underneath.'

'Gordon, too?'

'Gordon perhaps, as the eldest, most of all.'

Ana was doing the pastry now, rolling it on the chopping board. She refloured her hand and ran it up the rolling-pin. 'I think that's about the thickness, don't you?' she said a moment or two later.

Claudine stayed another day. There was no more talk on the subject. But Gordon was pensive. He had made a verbal repair to the fence which surrounded his magisterial assurance, but behind it she knew something had changed, perhaps permanently.

As for herself, she was sure things would never be quite the same again and that this was a good thing. Gordon wouldn't accept the loan. Billy, as always, had gone much too far. He had gone off - a temporary casualty of his own outsized generosity. She determined that as soon as possible she would let him know that he shouldn't feel this way, that he had been right in what he did, and that in some other less ostentatious way, assisted by readjustments in Gordon's mind, in the course of time . . .

When she left them, she kissed Gordon quickly on the cheek. He was too surprised to object, and gave her a sort of sideways peck back. Ana she embraced warmly. Driving to her flat she felt a light-hearted happiness. Good old Billy. Who would have thought it would be him who put the pieces back on the board?

DARLING, HOW LOVELY TO SEE YOU

For a moment Alistair thought he had mistaken the house. It looked as if it had been skinned. The massive mantle of ivy had gone, the walls had been re-rendered and painted brilliant cream. The garden, once the jungle Father had always insisted on, was neatly parcelled into level manicured lawns, bordered with gaudy bloom. Most surprising of all, on a sloping bank on one side of the now tarmacked drive, small flowers depicted the arms of the Royal Air Force with the words 'Per Ardua ad Astra.'

They must have been on the look-out for his arrival. As he drove in, the procession came out. Alistair had a vision of them lined up behind the door like a guard of honour waiting the order. First came mother, with arms outstretched as if she were sleep-walking, his sister Jenny next - she at least, Alistair noted with relief, seemed to have undergone no outward change - and last Giles, new master of the refurbished ship.

The Braithwaites had never been kissers. Returns from absences, even perhaps one as long as his, could be expected to pass off without comment, as if the absentee had just been down the road. Alistair found himself engulfed in an unprecedented embrace. 'Darling, how lovely to see you.' She stepped back as if to steady herself. 'And this, Alistair, is Giles. He has been so looking forward to meeting you.'

Alistair had no reason to doubt it. There he stood in the doorway, in blue summer-weight trousers, white shoes, and an open-neck white shirt sporting a brown silk scarf. His huge domed head was like an overrisen loaf. Sunshine flashing on his spectacles, he was grinning ruefully. 'Welcome home, Alistair,' he said. A long arm came forward on the end of which was a hand the size of a dinner-plate. 'Still just about *recognise* it as your home, eh?'

Alistair made a rapid adjustment. When Father died two years ago, Mother wrote that nothing would ever console her for her loss, but if Giles had so miraculously filled this deficiency, who was he to make comparisons? Mother's life, as ever, was her own.   Jenny was sending him eye signals, but he avoided them.   Whatever Jenny thought, he would be amiably neutral.

There was a moment of tension after the introduction.   But Giles had been peering under Alistair's car. He seemed suddenly to go berserk. 'Emergency, scramble,' he shouted, and rushed off frenetically towards the garage.

Alistair looked at Mother.   She seemed as mystified as he was, but she was smiling benificently as if to assure that all would be revealed.   It was Jenny who saw what was happening. Bending over, she was also peering under Alistair's old Escort. Alistair did likewise.   Pleased to be at rest after the long journey from London, the engine was quietly leaking oil on to the immaculate tarmac.

Giles reappeared at the double with a tin box and a metal tray which seemed to have wheels.   Lying on the tray he shot under the car.   Seconds later he reemerged, clashing his hands together like cymbals.   'Well, finger in the dyke at least, the tin'll catch it now. Probably only a gasket.   Want me to take a dekko, Alistair? No time like the present.'

They peered together under the bonnet.   The haemorrhage turned out not to be a gasket, no more than a loose screw, which Giles's spanner soon fixed.

The emergency dealt with, they found the women had gone in. Alistair found himself being regarded conspiratorially.   'Seems we've been left alone,' he said. 'Care to inspect one or two of my little improvements before you go in?'

Alistair was shown a new summer house on the bottom lawn. Behind a discreet ring of conifers at the top of the garden, there was an incinerator - Giles's own brickwork, he was told.   A home-made concrete sundial had to be admired, also a minor saw-mill where the trees, which once had shielded the Braithwaites from the stare of the outside world, now lay severed and stacked in architectural heaps of logs. They returned finally to the garage, outside which Giles stopped.   'Prepare for the biggest surprise of all,' he said.

They entered.   It wasn't the garage itself which, though now clean and uncluttered, housed a car as it always had.   It was the large room beyond, Father's laboratory - always Alistair's favourite in the whole rambling house - which had undergone the change. On one side had been a long mahogany bench, fitted with two gas burners, retorts, test tubes of every shape and size, two small adjacent sinks. Behind the bench, attached to the wall, had been shelves filled with romantic ceramic jars which announced the chemicals they contained in gothic letters. The rest of the room, from floor to ceiling, had been filled with books, books of every sort, for though Father had been a free-lance research chemist who did work for large pharmaceutical firms, he was an avid reader, of catholic taste.

The place had been purged. There was not a book (or a cobweb) to be seen. The old worn lino had been replaced by spanking tiles on which, at the far end stood a brand-new metal structure standing over a wide metal tub. It looked like a corking machine. The bench was still there but held now, instead of retorts, four rows of a dozen or more large demijohns, the front ones corked with S-shaped gas escape-valves, each with a printed name on its side. 'Elder-flower Cordial, Apple-Juice Elixir Extra Sweet,' he read. 'Loganberry Liqueur, Wortle Brew, Home Sloe Gin (in brackets 'Mother's Ruin.') . . . Like officers inspecting troops, they went down the line, Giles keeping up a non-stop flow of instruction on his wine-making processes. The front jars were fermenting, he explained, the rear ones contained the finished product, which would soon be bottled. Finally, Giles opened a cupboard under the sink. A glass was produced, and he was given a sample of 'the Elder Flower.' Though oversweet it was not unpleasant.

Giles chortled. 'Not bad stuff, eh? My latest. It's the natural juice, you see. Organic, no impurities. Not like the poison they sell in the shops, full of chemicals. People will take to it, I tell you. In a year or two they'll be clamouring. This little hut will be a mere outhouse. Your mother hasn't realised the full potential yet. There's a fortune pending.'

'You mean you're hoping . . .'

'Not hoping, Alistair, full scale commercial production is *imminent*. I have the sources of fruit, the bottling, the logo, the labelling, sorted.   The outlets are already identified, among them a supermarket.   The supermarket is jibbing a bit, as they would at something so new, but pretty soon it and the others'll be falling over themselves.   In a few years your Mother and I will be comfortably off, I may say a great deal more comfortably off than your old Pater was able to leave her . . .

'Now I can guess what's in your mind.   You're wondering how all this has come to pass *financially*.   Quite a proper thing for a son *to* wonder, who has an inheritance to consider.   Well, I won't conceal that your Mother has helped with the initial outlay. A service pension doesn't exactly capitalise a venture of these proportions.   But fear not.   The talents will not be buried, they will be multiplied an hundredfold.'

Alistair's attention was wandering.   Despite his earlier resolution, he was thinking why Mother, normally so outspoken, had been totally silent about all this in her letters, and how it was that a woman who, whatever her occasional remonstances at Father's eccentricity, had been proud of his learning and his contempt for material display, could have apparently switched her preferences so radically.

One thing hadn't changed.   Temporarily at least in her domain, at lunch Mother stood at the serving end of the table sluicing brown gravy over fat pork chops whose isthmuses embraced steaming mounds of apple-sauce, home-grown runner-beans and new potatoes.   Just for a moment Alistair felt Giles was the visitor, the odd man out.

The anomaly was short-lived.   Giles began to describe the improvements he had made inside the house, how the perilously thin water-tanks had been replaced - thus saving them all from certain inundation - how the wiring system, allowed to fall into 'astonishing decay', had been 'rooted out' and replaced. Throughout, Mother said nothing, eating with a faint complacent smile, her eyes lowered.

In a small interstice in the monologue Alistair asked Mother about her painting.   She had made quite a name for herself in the local Art Society.   'Oh all that,' she said dismissively, 'I don't have too much time for that sort of thing these days.' She brightened. 'But Giles is something of an artist, you know. As well as all the other things he has done, he has produced that.' She pointed to a ship in a bottle mounted on a piece of wood on the sideboard. Alistair gave up.

When they had got through a large bowl of raspberries and cream with cheese to follow, there was a noticeable change in the atmosphere. Giles stopped talking and glanced significantly at Mother. Mother seemed cued by this. 'Had enough, everyone?' she said in a different voice. 'Jenny? Alistair?' Her jaw took on a more familiar stubborn set, and a peculiar hush descended. Giles closed his eyes, Jenny kept hers open but inclined her head marginally, and Mother, gripping the edge of the table with both hands as if she feared levitation, also squeezed her eyes shut as if she were peeling onions.

'For what we have received may the Lord make us truly thankful,' Giles rattled off. There was a slight pause as he reopened his eyes. 'And all the other stations to Brighton,' he added.

Alistair expected a pentecostal change, but there they all were, Giles grinning over his spectacles, Mother, firm-lipped now, getting up to clear.

Religion to Father had been anathema. 'It's no good thinking you can tidy up the mysteries of cosmic chaos with fairy-stories,' he had said once. Mother had seemed to echo this indifference to institutional explanations of the universe. Jenny and Alistair washed up alone. It was the first opportunity they'd had to talk.

'How has it happened?' Alistair said. 'How can she have swivelled a hundred and eighty degrees like this?'

'She'd certainly qualify as a whirling Dervish these days,' Jenny said.

'Yes, religion, too, apparently. Do they go to church?'

'Indefatigably. Giles is a sidesman and sits on the Church Council.'

'Is Mother happy?'

'As a sandboy, I'd say.'

'It's as if she were never married to Father.'

'Perhaps she never was.   Perhaps it's a figment of our imagination.'

'Well, I suppose it's a good thing, isn't it?   Giles is certainly amiable enough.'

'That's what I tell myself every day.'

Alistair decided three days would be the minium period of decency he could stay.

They had coffee in the sitting-room.   Books, which had abounded throughout the house as well as the lab, had thinned noticeably.   But he thought he would like to have one or two quite valuable volumes on anthropology - his subject - if Mother would spare them.   They surely had been kept.   'I think they used to be in a glass case in the hall,' he said.

There was at once an atmosphere.   'Oh yes, dear,' Mother said, attempting the off-hand, 'the old case which had broken glass.   I think you gave the case away, Giles, didn't you?   But I'm sure you have the books somewhere safe?'

Giles dropped a spoon and dived under the table to recover it. Mother had to repeat the question.   'Books dear?' he said innocently.

'Yes.   They are rather valuable ones, which of course Alistair must have now.   You remember I told you that at the time.'

'Did you?'

'Giles, you know I did.   You don't mean to tell me you gave the books away, too?'

'Must have done.'

Something seemed to snap.   Complacent, benevolent smiles, had he thought?   A sea-change in Mother's character?   A storm of Beethovian fury broke.   'Well, you had absolutely no right to do it without asking my permission,' she said.   'I'm quite surprised you should be capable of such a thing.'

'I'm an amazing fellow,' said Giles, looking at Alistair.

'It's not a joking matter.   I'd've thought a person of your sensibility would have known they were valuable even if I hadn't told you.'

'I can't be very sensible then, can I?'

'*Giles.*'

'Yes, dear?'

'Alistair would have liked those books, they were his Father's, they will help with his work. And there is another point while we're on the subject. That grace you said at lunch - what you said after it.'

'What about it?'

'In my opinion that was inconsistent of you.'

'Oh that - learnt that in the services.'

'In the Air Force perhaps, but why should you feel it necessary here? You believe in grace, don't you? You introduced me to it. Why should you now want to apologise for it?'

'Apologize? Did I?'

'Of course you did, with that phrase.'

Giles rocked in his seat and looked embarrassed. 'Well, what if I did,' he said with a wink at Alistair. 'After all we've got a couple of heathens here, haven't we? Can't have them feeling uncomfortable.'

'Alistair is not a heathen,' persisted Mother, 'he's an agnostic. I'm quite sure, even if he doesn't agree with grace, he would be sympathetic to it without any apology from you being necessary. To my mind it shows a feeling of uncertainty on your part.' She rose. 'I'm sorry, Giles, you have disappointed me over these two matters. Alexander did not have your practical abilities, but he was a deeply thoughtful man. Alistair has inherited that quality. Getting rid of those books has shown a lack of respect. If you'll excuse me, I'm going upstairs. Alistair's coming home has made me want to paint again. We'll all meet at tea-time.'

Alistair was sorry for Giles. Father and Mother having been what they were, he and Jenny had been brought up to ride such brutal revelations of the truth. Giles, presumably, had not. When Giles suggested an inspection of the new electronic security system he had installed, he agreed. But from the word go this was a non-starter. Giles had lost his enthusiasm. Probing in the fuse-box, he gave himself a shock. This seemed to do final damage to his spirits.

'Well, I don't know if you really want to see any more of my stuff, do you?' he said. 'You're not a gadget freak like me.'

'I don't mind,' Alistair said.

'Decent of you. But look . . .' He seemed to brighten. 'Look there is one other item I think might interest you. Something more in your line, being a seasoned traveller and a man of the world.'

He led the way back to the garage. He entered the laboratory by its own outside door and marched towards the far end. He took something from his pocket and pointed it at the ceiling where there was a trap door, which in Father's day led to a loft room where unwanted junk was stowed. There was an electronic clonk, and the trap began to fall, opening behind it a concertina-ed staircase which extended itself slowly downwards until it reached the ground. Giles's eyes flashed. 'How about that for a marvel of modern science?' He again pointed the gadget in his hand, clicked twice, and a light sprang on above. 'Follow me,' he said.

The attic had clearly become another workshop. Gone was the rubbish, instead was another, much rougher bench on which there were two vices, an electric saw, and a small lathe. Hanging behind it was a gallery of gleaming tools - saws, chisels, hammers and clamps. But these apparently were not the interest. Producing from his pocket a bunch of keys attached by an umbilical silver chain to a trouser button, Giles selected a small intricate-looking one and got on his knees to open what appeared to be a cupboard built into the plaster-board panelling at floor level. It would not have been noticeable had he not called attention to it in this way.

Swinging open the door, he reached inside. 'I have something here even your mother doesn't know about,' he chuckled. 'Something she wouldn't necessarily approve of. It's by way of an experiment.' He brought out a small glass and a half-size bottle containing a colourless liquid. He regained his feet, put the glass on the bench and, holding up the bottle, tapped it with the joint of his first finger. 'Potato-base, seventy per cent proof. Shan't tell even you where I keep the distillery. To be honest I don't know how legal it is. You'll understand the need for discretion.'

The first sip was like a karate-blow to the side of the neck. At the end of the glass, which they handed back and forth between them Alistair could feel blue flames light in his stomach and creep up to his throat. After the second glass, his stomach blazed like a furnace. The sensation was not unpleasant.

Apparently Giles was no more immune. Alistair received a sudden blow with the flat of his hand on his back. 'How about that, Alistair? Bit of the all right, eh? *Not* quite what you expected from your new Dad.'

There was another refill. Giles was now unstoppable. 'Not that I'm a tippler, far from it,' he chattered on. 'You don't get where I got in the Service with that sort of thing. Finished Squadron-Leader, you know, and that's no mean achievement nowadays. And one has principles of course. Take religion for instance. Oh, I know your Father didn't go in for religion too much, and quite frankly I don't go so much on parsons - perfectly ordinary chaps like us when all's said and done. But one's got to hang on to something, that's what I say. Like grace. I've always said grace and I see no reason to stop. Your Mother likes it, too, really, whatever she said just now. She likes to have a strap to hang on to. Why, I daresay even your Dad offered a silent prayer or two before he was mixing up his brews of chemicals. We're all the same when it comes down to it. That's what I tell your Mother. You know there are times when she wonders whether she did the right thing hitching up with me - after your Father. But there's no need to make comparisons. Every man his own kit-bag, don't you agree?'

'Well, yes . . .'

'Of course you do, Alistair. I can see you aren't one to stand on ceremony. Saw it the moment you arrived as a matter of fact. There, I said to myself, is your best type of modern chap - easygoing, yet not sloppy. I knew we'd get on, have another?'

At tea, Mother appeared in her old smock. She lay back in her chair, eyes closed, letting Jenny do all the work of putting out plates and pouring. It was a posture Alistair well remembered, indicating creative exhaustion after hours at her easel.

'Well, I think Alistair is now conversant with the estate of our little realm, Mother,' Giles said loudly, giving Alistair an ill-concealed wink. 'We have visited the various marvels and also examined some of my - er - gear in the lab. A cursory glance, mind you, but enough to let our friend here know what has been achieved.' He giggled drunkenly.

Mother's eyes opened wide as she turned to Alistair. It was as if she hadn't heard. 'Alistair, I am ashamed. Since you arrived you've heard of nothing but us. We've asked nothing about your wonderful doings in America. We don't seem to have corresponded much lately, have we? Those Shaker People you have been studying in Ohio, sound quite fascinating. Your Father would have wanted to know all about them.'

Alistair was wheeling like a roulette wheel. 'Oh, they're a long story,' he said.

'I've been reading about them, you know, knowing you were coming home. I did take your advice on that book you recommended a long time ago, and have consumed it. The cultural aspects of their life are very enthralling . . .'

'Lot of dear old Yankee Doodlers,' Giles interrupted.

'Utterly enthralling, and I . . .'

'What do you know about Yankee sects, my dear? You've never been over there. You forget I was in Canada five years training their pilots.'

'Giles, if you don't mind, just for a few minutes I would like·. . .'

'Five years. As for Shakers, I've read all about them in The Digest. Fine magazine, that one. None of your arty-crafty nonsense, gets things pared down to their essentials. There was a piece on - well not Shakers actually, but Moonies. Same sort of stuff, though, wouldn't you say?'

'Giles, will you please, just for once . . .'

'Shut up? Course I will, my dear. Talking too much as usual, but it just happens that Alistair and I . . .'

'Have been drinking. That is plainly obvious.' Tight-lipped, she rose, holding her tea-cup. 'If you'll excuse me, Alistair, I'm going upstairs again. Perhaps you'd like to pop up later when you've had tea. We can have the talk I am so looking forward to.'

After tea Giles began to mow the lawns at frenetic speed. Jenny disappeared, and Alistair saw no alternative to doing as his mother had bid.

He had expected to find her at her easel, but she wasn't painting. The curtains were half-drawn, and she was sitting very upright in her chintzy chair with Boris Pasternak's *Dr Zhivago* held before her in one hand, like a breviary. There were no traces of her anger.

'Have a seat. What a truly great book this is,' she said, lowering it reverently.

'Yes.'

'Such breadth of view, and right in the Russian tradition.'

'Mm.'

'It lifts one from the trough of life.' She placed the book carefully on the table beside her. 'One does of course need something like this now and then.'

'Yes?'

'I can no longer paint, you see. I did try this afternoon but for some reason the urge has departed from me. But one can still read to keep contact with the past.' The clock on the mantelpiece seemed to tick faster. 'I need contact with the past. As you can see, wonderful man as he is, like all human beings Giles does lack certain qualities which, well, your father had. Humour perhaps, too. A sense of proportion.'

'Yes, but . . .'

'Qualities which you have got, which *I* have got to a lesser extent. And you must realise, dear, what a very good man Giles is. He has been so kind and sweet to me.'

'Of course, Mother.'

'And another thing, he never bears any ill-will, however much I tell him off, which I'm afraid I do sometimes.'

'But I have never . . .'

'You see he has led a very different sort of life.' A
Pre-Raphaelite glow suffused her face. 'To be quite frank, I
think Giles even has a touch of genius about him, and geniuses
must be allowed a little eccentricity. You must certainly not
look down your nose at him, or that would rebound on you. In
fact, if Giles has been a bit excited today it has probably been
because of his awareness of your criticism. He is hyper-
sensitive.'

'Look, Mother . . .'

'Now I know what you're going to say, dear. But you
mustn't. You mustn't even *think* it. All right, I too was myself
a little short-tempered just now until I gave myself time to think
and restore the inner truth of the situation. But now I have done
so.' She rose, and went to the window. 'I see Giles is finishing
the lawn. What I suggest is that in half an hour or so we all
foregather for a nice drink. I'm sure Giles will supply us with
one of the low alcohol *wines*.'

Alistair couldn't remember afterwards the exact train of events.
He had reinforced his decision to ride it out. If Mother had
decided to precipitate herself into another incarnation, why
should he care? It was another sign of her immense versatility.

He was sure he felt no different when, all of them seated and
well-supplied with 'Parsnip Champagne', Mother and Giles
began a loud conversation with each other about Church affairs.
If it went on any longer, Alistair was thinking, he could quietly
move to sit next to Jenny, who had parked herself somewhat
apart. They had hardly talked. But Giles prevented it.

'But look here, Mother,' he said, 'here we are gassing away,
and we're forgetting our Alistair, who probably isn't in the least
interested in our little goings-on. You must feel all this is very
small-fry compared with what you get up to?'

He meant it kindly, Alistair was sure, and he was about to
compose a suitable denial. Something happened to Mother. A
flush sprang to her cheeks.

'If he thinks that, he is quite wrong,' she said briskly. 'Our
local church affairs are in no way "little". You don't have to be

an intellectual to qualify for importance.'

Giles smirked. 'Oh, I don't know if I'd put it like that,' he said. 'If I could be made an egg-head tomorrow, I'd become one like a shot.'

'No, you wouldn't. You would be very foolish to. Intellectual pursuits are not the bee-all-and-end-all of everything. If Alistair thinks that, he is quite wrong.'

'But I don't think Alistair does, Mother. Alistair and I have been . . .'

'Alistair, like his father, is apt, I'm afraid to put his head in the clouds sometimes.'

There was more. He remembered something about living in the past, living among weird communities - and about living abroad - which had somehow severed him from reality. Then he lost control. The last thing he remembered clearly was the urgent look on Jenny's face, trying to restrain him.

'Will you kindly shut up, Mother?' he must have said, or something to that effect. 'I have made no comment on anything since arriving here, and have no wish to. If anyone's burying their head in the sand it's you. You're jumping to conclusions of pole-vaulting dimensions about what I'm thinking.'

What he said, he knew, would probably no more than confirm Mother's charge against him. But it certainly brought things to a close.

It was Giles who brought them back from the abyss. He said a great deal more about the Moonies. By supper they had returned to something like normality. But it decided him. At breakfast he announced that he really thought he would have to depart today.

There were no remonstrations. 'He's got his flat to see to, friends to see,' Giles said to Mother. She also apparently took it in her stride. 'I understand, dear, I'm sure you have an immense amount to do.' The parting scene seemed as normal as any family departure in the past.

'It was *so* lovely to see you,' Mother said. 'I'm sure you'll be coming down again soon.' She felt for her lover's left arm.

Alistair shook hands with Giles's disengaged right hand.

'Bye, old chap,' he said.   He winked.   'Probably have some new prototypes next time you come.'

He looked sideways at Mother.   She grinned.

LIKE IN THE COUNTRY

Ken started the gardening job during the strike. He didn't want to be out. Most didn't. It was Waites again, and the other stewards, that brought it on. He didn't like being without the money, especially with alimony to pay. Above all he didn't like doing nothing, now he was alone.

The job at The Limes was a godsend. He had tried most of the other houses on the hill and was going to give up. Mrs Prideaux opened the door to him herself. While he stood there telling her what he could do - decorating and the like - she eyed him from head to foot. He didn't mind this. The others had just been polite in the usual way, this at least showed some interest.

'You wouldn't like to do some gardening, I suppose?'

She kept her distance. No question of any liberties, even if he'd wanted to take them. The money wasn't much, the work hard - she wanted a whole area cleared and dug. But she made things clear before he started, looked him in the eye, and some days came out to work with him. She could certainly lift a spade. 'I can work with you, Ken,' she said once. 'You don't cut corners, and give value for money.' He did that, he thought, more than most.

When the job was done and the strike over, she offered him three hours regularly, Sundays. He enjoyed the work. In the winter it was more digging, and weeding. When it was wet, wood-cutting. In the Spring he took on all the mowing. He could have done with a sit-machine like the one next door, but he took a pride in keeping the three lawns trim, edges too, and it was nice to be out in the air after a week in the works. He liked the neighbourhood, peaceful. Where he lived there was always a dog barking, or a young madman racing his car up the street, and raised voices in the other half of his house. Sometimes when he turned the mower off it seemed like he was in the country. He'd been brought up in the country. The big house dozed among the trees and the massed flowers and shrubs.

Mr Prideaux was a banker. A large, bald, quiet man, he

didn't come out into the garden, only to the garage to get into his German car. Ken saw him standing in one of the bay windows sometimes, hands in pockets, staring towards the horizon at nothing in particular. There were three children. On fine mornings, the eldest, Jennifer, went off to play tennis, serious but eager. 'Good morning, Ken,' she said as she came across the lawn in her white dress. 'You *are* making the lawns look nice.' Learning to be grown-up, he supposed. James he didn't take to much. He wasn't home a lot, but when he was, came out to interrupt his work. He wanted him to talk about the firm and the strikes. 'Why do you go along with them then?' he said when he learnt he wasn't keen on being out. 'Why don't you speak out at the meetings?' Cheeky ponce. Studying social something-or-other at university.

Lorinne was the youngest. Left school when she was sixteen and as far as he knew was helping Mrs Prideaux with the house. Right away he saw she was different. She didn't seem to belong to the others. She was always busy, self-contained, usually with her pets. She had rabbits, budgerigars in an aviary, and a large white cat. One Sunday she came looking for the cat, which was missing. 'You haven't seen him by any chance, have you?' she said, 'he's been out all night.'

They had a conversation about the cat and where it might be. He really tried to think for her. Someone had fed it perhaps, it was a handsome beast. It'd be back for its next mealtime, he said. But he had the sense she was no longer so interested in the cat. They were in the shed, where he was changing the mower oil. She was looking round.

'I used not to like this place,' she said, 'you've made it nice.'

He got out his pipe, knocked it on the bench, he was due for a break. As he lit up, she looked at the pile of wood he'd cut and stacked.

'Do you like working here?' she asked, still looking at the wood.

'It's all right.'

'But don't you think we're all so, well, *isolated*, up here in these *compounds?*'

He had to ask her to explain what she meant. She didn't explain really but wanted to know where he lived. 'I mean I'm sure people where you live don't cut themselves off from each other.'

He had to laugh at that. What did she know about where he lived? 'Oh, but I do know a lot,' he was surprised to hear. 'I know exactly where your house is. You gave my mother your address and I went to look.'

This alarmed him. He thought about it all week. What on earth would she want to do a thing like that for? Some kind of an intellectual trip like the boy, was it? He didn't think so.

The next week it was raining and he was in the shed most of the morning. She came in again. He noticed her clothes, dressed up a bit. Was she going out?

'You know where Simpkin was, don't you?' were her first words. 'In here. All the time we were talking last week he was curled up behind those potato sacks. I came back here after you'd gone. You see, you've made it so nice in here, Simpkin knows what's good.'

He knew for sure something was up that day. She asked him if she could come and see him at his house one evening in the week. He'd imagined a quick visit, a cup of tea and, after thinking, said he didn't see why not if she really wanted to. But as soon as he agreed, she said she would cook his 'dinner' as she called it. When he said that wasn't necessary she danced away. 'Leave the front-door key under the mat and I'll have it ready for you when you come back from work. I'll buy all the food and it'll be a surprise. Tomorrow. Don't forget the key now,' she said, as she tripped out.

He didn't like it. Either it was a lark or, if it was leading to something more serious, out of the question. For a start he was twice her age - apart from other considerations. But he was intrigued. He decided to let it happen, just the once. It was only her curiosity, and perhaps his, which would soon be satisfied and that would be the end of it.

He was nonetheless dumbstruck when Lorinne opened his own door to him. He not only smelt delicious roast pork but saw a spring-cleaned house. She'd done out the whole of the ground floor, it seemed.

'I've been here all day,' she laughed. She made him sit in the chair. 'I don't know if you prefer beer, I see you have some in the fridge. Or gin and tonic - I've brought some.'

He was confused, holding one of the chair arms with both hands and looking at her over them like an invalid. 'You shouldn't have gone to all this trouble, Lorinne, really.'

'It can't be trouble when it's a pleasure, can it? Beer or gin?'

'Well, it'll have to be the gin then.'

'Good. Me, too.'

He was ashamed there wasn't a proper glass. He and Marge never drank spirits. She brought two tumblers from the kitchen, poured, and made him clink glasses.

He'd never been so embarrassed in his life. All he could do was look round the room as if it were a strange house. Meanwhile, she talked. She'd had one of the happiest days of her life, she said. She hated home. Father didn't know what to do with himself when he wasn't at the bank, for 'the bank was all he was'. Mother was overbearing and bossy, Jennifer was 'a prude', James a 'cocky ass'. For the first time in her life, she said she felt she had some use. 'At least I hope I've been some use.'

At first all he could do was stammer and start. But she'd brought wine to go with the meal, too. Suddenly he found his tongue. The food was excellent. She was a nice little cook - baked potatoes, peas, apple sauce, the lot - and she as neat as a pin in her summer dress. What was he thinking about, if she wanted to do it? If a horse won for you, you collected, didn't you?

'Well, this is really nice,' he said, spreading his arms on the table. 'You're a dab of a cook.'

She grew serious. 'You really like it, Ken, like what I've done?'

'Like? This is the nicest thing that's happened to me ever.'

In a moment he was telling her about Marge, what a slut she was and how he'd had to do all the cleaning and how all she'd

thought about was the pub and her Bingo.   Then she began.
She said how she hated all the people she knew, all so smug and
self-satisfied.   She said how she always had more sympathy and
kindness from working people she met.

They were back in the sitting-room, sitting beside each other
on the small sofa.   The wine was wearing off - the excitement,
the confidence, too.   But it was supplanted by something he
hadn't expected.   He'd forgotten for so long what feeling for a
woman was like.   She was so young, and tender, and surely,
also willing?

But he mustn't.   It was too easy.   She was too fine to muck
about with.   He was old enough to be her father.   And a sort of
father was what he should be, if she'd let him.   He didn't touch
her, though he thought she wanted him to.   He walked her
half-way home.   It was she who kissed him quickly on the cheek
as they parted.

He kept to his decision.   He saw her every Sunday at the house.
Once or twice they went for secret walks when he had finished
the work, and a meal at his place became a weekly event, though
he insisted on paying for the food.   On her suggestion, he agreed
not to mention anything to Mrs Prideaux, but there was no
hanky-panky.   He thought he was playing a nice-old-uncle role.

It moved him, though.   Nobody had ever asked his advice
about anything serious before.   Lorinne had some problem for
him every time they met.   He didn't think what he said could be
of much help.   Usually he just told her not to worry about her
father's rudeness or her mother's chivvying.   But she always
said how helpful he was.   Then there was a young man, a
university friend of James's, who started showing an interest in
her.

Ken saw him one Sunday at the house.   He didn't think any
more of him than he thought of James, but he kept it to himself.
If that was what Lorinne wanted, he thought . . .   But it
saddened him, not the least because it would be the end of their
times together.   But he made up his mind to give it his blessing
if she asked him.

But she didn't ask him. Beyond her original remark that he'd made a pass at her and that her mother, as well as James, was keen on the idea, the subject wasn't mentioned. One evening when she was due at his place, the key was still under the mat when he got back, no smell of cooking. It hurt. Not even a phone call or a letter. For days, silence. Almost he didn't go up to The Limes on Sunday. When he finally did go, the morning passed and she didn't appear. He didn't see any of them as a matter of fact. His wage was in an envelope left on the bench. Yet both the cars were in. It seemed as if there had been a death.

That afternoon he just sat at home indoors. It was hot and he would normally have taken his shirt off and sat in the garden to get a spot of tan, but he felt really low. Then he heard the gate whine and quick footsteps. He rushed to the door. Lorinne was carrying a suitcase. She put it down, fell into his arms, and burst into tears. 'They're horrible, I've left home,' she said. 'I can't bear to stay another moment.'

He had to hide the joy he felt. He sat her in the chair and made tea.

When he came back with the tray she had dried her tears and was smiling. 'It's happened, hasn't it?' she said.

'What's happened?'

'You feel the same as I do. You're pleased I've come. You've suffered as much as I have in these last days. You love me Ken, as much as I love you. That's true, isn't it?'

It frightened him. She'd given the young man his cards, but he pulled out all the stops to make her go back home. How could she live with him, just like that, he told her. For starters, what would his neighbours think, and say? And - he didn't know which way to look when he said this - it wouldn't be right . . . in such a hurry . . . Privately, he thought that, though seventeen, she could be a virgin.

'Don't worry, Ken darling,' she said. 'I know what you mean. *That* side of things needn't be rushed, I agree. I'll sleep in the front room for the moment. But I want to be with you. I love you. I'll never go home again, they were so nasty to me. We're going to be married.'

He thought of legalities, and wondered if he shouldn't go out at once and phone Mrs Prideaux from the box at the end of the road. But he didn't. He was dazed. He allowed her to take her suitcase upstairs and move in. She cooked them omelettes, told him at length, amused now, how she had told the young man he was wasting his time, told her mother the same, too. When she wanted them to kiss each other goodnight, he felt more of an uncle than ever, but Lorinne laughed. 'My life's begun today,' she said.

He went to work in a state. He'd lain awake thinking half the night. What would the Prideauxs do? How could an unskilled labouring man like him make a girl like Lorinne happy? Where was the money coming from? There'd been talk of that already that evening. She'd said she'd get a job, and that he must do a course and gain a skill. Had he the ability? Did he want to? All day he was silent. His mates ribbed him. Was he in love or something, they asked. He kept away from the canteen, went out to The Seven Stars.

Days passed. Nothing happened. He made Lorinne write to her mother to tell her where she was, and that he wouldn't be coming up to The Limes any more, but there was no word from her or Mr Prideaux. Lorinne got a job at the tobacconist's. He didn't like this, they could manage. But, as she said, she couldn't sit at home all day, the whole house had been done over by now. It began to seem more normal. One night she came to his bed. They made love. She wasn't a virgin. Somehow this was more of a relief than anything. Tenderness overcame him. She was so fresh and sweet and willing. She took everything so naturally he began to believe in it, too. People won on the lottery, he thought. He'd won on happiness, it was as simple as that. When he found people in the street were looking at him in a new way, with respect and curiosity - Lorinne had been talking to everybody quite openly - he was finally won. It was because *he* had always been different, too, he thought. He'd never accepted second best. That's why he and Marge had come to grief. It was a new life, which he deserved.

Lorinne had gone away for a couple of days to visit a female cousin she was friendly with. There was the BMW parked when he came in from work with half the neighbourhood craning their necks. It was Mrs Prideaux. She was sitting in the car, and got out when he approached.

'I'd like to come inside please, Ken,' she said, quite civilly.

She turned down his offer of tea, or a drink. 'No, Ken, I want to talk. I know Lorinne's away. We've *got* to talk.' So, when he had been upstairs to wash, which he delayed over, there he was sitting opposite her not knowing where to put his hands.

'First, I don't blame you, Ken. I should guess that you have behaved honourably throughout. You didn't seduce Lorinne. I have eyes, she made all the running. I know when Lorinne first went away you tried to make her come back, she said so in that letter you got her to write. I won't even blame you for giving way. She's an attractive girl, you're a lonely man.

'I thought it would pass. Lorinne's like me, she's headstrong. I thought she would make her point and that, in a day or two, that would be that. It would be you who was hurt, I felt sorry for you. But now I fear it could get out of hand. Lorinne knows about - love-making - but there could be a mistake. Supposing she had a child? Her life could be ruined. Have you thought about that?'

He was surprised, now it came to it, how calm he felt. 'We have thought about it actually, Mrs Prideaux,' he said, quite clearly. 'We are going to get married.'

Her manner stiffened. 'It cannot happen,' she said. 'It *must* not happen. You must stop it now. I'm not a snob. My husband's a merchant banker and we're quite well off, but my father was a builder and Tom's was an auctioneer. It's straight facts I'm talking about. You must be nearly twice Lorinne's age, you have an ex-wife to support, and you have no skills. Neither has Lorinne for that matter . . .'

She went on, hitting him with every sentence until she had finished. After a while he stopped listening. He concentrated on a twitch she had in the corner of one of her eyes. Then she

214

was expecting him to say something.

'We love each other, Mrs Prideaux,' was all he could think of. Perhaps it was all there was to say. That made her angry. She got up. 'Well, don't expect anything from Lorinne's father. He says he won't speak to her again if she goes through with this idiocy. So if *that's* what's at the back of your mind, forget it. You won't get a penny out of him, and Lorinne's used to living well.' He went to the Stars that evening and had more than was good for him.

Nonetheless, the wedding wasn't so bad. He didn't enjoy it, neither did Lorinne. But Mr and Mrs Prideaux came to the registry office and there was tea afterwards at The Limes. A few friends of Lorinne's came, Jennifer was there, and they were all decent enough. But they were both pleased to get home.

The marriage was a success. Lorinne was transformed. Even Mrs Prideaux said so. The pets were forgotten. She was still only eighteen, but she set about her new life with an energy and an inventiveness which was a delight to Ken. He had imagined awkwardness with people in the street. There was none. Lorinne made friends with everyone, and she began to affect their lives. She got people who had never thought of it to cut their hedges, put in plants, decorate and repair. The street was getting a new look. And their own home was the model. Ken spent all his evenings at it, too, inside and out, and every inch of the small garden was used for herbs and the like. He began a welding course - three evenings a week at the Institute. When he got his City and Guilds and a better job they would be able to move, Lorinne said.

The welding was all right. He quite enjoyed it, and thought he was making progress. But the instructor seemed to think otherwise. Ken noticed he seemed to be getting less of his time. One evening towards the end of the second term, the instructor told him it was no good, he wasn't going to make it. There was no point in him going on and taking the exam.

He didn't mind so much. It was a lot after a day's work. But when he told Lorinne, she was furious, first with the instructor, then with him, for accepting the judgement so 'meekly'. 'You can't just cave in like this at the first obstacle. Try harder. You'll make it if you try.' He did try again, but it was hopeless, he just didn't have the knack. One evening he played truant and went to The Stars. She smelt the beer on his breath and made him confess. They had their first real row.

'You're spineless,' she said. He said she was chasing her tail. 'What's the sense?' he said, 'you only live once. Take things as they come. I thought you believed in that.' She said he was lazy and lacked ambition. Didn't he *want* to better himself,' she cried finally.

They made it up, but it was the beginning of a recurrent theme. He gave up the course. She got a job in the five-star hotel in the centre of the town. In six months she was promoted to a management job. She met someone, a manufacturer. She went with him, and left Ken.

For a month or more Ken didn't care if he lived or died. Every evening her not being there was a torture - her cheerful, excited voice, her delicious meals. He didn't know which way to turn until, one Saturday morning, he thought of going up the hill. When faced with that glass front-door he nearly turned away, but he rang the bell and Mrs Prideaux opened it.

She looked at him for a moment with that stare she'd given him the first time he came up here. Then 'you'd like your job back, wouldn't you?' she said. 'All right. The garden's never been the same since you stopped looking after it.' He explained it wasn't just the money.

And it wasn't, neither. He liked the peace, the smell of the mown grass, and the sight of Mr Prideaux at the window, staring away at nowhere. That's how he felt himself sometimes. It was nicer now that James and Jennifer had gone away as well as Lorinne. Sometimes, when he stopped for a smoke, it really did seem like in the country.

UNPLEASING SUSPICIONS ABOUT ROD WOZCEC

It's enough to say about myself that I am an Englishman, a trombone-player, and that, because of an exchange arrangment, I was playing for a year with the Cleveland Orchestra in Ohio. I found myself renting a nice flat on the fringes of the famous Shaker Heights - which has been described as the richest suburb in the United States.

What time of day shall I choose to describe this urban paradise when I arrived in early September? 4pm perhaps? Down in the city it is hot, not so in these tree-lined boulevards. The spacious houses are shielded by bodyguards of plane, elm and sycamore, and are set back from the road by sweeps of lawn kept lush by hidden sprinklers which go to work twice a day. A large car or two rears ahead from the numerous traffic lights which hang like lanterns in the trees, and a party of negro help pile cheerfully on to the bright yellow streetcar which glides silently up and down beside the main thoroughfare down to the town. Otherwise all human life is tidily out of sight. Even before I met the Wozcecs, I could imagine those well-dressed, air-conditioned, white, well-to-do American wives going happily and unhurriedly about their lives indoors, in the comfort for which their husbands worked so hard and to which their husbands would soon be driving home.

I took on some private pupils to make some extra cash. One of these was Polly Wozcec. After we'd had only one lesson, her mother invited me to dinner. Barny Wozcec, who made rocket parts, had wiry crew-cut grey hair but, though he must have been in his mid-forties, looked so young he could still have been involved in college football. Emma was slim, especially attractive on that evening in an expensive pure silk cheonsam. She was what the Italians call 'gentile' and the Americans 'gracious.' The couple were cheerful, welcoming, and pro-English. We sat down to what promised to be, and was, a delicious dinner amid more silver and cut-glass than I can remember seeing on any table, and served discreetly by a black

black girl wearing white gloves.

I noticed there was an unoccupied place laid. It seemed to get increasingly unoccupied as the meal went on. Polly hadn't described anyone else in the family. Why was it I got the feeling the absentee was deliberately not being spoken about? But Polly was at the age for making startling revelations. Aged thirteen, her teeth were encaged in a brace - I had indeed wondered about her choice of instrument from this point of view. She had largely been left out of the conversation so far, and was probably being required to produce table-manners which didn't come naturally to her. She caught me glancing at the untouched perimeter of gleaming cutlery.

'You're wondering who's missing, aren't you, Robbo,' she said steadily. 'It's my brother, Rod.'

The butts marker came up at once - a white sphere placed plumb on the bull. Polly was reprimanded for her racy abbreviation of my name, as if this had been the aberration.

'Rod's going through a bit of a screwball phase since finishing college,' said Barny off-handedly, after too long a pause. 'Though I guess he'll pull out of it soon enough.'

Emma's lips tightened. 'He won't pull out unless he's made to,' she said. 'And I *insist* he comes to meals, Barny, especially when we have guests.'

Again, the fifth column. 'Rod's interested in fish,' my pupil supplied simply.

The conversation thereafter was like a Bach concert I was playing in once when the soloist lost her concentration. The music stumbled, petered, searched manfully for the trail, refound it, but never again with the same brio. Later on, an object fell heavily in the upper regions of the house. When Polly suggested after the meal that I might like to meet Rod and see what he was up to, there was almost relief on the part of her parents. It had been getting like the Jane Eyre inhabitant in the tower.

Rod had turned the large attic room into his aquarium-laboratory. On the sloping ceilings were huge enlarged colour-photographs, representations I learnt of 'rare

Polonesian molluscs.' Round the sides of the rooms were cabinets of thin drawers filled with colourful hoards of sea-shells. In the centre of the room was Rod's workbench and at each end two large glass tanks, green with weed, in which lurked living specimens of those mute invertebrates which had taken possession of the imagination of the younger male Wozcec.

Rod looked a fair replica of his father, dressed in jeans and a check shirt. He hardly turned his muscular back as Polly and I entered. He was looking down a microscope with one eye and gently twisting the adjustment wheel. He was humming. As we approached he substituted for this a shrill whistle. 'Hey, what d'you know?' he said, 'this is really something.'

Just what was something we weren't to know. Polly interrupted him with an introduction and followed this with conversation.

'Ma's upset you didn't come to dinner.'

Rod looked only mildly concerned. 'Oh heck,' he said. 'I grabbed a sandwich in the kitchen. 'I have to finish this today, Polly. Don't they get that?'

Not receiving much encouragement from her brother, Polly turned her fact-giving abilities to me. 'Mum's sore because she thinks Rod ought to be doing something serious. She thinks he ought to be going in with Dad like the other college kids are doing with their Dads. She thinks he's wasting his time . . . Rod was high on the Honour Roll when he was at College,' she added with an apparently irrelevant rush of family pride.

Either Rod had reached a stopping point, or he didn't relish the drift of Polly's conversation, or it could have been a natural social impulse. 'Hey, d'you want to take a look at this, Robert,' he said. He turned to one of the tanks, and after a few moments of searching, with his sleeve held up with his other hand, pulled out a little crab. He held it delicately on either side of its shell like a cheese biscuit, with its little claws working in the air like a disengaged engine.

'Got this little fella this morning by mail.'

'Mail?'

'From the National Institute of Crustacean Research. They send them in cans, you know. Now this one is quoted as having the most remarkable habits. It's said the gentleman crabs remove the ladies' shells before having sexual intercourse with them and good-naturedly replace them when they have finished? Real tidy, isn't it, if it's true? Think I'll write an article one of these days. "Sermons from the Deep," how about that? "There is so much we can learn from these little creatures, do you not think?"' He put his hand horizontally round his neck as he said this, imitating what Polly later explained to me was the voice of their episcopalian minister. The elder Wozcecs were pillars of his church.

I began to see why Mrs Wozcec was worried.

Polly was not only a retailer of facts - a service which she supplied with the detachment of a Gallup Poll - she went out of her way to gather them. She became a tachygraph in the Wozcec household. I had to admit that her playbacks were more entertaining than her trombone-playing.

Emma's dissatisfaction with her son's 'bum' attitude to life reached an apogee, it seemed, when an adventurous sea-snail laid a tell-tale trail across her sky-blue bedroom carpet and was waiting to make her acquaintance on her dressing-table one morning when she came to brush her hair. She spoke 'seriously' to Barny about it. He had got to do something to 'get Rod up off his fanny' and do it fast. He'd been at it for a year now. Her friends were beginning to question her about him. She couldn't go on saying he was resting after his exams.

I could imagine Barny's embarrassment. His son was doing what he had never got round to doing - what he wanted. Rod was doing another thing he had never done - resisting Emma's wishes. But he grasped the nettle. The interview, I was told, took place in the attic. Barny began by talking about Rod's college career, how successful he'd been, how they'd got the habit of thinking of him as a success, and what a contrast this was to finding that what he wanted to do was . . . well, he didn't want to downgrade Rod's activities with sea-creatures . . . but . . .

This didn't get much moving apparently. Rod could quite see what his father was driving at, he said. He could see how he (and particularly Mum) would view his researches in this light. But didn't Barny think it was important for people to do what they wanted? He was sure he did. He, Barny, had made rocket parts all his life for example. That was what he wanted. It was just that his own interests happened to be a bit different.

One could imagine Barny sitting awkwardly on the edge of the work-table or lolling against one of the tanks while this was going on. Not quite the best position for fathers delivering life-orientating speeches to their sons.

There was a switch in Barny's tactics at this point. What did Nancy Jane think of it all, Rod was asked. Nancy Jane, Polly told me, was Rod's steady. They had been going steady for years. Nancy Jane had apparently, out of Rod's earshot, expressed views similar to Emma's about Rod's post-graduate researches. Once more the elder Wozcec was met with bland affability. He was sure his father was right. It was just the view he would have expected from Nancy Jane, she being a woman, and women having a more materialist attitude to life than men.

I guess it was this remark which brought out the heavy artillery. Circling the walls with trumpets wasn't getting Barny results. Indeed at any moment the besieger looked like becoming the besieged.

'And just how do you propose to finance all this?' Barny apparently said, a lot more bluntly.

Polly reported that some interesting facts came to light here. Rod had an evening job five days a week, washing dishes in a restaurant. He paid rent to his mother, and anyway wasn't eating much. What did Barny mean? Was he saying that all this didn't balance the books, that Barny wanted him to move out? If so, he would do so very willingly. He knew Mum had been bothered recently by an errant gastropod. Of course it had been insensitive of him not to mention it before.

It was unconditional surrender. No, of course they didn't want Rod to move out, Barny said. It appears there was a handshake. The last words were Rod's, on a cheerful, almost a capitalistic note. 'You might like to know, Dad' - words to this effect - 'I'm currently working on some coral anemones. They secrete a substance which I believe can revolutionise the manufacture of perfume. You know the principle of perfume manufacture? The bigger the stink, the better the mixitive. We sure do have a stink here. Put civet cats right out of business. Could be a breakthrough.'

Soon after this, the Cleveland newspaper, *The Plain Dealer*, came out with a feature on Rod Wozcec, the missile manufacturer's son, who preferred amateur marine studies to big business. There was a photograph of him holding a live Kurtus in his hand. Alongside him was Nancy Jane, whose expression either communicated her uncomplimentary attitude to this Australian fish or to her lover's chosen career, or both. She wore on her lapel, however (this was arrowed in the photo) a cameo which the article said Rod had laboured five days to create - for Rod had artistic as well as scientific skills. Nancy Jane had commented (with stiff upper lip) that it was a 'truly lovely gift.'

Rod's immediate projects at this time? Why, lobster. He was at work on an article which he had entitled 'One Man's Poisson Is Another's Poison.' He had been plotting the incidence of lobster catches in relation to sewer outlets on the east coast and had found a remarkable correspondence.

I don't mention the newspaper article lightly, for without doubt it was the cause of the next development. Hitherto the problem of Rod Wozcec had been confined to his family and fiancée. It now assumed more ecumenical proportions. A week or two after the article, I happened to be in a local fishmonger's shop run by an Italian called Simon Mentone. He complained of an almost hundred per cent fall-off in his sales of lobster and shrimp, and unequivocally blamed this misfortune on the ecological studies of Rod Wozcec. This was straightforward enough, but it wasn't much later that a strong rumour began to circulate in the neighbourhood of serious 'anti-American' activity. There was nothing at all specific about what the origin of this might be, but various possibilities were posited, among them Afghans, Hezbollah, and a selection of religious 'crackpots.' The phrase 'germ warfare' was also breathed. Was Mentone the originator of the story? I couldn't help wondering.

At first only minor attention was paid to the unspecified rumour by sophisticated citizens, surely immunised against witch-hunting by the McCarthy episode years ago. But when Rod's new laboratory went up in the Wozcecs' yard, a few active minds did make a connection. One sensed a certain air of anxiety and vigilance. With my contact with the family, I was cross-examined by several people. Had I any evidence of links with undesirable terrorist groups?

The unease was no doubt increased because of the numbers of teenagers who hung about this new wonder. The families of these kids heard emotional accounts of the new enterprise - the exciting watertanks, the wonders of the dissection bench, the growing number of specimens, the photography room which was at present illustrating the visual wonders of the sponge kingdom. Suspicious ears were cocked when one exuberant child told of an investigation into the disease-bearing qualities of whelks.

It was the affair of one Sunday morning, however, which abruptly drew together these hitherto separated impeti of suspicion and made what can be described as a movement of opinion. It wasn't insignificant that it was an ex-suitor of Nancy Jane who first made the discovery. Living only three lawns from the Wozcecs, he came down one morning to find a large part of the ground floor alive with worms. At least, 'alive' is a misnomer, for a good proportion of them were dead or dying, being, as was later announced by their keeper, a species of marine worm, the Sand Worm, which couldn't for long survive the massive escape from their natural habitat. Very quickly other families were finding further invasions of the obnoxious creatures. When a few days later a girl went down with a vicious stomach disorder, the neighbourhood was abuzz. Admittedly the girl lived well outside the perimeter established by the most adventurous and long-lived worms, but there comes a point when even a fair-minded person fails to examine each new piece of evidence in isolation.

It was not only Rod, now, who fell under suspicion, but his entire family. Several important business associates were quoted as saying they had always suspected Barny Wozcec's success in life. Hard-working he was, business flare and drive he possessed, but hadn't he always been a man with no loyalty but to his own interests? It was clear to many at the golf club that Barny's puzzled and humorous references to his son's activities were a cover-up. He had after all put up the money for the 'extravagant thing in the yard', why should he now deprecate it? He was clearly behind the project. Several people wrote clandestinely to the CIA.

Rod's ex college friends also came into the picture. Several of them were already in harness. The least vindictive among them subscribed to the charge Nancy Jane had made one day that she feared her fiancé was suffering from some kind of an 'infantile regression'. Others found a less psychological explanation. Great ball-player he might once have been, but now Rod Wozcec was clearly a traitor. Something had to be done, and done fast.

There was then a surprising development at the Wozcecs' Christmas drinks party, which apparently only a third of the people who usually came attended. I was talking to Rod, who had been conscripted to put in an appearance. He would have normally sat alone, I suspect, probably reading a book - I had seen him doing this before at a family function. But he seemed to think I was interested in his work. Quite unaware, as far as I could tell, of the furore in the suburb and of the distress he was causing his family, he was describing to me with particular enthusiasm the habits of a tropical jellyfish.

Our conversation was abruptly severed as Nancy Jane skipped up to us, looking, I thought, her most ravishing and, more to the point, more positive than I had seen her for some time.

'Ah Robert,' she said, placing a white, manicured hand on my sleeve, 'I'm glad you're here. You know all about Rod's work.

You can witness my confession. Yes, confession, Rod. What I've come to say is that I owe you a deep apology. It came to me in bed last night with blinding force. I admit that I have been guilty of disloyal thoughts just lately. With everyone talking about you so much, I really did begin to wonder about your work and about where it's leading. But then the simple explanation came to me.' She lowered her voice. 'Of course, it's government work you're doing, isn't it? Top secret work. *This* explains your silence.'

Rod looked perplexed. 'Government work?'

'Don't worry, dear. Robert's English, he won't betray us. Not that I'm going to keep it mum exactly. No siree. Two can play at the rumour game. No one need know *exactly* what you're doing. I shall just say one or two well-chosen words and leave it at that. I don't want you to say anything in fact, Rod. You don't even have to speak now. Just leave it to me to counter all these cruel and stupid lies. What I'm saying is that from now on you can count me on your side one hundred per cent, as any husband-to-be should be able to count on his wife-to-be.'

'Lies? What lies?' said a bewildered Rod. Polly had told me Rod was the only person in Shaker Heights who didn't know what he was being accused of. He thought people were still bothered about the worms, which had clearly been a one-off.

Polly went dancing away, and I told him what was happening as far as I knew. When I had finished he shrugged his shoulders.

'Well, let Nancy do her stuff then, if she wants to,' he said with a chuckle. 'If it takes a lie to defeat a lie, so be it.'

Emma Wozccc was Nancy Jane's first convert. I heard it from Emma herself. She, too, had been guilty of doubting her son, she said. She was grateful to Nancy Jane, who had come to see things in 'such mature perspective.' What they had to do was to work together now to restore the Wozcec name to its rightful position - at the top of the list. She had been able to contribute something that very day. Did I remember the girl who had gone down with an upset stomach? She had obtained first-hand evidence that she had eaten lobster the day before.

Now if her parents had heeded Rod's warning about contamination, she wouldn't have been ill. As for the worms - did I know what really happened? Some of the kids who hung about Rod all day had let them out. One had confessed. She had little doubt they had done so on adult instruction, so that wicked rumours could be manufactured about the exodus.

And it wasn't long before the tide of rumour in the neighbourhood turned and began to flow the other way. People went up to Rod in the street, shook him by the hand, and made complimentary remarks, which mystified him. Simon Mentone's shop, ostracised, was closed down. It was said he had left the area.

I was in Cleveland long enough to witness the full triumph of this family effort - surely the largest most expensive wedding ever staged in the area. I cannot report anything very striking about the bridegroom, who spent most of the service looking at his fingernails. His speech was indecisive. He mumbled something about gratitude for favours he had never sought, which well-wishers took to be modesty and his enemies poor taste. Nancy Jane, however, was radiant. She talked much about Rod's newly-patented coral anemone perfume, recently, with her assistance, taken on by a manufacturer, which even Jeremiahs conceded would make him a lot of money. The wedding presents, put on display, were of course magnificent. The gift Nancy Jane was proudest of and which she showed repeatedly to the guests was Rod's present to her. Given pride of place, mounted on a block covered with black velvet, it was a simple glass cube in the centre of which was imprisoned an ostracon which, as the initiated will know, is among the smallest and most beautiful of the crustaceans.

THE PECCADILLO

'Someone's palm is glistening with grease.'

Whitlow knew Hardy's comment on George Roebuck's knighthood was aimed at him. It was timed for peak ratings during mid-morning break. Whitlow was standing by the notice-board on which he was about to pin an announcement about the Geography Sixth field-trip. For a moment Hardy's mocking eyes met his before they continued on their self-congratulatory sweep.

Whitlow had to control a surge of annoyance as he turned back to the green baize. How could Cuthbert even consider so negative a personality as Hardy's to head the Modern Side? What morsel of evidence was there that George Roebuck had bought his title? The fact was Roebuck had been successful in life, and that was enough in itself for Hardy to want to denigrate him. It was also, Whitlow was certain, that he was jealous of his own relationship with Roebuck. Did he really have to consider Hardy as a serious rival for the post he hoped might come his way?

Sir George lived in Beacon Place, the fine eighteenth century 'Nabob's palace', which crowned the hill overlooking the school. How appropriate, Hardy had sneered, that Roebuck, rich managing director of a large international company, hardly out of even a middle drawer himself, should so continue the tradition of greedy, upstart commerce. But though Whitlow owned that Roebuck could be over-forceful sometimes, and perhaps a little repetitive about his humble origins, he liked and admired him. Whitlow and his wife lived, at a very reasonable rent, in one of the houses on the estate. This was not the only advantage they derived from knowing the Roebucks. Quite often they were asked to dinner parties. Recently, on separate occasions, they had met two cabinet ministers and the President of an African state who was staying with the Roebucks for the week-end. What was especially gratifying to the Whitlows was the way George treated them. He would talk about the suspension of their old Citroen or the imperfections of his own tennis backhand with the same weight, Whitlow suspected, as he gave to matters of high policy in his company.   It wasn't very common, he guessed, that people in high positions should be so unhierarchical.

Whitlow forgot the common-room incident about Roebuck's knighthood until three weeks later.   It was after lunch, when bald heads lolled in leather armchairs, a game of bridge was in progress in one corner, and the air was blue with pipe smoke. For once Hardy was not talking, but sat reading the Daily Mail. Even this he couldn't do quietly.   Every few moments there was a sigh or a click of the tongue or an impatient rustling as he turned a page.   Whitlow was aware of the annoyance peripherally, as he corrected books at the table.

Suddenly Hardy snorted.   'Here, listen everybody, how about this?' he said loudly.   All eyes turned to him, the game of bridge stopped.   'New knight shoplifts.   Yesterday evening, Sir George Roebuck, managing director of Unicape, awarded a knighthood in the Birthday Honours List, was stopped in the street by a store detective employed by Harrods and accused of stealing an expensive bottle of perfume from the cosmetics department. When telephoned at home, Sir George refused to comment.   But, according to the security agent, he denied that he had failed to buy the goods.   The case will be heard at the Bow Street Magistrates Court.'

Hardy was immediately surrounded by a knot of people eagerly reading over his shoulder.   'So much for our titled magnate,' Hardy said triumphantly, 'and for those among us who slavishly follow the retinue.'

Whitlow couldn't believe it.   There had been a mistake.   He was teaching George's son, Bob, that afternoon.   He didn't like approaching the boy if his father was really in trouble, but Bob seemed to be behaving so normally he didn't feel too badly about it.   He took him aside at the end of the class and asked him if was true.

Bob had his father's complete assurance in life.   'Oh yes,' he said. 'Father's most amused.'

Whitlow paused. 'Is it all right then? I mean, did he have the receipt?'

'No, that's the point. He'd thrown it away.' This appeared to make the incident even funnier. Bob shouldered the rucksack in which he kept his books and departed.

Whitlow was relieved. The boy obviously wasn't upset, and this reflected what must be his father's lack of concern. Obviously, there *was* a simple explanation, which would come out in the hearing. Hardy was going to look pretty stupid, he thought. It would be tempting to make a remark in the common-room himself about rash minds leaping to conclusions too readily. He knew he would never stoop to such undignified depths, which would put him on Hardy's level, but he blushed with pleasure at the thought nevertheless.

His relief continued until, driving home one evening, he saw the placard outside the local newsagent. 'Local Knight Guilty of Theft.'

It was right over the *Evening Standard*, with George's photograph - taken as he came out of court. His face was strange. Whitlow had never seen the look before. It must be outrage, he thought. He had only been fined, but he had been the victim of a gross miscarriage of justice. That would upset anyone.

It appeared George had rushed into Harrods after work to get his wife, Cynthia, a birthday present. He had 'confessed' he was in a hurry. He had picked up the perfume from the stand and taken it to a cash desk, where the security tape had been neutralised and the box wrapped in a green Harrods bag. At this point the till had jammed. George had asked if he could pay at the next cash point. The girl, flustered, had agreed. George said he went to the other cash point and paid. The first cash-point girl said that, having asked for the services of the engineer to see to her machine, in the company of one of the floor detectives who happened to be present at that moment, she watched Sir George at the other till. There was a queue of people waiting to pay and the queue was moving slowly. She saw Sir George look at his watch, then leave the queue and walk to the exit. The floor detective followed, and arraigned him in the street.

The next day, Whitlow had to face Hardy in the common-room. 'Still supporting your distinguished benefactor?' Hardy said in the middle of break.

Whitlow kept cool. 'I'm quite sure we haven't heard all the story,' he said quietly.

'Story's the word. Which you no doubt, enjoying your private access to the great man, will be privy to? We shall all be agog.'

The Whitlows were sometimes asked up to the house at week-ends for tennis and tea. Whitlow wondered if this would happen again. But to his suprise, that same Saturday, George's boyish voice came on the phone as if nothing had happened.

The afternoon proceeded along ritual lines. Lady Cynthia, cool in her light summer dresses, never played tennis. After gracious and hospitable greetings she disappeared. Bob Roebuck made up the four. As usual, they played family against family. There wasn't much to choose between the Whitlows and George. The deciding factor was Bob. He was the best player, but he was also rash and insouciant about the score. The outcome depended on the extent to which George could control his excesses. Was it possible to believe, Whitlow kept thinking as George rushed energetically from back line to net and back again to take a lob, talking incessantly to Bob about the game, that such an enthusiastic man, rich enough to buy the whole cosmetic department of Harrods for Cynthia, could be guilty of petty theft? He couldn't think so. Yet nothing had been said. He knew what Hardy would say. Roebuck was guilty and would shut up about it. What else could he do?

It seemed this was so. Ritually, Lady Cynthia served tea on the terrace, distributing small plates to each of them, pouring tea from a silver pot with her hand on the lid. She wove webs of polite conversation.

The Whitlows were expecting two more sets after tea, but when Cynthia got up to take away the tray Bob also disappeared.

George made no sign of getting up.

'It's of course quite monstrous,' he said as soon as the coast was clear. 'I'm a victim of a sordid little conspiracy. That magistrate should be removed from the Bench. When the appeal is concluded I intend to press for him to be disciplined.' He scratched the back of his hand. 'Now look,' he went on, 'I know you two will have been giving the matter a lot of thought. I'm referring to Bob of course and the need to protect him at the school. I shall give you the full facts in order that you may play your part successfully.'

Whitlow swallowed. 'Part?'

'I've already written to Cuthbert and no doubt he'll make a statement to the school in Assembly. But I'm relying on you to put the real story round the shop-floor. It's all the doing of that lefty shop assistant and her cohorts, you know. She must have recognised me and saw her chance of a juicy anti-establishment press story. I'd also like you to approach Cuthbert and reinforce my letter. You're in a senior position now, and he should listen to you.'

Whitlow remembers the moment to this day, for it was the last time he could have backed out. He could have said he would do his best, then found some reason later for not seeing Cuthbert. But, involuntarily it seemed, all his nature came to the surface at this moment with unexpected power. Here surely was a clear call to duty, not only to support a friend who had given him his word that he was innocent, but also to uphold against Hardy's glib certainties an old English principle - that a man is innocent until proved guilty. An appeal was in progress, the matter was still *sub judice.*

He didn't like whispering in corners. For once he would say something publicly in the common-room, he thought. He chose his moment with care. Hardy had been jubilant when Roebuck was fined, but Whitlow noticed a doubt under the swaggering exterior when the appeal was announced. 'Of course the man will probably get away with it,' he pontificated. 'It'll all be fixed behind the scenes at a St James's Street club. A technicality will be found, a capitalistic half-Nelson applied.'

Hardy was hedging his bets as usual.   What a coward he was. Whitlow pounced.

'I think that's rather glib and prejudiced, Hardy, as your statements sometimes can be.   I think most decent people would prefer to withhold their judgement until the facts are finally established.'

Even Hardy took a second or two to recover.   'I see,' he said, 'and I suppose we are to understand you *have* now been made privy to facts we ordinary mortals are denied, is that it?'

Whitlow felt calm, calmer than he had ever felt in an exchange with Hardy.   'As a matter of fact, Sir George has told me he's innocent, yes, and given me an explanation of what happened.   I should have thought therefore it was our duty, both as teachers of his son, and as human beings generally, at least to suspend judgement.'

'How much remission of your rent are you getting for this?'

Hardy had overstepped it as usual.   The bell had gone for sixth period.   Effectively silent, he felt, Whitlow made a dignified move to the door.   He was more than pleased.   When pressed, he had been forthright, as he would have to be if he became Head of the Modern Side.   Raymond Armitage, another senior colleague, later told him he agreed with his view.   It was right they should all suspend judgement, he said, until the appeal had been heard.

Whitlow shrank from fulfilling Roebuck's other request. Cuthbert, a weathervane, was a tricky fish to play.   Yet for this very reason, Whitlow thought it vital he saw him.   Hardy was in and out of his study every other moment on some pretext, no doubt leaving behind him his hints and innuendoes.   For Bob Roebuck's sake, these must be countered.

'Ah, come in, come in, Whitlow,' said Cuthbert as he jumped up from the enormous desk.   Like many men uncertain of their position he did everything at the double.   'A pleasant interlude to a dull morning.   Sherry?'

The first minutes had to be an account of Cuthbert's latest doings, in this instance an Elizabethan knot garden his wife was creating in their garden.   It was possible, Whitlow thought, that if allowed the interview could go on in this vein and end with no mention of what he had come about.   He chose his moment.

'Headmaster . . .'

The bushy eyebrows twitched.   'Ah yes, of course, enough of herbs and remedies.   Now you've come to discuss something. Not a miscreant, I hope.'

'It's about Sir George Roebuck.'

The eyes went down, in memoriam.   'Dear me, yes, a sad case, a man of his eminence . . . it only goes to show . . .   Do you know, I've had a letter from him?'

'Yes, I gathered he was writing.   But what I've come to say is that I think there's rather a witch-hunt going on - in the common-room.'

The eyes came up.   'Witch hunt?'

Whitlow knew Hardy had been at him and that he had arrived just in time.   He proceeded step by step to build the counter-case. Whatever the outcome of a certain legal appeal, of whom no one could be sure, did Cuthbert think it proper that quite senior members of staff should voice their feelings in public about a parent who, yes admittedly, did speak his mind about his son's education from time to time in a brusque manner, but who was a highly respected businessman?   Would not the opinion soon pass to the boys - which was hardly the way to protect Bob Roebuck?   Far be it from him to name any individuals, but in a *general* sense, would not the Headmaster agree, an injurious mistake was being made if allowed to continue?

Whitlow's effort induced the most polished performance of Cuthbertian fence-sitting he had witnessed to date.   During his exposition Cuthbert had embarked on an ambitous doodle on his blotter, this being interrupted by an exploration of his left ear with a screwed up corner of his handkerchief.   Exposed to the need for a reply, he lifted and extended his arms, gripping the edges of the desk with both hands as if he were a pianist playing a wide Chopin chord.   On a 'personal level' he had a great deal of sympathy for Whitlow's point of view.   Though a 'rough diamond', Roebuck was a decent enough fellow.   He might well be innocent of the charges brought against him.   But of course on the other hand Whitlow must see, as Sir George must see (he had replied to his letter) that he couldn't in his official position indulge the luxury of a private view in a matter which was still in - er - legal suspension.   Whatever he thought behind the scenes, publically he must remain silent.

And silent about other people not being silent?

On the whole, silent about that, too.

Whitlow wasn't dissatisfied with the interview.   Cuthbert had made no commitment, but he had been served with the liberal counter-view.   He could no longer ignore it.   Whatever the outcome of George's litigation, he had surely put on record a firm attitude, a great deal less judgemental than the one which had no doubt been currency hitherto.   If this was instrumental in his obtaining the post to which he felt he could contribute a great deal, so be it.

One evening a week later, Whitlow was cutting the yew hedge at the bottom of his garden when he caught sight of an elegant flutter approaching down the hill which could only be Lady Cynthia.   Out with the dog, he thought.   Even when it was clear there was no dog and that she might be visiting their house, he wasn't alarmed.   It wasn't unprecedented that she had something to say or give to his wife, Lucy.   He continued with his clipping. She was soon obscured by the house.

In a few moments Lucy came out.   'Cynthia wants to see *you*,' she said anxiously, 'alone.'   This was unusual.   He went in.

Cynthia didn't beat about the bush.   'George has lost the appeal,' she said, as soon as he entered the room.   He began to express his regret, but she interrupted.   'It was rather to be expected.   I have come to tell you, because I am worried about George and I think you can help.'   She paused, like a patient mother feeding a windy child.   Let that sink in first, her manner implied, the spoon poised, her head turned aside.   'Whatever the truth about this incident, in my opinion George is behaving very foolishly.   The law has declared itself.   It's a matter of minimal importance, and it should be dropped. I'd like you to tell George that.'

'Me?'

'You teach Bob. George has a regard for what you think.'

'You mean you think . . .'

'In my view we don't need to think beyond a certain point. The *practical* point is that a court of appeal has decided, and that is surely enough for all our sakes. George is a very stubborn man - he is talking of the House of Lords - but you can bring in the school and Bob. At all events, get him to withdraw, otherwise I don't know where we shall all finish up.'

Whitlow found the approach flattering, but his first thought was that he would refuse to see George. He would write Cynthia a short note. It was really no business of his. But he was moved that Cynthia had revealed her innermost feelings to him. He was conscious also of a higher motivation. He was persuaded now that George was guilty - hadn't Cynthia made this plain? What was the Christian attitude to sin? Why, the guilty party must be brought to confess in order than he may be forgiven. Supposing this happened? Supposing he persuaded George to own up? Everything then would change, for who can resist a contrite sinner? He might even himself gain some small kudos for having been the loyal friend who had brought sense to a difficult situation.

Whitlow had borrowed George's rotivator. The next morning, it being a Sunday, he took it up in his car. From the drive, Whitlow saw George in his conservatory watering his cactuses. He approached the glassed-in area directly, which had an outside door.

He could see at once it was going to be the most difficult interview of his life. 'Brought back your machine, George, many thanks.' He got a grunt. 'Violated the virgin sods very nicely.'

Not even a grunt. George had hardly glanced at him as he came in. Whitlow didn't have the equipment for a stealthy approach. He shut his eyes and plunged. 'So sorry about the appeal. Cynthia told me.'

This at least got a line aboard. 'So will a lot of other people be sorry,' George said, who went to the tap to refill the can.

'You mean you're contemplating further action?'

'Further action is already taking place.'

Here it was, now or never. 'George, don't do it. Drop it. It can't do any good - whatever the circumstances were. As Bob's teacher, I must tell you. At the school they're saying . . .'

George's face came up, red and fiery. He would have done well among Genghis Khan's front riders. 'What the hell do you mean "whatever the circumstances were"'.

'I mean - well, have you considered . . .   I have to say this . . . have you considered that perhaps you *did* walk away from that cash point.   It's obvious that you intended to pay, or you wouldn't have queued there, but perhaps you thought of missing your train, perhaps your mind . . .'

'Get off my property.'

'George, be reasonable. Think of Cynthia, of Bob . . .'

'You impertinent busybody, you half-witted schoolmaster.'

Bowled over by a torrent of abuse, Whitlow remembered afterwards only fragments of what George said - something about sleuths hired to investigate the private life of a shop-girl, a great deal about pedantic high-minded schoolmasters who knew nothing of the world - remarks about effete southerners and phoney Christians.

The Law Lords were never troubled with an appeal, leave for which was not given. No action for defamation of character was brought against a shop-girl. By the end of the summer Sir George had been ousted from his company with a golden handshake, but apparently with no golden hallos from elsewhere. Bob did not return to school for the new academic year. It was then learnt that the Roebucks had left Beacon Place, and the district. Finally it was known that Sir George had divorced his wife for desertion. There was no defence.

After his disastrous interview, Whitlow closed his ears to Hardy's quips, and concentrated on maintaining a detached dignity. This wasn't so difficult, he told himself, for whatever the outcome had been, all along he had been on the side of decency and moral right over Roebuck. This would be recognised by level-headed people like Raymond Armitage and the silent majority - therefore also, surely, by Cuthbert. He practised a philippic, which in some way he would be pressed to make by his collected colleagues. 'Which is worse,' he aimed to say, 'George's outsized pride which, there is no doubt, caused his unnecessary fall, or the smug certainty, based on prejudice, practised by a certain individual? Sinners or Pharisees?'

But, as he knew would be the case, there was no opportunity for this speech. Hardy continued to make hay as each new piece of news about the Roebucks emerged. Whitlow continued to say nothing.

Neither Whitlow nor Hardy became Head of the Modern Side, Raymond Armitage did. Cuthbert, seeing Whitlow about it to explain why he hadn't been chosen (as, Whitlow understood, Hardy was also seen) distinguished himself by stating a view. If he was absolutely pressed to say it (which he wasn't, by a subdued Whitlow) other things being equal - as they were, Cuthbert said, other things were very equal - in the end it had to be a matter of which man had the best judgement. It was only a small difference they were talking about, but in his (Cuthbert's) fallible opinion, as recent events had rather borne out, a middle way between two extreme positions was usually the best.

Whitlow has never understood what was meant by this, if anything. Hardy was an extremist, yes - he could understand Cuthbert's thinking that. But himself? Was it fair to couple him with Hardy in this way - at the other end of the spectrum? He didn't think it was fair at all.

Recently, he heard that Roebuck had gone from bad to worse. Someone said he was living on his own in a small flat somewhere in London. Whitlow has constantly to fight a bitter satisfaction about this. For wasn't his failure to gain promotion the result of Roebuck's peccadillo and his stubborn refusal to admit it until proven? He believes it was.

THE HARRINGTONS

Before the war, for many residents of the south coast resort, the tennis club seemed like a haven from the hordes of summer visitors who overran the rest of the town. Shaped like the after end of an ocean liner, three levels stepped down like decks - each with three grass courts. Around, as if protectively, stood a rectangle of tall Victorian houses, most converted tastefully into flats, a few still owned in their entirety by well-to-do families.

On week day afternoons there were ladies' fours, busy groups of all ages in a mixture of attire - though always white of course. The younger ones wore one-piece tennis dresses, some of the older ones white stockings and pleated skirts. There was a green eye-shield or two, hairnets attached, cocked saucily, some ladies served under-arm. By five-thirty the men arrived. Typically, twice a week if weather permitted, always on Court 7, a doctor, a bank manager, a solicitor and a retired naval officer battled it out. Intense, absorbed, cutting and slicing, they ran to the net with little panicked steps, volleyed, ran back, covered each other, shouted 'mine' and 'yours', 'watch it' and 'played, partner', until fading light at last drove them to the gentlemen's dressing-room and finally to the bar where, showered and blazered, they would play another, verbal, match, concessively analysing each other's 'form'. There were many other such meetings of friends.

A most ardent younger supporter of the club was Adam Webster whose father, being the manager of a department-store in the town, would not automatically have been elected to membership. But he was good at tennis. Runner up last time at the age of fifteen, this year he was expected to win the junior tournament.

The apogee of Adam's summer was the open tournament, when the stop-netting dividing the courts was faced with dark green Slazenger canvas, when the referee's assistant bellowed through a megaphone, when the club was thronged (in this one week in the year, entrance-paying visitors were permitted to tread the sacred turf) and when tennis celebrities were among the contestants. Adam had free entrance, for he sold programmes for no wage and ran countless errands for Captain Breakspear, the club secretary. At this exciting time Adam felt touched by something soaring far above the commonplace. Even Captain Breakspeare and club committee members seemed to pale into insignificance beside these grandees of the game who had descended out of the blue.

During the rest of the season there was only one event which produced anything like the excitement of tournament week for Adam. This was a rare visit by the Harrington family. It would take place after tea, always with the same ritual. First to be seen coming through the car park entrance was the chauffeur, a capped black-suited, leather-gaitered individual, who was leaning back to restrain the energy of two huge Pyrennean sheep-dogs panting on their leashes. Just behind him came 'the old man', Mr Harrington, President of the club. A kindly-looking, white-haired octogenarian, he had a gentle regal air. On his way he would make a point of stopping to talk to the groundsman, whom he would ask 'how he was going along.' There was sky inspection, and ground inspection, before progess continued towards the clubhouse. Meanwhile, his two grandsons, Lawrence and Ronnie, would have caught up, one on either side of their grandmother, a voluminous lady with a mauve parasol, who didn't move with ease.

Captain Breakspear seemed to know of the visit in advance. Staying in his office until the strategic moment, he would then come bounding out like an energetic terrier, spectacles flashing, to make his greetings and especially to look after Mrs Harrington. Having got her seated in a folding chair, he would bring people up to introduce them to her, usually new club members. Mrs Harrington, Adam noticed, didn't always seem to appreciate this. Really, he thought, she wished to be left to sit in the warm evening air. She would break off in the middle of a sentence to rummage in her huge handbag. When she had found what she was looking for, her cigarette-holder, she had forgotten what she was saying, or the new member had withdrawn, thinking the conversation over.

While the boys changed, Mr Harrington was active in conversation. He spoke to senior club members, and listened, head aside, with that attentive kingly stoop. The boys then appeared from the gentlemen's changing room in immaculate long whites and Mr Harrington joined his wife to watch them play.

The Harrington boys, aged seventeen and fourteen respectively, were certainly not top class players, but Lawrence, though still a junior, had played with county representatives, and in style at least dealt on something like equal terms, in attitude certainly. He always brought onto the court, not one but three racquets whose tension he would test by biffing the gut with the palm of his hand an inch from his ear. Six brand-new balls would also be thrown out each time they played. Perhaps for this reason - though more likely it was a gesture to the Club President - Brakespear always put a net up for them on the centre-court, never normally used on ordinary club days. This was not viewed with universal approval by other club members.

Generally the boys played a single, often knocking up for most of the time to show how unconcerned they were about the score - a bourgeois concept beneath them. Sometimes they brought two friends, either two men considerably older than they were, or two girls nearer their ages. In these cases a game was played, as it was assumed the guests would expect it. One evening they came with only one man. Adam's ears pricked as he heard Mr Harrington explaining the dilemma to Captain Breakspear in a lowered tone. He was wondering if Breakspear knew of anyone who would 'care to stand in.'

Adam knew instinctively the pressures which besieged the unfortunate secretary. To select wrongly, either socially or from the point of view of tennis standard, would never openly be referred to, but a gaffe would be silently attributed to him. His eyes, Adam noticed, showed the strain. Enlarged by his double-lense spectacles, he was glancing round at members present as if his life depended on it.

Something came over Adam. Never had he remotely thought of being included in the Harrington circle, but as

Breakspear's eyes ranged, the notion came to him - not only that he wanted to be selected - but that, as potential junior champion, he had a right to be.   He must have somehow communicated this, for when Breakspear's sweep met Adam's eyes it faltered, went on, returned.   Adam saw doubt become possibility, possibility certainty.   Something was said in a low voice into the stooped ear.   The next thing Adam knew was that Mr Harrington, too, was regarding him.

On court, Lawrence seem to assume he, being the eldest, was the best player and Adam the weakest.   'We'd better play together then,' he said to Adam, taking charge.   Ronnie had other ideas. 'No, why don't Adam and I take you two on?' he said, and before any more could be said spun his racquet.   Lawrence looked nonplussed, but a scene in front of a stranger was unthinkable.   'Very well then, if you prefer,' he said in a tone which suggested a very lop-sided result.   'Smooth.'

Adam was inspired by the challenge.   To begin with Ronnie had used his name, which had been avoided until now.   'Do you prefer left or right,' Ronnie then enquired as they walked together to the baseline.   The tone offered, if not friendship, at least temporary alliance.

'Right.'

'Good, I prefer left.'

The new allies played like heroes.   They lost the first set, largely because, taking his cue from Lawrence, Ronnie was too concerned with style and appearance.   Thereafter a grimmer mood set in.   They started to keep the ball in court, to avoid unforced errors.   There seemed a crucial moment.   Lawrence served a double fault, then, shaping magnificently to play a smash, hit the ball several feet out.   The younger pair began to win.

To someone less versed in Harrington attitudes than Adam, it would seem Lawrence lost his nerve.   He cursed the court ('like a ploughed field'), the balls ('sodden'), and finally his partner. 'Do cover me, Charles,' he said, when he had put himself right out of position by running round his backhand, and was beaten by Adam's drive down the middle of the court. Ronnie and Adam won with increasing ease as Lawrence grew slacker and 'tried out shots.' They won the second set and were on the way to winning the third. Lawrence changed his racquet twice. At five-nil down, after stretching to retrieve a good drive by Ronnie down the sideline, he began to hobble. It was his service. The next one he served underarm. Adam hit it hard to his backhand. He made no attempt to get it back.

'Sorry, old boy, ricked my back. Old trouble, I'm afraid. Have to stop.'

Adam was furious. Wasn't it patently obvious that this was a ploy to avoid defeat? He looked pointedly at Ronnie, but Ronnie now was apparently as concerned about his brother's back as Lawrence was himself. Ronnie moved to the net, there was a short exchange, and play was abandoned.

In the gents, Adam sat next to Ronnie on the lockers. Lawrence was in one of the shower cubicles, making a great deal of splash and noise. Hot and sweaty, Adam still felt cheated and annoyed. 'A pity we had to stop like that, we had them cooked,' he said.

Ronnie, having had his shower, seemed to have lost his earlier bout of competitive spirit. He was sitting with his own large woolly yellow towel wrapped round him - not one of the worn club ones. 'Oh, was it?' he said, distantly.

'A tactical move on your brother's part if you ask me.' There was no reply. 'Does Lawrence really have a bad back?'

'I'm afraid I don't quite follow you,' Ronnie said, moving forward to inspect his toes.

Lawrence emerged, pink, athletic and whistling from the shower, with no sign of his disability. Far from suffering any loss of dignity because of his behaviour, he seemed to have a resurgence of spirits. Adam, who went home to change and had only come into the gents for a brief wash and out of courtesy to the Harringtons, by now was thinking only of escape. He got up to say a perfunctory goodbye, and to thank for the game.

'But, my dear fellow, you can't rush off like this,' Lawrence said, fastening a cuff-link. 'You must have a noggin with us.'

Having pulled a pair of grey flannels over his shorts, Adam had an embarrassing wait while the two boys finished dressing.

In the bar, where the elder Harringtons had now repaired, Lawrence ordered Charles and himself gins and orange and a half of shandy for Ronnie. 'Shandy OK for you, too?' he said to Adam. There was a further conversationless period for Adam while the other three, Ronnie included, discussed a local horse-race with their backs to him.

Adam took his empty glass to the bar. The room was full of adults, there was no one else to talk to other than the Harringtons, and there wasn't much point in hanging about, he thought. He would say a brief goodbye and be off. He picked up his racquet.

Lawrence was by now sitting at a table with his grandparents, As Adam approached, he turned his head languidly. 'My dear - er,' he said, fingering a multi-coloured silk scarf. 'Not going, are you? So soon? Must you? Sorry about the old back, you two were putting up a good show, some nice shots. I say, you'll have to come and play on our court some time. Better surface than down here.'

Adam made an adjustment to his view of the Harringtons. Not the grandparents - who remained in his mind as they had been, county-class gentlefolk who dispensed courtly charm - but Lawrence and Ronnie? Would he have quite the same feelings about them after their behaviour? He thought not. But he dismissed the matter. There was little chance he would have further contact with them, anyway.

It was for this reason a week later, when his mother gave him the message, he was taken off guard. A 'Master Lawrence Harrington' had called and wished him to phone back. The flattery involved immediately overcame any thoughts of ignoring the call. Perhaps he had misinterpreted their behaviour, he thought. Perhaps they had not wished to make him feel small. Could it be they were inviting him to their home?

Lawrence answered when he rang. 'Adam? Adam who?' he was dismayed to hear. 'Oh yes, of course, you're the fellow who made up the four at the club.   Yes, we'd thought of inviting you over.   Sunday at threeish any good by any chance?'

Adam was surprised the Harringtons lived in the town.   He had imagined a country mansion.   But it was a large house in the most desirable quarter, a wooded hill overlooking the sea.   At five minutes to three, he was the only passenger to get off the bus, carrying his racquet and a box of balls, and as usual wearing a pair of grey flannels over his tennis shorts.   As the noise of the bus receded, he had a moment of panic.   What was he doing in this silent neighbourhood, the large houses standing off from the road in the trees?   What had made him accept?   But then he felt that resurgence of confidence he had felt at the club.   Why not?   What difference did it make that his father was a shop manager?   He could beat them all at tennis.

The drive, a curve of newly-laid tarmac, was flanked by a well-kept rockery where a waistcoated gardener worked.   The man put a finger to his temple as Adam passed, but didn't answer his greeting.   He approached an open front door and rang.   An inner glass door was closed.

Not a sound came from the sleeping building.   Had he mistaken the day?   He rang again and still there was no stir.   He was going to consult the gardener, when there were footsteps coming round the conservatory attached to the front of the house. A woman appeared, wearing a flowered silk dress cut very low in the front.   Her lips were bright scarlet.   Was this Mrs Harrington Junior, the boys mother, divorced daughter-in-law of the Club President?   Adam's   mother,   a   lexicographer   of   town personalities, had supplied this information.

'Who are you?' the woman said offensively.   Apparently a reply wasn't necessary.   Stepping back a pace or two she called round the corner of the house.   'Lawrence, Ronnie?   There seems to be a person here for you.   You'd better go round,' she added to Adam.   She went into the house and shut the glass door behind her.

Lawrence and Ronnie were sitting in deck-chairs in front of open french-windows, reading the Sunday papers - the more sensational variety, Adam noted.   Lawrence stirred with visible reluctance.

'Hallo there,' he said, not getting up. 'I say, you're a bit on the early side, aren't you? Still, I suppose it's time we had a bit of exercise. Esther?' he called up to an open window above. A female voice sounded within.

'I thought we said three o'clock,' Adam said.

'Did we - and is it? My God, it *is*. Too good a lunch, I'm afraid. Yes, well, we must think about changing then. You can use one of the spare rooms. But, look here, where are your things?' He gazed at the empty space where there should have been a tennnis case in Adam's hand. The novelty of grey trousers pulled over a pair of tennis shorts had to be explained.

'Oh, I *see*,' Lawrence said. 'Well then you'd better look at the papers while we go in. Ronnie and I'll be down directly.'

'Hello, Adam. You are Adam, aren't you? I'm Esther, I'm so glad you could come. I hear you're terrifyingly good.'

Adam jumped to his feet, the well-creased copy of the *News of the World* falling to the ground. Coming through the french-windows was the prettiest girl he had ever seen. She was neat, hardly made-up at all, had wide blue eyes and lovely auburn hair parted in the middle and done up at the back in a high bun, Greek style. She wore an aertex shirt, a dainty pleated skirt which showed most of her brown legs.

'Oh, please sit down,' she said, jumping deftly into the swing seat and setting it moving. 'You don't have to be polite to me, you know. In fact I love impolite people, especially when they're male. Are you polite, Adam?'

'I - er - well, I suppose it depends.'

'Yes, I suppose it does. But will you promise not to be polite to me?'

'I'll try.'

'That's settled then.' She hummed. 'Do you get on with my brothers?'

'I hardly know them.'

'You're being evasive. Most people decide whether they like someone at once. I've decided I like you right away. You're nice and straightforward. Lawrence and Ronnie aren't straightforward. Quite honestly I think they're spoilt. They have no manners at all - and by that I mean real manners, thinking of other people. Mummy's worst of all. Daddy ran away from her, you know, and I'm not surprised he did. This is Grandad's house and he pays for us. We're really not very nice people - we, the younger Harringtons, I mean. Don't you agree?'

Adam was fortunately given no time to answer this. Esther asked him if he would be her partner in the coming tennis match.

For the second time, partnerships were fixed over Lawrence's head. Esther said she was going to play with Adam, and that apparently was that. But this time it was an unequal contest. Esther didn't play badly, but she didn't over-exert herself. Ronnie and Lawrence played today with some concentration. Adam and Esther were beaten, not ignominiously, but decisively. For Adam, however this wasn't the point. What mattered to him now was the way Esther handed him balls to serve - with a certain kind of smile - and the way she spoke to her brothers, which seemed more a communication with him than with them.

'Out,' she cried triumphantly when a finely executed stroke of Lawrence fell beyond the baseline. 'Brilliant, but out.' She gave Adam a little glance of conspiracy. When Adam won his service after a particularly long duel of deuces she ran to pat him on the shoulder. 'My knight,' she cried.

Tea was brought on the terrace on a silver tray carried by a butler in dark trousers and a white coat. Adam had been hoping to sit next to Esther, but as they were about to take their seats round the iron table Mrs Harrington appeared - in a different dress, equally low-cut. Esther seemed almost to change personality. Light-hearted, skittish, before, she seemed now to go into a sulk. She went to sit apart on the swing-seat, and when summoned by her mother to the table said she didn't want any tea. Adam tried to catch her eye but she took up a book and apparently began to read.

This didn't seem to worry Mrs Harrington. Ignoring the guest as well as Esther, she talked to the boys about the town and what a 'fantastically boring' place it was, 'gauche to a degree',

and 'full of tedious shopkeepers'. It was all right for Lawrence
and Ronnie, she said, they at least got out of the place during
term time. They could not imagine what she suffered when they
were away - left 'in this cultural desert'. She didn't think she
could stand it much longer, she would have to 'talk to the old
man about it' when he and 'Mother' returned from London.

Her monologue seemed to destroy the afternoon, even after
she had returned inside. Nobody seemed to want to play after
tea. Lawrence, looking at the sky, which seemed to Adam
perfectly blue, said it was 'getting a bit muggy.' Ronnie said he
had something to do indoors. Just for a moment Adam had the
wild idea that he and Esther might go back on the court alone.
She was still sitting reading on the swing seat. Was she waiting
for them all to go?

Lawrence scotched any hope of this. 'Well then, er, Adam, I
suppose you'll be wanting to get back. How are you going?
Someone picking you up, I suppose. Want to phone?'

'I'm going by bus,' Adam said.

'*Bus*?' But my dear chap, you can't possibly go on a bus
dressed like that, can you? Piggot will run you over. Live in
town somewhere, do you?'

'Take the bus', a voice advised Adam, 'what was *wrong* with
a bus?' But, half-looking towards Esther, he hesitated, and it
was too late. Lawrence went off to arrange it. Ronnie had
gone, he and Esther were momentarily alone.

She put down the book and got to her feet, yawning. 'You
see what I mean?' she said. He saw what she meant exactly, but
was that the point any more? Wasn't the point how they were
going to contrive to see each other again?

He stood there holding his racquet and box of used balls,
which hadn't been played with. 'Perhaps . . .' he began.

To his amazement she came up to him and kissed him
briefly on the cheek. 'Leave it to me, I'll fix something,' she
said. She walked calmly through the french-windows.

Had she said that? Had he imagined it? Had she kissed
him, or was it an illusion? When Lawrence returned, he was in a
state of blushing confusion. Fortunately Lawrence didn't seem

to notice. 'Transport' was 'laid on'.

His next clear thought was that he was being born smoothly homewards in a black Bentley, Piggot making no secret of his distaste that his sweat-soaked tennis shirt might soil the spotless upholstery.

Adam's mind raged in the succeeding days with the memory of Esther's very small but feminine breasts lifting the light aertex shirt, the graceful way she bent her knees together and tilted sideways to pick up a ball. Like a detective, he raked through the handful of evidence. Had she feelings for him, like his for her? She would 'fix something', she had said. What had she meant? What could she possibly fix - another tennis afternoon? That would be less than satisfactory.

Nothing happened. He was obliged to continue with his normal schoolboy's summer holiday. A wet afternoon a few days later, he was in the indoor municipal swimming baths with his schoolfriend, Neil. Neither Neil nor Adam were expert swimmers, a frog-like breaststroke being their limit. Neither were they divers. Noisy, untidy plunges from the springboard and feet-first leaps from the high board was the summit of their achievement. Neil had just completed one of the latter and had hit the water only a few feet from a young male swimmer. Adam realised it was Ronnie Harrington. Just at this moment he saw Lawrence emerge from the changing-cubicles in a pair of white swimming trunks of a shiny skin-like material. Clearly he had seen the incident and went towards the corner ladder Neil was making for, where Adam was standing.

Lawrence addressed Neil. 'I say, do you realise you nearly landed on my brother? Those boards are for divers not skylarkers.'

Adam knew at once who would emerge better from this dispute. Neil - fearless, guiltless - pointed out amiably that he had missed his brother by at least three feet and that the boards could be used by divers and skylarkers alike. He invited Adam to make a double jump with him. This was no defiance, he would have done so anyway.

Adam wished he was elsewhere.   He hesitated, met Lawrence's gaze and dawning recognition, and was obliged to greet him.   Neil continued on his way up the ladder.

'I say,' said Lawrence, looking after Neil, 'what an uncouth fellow, a public menace.   Not a friend of yours, is he?   I've a good mind to have a word with the superintendant.'

'How's your family?' Adam said.

Lawrence was easily distracted.   'Er - fine, thanks.   Mother's a bit under the weather - literally with all this rain, ha, ha - but nothing serious.'

'And Esther?'

'Fine, too.   Coming to join us for tea upstairs as a matter of fact.   I say why not toddle along and join us.   Fourish in the restaurant?'

Neil found it incomprehensible that Adam should wish to consort with 'such a prick' as Lawrence.   They parted company after dressing.

Adam had been once or twice to the restaurant with his mother.   At tea-time, ladies in hats and Henry Jamesian gentlemen with tie-pins sat at tables ranged about a polished dance floor, eating scones and cream cakes with double-pronged forks.   On a raised stage a small orchestra played a medley of Strauss and Humperdinck and, to give the dancers a rest, an occasional touch of Elgar.   Dwarf palms in pots and other semi-tropical foliage were placed about the room, a 'hostess' in a black dress showed you to your table.

He was worried by his damp bathing things stuffed into a scruffy bag he was forced to carry into the genteel gathering. He was sure the Harringtons wouldn't be carrying bags.   What would Esther think?

Apparently she didn't think anything, nor did the boys.   They greeted him quite warmly, Lawrence actually going to the next table to get another chair.   'There are muffins today,' he said.

Adam had eyes only for Esther.   She looked enchanting in a pale blue fluffy jumper and a crocheted beret to match.   She looked up briefly to smile at him but seemed more interested in the menu.   Was she shy of making any signal in her brothers' company?

It was Lawrence who continued to make the running - he who collected their orders for food and he who passed them on to the uniformed waitress.   Esther made a remark to Lawrence about his eating too much, and when the food arrived grabbed the pot of strawberry jam an inch ahead of Ronnie and said 'ladies first.' Otherwise she seemed content to take a back seat - while Lawrence discoursed on the Spa restaurant, which, 'he had to say, did put on a decent tea.'   While he talked, she looked round the room distantly as if searching for something which would interest her.

Adam became increasingly anxious.   Was this a sign off? Had he leapt to stupid conclusions because of the other day? Had she behaved as she had simply out of one particular afternoon's boredom?   He drew comfort only from his apparent easy inclusion in the Harrington circle.   He had a sense of them suddenly, not as the amazingly sophisticated family he had thought them, but just three teenagers like himself, a little out of their depth at a public thé dansant.   When the music struck up and dancers began to take the floor, he had a moment of panic, until a highly painted girl in a scarlet dress at the next table came to ask Lawrence if he would like to dance.   To Adam's amazement, Lawrence blushed.   'Oh no, I don't think so, thanks all the same.   Bit occupied right now.'   Rather vulgarly, he raised his jammed muffin to prove his point.   Ronnie pointed out the pianist who, temporarily unemployed, was picking his teeth behind his hand.   It was a pleasing distraction.   All four of them laughed, Esther, too.   The girl retreated, abashed.

Suddenly, Adam's world was transformed.   Out of the blue, Esther asked him in the most matter of fact way if he would come to a 'do' their grandparents were organising for their grandmother's birthday.   It was only the mother who upset things, he thought.   When the three of them were alone, things were perfectly easy and natural.   He gave his acceptance also in a natural way, as if they were old friends.   And then, while Lawrence was paying for everyone - he had insisted on this -

Esther winked at him. As they walked to the door she brushed his arm with hers. He was sure it was deliberate. His spirits ignited.

But a 'do' - what on earth was that? He imagined a party at the Harringtons' house, perhaps with games. When the gilt-edged card came he was terrified. 'Mr and Mrs Harrington, and Mrs Harrington Junior, request the pleasure of your company at a buffet dinner and dance at the Castle Hotel. Dinner jackets optional. 8 until 12 pm.'

The Castle Hotel was enough in itself to cause concern. The poshest hotel in the town, it had for Adam something of the aura of a royal court. In the front hall, fragrant with cigar smoke, managers walked about in black coats, silver ties, and striped trousers, like cabinet ministers. Women were invariably beautiful and aloof. Passing through on the way to the squash courts below, Adam had caught the heavy stifling atmosphere of wealth. And dinner jackets - he hadn't got one. 'Oh there'll be plenty of boys of your age in suits, I'm sure,' his mother said. He didn't believe her. Until he thought again of Esther, he nearly resolved to make an excuse and not go. It was an adults' party after all.

From the hotel front hall Adam could see that the large central reception room had been hired. Tables were set on the carpeted area round a square of polished boards. On a raised platform musicians were taking their seats, and it seemed to Adam at first glance that all the males, young and old, wore dinner jackets. He caught a glimpse of Lawrence who was wearing one, and with it a frilly white shirt and a purple velvet tie.

He had no time to reflect. Mrs Harrington Junior and her father-in-law were receiving at the door. The old lady was nowhere to be seen. He found himself sandwiched in a queue between two middle-aged couples who talked over his head. As he drew level with the hosts, Mrs Harrington Junior, sparkling with green sequins, looked at the couple behind him as she offered a limp hand for him to shake. But Mr Harrington rescued him.

'Ah, our young tennis player,' he said affably, shaking Adam's hand with a pleasing horizontal movement. 'You'll be playing for the county at this rate.'

Esther came skipping up in a haze of pink frills. 'Hallo, Adam, you're late,' she said. Adam noticed particularly her shoes which were also pink, with a strap buttoned over her dainty feet. 'How unkind to keep a lady waiting.' Stooping, fatherly, Mr Harrington yielded him to her. 'Always the best policy,' he said, winking.

His suit. Colour rose to his cheeks like a firework, but Esther seemed to bug his thoughts. 'Thank goodness you're wearing a suit,' she said. 'I do hate men in those black and white things. Ronnie and Lawrence look completely absurd in my opinion. Do you want to get me a drink?' She took his arm and impelled him in the direction of the bar, which was on a lower level, down a few stairs.

'Gin and T?' said Esther, 'it's all free, you know. Grandad's paying.' Standing with their drinks she continued in her breathless way. 'I'm so glad you could be my partner. I was dreadfully afraid you'd have another engagement or wouldn't want to come, or something.' She took a gulp of gin. 'Look at Lawrence there with that girl. He doesn't *like* her, you know, her head is as empty as a box. He *poses* with her.' She appeared to describe the relationship accurately. Lawrence, foot on the bar rail, was talking in a raised voice, the girl stared, her head tilted upwards with speechless admiration.

'Where's your grandmother?' Adam asked. 'She wasn't doing the greetings at the door.'

'Oh, she's got more sense. She's over there somewhere at a table they've reserved for the family. I'm not going near it by the way.' She took his arm impulsively. 'We're going to have fun. Nobody'll bother about us tonight.'

The band struck up. 'Let's dance,' said Esther.

It was a quick-step, surely it was a quick-step, Adam thought, as they threaded to the floor. Desperately he tried to conjure the diagram in the book he had found at home filled with Man-Friday footprints, showing the steps of different dances.

Long-long, short-short-short, wasn't it? He tried to marry this with the beat of the music. As it happened, it wasn't very important what dance it was. The small dance floor was soon thronged and there was no space to do more than rock. Infiltrating into a corner they rocked together. Adam felt Esther's hair on his temple and held her closer. The music changed to a slow tempo piece. Adam had feelings he had not experienced before.

'You dance divinely,' Esther said, as they left the floor.

'You *are* divine,' he said.

The evening drifted deeper into an abstract ecstasy. Only here and there solid images emerged. Lawrence strode up once and said 'I say, it's about time you two broke up, isn't it? Want a gallop, Esther?' He had to spend an empty ten minutes talking and dancing with Lawrence's partner, who was as hostile to his small talk as she was to his dancing. But Esther returned to him. They went off to the buffet.

The new feelings rose to envelop Adam. Dancing now was no ordeal but a further opportunity to hold Esther's body against his own. They danced every time the music played, once even a tango. In a slow dance, he danced with her warm forehead against his own.

It was a fine night. Adam had seen several couples drifting through the bar window on to the terrace. Towards midnight, when some people were going, by tacit consent they glided out. At the end of the terrace a cluster of lights had amorously fused. He led her to an unoccupied garden seat.

They were not inconceivably first kisses for Esther, for Adam they were. He was aware at some point that the music had stopped, that there were other couples on the terrace who weren't talking too much. Once the moon came out, but went behind a cloud again as if it had put its head round the door, seen what was going on, and discreetly withdrawn.

A torch flashed and an unmistakable voice spoke behind it. 'I say, I've been hunting for you all over the garden. Mother's ready to go.'

Adam jumped up. 'Isn't this rather . . .' he began.

But Esther was also getting up. 'I'm coming,' she said briskly. She whispered 'goodnight' to Adam, hugged his arm briefly, and kissed his ear. 'I'll phone.'

A small hand fluttered over his, and she was gone.

Four days passed. Esther didn't ring. Adam was forced to ring the Harrington number. A male voice answered - he thought it was the butler. When he asked for Esther it was not her voice which came on the line but Lawrence's.

'Sorry, old boy, it's all off. May as well face it. Understand how you feel and all that, but it's just not on. Much too young, both of you - apart from other reasons. Mother's adamant. Tootle-oo. Maybe have another knock at the club some time.'

'But I want to speak to . . .' Adam was talking to a buzz.

He planned a Romeo-like invasion of the Harrington house at night. He thought of plans for elopement. He didn't go out in case Esther phoned. He was sure she would phone. She would sneak out of the house and use a public box probably.

But it was not a phone call which came, but a letter. Three lines. Sweet and lovely as it was, it *had* been midnight madness, hadn't it? Lawrence, though awful, was right on this one occasion, it could never be anything permanent. She was still most glad Adam had agreed to be her partner at the dance. She had *so* enjoyed it - 'especially on the terrace!!'

It was the banality of those exclamation marks which wounded him most, as if it was all something to be jested about, their kissing reduced to a momentary skylark. Nonetheless Adam wrote many letters, all a great deal longer than three lines. He did more plotting, actually going once to stand outside the house hoping Esther might come out alone.

The new school year began. Adam went to the local grammar. Esther presumably had gone away to her boarding school. He dreamed of the Christmas holiday. Then in the tennis club he heard a member say that Mrs Harrington Junior had 'flown.' She had grown tired, it seemed - as the member reported her words verbatim - of 'slumming it in the provinces'. She had returned to London - taking with her, it was to be presumed, her three children.

'Well, there's one good thing,' someone else said. 'Breakspear won't be dishing out the centre court again - for those young peacocks .'

Also available from Benchmark Press by Guy Wilson:

'A Healthy Contempt.' Maynard Temple, a worldly Cambridge don and successful TV historian lives with his talented wife, Rachel, a biographer. They have a young son. Their relationship is open, loving, rooted, until Rachel's sister, Rhoda, comes out of prison where she has served a sentence for an episode of violent idealism. Maynard contains his distaste for Rhoda's strident martyrdom to causes until he suspects her attitude to him goes beyond random dislike. Against all his liberal principles, he is driven to an extreme act which tears his life apart. (Hard back. First published in 1993. UK price: £14.95 UK postage included).

'The Carthaginian Hoard.' Sir Alan Silverman, eminent archaeologist and discoverer of the legendary hoard in the Central Sahara in 1936, is buried in Westminster Abbey with full state pomp. But does he merit the international reputation he has won? Claudia Drake, his biographer, thinks so. But left-wing freelance journalist, Michael Strode, has another opinion. He guesses Silverman knew a lot more about the murder of one of his British assistants than ever came out. In an unlikely alliance the two go out to Sahara, now independent and a vicious dictatorship, to find the truth. Amid unforeseen perils and hardship, they find their courage challenged and their view of each other changed. (Hard back. First published in 1997. UK price: £15.95 UK postage included).

'Second Time Round'. 'Rent a muscle . . . you must frighten him,' Jocelyn is told. 'Take out an injunction,' advises her daughter. Jocelyn thinks otherwise, for she knows violence, the law, will be ineffective against anyone like Leo, her ex-husband, who is pursuing her. She knows she must change her name, and disappear.

She takes a job in a large garden in Devon open to the public run by Henry Bordeaux, an ex-commando. Henry is a kind and sympathetic employer and for a while she is happy at a job she finds she is good at. But she is threatened from two directions. Delia Bordeaux, afflicted with a terrible injury, and bedridden, is jealous of her and willing as it turns out to go to any lengths to discomfort her. Then, when this problem seems resolved and a chance of real happiness dawns Jocelyn is assaulted anew. Has Leo discovered her whereabouts and will he reappear? What will her feelings be if he does?

'In a second marriage there is always a locked room.' (Paperback. First published in 2000. UK price: £6.99 plus postage).

Available from Benchmark Press, Little Hatherden, Andover, SP11 0HY.